The Artist

and the

  Cop

(The Death of Margie Sloan)

-by Barbara Lee-

PublishAmerica
Baltimore

First printing

At the specific preference of the author, PublishAmerica allowed this work to remain exactly as the author intended, verbatim, without editorial input.

ISBN: 1-4241-1016-5
PUBLISHED BY PUBLISHAMERICA, LLLP
www.publishamerica.com
Baltimore

Printed in the United States of America

This book is dedicated to my wonderful children and their families,
Deborah & Andy
Mike, Dianne, Natalie & Audrey.
Brad, Linnae, Matthew & Leah
Kirk, JoAnne, Cameron & Michael
Carla, Mike, Thea & Megan
Special Thanks to Brad for being my reader.

Chapter 1

The state highway to Easton was only two lanes, but traffic was light, so it was safe enough. It was barely daylight when Karen left Dinsmore and headed to the art colony that Monday morning in October. Fall leaves were at their best. Oranges and yellows intermixed with the green of the cedars. She enjoyed driving in her little red Toyota, with the window down, listening to the FM station on the radio. The talk was about the national news, mostly the upcoming presidential election. She was hoping they would start the classical music soon.

It was the first time Karen has attended an art workshop. Since she had retired from the police department, she had been painting a lot more and was hoping to be inspired by working with other artists. She also knew it was the best way to network and gain some new friends in the business and perhaps supplement her retirement income.

Her hometown of Dinsmore was only populated by about seven thousand citizens but since it served the whole of Smith County, their little police department had stayed busy. It's a small town with wide streets bordered by beautiful maple trees. Main street has the usual shops, the barber and beauty, "Hairs to You," two dress shops for the ladies, one specialty store for the men, and the Regal Department Store. The main activity took place at "the Café," the only locally owned eatery where everybody from bankers to farmers met for good food and conversation. One grocery store was the Piggly Wiggly on the north end of Main Street. A State highway went to the interstate. There was a strip mall with a Super Wal Mart, McDonald's, Wendy's and the Holiday Inn for the interstate travelers going to and from Chicago. The whole county shopped out there.

The local crimes were mostly fender benders, public drunks and teen age punks who had nothing better to do than bust up mailboxes with baseball bats. Once in a while they would have a shooting and they did have a murder about ten years before Karen retired.

Ed Hawkins was her partner or she was his partner. They never decided who was in charge and became good friends enjoying their work together. Ed was a bachelor, a confirmed bachelor. Rich, her late husband and Ed became extremely close friends. They hunted together, golfed together, went fishing together and just hung out together. They were both easy going guys and neither of them liked the party life so they got along well. Karen was always invited to join them on their trips but she liked to use her spare time to paint. Occasionally she would go along to take photographs. When Rich was killed in a car accident, Ed was as grief stricken as she had been. She had quit painting for a while and buried herself in police work. After Rich's death she only saw Ed at work. They never talked about Rich, not even once, after his funeral.

Karen had worked the one and only murder case with Ed and they had successfully solved it. The guy was serving time now for killing his ex wife's new boyfriend. Let's face it, it happens even in the best of places. The guy was your usual dumb jerk with a hot temper. There were many witnesses to the crime but it took a while to get them to come forward but they finally saw the light and turned him in.

Karen was an attractive blonde with a nice figure for a fifty-year-old who kept trim by walking every day. She rode her horse at least once a week and kept busy gardening and doing yard work. It took a lot of time and effort to keep up since she had five acres. And of course she had her painting. She did a lot more painting in the winter. Winter in Illinois is bitterly cold. It's flat and the wind can blow snow into big banks that will keep one in the house for days at a time. High top boots or overshoes were fashion accessories in Smith County.

Karen did her artwork from photographs taken every chance she got. That made it possible to paint in her studio year round. Her new digital camera was kept in the car to take photos of things seen while driving around the area. She was getting close to Easton now and stopped to get a shot of an old red barn and a little white house. There were colorful maple trees in the well-manicured yard which had a little white picket fence around it. She thought, this is going to be a great subject, I can't wait to start on it.

Close to the edge of town she spotted the Golden Arches and pulled into the drive to order an egg and sausage McMuffin and a cup of coffee. She pulled to a parking place and ate her breakfast with the motor running so she could keep listening to the radio. Finished eating, she got out her map with the letter from the colony to figure out how to get to the campground where she would be for the next three days.

Ann Neal was the lady in charge of the affair. Karen was looking forward to meeting her. She was a very well known artist and would be a good one to know. Karen was more than a little concerned about painting with a group of artists but she was determined not to be intimidated by the more experienced artists that would be there. At least that is how she had imagined it would be.

She took off down the highway again, going through the town and turned left on Maddox Road. There were some nice new homes along the road with big yards. Some of them had big barns with horses grazing in the fields near them. Some of the houses were so big they could be described as mansions. She wondered about who lived in them, thinking they are probably doctors or lawyers. She smiled to herself, thinking, always the detective. She wondered if she was just naturally nosy. After three more miles, there was a lane with a sign pointing right. It read Easton Art Colony in big red letters. She drove down the gravel lane another two miles and came upon a little log cabin that had a sign, "Office" on it. Before she went in, she took a photo of the "Office." There were three other cars parked in front so she pulled around to the side of the building.

She put her camera back in the car, got her purse, and went up the wooden steps to the door. As she entered a very pretty, blonde lady in blue jeans and a red plaid flannel shirt greeted her with "Good Morning, welcome to Easton and to the colony." She stuck out her hand to shake.

"I'm Ann Neal" she said. Karen introduced herself and shook the extended hand. "I'm here to participate in the workshop and need to pay the rest of my fee."

Ann got out a ledger and told Karen she owed $200 more dollars. She had already sent in a deposit of $150. She wrote a check for the $200 and then asked "Now where am I staying and who are my room mates?" Ann was busy writing her a receipt and didn't answer right away.

As she handed her the receipt, she told her "Let me look in my directory and find where you are. Let's see you're in Cabin C with Loretta Hawthorne and Susan McComb. They're both from Chicago and I'm sure you'll enjoy them."

She gave Karen the directions to her cabin but then asked her if she would like a cup of coffee before they went to the cabin. Karen accepted, and they sat on a wooden, parson's bench to drink their coffee. Ann asked her, "How long have you been painting?"

Karen smiled. "I've been painting about twenty-five years as a hobby but I just retired from the police department so I'm devoting all my spare time to my art now."

Ann told her that the instructor would be John Whitcomb and that he was

7

a very talented artist who lived in Taos, New Mexico and traveled all over the country doing workshops. They would attend a lecture by John today to get acquainted and tomorrow they would begin to paint. The food would be catered from town for breakfast and lunch. They would go to town and be on their own for dinner.

Chapter 2

Ann and Karen drove down to her cabin. There were eight cabins and they all were made of logs. Opening the door she found one of her room mates already ensconced and reading a book. "Loretta, this is Karen, one of your room mates, she's from Dinsmore."

Loretta responded with a big smile, "Oh, yes, I drove thru there yesterday and went into town for breakfast at a charming little cafe."

"Yes, it's the most popular place in town. I'm glad you went there instead of staying on the interstate."

Loretta, a large woman with her graying hair in a big bun on top, had a lovely pink face and looked like everyone's ideal mom. She had on a purple mumu and was barefoot. She gestured toward one of the three twin beds and said, "I like to get off the beaten path and see the little towns. Take your pick and make yourself at home. I'm so glad to meet you. We are going to have a great time this week."

"Yes, I'm sure we will. It's nice to meet you, too. I'm a little concerned about my painting ability but looking forward to being inspired by other artists."

"Oh my word, I just do this for the fun of it so you don't need to be intimidated by me. At my age you don't take anything too seriously. Just enjoy and learn, trying to keep the old brain busy so "Oldtimers" won't set in." Karen thought, "yes, this is going to be fun."

The cabin had a lot more room than one would think, looking at it from the outside. There was a bed and chest for each guest and a small rack to hang clothes on. It had a large bathroom with a tub and shower, a double sink with one end that had a bench to sit on and apply one's make up. It was decorated with blue and mauve floral chintz on the beds and there was a little round pine table with two chairs by the window. The chairs had blue plaid cushions on them. She put her luggage on one of the beds and began to unpack some things that she needed to hang. Ann and Loretta had gone out on the stoop and were still talking.

Back in Dinsmore Margie was getting ready to go out. She had been feeling like she was coming down with a cold but she had looked forward to this date and decided that she would feel better if she had a nice evening out. She was meeting Daniel Carmody at the country club for dinner. She put on her favorite little black dress and the new four inch heels she had bought that afternoon. The dress was a low-cut V so she selected a diamond pendent that she had inherited from her grandmother. It was easier to meet Daniel than to have him pick her up. Just in case she needed to get back home for some reason. She had a daughter away at college, and her mother in a nursing home with poor health. This meant she could get an emergency call at any moment. They hadn't been on many dates, once to dinner and the movies and another time they went to a football game north of Dinsmore. She got her purse and keys off the hall table, had a last look in the full length mirror. She was a striking brunette, very petite, not even one hundred pounds. She worked out in the church gym or jogged to keep herself in good shape. Locking the door behind her, she went down to the parking garage to get in her car.

When she pulled up to the club she gave the valet the keys to her little blue Cavalier and went in. The club was a pretty stucco Spanish style building with a big blue awning over the entrance. When she went in the maitre'de recognized her and immediately took her to the table where Daniel was already having a martini. He was very handsome in a blue pinstripe suit with a red tie. The diamond in his tie pin sparkled like his deep blue eyes. His white hair was in a sort of modified crew.

He got up and helped seat her then took her hand and kissed it. Then he ordered a Chablis for her and another martini for him. "You're a little late, I was afraid something had come up and you weren't going to make it"

" I took too long getting dressed, I guess. I'm sorry, the time just got away from me. I went shopping after work and that made me late getting home."

"Well, you were worth waiting for, because you look beautiful."

" Thank you kind sir, but we'd better look at the menu because I can't stay out too late. Work day tomorrow you know." Smiling, he told her that he understood she had the goods on her boss and could probably be late without getting fired. Margie was a teller at the Bank of Dinsmore where he was the vice president.

When the waiter came, he ordered what they had decided on, Veal Parmesan for both of them with a dinner salad. He asked if she'd like another drink but she said, "Let's have coffee with our meal." After the waiter left, he asked if she had talked to her mother today and she told him "No, I'll call her tomorrow."

He told her he was going to Chicago on business and might be gone until the end of the week. "That's why I wanted to see you tonight." She asked what he would do in Chicago and he said it was just business and he quickly changed the subject. " How is Melanie doing in college? It won't be long before Thanksgiving vacation. Have you told her about us?"

"No, I think it will be better to tell her when she's home and we can talk face to face. She'll be okay, she knows I had good reason to divorce her father. But you are the first person I 've really dated since the divorce, so she may be surprised."

"Well, speak of the devil, look who just walked in." Daniel whispered. "Don't turn around. It's your ex and his date."

"I didn't know you knew him. I certainly hope he doesn't come over here."

"You didn't know he came to the bank to apply for a loan? You must have been out that day. I think it was when you went to visit your mother."

"Oh, I'll bet he planned it that way because knew I was going to see Mother. Did he get the loan?"

"No, he wanted $10,000 and had no collateral to cover it. His credit rating is not very good."

He joked, "Did you take him to the cleaners when you divorced him?"

She wasn't amused. "There wasn't enough left to take after all he spent it on her and trips to Las Vegas, a new car and on and on. I was lucky to get a little alimony and Melanie's college tuition."

Much to her chagrin, Larry Sloan came right over to their table, grinning from ear to ear, with his little blonde, Pamela, on his arm. Larry was not a handsome man. He had the kind of face that looked as if he'd had a bad case if acne as a teenager. He had a pug nose like a boxer and bright red hair. When they had first met, Margie thought he had a great personality and he had plenty of friends. They began to disappear when he took up drinking to excess. His face was always flushed, maybe from his habit of heavy drinking. Larry was the manager of the largest department store in town, The Regal Department Store. Pamela was his secretary at the store. He knew most of the people in the room and they knew him. In other words he was well known, in more ways than one.

Sticking out his hand to shake Daniel's and turned to look at Margie and said too loudly, "Now I know why I got turned down for that loan, I guess."

Margie blanched and she could hardly speak. She was angry. " I think you probably know why you didn't get a loan better than I. I didn't realize you were having financial problems."

His face turned beet red. He turned to his girlfriend, "Pamela, I want you to meet my first love and ex wife, Margie. She was a very sweet girl when we first met but this is what twenty-five years of marriage does to you."

Daniel seeing things were going badly said "It's nice to see you again, Larry, but I think you'd better go to your table because I see our food coming. Have a nice evening."

Knowing he was getting the brush off didn't improve Larry's manners. "Well, I wouldn't want to interrupt your dinner, asshole."

With that Daniel rose from his seat and before he had straightened up, Larry took a swing at him. Apparently, Larry had a little too much to drink, because he missed and fell on his face in the floor. It seemed, to the onlookers as if Daniel had hit him, but he hadn't even raised his hand. The maitre'de rushed to the rescue, helped Larry up and led him quickly out of the dining room to the door. He told him he'd better go home and sober up. Little miss Pamela dressed in pink satin off the shoulder top and a very short mini skirt followed sheepishly behind him attracting a lot of attention from the men in the room as they left.

The two of them didn't have very good appetites after that scene but they both agreed the best thing they could do was to act as if nothing had happened and go on with their evening.

Margie asked, "Do you want to come back to my place after we finish?"

"Of course I do." he smiled, "Are you sure you're going to be all right?"

"I'm not going to let him ruin things for me. I intend to enjoy the rest of my life. He's such a fool. I guess he thought I would be home feeling sorry for myself. It probably took the fun out of it for him after I found out what he was up to. I didn't waste any time getting a divorce. I don't especially believe in second chances after I'd been married twenty five years and doing the right thing. He had no excuse and I certainly didn't feel guilty so I've had no problem getting on with life, without him."

"Okay, let's forget it and enjoy this meal, it really is very good. Would you like dessert?"

"No, we can have that at my place." She murmured. She blushed at her own words.

Daniel signaled the waiter and paid the bill. They smiled bravely and walked out as if nothing had happened. He walked with her to the door and asked the valet to bring their cars. He told her he would meet her at the apartment. Then he got in his car and waited until she was out of the drive and well on her way so that anyone watching would not think they were going the same way. There was no need to add fuel to the gossip that was sure be all over town in the morning after Larry's big act.

He drove to Margie's apartment and choosing not to park on the street; he found an empty spot in the building parking lot. Margie was waiting for him by the elevator and they went up together. He kissed her on the cheek after the doors closed and she turned and kissed him warmly on the lips. They got off the elevator at her floor and after she unlocked the door they entered. Her apartment was small but nicely decorated in an eclectic sort of way. She liked to mix modern with the antiques that had belonged to her grandmother. There was a huge caramel-colored sofa with colorful pillows and a hand-crocheted afghan across one arm. A big white shaggy rug was in front of a rough-hewn fireplace. Two side chairs in a teal green, floral pattern were placed nearby with cherry end tables and cut glass lamps with white shades.

"Would you like a glass of wine? That's all I keep in the house." She asked as she went toward the huge eat-in kitchen with it's stainless steel appliances and white cupboards.

"That sounds good, can I help?" "No, just give me a minute to get more comfortable and I'll get it. Why don't you take off your jacket and turn on the fireplace?"

She went in her bedroom and got out of those four inch heels and then exchanged the dress for a robe. Nothing sexy just a nice white terry robe. When she came out, she went to the kitchen and got down the wine glasses and poured the wine. Then she took it into the living room where he was lighting the gas logs in the fireplace, sat on the rug and waited for him. He had taken off his jacket, rolled up his sleeves and loosened his tie.

He sat next to her and she leaned over and kissed him. He smiled at her. "This is really nice. I could get used to this, you know."

"We don't want to go too fast and get too serious, too soon. Let's just enjoy each other's company while we may."

He frowned at that. "That sounds ominous, are you planning to leave, or something else?"

"Oh no, I just want to be careful. You know, I don't want to get my heart broken by such a good-looking man. We really don't know that much about each other. However you probably know more about me than I do about you."

"Okay, one of these days I'll tell you the story of my life," he quipped, "but not tonight because I can't stay that long and I don't want to waste what time I have." She moved closer to him and he leaned forward to kiss her.

Chapter 3

Karen and Loretta welcomed their new room mate Susan when she arrived. Susan was a tiny little lady with a pixie haircut, wearing blue jeans and a navy tee shirt. They were all heading to the recreation center to have lunch and listen to the art instructor's lecture. There were about twenty people already there and the tables were set up cafeteria style. There was a buffet that featured chicken salad on a bed of lettuce, garlic French bread and chocolate pudding or fruit cup for dessert. They had a choice of iced tea or coffee to drink.

They got their trays, filled them and made their way to a table. After introductions, they all began to get acquainted. There were more women than men, about three to one but the men didn't seem to mind. Everyone was really friendly and Karen was beginning to relax. When they began eating dessert, Ann got up and went to the front of the room where there was another table turned sideways and introduced the instructor, John Whitcomb. He was a very handsome man. He had dark wavy, medium length hair left to it's own natural arrangement. He had on a maroon pullover sweater, blue jeans and loafers without socks. She talked about all of his credentials. He began the lecture by telling them that rather than talk, he was going to do a demonstration painting while he talked. They all applauded at that. He told them they could ask questions and his answers would be the lecture. In order to keep it organized, Ann would acknowledge them and then they could ask their questions. It was a lively afternoon and he did an impressionistic painting of a fall landscape similar to the scenery Karen had seen on her drive from Dinsmore

While he painted, he told of all the wonderful places he had gone to study with other artists. Rome, Paris, the Greek islands and even Japan to study the art of paper making. It only took him about an hour. They all seem to enjoy his presentation and afterward they milled about and got better acquainted. Ann made some short announcements about the next days activities and told them that they would be on their own for dinner. She made some suggestions of restaurants in town where they might go and dismissed them.

The three of them made their way to their cabin and took turns taking showers and changing to go to town. Karen put on a white blouse with black slacks. Loretta put on A shaped black dress and Susan wore navy culottes and a red tee shirt. Karen volunteered to drive and they agreed. So after deciding to go to a chain steak house they took off. It was cafeteria style. After they ordered, they got their salads and sat down at a table in the back. The waitress brought their drinks and soon their orders. They exchanged abbreviated life stories while they ate their dinners. Then they agreed it was time to get back to cabin so they could get to bed early and be ready for a full day tomorrow.

When they got back, they all got ready for bed and then had a lot of girl talk before finally settling down and going to sleep. Loretta told all about her seven grandchildren and how much she enjoyed them and Susan talked about her three children from twelve to six and how crazy they made her. Karen didn't have her own children to talk about but she told them about Melanie, her best friend, Margie's daughter, a budding artist that she adored.

Chapter 4

Tony Distefano opened the door to the Café at five a.m. that Monday morning though he had been working since four. Maria had just come in and they were ready for the early risers. Tony is a short little Italian guy, only thirty-two and the father of five. He has dark skin and is balding but he's still rather handsome. His wife Maria is petite, twenty-nine with beautiful black hair that curls all over the place and she is the mother of those five children.

Two postal workers were the first customers. They ordered breakfast. When Maria took them their coffee, she overheard one say, "Did you hear about the scene at the country club last night?"

The other guy said, "Are you kidding? How would I know what goes on at the country club? Since when did you go to the country club?"

"Oh, I wasn't there, my daughter works there part time for special events and she told me that Larry Sloan was in a fight with Margie Sloan's new boyfriend."

Maria couldn't wait to get back to Tony to tell him what she had heard. She couldn't tell him right away because a short, sort of wiry, white-haired stranger in blue jeans and wearing cowboy boots had come in and was sitting near the postal worker's table. Maria went to wait on him and as she gave him the menu he ordered coffee and orange juice. She got the drinks while he looked over the menu. When she came back with his drinks, he ordered the Country Breakfast. She called the order to Tony and he started cooking the country- fried steak and eggs.

Maria asked, "Are you new in town?" The stranger just sort of growled. "Yeah, I'm just passing through."

He was reading a newspaper and Maria could tell he didn't want conversation so she retreated to the counter. He seemed to be listening to the postal worker's conversation. Maria was watching the stranger as he watched the postal workers pay their bill and leave.

She finally had the chance to tell Tony what she'd heard, and no sooner were the words out of her mouth, when Daniel walked in. He came to the counter and ordered a black coffee to go. Tony said, "You're out awfully early for a banker."

Daniel smiled ruefully, "Yeah, I know. I'm on my way to Chicago for a business meeting and I need an eye opener. Let me have one cup while I'm here, too."

Tony didn't know whether to risk asking about the country club event or not but decided to plow in anyway. "Heard you had a little ruckus at the country club last night."

Daniel looked shocked, "I can't believe that you could have heard about that already."

Tony asked, "Did you knock him on his butt?"

Daniel was quick to answer, "Are you kidding? I didn't touch him, he was so drunk, he fell on his face and they led him out of the place. How did you hear about it?"

Not wanting to cause any trouble Tony just said, "Oh, you know word gets around and especially in here. We hear everything and believe very little. Actually, Maria told me."

Daniel was just amused by it. "Well, it's no problem, I'm sure anyone who knows Larry will understand. He doesn't exactly have a squeaky clean reputation. I'll take my coffee and get on the road now. By the time I get back the story will probably be even better, after the gossips get through with it. I'm not worried though, anybody who knows me knows I'm not into bar fights."

Daniel had finished his coffee and left. Tony watched as he went out and got in his silver gray Lexus, to leave town. Then he went back to his grill.

Just minutes later, he turned around, as he heard the door open again. Larry Sloan came in looking disheveled. His suit was wrinkled and tie askew. He came right to the counter and ordered black coffee not speaking to anyone in particular. Tony waved Maria off and took him the coffee. "You're looking kind of beat, Larry. What's the matter?"

Larry just mumbled, "Oh, I guess I had a little too much to drink and now I'm paying the price. Got to go home and change for work, just needed some coffee to clear my head. I'll come back for breakfast later if a shower and change of clothes help." He gulped his coffee and headed out the door.

Maria yelled, "He didn't pay!" "Oh, he'll be back, don't worry about it."

The stranger said, "You surely are a trusting soul."

"It's a small world here and I know everybody so I don't worry about a cup of coffee."

Maria took the coffee pot to the stranger's table and asked, "Can I get you anything else?"

"Just a refill on the coffee and the bill."

By now it was six-thirty and the farmers from the surrounding area were coming in. They all showed every week day to cuss and discuss their various crops and cattle. Sometime they talked politics and whatever was on their minds. The same six men had been coming in for the five years Tony and Maria had owned the Café. It was hard telling how many years before that. Some of them were getting up in age but occasionally they would be joined by a younger son or two. The farmers all hoped to pass the family farm on, to their extended family.

Maria served them while Tony did the cooking. They all ordered breakfast and she didn't have to write it down because they ordered the same every day. Tony knew what to cook, too.

At seven o'clock, Ed Hawkins came in with one of his detectives, Chip Carter, the newest member of the police department and they sat at the counter. When Maria went to wait on them, she overheard talk of the country club scene again. "Everybody must be talking about that. I just heard two other guys who were discussing it."

Ed asked very seriously, "And just who were they?" Maria told him it was two postal workers that had heard it from a waitress.

"That's the trouble with this town. By the time it goes around, they'll have Daniel murdering Larry."

Maria looked shocked and Ed said, "Oh, hell, Maria, I'm just kidding." She went to get their usual coffee and donuts and after she had served them, she left to wait on some other customers who had come in.

When Ed started to get his billfold out, Tony waved him off. "Have a good day and keep on protecting us from all those bad guys, Ed." Ed thanked him and the two of them went out to the unmarked Mercury, climbed in and took off in a hurry.

The stranger asked, "Who were those two?" Tony told him, "That's the best detective in this county and one of his new cops."

The stranger asked, "Have a lot of crime around here?" Tony said, "No, but when you do, you like to have dependable cops."

The stranger paid his bill and went out of the door. A little later, Tony went to the window to see what he was driving. He wasn't driving though. He walked down the street crossed over, and went toward the post office. Tony shook his head and wondered what the guy was up to. He obviously didn't want to reveal his identity to Maria, when she had made it easy for him to tell her his name.

Chapter 5

Daniel made it to Chicago at nine o'clock and went directly to the courthouse. He had been served divorce papers the week before and was there to settle the divorce and get on with his new life. He met his lawyer and hers in the judge's office, agreed to pay alimony and child support to his wife and a twenty-five-year marriage was over in the matter of a few minutes. His two children were in college and away in the east and he would just have to deal with them later.

He was relieved that his ex hadn't been there so it had been simpler than he had thought. She suffered from bi polar disease and had harangued him for years, accusing him of affairs that never happened, until he finally had enough and left. She accused him of desertion and rather than go through another fight, he gave up. The children would soon be grown so child support would run out and he could afford to pay her alimony. She was too sick to hold a job for any length of time because she would go off her medication and become manic enough to lose whatever job she had managed to get.

He had written to kids to explain his reasoning but had not heard back from them so he wasn't sure how they were taking it. He loved his children and was hoping they were mature enough to understand. Now he didn't have to even stay overnight. He could make it back by midnight. He planned to see Margie again, soon and tell her about his past before she heard it from someone else. He was feeling better than he had in years, now that he was a free man. He felt he had a future to look forward to. The drive back to Dinsmore gave him time to think about it.

Chapter 6

It was the first day of the artist's workshop in Easton and Karen was a nervous wreck. Loretta fussed at her and said, "Girl, you'll be just fine. Just do what you do and don't worry about what the instructor thinks or says."

Susan chimed in. "She's right, we're here to learn but we're going to have fun, too. It's not brain surgery. It's just art. Our art. Our expression, not his so have a little faith in yourself."

By the time they finished, she was feeling silly for her angst. They were all in casual wear. Karen was in a sweat shirt and pants. Susan had on jeans that already had paint on them and a chambray shirt that looked like a paint rag. Loretta had on a blue mumu to hide her bulk, which was hard to hide. They drove up to the recreation center because Loretta didn't feel like walking. They got all their supplies out and went in to join the others for the morning session. Karen planned to paint from a photo of an old abandoned farm house, she had taken last summer. She had stretched a large canvas for the project and started to work on the sketch.

She finished a preliminary sketch and was working on enlarging it when John, the instructor came by and asked, "Do you always work from photos?"

"Yes, I really don't like painting out in the elements like heat and bugs."

He smiled and said, "Yes, I understand, that's why I paint from my imagination."

"I'm afraid my imagination is not that good. I'm kind of unimaginative type of person. The detective in me says "Just the facts, Mam. I might need to try it sometime though."

"I would think a detective had to have an imagination to be able to find clues and solve crimes."

She was slow to answer, "I never thought about it that way but you're right. Maybe my imagination is better than I thought."

He suggested, "Why don't you put away the photo and just for fun, try painting it from memory or using your imagination to improve upon nature. After all we do have the right to arrange things as we wish."

"Well, I'm here to learn, so maybe I'll take your advice and try it."

Loretta and Susan were both watching and listening to this conversation and giggled as he walked off to other students. Loretta whispered to Susan, "I knew he would go right for her because she's so attractive and she doesn't even know it."

Susan said, "Yes, I noticed that. She could be stuck up but she's so nice and easy going that you forget how pretty she is and just enjoy her companionship. She surely doesn't look like any cops I've known."

They didn't want Karen to know they were talking about her so they got busy working on their own paintings. There was a wide array of art being done. Impressionists to super realism and everything in between. They painted for two hours before they took a break for cokes or coffee. When they returned to their painting, the instructor told them that he would expect them to finish a painting today. There were groans all around and everybody began to work furiously until noon when they broke for lunch. The caterer had delivered sub sandwiches of various meats and buns with strawberry tarts for dessert.

They chatted and ate for an hour and then went back to work on their painting. At four o'clock, Ann rang a little bell. "Times up, folks. Let's see what we have accomplished. Anyone who wants a critique may come up now. Just line up to the left and John will do his critique. Don't be afraid. He won't hurt. It will be the positive approach and a learning process."

A few people got in the line, but very few. Loretta went over to Karen and said, "You've got to get up there. You've done a great job and you need to get his input."

Karen told her, "I don't see you rushing up to be criticized." Susan chimed in, "Yes, but ours is not as good as yours. I will go if you will." Karen agreed, took up her canvas, and headed for the line.

When he came to her, he said, "Well, I'm impressed. It's obvious you took my advice and it worked very well. You used some unusual colors and made this a truly unique work of art."

Karen was blushing because she had not expected to receive a complimentary critique. She thanked him and went back to her seat. Loretta leaned over and whispered, "See, I told you so."

After getting back to their cabin, they showered and dressed to go to dinner. They had decided to go to a little Italian restaurant they had spotted the night before. They got in Karen's Toyota and headed for town. On entering the restaurant, they saw that Ann and John were there. Ann waved at them and motioned them over. "Why don't you join us? We'll pull another table up and make it bigger."

Karen was about to make excuses when Loretta said, "Oh, that sounds like fun. We get to have dinner with a handsome young man. Maybe I'll be teachers' pet tomorrow."

Everyone had a big laugh, Loretta, loudest of all. After they were seated and reintroduced they ordered drinks and started to look at the menu while they had conversations about their day.

John said, "All in all I was pleased with the work I saw. I seem to have been lucky to get several really talented artists in the group." Loretta started to speak and Karen interrupted to say the waiter was here and did she want to order. Karen ordered chicken Alfredo and after the rest had ordered she excused herself to go to the rest room.

Loretta followed her and after they got inside she asked, "Why did you stop me from finding out who he was referring to?"

Karen said, "I didn't want to know and it would have put him on the spot. Please, don't embarrass me, Loretta. I'm just not comfortable talking about my artwork. It's very personal to me and it took every bit of nerve I had to come here for this workshop."

Loretta looked sad and apologized, "I'm sorry. I didn't realize and I promise not to do it anymore. I don't want to hurt your feelings, and I surely never want you to be angry with me."

Karen was smiling when she said, "Who could be angry with you? You're such a curmudgeon."

Soon after they returned to the table, their food was served by a handsome young waiter that Loretta embarrassed by asking him if she could take him home with her. He blushed but answered, "Well, Mam, I would but I'm afraid my mother wouldn't like it."

The joke was on Loretta then. "That will teach me not to be so cute." Then there was more laughter. John did get around to mentioning that he really liked Karen's work in spite of her efforts to avoid the conversation. She managed to thank him, and change the subject to what they would be doing tomorrow. Then Ann asked if anyone would join her in dessert and Susan said, only if she wanted to share one. She ordered a big Chocolate Fudge concoction and six spoons.

Karen asked her companions if they were ready to go. "You know we have to get our rest so we'll be up to the instructor's orders tomorrow." She was smiling at John.

They were in the car and on the way back to their cabin and Loretta said, "I think he likes more than Karen's art, don't you, Susan?"

Susan agreed. "Yes, one could get an inferiority complex around this talented teacher's pet."

Karen groaned, "You girls just won't give it a rest, will you?" They all laughed and agreed it had been a great day and evening.

Chapter 7

When they got back to the cabin there was a note for Karen to call Ed Hawkins at the police station in Easton. She went to the main office and placed the call with her credit card. The desk sergeant answered and when she told him who it was, he told to hold and he would put Ed on.

"Hello. This is Ed Hawkins. Can I help you?"

"Ed, Karen here, I got a message to call you. Whatever is going on?"

He hesitated before he began to explain, "Karen, I hate like hell to tell you this but your friend Margie Sloan has been found dead in her bathtub and it looks like suicide but I'm just not sure about that."

Karen went weak in the knees and looked for a place to sit down, finding none she leaned on the counter and groaned, "That can't be true. Why would Margie commit suicide? She's such a wonderful person and…Oh, My God, how will I tell her daughter?"

"I sure wish I hadn't needed to call you but I thought you would want to come back and try to help."

She was crying now and told him, "I'll leave early in the morning. I don't like driving on that two-way road at night. Don't call Melanie. Let me take care of that. She's like my own daughter and it will be better coming from me, unless that stupid Larry calls her. Have you talked to him yet?"

"No, he had a run in at the country club with Margie and Daniel last night and he didn't show up at work today. Called in sick. His little girlfriend is missing, too."

Stunned by that news, she told him she would meet him at the café in the morning as soon as it opened. She asked, "Where is Margie's body?"

"At the coroners. He'll be doing the autopsy tomorrow. We didn't find her until nine o'clock last night when Daniel got back in town and went to her apartment. He is beside himself because he is the last one to see her alive, and there's the fact that he was obviously serious about their relationship. I think I'm going to need your help on this one because I just can't believe it's suicide, think you're up to it?"

She didn't waste any time saying, "I wouldn't have it any other way. Let me go now so I can try to get some rest for the trip back." He told her, "Bye for now."

She sat in her car for a few minutes just mulling over the horrific news and trying to convince herself it was true. She went into the cabin and told her room mates the awful news. She would have to leave early and would try not to wake them. They hugged her, told her how sorry they were and was there anything they do to help. But of course there was nothing that would take away the heart wrenching sadness she felt. She kept telling herself that she had to be strong for Melanie. She silently vowed to find out what had really happened. Sleep did not come easy but she did get a couple of hours before she got up and dressed in her sweats, loaded up her car and slipped out of the park. Her room mates had heard her but pretended to be asleep because they knew she wouldn't want to talk about it anymore.

The trip back was uneventful and even though she broke the speed limit, she wasn't stopped on the way. She went directly to the café and Ed was there already waiting for her. Ed was about 5'10," strong looking with wide shoulders. He was in his late fifties and stayed in shape by working out at home on his own exercise equipment. He was ruggedly good looking with salt and pepper hair and blue eyes that could look right through you. He had on a black windbreaker, white dress shirt and striped tie with khaki pants and brown suede casual shoes. He smiled when he saw her approaching and got up to pull out a chair for her.

Tony and Maria both went to her and told her how sorry they were. Everyone knew that she and Margie had been good friends for years. She and Ed were at a table in the back and he started to fill her in on the details after Maria brought them coffee. They didn't want to be overheard.

Chapter 8

In the small town of Pocahontas in the Ozarks of Missouri a little red Mustang does not go unnoticed. Larry and Pamela had called the Regal and told them they were going to St. Louis to a buyer's market and wouldn't be back until the following Monday. They drove through town and out into the countryside.

Pamela told him to turn at the next road and he said, "It sure is dusty. I hate to take my car down this road."

"It's the only way to my house if you still want to go." He turned in and when they had gone about three miles she told him to pull in the driveway on the left.

He was shocked since it looked like a junk yard. Chickens and dogs were all over the place. An old man with a cane came out on the rickety porch and yelled, "Whatch ya' want? We ain't sellin' anything and we ain't buyin' anything."

Pamela jumped out of the car and yelled, "Daddy, we don't want to buy anything. You don't even know your own daughter?"

A big toothless grin showed on his wrinkled old face then and he said, "Girl, you are a sight for these old eyes. I never thought I would live to see you again."

She told him, "Well, I came back to introduce you to the man I'm going to marry."

He frowned. "I don't know if I like that news or not. He'd better be a good one."

By then Larry had managed to get out of the car and amble up to the two of them. "Daddy, this is Larry Sloan, the man I'm going to marry this afternoon."

"What's the big hurry?"he asked, "Are you pregnant?"

"Good Lord, Daddy is that the only reason for getting married?"

Larry spoke up. "No sir, it's not that she's pregnant, it's that we're in love and thought we'd come down here to get married so you could be there."

The old man told him, "You're kinda old to be marrying my little girl. Ain't you ever been married before?"

Larry was taken aback by the old man's frank assessment of him and answered, "Well, I was married but it didn't work out so I got a divorce. Pamela came to work for me and we started seeing each other."

The old man said, "Well, I guess it's okay with me but I ain't goin' to no wedding so you can do it without me." He turned to go and asked, "Want to come in and have a glass of tea?," he acted as if they had answered, so they followed him up to the porch and into the ramshackle house. It was a mess. Dirty dishes were every where and a cat was sitting in the middle of the table licking his paws.

Pamela explained that they wouldn't stay for the tea but that she just wanted to see him and tell him about getting married. They would be going back to town to get the license and the justice of the peace would marry them.

He looked sad. "Well, this will probably be the last time you'll see me alive. Doc told me the old cancer had me and I wasn't long for this old world so I hope you'll come back to bury me when the time comes."

Pamela started to cry. "Ain't no need to cry. Mama's been waitin' for me for a long time and I'm tired and ready to go meet up with her. I know things will be better up there. Preachers' told me all about it and it sounds real good." Then he grinned at Larry and told him, "You all go on now and take care of your marryin'. I'll be fine right here. You better be good to my little girl or I'll send some of these country boys to take care of you."

They walked back to the car and waved goodbye as they took off slowly down the dirt road. Larry was driving slowly to avoid being covered with dust. They headed back to Pocahontas where you could get married in an afternoon. They'd get the blood test, the license and the JP and have it all over within a couple of hours.

Larry looked at Pamela as they turned onto the highway again and asked, "Did you really grow up in that house?"

"When Mama was alive, it was much better. It wasn't much but it was as clean as could be. People here are not used to having much. If it wasn't for movies and television, we wouldn't have known there was a better way to live."

He asked, "How did you manage to get out of here?" "Mama made sure I talked to the counselors at school and they knew I was a good student. Even though I couldn't afford to go to college, I was able to go to the community college on scholarship and took the marketing courses that eventually got me the job with you." He reached over and patted her hand as if to say everything would be all right now.

Chapter 9

Ed and Karen were still talking when the police chief, Bradley Stone and another detective, Jeff Collins, came in and made their way back to the table. Jeff, thirty years old, had been Ed's partner since Karen retired. Ed asked the chief, "Have you heard from the coroner's office?"

"No, not yet but we should before too long. I'm really sorry Karen because I know you were very good friends."

She said, "I'm sort of waiting to call Melanie until I have a little more information but I'm going to have to soon or she'll hear it from someone else."

"Don't you think her father ought to do that?" "He's nowhere to be found, I understand," she answered. "He and Melanie don't get along very well since the divorce, anyway. She's always been the nearest thing to a daughter I've ever had so I think I can handle it best."

Stone looked at Ed and asked, "What do you mean when you say Larry is nowhere?"

"I went to see him right after her body was found and he wasn't home. Then I went to the store and they told me that he and Pamela had gone to St. Louis to a buyer's market. No one seemed to know that it had been planned. The assistant manager was even left in the dark."

Maria was refilling their coffee and she said, "I don't want to be nosy but I'm sure you all heard about the incident at the country club."

Chief Stone said, "Why no, we're always the last to know the local gossip. What about it?"

"Oh, now it sounds like I'm gossiping but you know we hear everything in here and a lot of it's not true. I don't know if I should repeat it to the law."

Jeff laughed and said, "Take a chance, Maria, we won't drag you in if it's just gossip."

She told them what the two postal workers had said and that Larry had come in looking like he hadn't been to bed, saying he was hung over. Karen said, "I can't believe Daniel really hit him."

Maria said, "Oh, no, Daniel came in on his way to Chicago and told Tony that he didn't touch him. Said he was just was so drunk he fell on his face and they had to escort him to the door."

"Well, now that sounds more like it." Karen muttered, "He's been drinking even more than before. He's going to mess up and lose his job if he doesn't watch it. I've heard that his assistant manager is a smart cookie and I'll bet she's just waiting for him to screw up enough to make it easy for her to step up a notch."

Ed just shook his head and said, "Maria forgot that she already told me this story when I was in here with Chip Carter. I never took it seriously."

Karen got up to go saying, "I need to get home and call Melanie." She would just have to wait for the coroner's report later. They assured her they would let her know immediately after they knew something.

Ed walked to the door with her and asked, "Do you want to be involved or will it be too upsetting for you?"

She said, "I definitely need to be involved if the chief doesn't object." He told her, "I'll call you later and we'll get together."

She went to her little house just outside of town. She and Rich had bought five acres so she could keep her horse and other pets. She had a big yellow lab, Jazz, that came running out to meet her as she drove in the driveway. Her calico cat was laying on the back steps enjoying the sun when she went to the door.

She unloaded some of her supplies and laid them on a lawn chair while she unlocked the door. Her neighbors up the road, the Barrys had been feeding her animals while she was gone. She went into the house and it felt good to be home but she was so sad thinking about what she had to do now. Her house was not fancy, just cozy country. Quilts and cotton slipcovers in a checked pattern. Lots of country blue and cross stitch pictures on the wall.

She didn't display much of her art. It was kept in her studio which was really a sun porch on the north side of the house, where she did her painting. She took her suitcase into the bedroom and sat on the bed while she phoned Melanie.

She was surprised when she heard a bright young voice. "Hello. This is Melanie"

She waited for the rest of the message.

The voice on the other end said, "Is anybody there?" Karen spoke hesitantly, "Melanie, this is Karen, I thought I had the answer machine. I have some horrible news for you. You'd better be sitting down."

"Oh, Karen, you're being so dramatic, it can't be that bad." Karen answered, "Yes, Melanie, it is. Your mother was found dead in her bathtub yesterday."

"Oh, My God, that can't be. Not my mother, she's too young and she's healthy. She's never sick. Oh, no there must be a mistake."

She was howling by now and Karen was trying to get her to listen. "Melanie, you need to make arrangements with your professors and come home. I'll arrange a flight to Chicago and pick you up there tomorrow if I can get the reservations." Melanie wasn't responding and Karen said, "Are you there? Listen to me now. I will call you back and give you the details for your trip. Okay?"

Melanie finally answered sobbing, "Okay, I'll get packed and wait for your call." Karen asked, "Are you going to be okay?"

"I'll be all-right but I just can't believe this is happening. I hope I'll wake up soon."

"I know, dear, I feel the same way and I'm going to hang up now and get on with the airline." Melanie was still sobbing. Karen waited for her to hang up first. "Okay, bye Karen."

She called the airline and was able to get reservations for the next day on Delta but she would have to take Ozark from Columbia to St. Louis and then on to Chicago.

She called Melanie back and gave her the information. She asked, "Do you have a way to the airport in Columbia?"

"Yes, my room mate has already told me she would help me. She even offered to drive me home but I thought I'd better fly."

Karen told her, "I'll be there to meet you so don't worry about that and we'll come right home to Dinsmore. You can stay with me."

Melanie asked, "Have you talked to my dad?" Karen hesitated before she answered. "No, I'm sorry to tell you that he hasn't been seen lately. Seems he went to St. Louis with his secretary on a buying trip but nobody knows where they're staying."

"Well, that's typical. Never there when you need him. I've got to get busy now and contact my professors. Thanks so much for taking care of everything, Karen. You're a dear and I don't know what I'd do without you."

"Okay, bye for now. I'll see you tomorrow." She waited again for Melanie to hang up in case she wanted to say something else.

As soon as she hung up the phone rang. It was Ed sounding impatient. "I've been trying to call you for an hour and the phone's been busy."

She explained what she had been doing and asked, "Do you have any news from the coroner's office?" He answered slowly, "Yes, and it's weird. She didn't have an overdose of sleeping pills. Actually none that he could tell. He can't figure out what made her heart stop. She doesn't have any bruises on her or any signs of distress. Her heart was fine but it quit beating all the same. Why? We just don't know."

Karen was mulling that over and didn't answer for a while and then she said, "It doesn't make any sense at all but I just know that Margie did not commit suicide."

"You're right. We're going to have to check this out more but I may be stopped and you will have to do it on the sly if the chief thinks I'm making trouble over nothing."

"Yes, I understand, I know how the chief thinks. Just close the case and forget it. Another mystery solved. I am going to pick up Melanie tomorrow and I'll have plenty of time to think. I'll see what I can come up with. I'll be back by four in the afternoon. Don't let them release Margie's body yet. Think of something to keep her there. Don't let them embalm her until I can check some other, so called perfect murders, because this has got something like that. I don't know who would want to do it but somebody sure as hell tried it."

Ed said, "I'll check in tomorrow when you get back and let you know the latest. If you get back early, you call me."

"Okay, bye, talk to you tomorrow."

She went out to the car to finish unloading it and the neighbors came driving up in their little pick-up. They both got out and Joseph said, "What are you doing home? I thought you'd be gone all week."

Ruth chimed in, "Just couldn't stay away from your babies, huh?" Karen paused and said, "You obviously haven't heard about Margie. She was found dead yesterday in her bathtub."

Joseph leaned against the car and held his hands to his heart, "Oh, my goodness, how can that be? What happened?" Ruth just stood there with her mouth open, unable to speak.

Karen told them what she knew and then said, "The hardest part was telling Melanie. I will be going to Chicago to pick her up tomorrow morning." Joseph asked if there was anything they could do to help. She told him that it would help if they could keep on checking on her animals because she was going to be so busy in the next few days with all that was going on. She didn't tell them she would be investigating the death. After they left, she finished unloading the car and putting everything away. Karen was a very neat person and did not like clutter except in her studio. She went back outside and hugged Jazz. He had been a big comfort ever since her husband's death. Then Callie, the calico got jealous and started rubbing on her legs and purring. She pulled her into her lap and just sat there staring off into space, thinking about what she had to do next, unable to fully comprehend all the events of the past two days.

She went into the house and put on the coffee pot, planning to stay up and do some Internet searches for poisons and their effect. She got on the net and checked her email. There was one from Daniel asking her to contact him by phone. She emailed him, told him what she would be doing and that she would get back to him tomorrow. There was another that Margie had sent before her date with Daniel. She was so pleased to be seeing him. Karen had a good cry at that one. She made a silent promise to Margie to find out what happened to her. She zapped all the other email and went back to her investigation.

Chapter 10

In Pocahontas, Arkansas, Larry and Pamela had done all the tests, got the license and looked up the local Justice of the Peace. He married them with his wife as the lone witness, wished them well and after Larry paid him, they got in the Mustang and took off for St. Louis. They stopped at the first Holiday Inn they came to and got a room. Larry got the bags from the trunk and when they got in the room, he produced a bottle of champagne. He grabbed Pamela and kissed her and told her to get comfortable and he poured the champagne. They used the little plastic glasses and toasted their future. They talked about what they would do tomorrow and then undressed and got ready for bed. Instead of romancing his new wife, Larry drank all the champagne and passed out on the bed. Pamela spent her wedding night watching the television.

Melanie was in Columbia busy getting to all her professors and making arrangements for make up work. Not knowing how long she would be gone was a problem but unavoidable since the plans were up in the air. She packed her bags, showered and went to bed early because she had an early flight. Her room mate wasn't in yet so she left a note on her bed to tell her what time they needed to leave. She didn't think she would be able to sleep but she was so exhausted and cried out that she fell into a deep sleep immediately. The next thing she knew was being shaken awake by her room mate, Shirley.

Shirley said, "You were worried about me getting up. Girl, you'd better shag. Remember you have to be extra early these days at airports."

Melanie groaned and answered, "I'll be ready in five minutes. I've got my clothes laid out and I'll just wash my face and put on some lipstick and we'll go."

Shirley told her, "I'm taking your bags on down right now. Hurry up and come on down." They got to the airport in plenty of time and there was no problem at the reservation's desk with Karen's plans. The plane left thirty minutes later and arrived in St. Louis on time. She had an hour layover which gave her time to grab a cup of coffee and a donut before her flight.

Karen was frustrated because she would have liked to talk to Ed before she left for Chicago but didn't want to take a chance on being late to pick up Melanie. She got in her little Toyota at six a.m. and went into town to gas up.

Then she took off to the interstate and started her trip to get Melanie.

The traffic was really heavy on the interstate but the weather was beautiful fall, not too cool, not too warm. Even on the interstate the fall colors were beautiful on the maples mixed with the deep greens of the cedars. She thought about what the girls at the art colony might have accomplished in their week and felt regret that she didn't get to finish. She thought she must drop a note to Ann to explain her fast exit.

Then she began to think of the reason she had left and sadness enveloped her once again. She was hoping to get back in time to see the coroner and check on what tests he had done. She also wanted to get back before Larry showed up and started interfering, if he even cared. She was trying to think of anyone who might have wanted Margie dead and no one could even vaguely come to mind.

Deciding she didn't need to be in a bad mood when she met Melanie she turned on the FM and listened to some classical music the rest of the way. She came to the exit to the airport and got to the parking lot. Since 9/11 one had to park away from the terminal and walk quite a distance. It took some time to find an empty spot and when she did it was the furthest one. She made it into the terminal, checked the information screen and went toward the gate that Melanie would be coming out on. She decided against going through the screeners since she didn't have a ticket and just waited there. The plane was due any minute anyway.

About twenty minutes later she spotted Melanie and was thankful to see she had a rolling bag. She waved and Melanie saw her and smiled. Karen thought, "She just as pretty as her mother. Brunette, but with auburn highlights, so tall and slim she could be a model. She had on blue jeans, a University of Missouri sweatshirt and black boots. When she came around the counter Karen hugged her and kissed her on the cheek.

Melanie moaned. " I can't believe this is happening, how can it be?"

"I know darling, I've thought the same thing all the way here. Do you have more bags?"

"Yes," she said, "We'll have to go to baggage, it's big because I didn't know how long I would be home, but it rolls, too."

"Oh, that's good," then Karen asked, "Would you like to get something to eat?"

"No, I want to get on home first." They went to the baggage area, got her bag off the merry go round and made their way to the car.

Earlier in Dinsmore, as the day had begun, Bill Wallace, the high school football coach was up before the rest of the family making the coffee. He stood at the back door and watched as the sun rose on a beautiful day. He was thinking of Margie because he had heard of her death and was devastated but dare not let onto his family. He had secretly begun to see Margie soon after her divorce. He had told her that he and Janet were separated and that he wanted a divorce. It was easy for her to believe him. Margie and Bill had been high school sweethearts until they went off to college at different universities.

No one knew they had been seeing each other. Her ex husband was very jealous and would have gone ballistic if he found out. Bill's wife Janet was even more jealous and didn't trust Bill. She was always accusing him of playing around with other women. That was one reason he had left their home for a few weeks. She had become aggressive and threatening lately, one never knew what would set her off. Bill was a handsome, six four athletic guy with brown, crew cut hair.

Janet had been a star basketball player in high school and college. She was six feet tall, with auburn hair that she wore in a pony tail. She had lost her once great figure and was now very overweight. She had been a beauty, even the homecoming queen their senior year when she dated the football quarterback. She seemed to have lost all interest in caring for her looks and seldom wore anything but sweats. She kept a neat clean home and was an excellent cook but had become more or less a recluse since gaining weight. She wouldn't go to the country club any more so Bill would go to some functions alone. That is how he became involved with Margie, when after her divorce she was alone also.

They sort of drifted together and eventually began to meet outside town where they hoped they wouldn't be noticed. At one time when he had been separated from Janet, he stayed at a local motel that was owned by a good friend who gave him a break on the rent. He had taken Margie there on occasion but only after everyone was asleep and the office was closed. There was a bell that people could ring for service after hours, because the owner had his living quarters in the back.

Dinsmore was a small town though and one never knew whom they might run into. He could see Janet was in extreme distress and she promised to get psychological help if he would come back. Also he had two great children, Amy fifteen and Tom, seventeen who were totally embarrassed by the separation and begged him to come home. Tom was the quarterback on the Dinsmore High football team and that was a source of much pride to Bill.

Sometimes he was accused of being a biased coach but everybody agreed Tom was the best quarterback they'd had in years. They had a winning record and were looking forward to playing in the finals. He didn't tell Margie he had gone back to Janet for quite a while. When she found out, she quit seeing him immediately. He called her and they just talked occasionally. He quit calling when he thought Janet might be listening in on the extension.

Janet never went to the psychologist as she had promised but he didn't push, thinking she would become miserable enough to go on her on. He had suggested they go for marriage counseling. She went into a fit of temper and threw a frying pan at him. He just stayed out of her way and spent a lot of time at the school working on plays for his team to learn. He was also the history teacher so he had plenty to keep him busy. The children were busy with all their activities and Janet just watched TV or read in her spare time. She didn't talk much but she would ask what they had been doing and acted as if she were interested.

When Amy joined an exercise class at their church on Tuesday nights she asked Janet if she would like to go. Instead of being pleased her daughter wanted to be with her she said, "So you think I'm so fat, I need to exercise, huh?"

"No, Mother, I thought it would be a good way to get out of the house and improve your health and mine."

Janet just huffed, left the room, and sat down in her recliner to read. Bill asked the kids if they wanted some ice cream and when they said, "Yes!" He went to the freezer and served it up. Afterward he cleared the table and Amy helped him load the dishwasher. Nothing more was heard from Janet.

He went to bed early and feigned sleep when she crawled in. He was thinking about Margie and he hoped Janet hadn't learned to read minds. How could Margie be dead? She was so young and beautiful. She had always been wonderful and even though he couldn't have her, he wanted her to be alive. He could have at least seen her sometimes at the club or at the bank or the store. Oh, God, why?

Chapter 11

Karen and Melanie got into town at four in the afternoon. Karen drove directly to her house and unloaded Melanie and the luggage. Then she retreated into her bedroom and called Ed at the station. The desk sergeant told her that he was out but he would get in touch with him and have him call her. She went out to check on Melanie. She was on the back porch petting the animals.

Karen went out and sat on the step and asked, "Melanie, is there anything you want me to do for you? How about something to eat?"

"No, I'm really not hungry. I'll find something when I get hungry. You don't have to treat me like company. I'm so glad I've got you, but I don't know what I'll do without Mom."

Karen smiled and said, "I'm here for you anytime. Listen, I'm probably going to go meet Ed soon and catch up on the latest but I won't stay long. Will you be all right?"

"Should I go with you?" Karen thought about it. "I don't think so. We'll be discussing some police stuff and he won't want anyone else there."

"Oh, fine, I'll be fine. How about I fix us some supper? That will give me something to do. I need to be busy. Okay?"

Karen said, "Oh, that's great! There's plenty of stuff in the freezer. Use the micro to thaw it if you need to and make yourself at home. I'll be back soon."

About that time the phone rang and she answered, "Hello." It was Ed and they made arrangements to meet at the café in thirty minutes.

She drove straight to the Café and they went to their table in the back again. Maria brought them coffee and asked if they needed anything else. It was the dinner hour but they said "No, thanks." Ed said, "I will order something later, though."

"Fine." She went to wait on others.

In the evenings Thursday through Saturday they had an extra waitress. Sundays they closed after the breakfast hour so they could go to the local Catholic church, St. Peters. Anybody that wanted Sunday dinner would have to go elsewhere. Most went to Holiday Inn Buffet out on the interstate. Even

Tony and Maria and their brood of five kids went there. The children were like stair steps, two years apart. Fortunately Tony's mother lived with them and did most of the housekeeping and kid rearing. She loved it, because Tony had been her only child and for an Italian Mama, that's just not enough. Tony was only four when his father had been killed on the job. Mama had never remarried. She doted on Tony and made their living as a seamstress, working at home making hundreds of outfits for the whole town. Anything from a simple blouse to a fancy wedding dress.

Ed leaned over closer to Karen and said, "I'm afraid we have no excuse for the coroner keeping Margie any longer. The chief said it was obviously suicide and no point in keeping the case open."

"Can I talk to the coroner?" "Well, he is working right now on a case of a child who died under mysterious circumstances." Karen said, "Let's go before we miss him."

Ed yelled to Tony, "I'll be back soon."

"Okay, buddy, later."

The coroner was just finishing up a non invasive autopsy on a little boy who had drowned in an apartment swimming pool. He said, "What a shame, it was just an accident, but they should have been watching closer. People don't realize how fast it can happen."

The coroner was Frank Peoples, he was an old country doctor that just wanted something to do after retiring. . It was an elected office and he beat out the local undertaker. Fortunately, he wasn't called on for many complicated deaths. When there was doubt, they could call on the state medical examiner in extreme cases that required a complicated autopsy.

Karen asked, "Frank, what do you think about Margie? Did she have a disease or was something wrong?"

He answered after a moment's pause, "There was nothing, but I sent some blood and urine samples off in case I missed something. As far as I can tell there's no explanation. I checked with her physician and he told me that she was in good health, no problems except she may have been going into an early menopause."

She asked, "Do you think it's wise to release her body yet? I mean we really don't know."

"Well, I guess we can hold up a few more days for the lab reports but I doubt if it will make a difference."

Karen told him, "Okay, her daughter is staying with me and we'll make the funeral arrangements but I don't want to do anything until we hear from the testing. I'll be checking back in a day or two."

They thanked him and went back to their cars. In the parking lot Karen asked, "Melanie's fixing our supper, why don't you join us? It would be good to have someone else for her to talk to." He looked doubtful and said, "You sure I won't be out of place?"

"Are you kidding? After all the years I've known you, I think this is the first time I invited you to supper but I think it is about time," she grabbed his arm, pulling on him.

He said, "Okay, I'll follow you. Lead the way."

By now it was after six in the evening and the sunset was beautiful. It made Karen sad to think that Margie would have loved to have supper with Melanie and watch the sunset on the golden fields at Karen's house. Before long it would be getting dark by this time of evening, then the weather would not be so pleasant.

When they got to Karen's house, Melanie was sitting on the back porch with the animals and got up to greet them. "Melanie, do you remember Ed Hawkins? You know I worked with him when I was a cop."

"Of course, I used to see him when I came to see you at the station. How are you, Detective HawkinsJ?"

Ed held out his hand and took hers saying, "I'm just fine. How are you doing? I know this is a sad time for you."

She shook her head, "It hasn't sunk in yet. I don't even know how to explain it. I still just can't believe that my mother is gone."

Karen interrupted, "What's for supper, Miss Melanie? Can I help get in on the table? I've invited Ed to join us."

They all went into the house and the table was set with Karen's best everyday dishes and she had put some linen napkins under each silver setting. Melanie hurried to get another place setting and said, "I fixed broiled chicken breasts and luckily I made extra. I must have had an inkling because I even baked four potatoes. The salad is in the fridge."

Karen said, "I'll get it and what kind of dressing do you two want? Ranch or thousand island? Oh, never mind I'll put them both out. Let's see we'll need some butter and sour cream."

Melanie said, "Oh, yes, I've got peas on the stove. I'll pour them into a bowl." She put the chicken on a platter, got a bowl for the peas and one for the potatoes."

Karen got some salad bowls out and put them by the salad and they all sat down. Melanie held out her hands to Karen and Ed and they all held hands as she said the grace like she did as a little girl, "God is great, God is good, God we thank you for this food. God thank you for giving me Karen and take good care of my Mama." After "Amen," it was quiet for a few minutes as they filled their plates and then Karen broke the silent sadness by starting to tell them about her trip to the art colony.

Chapter 12

Ed didn't leave until after ten and as Karen walked him to his car, he said, "You know Karen, I never thought it was a good idea to ask you out when we worked together. Now there's no reason I can't take you to a movie or dinner sometime." He smiled then and added, "Or even dinner and a movie. Would you be available or agreeable?"

She was a little surprised but answered, "Why, Ed, I would love to after we get this mess straightened out. I'll be busy with the funeral and helping Melanie for a while but after that it would be great."

He nodded his head indicating he understood. Then he took her hand in his, leaned over kissed her on the cheek, got in his car and backed out of the drive. She stood there a minute or two, contemplating what had just happened, then she turned and went in to help Melanie with the clean up. They watched a late show on TV and then they got ready for bed.

Karen had prepared the guest room for Melanie and she made sure she was comfortable.

She said, "Want me to tuck you in?"

She was surprised when Melanie said, "Yes." She had tears in her eyes, Karen brushed them away, pulled the quilt up, tucked it in, kissed her on the cheek and left the room fearing she would start to cry herself. She kept waking up all night long with thoughts of Margie on her mind each time. She just had to figure this out somehow, or she would never be able to rest.

Ed got back to town right before the Café closed. Actually they were closed but opened the door for him. "I didn't come back and I owe you for the coffee that Karen and I had earlier."

"You gotta be kiddin' man! Since when am I gonna worry about a cup or two of coffee?" He continued, "I am glad you stopped by though. Larry Sloan was in here earlier looking for you. Wanting to know what all this was about Margie committing suicide. I told him that all I knew she was dead. He was real upset and as usual seemed like he had been drinking."

"Well, he can find me tomorrow because I'm beat and I'm going home to bed. This thing has about got me down. Something's just not right and I can't put my finger on it."

Tony held up his hand and said, "Hey, man, that ain't all the news I've got for you. Him and that Pamela went off and got married. Poor kid, she doesn't know what she's in for."

Ed just shook his head and told Tony, "I'll see you in the morning, I can't take any more surprises tonight. What a mess!"

Chapter 13

Bill Wallace was watching a football game on TV with Tom when Janet came and asked, "Why didn't you tell me that Margie had died?"

Bill looked surprised, "I didn't know you knew her. She was older than you."

Janet sneered, "She may have been older but she was a hell of a lot better looking, wasn't she? You and her were an item, weren't you?"

Bill said, "Yes, we went together in high school and she was a very nice person."

Janet sneered and said, "Oh, you haven't seen her lately?"

"Look Janet, Tom and I are trying to watch the game. Don't start anything, please."

She turned on her heel and headed for the bedroom. Over her shoulder she yelled, "Oh, yeah, don't start anything, Janet, just wonder what Bill started."

Tom looked at his dad, shook his head and they went on watching the game. They were getting psyched up for the big game on Friday night. Bill went to sleep on the couch with the TV on after Tom went to bed. In the morning he showered, dressed and slipped out before the rest of the house woke. He went downtown to the Café.

Tony had just opened the doors when Bill came in. He yelled, "Hey, buddy, my first customer of the day! We gonna win the game tomorrow night?"

Bill said, "You bet, you can count on it. You know the coach don't you? And how about that quarterback?"

Tony was grinning as he brought him a cup of coffee. He said, "What is you gonna have this morning?"

Bill asked, "How about an omelet today? I'm really hungry and it's going to be a long day."

Maria came out of the back room and said, "Good Morning, Bill. How ya doing?"

He smiled and told her, "I'm fine, just hungry."

She turned to Tony. "Well, you better get this man something to eat, Hon.

43

Can I refill your coffee?" He nodded. "Okay, that will be good."

Just then the door opened and Larry Sloan walked in or maybe staggered would be a better description. He was slurring his words as he asked, "Did you ever see Ed Hawkins?"

Tony told him what Ed had said and he turned on his heel and staggered back out the door. Bill said, "God, I hope he's not driving."

Tony said, "Oh, sure he is. I just hope nobody gets in his path. I'd like to be a fly on the wall when he goes in the police station. That should really be a big joke to the cops. Bet ya ten bucks they arrest him."

Bill says, "I'm not betting on that one. He's a walking disaster. Poor Margie was smart when she got rid of him."

Tony says, "Oh, you ain't heard the latest. He just got married again to that Pamela girl that worked for him at the store."

"Oh, my God, what was she thinking? Bet she thinks he's got money." Maria brought him his omelet and he began to eat. More customers were arriving and that ended their conversation.

Chapter 14

Karen got up early, made the coffee and when it was done, poured a cup and took it out on the porch to watch the sunrise and think about the things she had to do today. Jazz and Callie both joined her. Jazz at her side waiting for a pat on the head and Callie at her feet looking as if she might jump in her lap any minute. The phone rang and Karen hurried in to answer, she had wanted Melanie to sleep late.

It was Ed, he told her, "We've got to release Margie today. The medical examiner has the blood and urine samples. If he finds anything, we can investigate further. We won't need her body to prove it's not suicide. You can call the undertaker and make arrangements for them to receive the body."

"Okay, Melanie will have to do that as next of kin so we'll get started on it when she gets up. I'll talk to you later when I know more."

She turned to see Melanie standing in the doorway. "What is that I have to do?" Melanie asked.

"Oh, I'm so sorry the phone woke you. We have to make funeral arrangements today and you will have to give the orders as next of kin."

Melanie began to sob and ran out of the room. Karen didn't know whether to follow her or let her alone. She decided to give her a few minutes alone. It was early and there was no rush. She heard the shower starting to run so she went back outside to wait.

Melanie came out on the porch fully dressed in a long grey jumper with a white long sleeved turtleneck. She had her brunette hair up in the back with a comb. She didn't have on any make up and her eyes were still red. She did manage a smile when she said, "Okay, I'm ready to do whatever I have to do. I have no idea what it is."

Karen was relieved and told her, "Honey, I'm going to be right there to help and we'll make it through. The undertaker will help us. I thought we'd call the Knight's funeral home. Is that all right with you?"

"That's fine with me. I'm going to have my coffee now. When do we have to go?"

"I'm going to fix us a little breakfast. Then I'll shower and get dressed and start the calls. They'll tell us when to come to the mortuary."

Melanie was petting Jazz and looked up at Karen. "I don't know what I'd do without you." Karen turned and went in to start breakfast before she got emotional.

Karen thought, "If I just stay busy, I'll get through this day somehow. After breakfast of oatmeal and cinnamon toast she went to shower and dress. She didn't feel like make up either but thought, "Melanie can get away with it but I sure can't." She chose a black pants suit with a pink satin shell, a pair of simple black shoes and put on her favorite diamond earrings. She stepped back for a final look in the mirror and decided she would do.

She went out to join Melanie at the kitchen table, but the phone rang. She looked at the clock and was surprised to see it was already nine o'clock. It was the minister from First Methodist Church where Margie and her family had belonged. "I understand Melanie is with you and I wanted to meet with her. When would it be convenient?"

Karen told him their plan. "We are going to make arrangements to go to the funeral home this morning. Would you like to meet us there?"

"Oh, sure that would be fine if I would be of assistance. I'd like to be there for Melanie."

She said, "I'll call you when we know what time. Will that be okay?" He agreed and after she had hung up the phone, she went back to the table. "Okay, Melanie are we ready to start this?"

"Yes, go ahead and make the appointment." After she had called the funeral home and made an appointment for eleven o'clock, she called the minister and told him when they would be there. He said he would be waiting for them at the home. She told Melanie she was going to feed the animals and after that they would go. She was thinking I should have done this before I got dressed. She went out to the barn to see about her horse, Candy. She still had plenty of food and after a pat on the nose she went back to feed Jazz and Callie. She was taking her time because she really didn't want to go but she knew there was no avoiding the inevitable.

It was a cool but sunny day and they decided they wouldn't need wraps so she locked up the house and they headed for town in Karen's little Toyota. She noticed the gas was getting low so she stopped at the first station and filled up. When she went to pay, she asked Melanie if she wanted anything. Melanie said, "A diet drink would be great."

She got two diet drinks and paid the clerk for the gas and drinks. She briefly thought about buying a pack of cigarettes because she felt the need for one. She had quit only a month ago and always thought of them when she was feeling stressed. Better judgement prevailed and she went back to the car.

"Well, Melanie, I have stalled as long as I can, so here we go to get this over with."

Melanie just smiled sadly, as she opened her drink.

Chapter 15

They got to the funeral home ten minutes early. It had been there for many years, a buff brick two story building, well maintained. Years ago the family lived on the second floor but these owners now lived in private residences. They entered the foyer that was tastefully decorated with a floral wallpaper in green and wine colors, with wine colored upholstered chairs at an ornate mahogany desk. Karen introduced Melanie to the receptionist, Mrs. Thorp, who was sitting behind the desk. Karen knew everyone there from having arranged her husband's services five years before. Unfortunately she had been to several funerals there over the past few years.

She said, "We're here to make arrangements for Margie Sloan. We're supposed to see Joe Froder. Is he available?"

"Yes, I'll see if he's ready. Oh, here's Mr. Froder now."

A tall balding man in his sixties came around the corner and held out his hand to Karen. "It's good to see you, Karen. This must be Melanie." he said as he took Melanie's hand and told her, "I'm sorry to meet you under these circumstances but I hope I will be able to help make it easier for you."

Melanie just nodded her head as she shook his hand. "Thank you," she murmured.

Karen asked, "Have you picked her up yet."

"No, we'll get Melanie to sign a release after we finish here." Karen told him they would go to Margie's apartment and find her insurance policies sometime today and get back to him with that. She was sure Margie had taken care of that sort of thing because she was always so organized.

They picked out a bronze casket with a soft pink lining, told him all the vital information. He told them he would order any flowers they wanted and Melanie told him what flowers she would like to have on the casket. Karen was glad she could mark that off her list. They decided to have the funeral on Monday at 10 o'clock in the morning. It was Friday by now and they didn't want to have it on the weekend. Karen was thinking she would have more time to do a little more investigating if she could get away today. Then she thought maybe it would be good for Melanie to be involved after all because the thought of suicide was bothering her, too.

Before they got ready to leave the funeral home she called Ed. After he got on the phone, she asked, "Did you take fingerprints from Margie's apartment?"

"I wasn't there but I don't think so. They thought it was suicide. They shouldn't have rushed to judgement but they did. Why?"

She told him to send somebody over to check for prints before she and Melanie got there because she wanted to know who had been in that apartment.

He said, "Good idea, I'll get right on it. You can go on over if you want. I'll go myself so it will be all right for you to be there as long as you wait to touch anything." She told him she'd meet him in thirty minutes.

Just as she turned to say "Let's go and get on with our business.," the minister, Gary Oldham, walked in the door.

Karen said, "My goodness, we were just finished with our business here. I had given up on you."

He apologized, saying, "I'm so sorry, I was detained by another church member who had a very distressing problem and I couldn't leave him." Karen was a member of the same church though she wasn't as devoted as she should be. He knew Melanie, too, because she had grown up in the church even before Gary had been sent to their church.

He was a young man probably in his thirties, brown, thinning hair but very tall and handsome, he was wearing a dark blue suit with a yellow and blue striped tie. He had married a local girl, Christine Foley, four years ago. They had two children, a boy and a girl, just toddlers. He hugged Melanie and told her how sorry he was. Karen told him the plans they had made and asked if he would be available to speak. He assured her he would and asked if there was anything he could do now. She told him that she would talk to him more tomorrow. He said if he wasn't needed, he would get back to the problem he had left at the parsonage. His wife was handling it right now. Karen was curious but decided against asking questions, as the cop in her always made her seem nosy. They said their goodbyes and headed for Margie's apartment on Avian Way.

Chapter 16

Friday morning Bill Wallace got up early again because he had the big game to get ready for and he was concerned that he had not prepared his team well enough. He hadn't slept well, tossing and turning all night. He made a pot of coffee after he showered and dressed in a green T-shirt and khakis. He had his coaching clothes in a locker at the school.

He went in to wake Tom so that they could go together. He was trying not to wake Janet and whispered to Tom, "Get dressed and we'll go to the Café for breakfast before school starts."

He started back to the kitchen and was surprised to see Janet was up pouring herself a cup of coffee. "Oh, I'm sorry, I tried not to wake you."

She whirled around and growled, "Ohhh, yeah, you didn't want to wake me so I couldn't ask you more questions."

"Good Heavens, what do you want to know?" he asked trying to be quiet so the children wouldn't hear them in another argument.

She screamed, "I want to know how long you've been screwing around with Margie Sloan!"

He put his finger to his lips to quiet her and that really made her crazy. She threw her coffee cup at him and it broke on the left side of his head, cutting a gash right above his eyebrow which immediately began to bleed profusely. He grabbed a hand towel and held it tight to stop the bleeding so his shirt wouldn't get soiled.

Tom and Amy came running into the kitchen. Tom said, "What is going on?"

Amy saw the bloody towel her father was holding to his head, and she screamed, "Mother, what have you done, have you lost your mind?"

Janet's face turned red and she raged, "Oh, yeah, I've gone nuts and daddy dear is just a little angel, isn't he? He can just chase any woman he wants and all is fine, but I'm the one who is nuts."

Tom said, "Mother, you have such a great imagination. Why don't you get your butt out of the house and see what the real world is like? Instead you sit around dreaming up ways to make us all miserable."

"Well, if you are all so miserable, why don't you just leave?," she sneered at him.

Bill interrupted and said, "Look I'm okay, just go get dressed, the both of you, and we'll go have breakfast before school starts." He went to the bathroom to check on his wound, cleaned it up with some peroxide and put on a band aid. It wasn't as bad as it looked at first.

Janet came by the bathroom on her way back to the bedroom. She growled as she went by, "Pooorrr baby, did it get hurt?" He pretended not to hear her, thinking it best to let it go, and just get the hell out before she had a chance to do more damage. The kids didn't waste any time dressing and getting their books together. They all piled in Bill's Ford pick-up and headed out. He drove by Margie's apartment on the way downtown and saw Ed Hawkins going in the building. He wondered what was going on but didn't let onto the kids. When they got to the Café they went to a table.

It was very busy but Maria came right over with a cup of coffee for Bill. She knew they would need to get to school soon. She asked, "What happened to your head, man? You've got quite a bump there."

Bill blushed and said, "Oh, I bumped it on the truck hood."

She took their order, after she left Amy whispered, "Dad, it is swelling up. Everybody is going to be asking you what happened."

He just laughed and said, "I know but don't you like my quick thinking?"

She shook her head and said, "I don't know how you can laugh. She's out of control and you've got to do something."

"What can he do?" Tom muttered. "Get her some help before she kills us all."

Bill waved his hand at her and said, "Don't you worry about it. I'll be all right and she will too. I know she needs help but I can't get her to go. I'll keep working on it. Let's just enjoy our breakfast and get to school. We've got the big game tonight and that's all I'm worried about right now."

Their food came and they ate in silence. When they finished Bill left a twenty-dollar bill on the table and they left without being noticed. They got back in the truck and headed for the school. He noticed that Tony had put a big paper sign in the window that said "GO TIGERS." He managed a smile at that.

Chapter 17

Ed Hawkins was waiting outside the apartment building when Karen and Melanie got there. Karen went into the parking garage and Ed came on in to meet them. He shook hands with Melanie and then gave her a hug.

He told Karen, "I got everything done and you're free to check out anything you want to." They got on the elevator and went up to Margies apartment. Ed unlocked the door and let them in. He asked Melanie if she had a key and said she did.

He said, "Well, I'm going to leave you girls to it, then. I've got a lot on my plate and need to get back. Do you think you can come in this evening, Karen?"

"Yes, I'm going to let Melanie drop me off and take the car to visit some of her friends later. She needs to be around someone young."

Melanie looked surprised, "Who would I go see? Everybody else is at school."

"I didn't think about that," Karen said, "I just thought you might like to take off on your own for a little while but it's up to you."

"Actually, I'd like to go back to your house and ride Candy for a while."

"That's a great plan and as soon as we finish here we'll go have lunch and do that."

She turned to Ed, "But I will come back in and meet with you later. I don't want to be too late though because I'd like to go to the game tonight. We need to get our minds off of this sad business for a while."

They walked with him to the door. He answered, "Yeah, me too, will I see you there, Melanie?"

She asked, "Do you think it will be all right? You know, with Mother gone and all? I don't know what people will think."

"Honey, if anyone thinks badly, it's their problem." Ed answered. "This town will talk no matter what you do, so do what you feel is okay. I hope you'll go to the game. See you girls later."

He turned to go saying, "Got to get my exercise," as he headed for the stairs.

Karen said sarcastically, "Oh, yeah, walking down steps is really good exercise." He did a backhand wave and disappeared.

Karen suggested Melanie go through Margie's desk. She noticed that the poor girl was starting to tear up again and said, "If it's too hard, I'll be glad to do it."

"No, I'll manage. I want to help."

"Okay, you do that then and I've got some other things I want to check on." She spoke as she went to the bathroom. She checked the medicine cabinet. There were no prescriptions there just the normal aspirin and ibuprofen. There was a tube of cortisone cream and the rest was facial cleanser and astringent. She knew that Ed had the bottle that had held sleeping medication which she presumably had overdosed on. She went to the bedroom and checked her jewelry box.

There was a diamond pendent laying right on the dressing table along with what had been her engagement ring. Most of the jewelry in the box was not expensive as far as Karen could tell. There was a little box that contained diamond earrings and some that looked like aquamarine stones. Karen knew that Margie had recently inherited some valuable jewelry and antiques from her grandmother. She looked in the closet, checked her pockets, looked in some boxes on the shelf. Finding nothing that looked interesting she went to the kitchen.

She looked in all the cabinets, under the sink and in the pantry type closet. No poisons, just cleaning aids, nothing that looked suspicious. She went to the living room and sat down, just looking around, thinking "What am I missing. There must be a clue here somewhere." She saw the answer machine and went to it but the tape was gone. Ed must have it, she thought.

She went to check on Melanie at the desk and asked, "Have you found anything of interest?"

Melanie answered, "Well, I do have her insurance policy and I was looking for her address book but can't find it. Have you seen her purse?"

"No, I imagine it's at the police department." Karen answered.

Melanie looked up surprised and asked, "Why would they have it?"

"Well, Melanie, probably thought it was evidence or might be. Ed and I just can't believe that your mother committed suicide. We are investigating further, just to be sure what happened."

Melanie said, "I'm glad because I don't believe it either. If you're ready, I'd like to leave now. It's creeping me out to be here without my mother. You know I've never lived here because I've been away at school during the divorce and all. I stayed for summer school because I didn't want to be involved in all the mess."

Karen said, "Fine, let's go. You can lock up with your key." They went down to the parking lot and got in the car. They pulled out and went to the Café down town.

They got a parking place right in front since it was mid afternoon and the lunch crowd had already gone back to work. When they went in, Tony looked up from where he was sitting at the bar and smiled.

He said, "Hey, girls, I'm glad to see you. How's it goin'?" He looked embarrassed. "Oh, I'm sorry Melanie, I know you've had a great loss and I really hate it. Your mom was a great lady and we will miss her."

Melanie smiled and said, "Thank you, Tony, I thought so too."

Maria came out of the back room and she said, "Oh, I'm so glad to see you two. Melanie please accept my condolences. I really admired her."

They sat down at a table and she brought them each a glass of water and asked what they would like to drink. Karen ordered coffee and Melanie iced tea. After she left, they both decided to just get a burger and fries. She came back with their drinks and they gave her the order. Tony started to cook and Maria came over and sat down at their table.

She leaned in toward Karen and said, "I don't want Tony to hear me. You should have seen Bill Wallace this morning. He came in here with both his kids and had a big bump and cut on his forehead. He joked about it and said he bumped it on the truck hood. The kids looked at each other when he said that and it was obvious he was lying."

Just then Tony yelled, "Orders up. Maria quit gossiping!" She shrugged her shoulders and went to get their orders. They started to eat right away so she went back to the counter and began to straighten up and wipe down. Karen hadn't wanted to pursue the conversation because she did not like gossip. As soon as they finished their lunch Karen got up and went to pay the bill. She told them that it was very good as usual and Melanie agreed. The four of them talked about the big game tonight and decided they would see each other there.

They got back to Karen's house at two thirty and Melanie couldn't wait to change to jeans and get out to the barn. Karen went directly to the phone and called Ed. They made plans to meet at the station at three thirty.

She asked Melanie if she needed any help with saddling Candy and she said, "No, I went out yesterday to see her and she still remembers me, I think. She's such a sweet horse and I love riding her. I'll brush her after we ride awhile. You go on and do what you have to do."

Karen went in the bathroom to brush her teeth. They had the burgers with everything and the onion breath would not be pleasant talking to Ed. She put on some more lipstick, ran a brush through her short hair and decided she would do. She went out to the car about ten after three and Melanie was on her way to the barn. She yelled at Melanie and told her not to forget to get ready about five thirty if she wasn't back. They would go to the football game and it started at seven. The weather was a little cooler as the sun got lower but it was going to be a good night for football. She thought they should take an extra blanket though just in case it got too cool.

Chapter 18

When school was out at three, Coach Wallace took his team out for some exercise and ran some scrimmages. At four thirty he sent them home to eat and told them to come back early to get ready for the game. Amy was still inside school, studying in the library so he sent Tom to get her and told them that he thought it best if they went to the Café to eat supper. They agreed and were both glad they didn't have to face their mother right now. They got their things together and went to the truck. They got to the Café at five fifteen and Tony greeted them as they walked in. The place was really busy but Maria waited on them in a few minutes. She brought them all some water and got their drink order. Spaghetti and meatballs were always the Friday Night Special so when Maria brought their drinks Bill ordered the Special for the three of them. Maria brought their salads and garlic bread and they began to eat. They didn't have much conversation because they were all thinking about their problem at home and didn't want to talk about it at this point. Bill and Tom needed to be in a good frame of mind for the game.

When they finished the salads, Maria and Tony both brought the main course and Tony said, "Okay coach, can I bet on the Tigers tonight?"

"You know I can't tell you to gamble on my team but you know we're going to win. Ain't that right, Tom?"

Tom answered, "You bet! Oops, I don't mean you bet, I mean yes indeed."

When they had finished eating Bill left a tip and paid the bill at the counter. Then they got in the truck and went back to the school. Amy was a cheerleader so she went to the girls locker room to change into her cheerleading outfit and Tom and Bill went to change to their football gear. After they changed, Bill and Tom went on the field and practiced passing the football. The rest of the team began to come back and then the visiting team from Union arrived on four busses. They had their marching band with them. Union's mascot was a bull dog, an ugly English bull dog.

When Karen got to the police station the desk sergeant grinned and said, "Hey, it's good to see you, girl. What are you doing, slumming?"

"I'm here to see Ed. Is he here?" "Sure go on back. He's in his office." She walked down the hall and when she got to his office, he was on the phone. He motioned for her to sit down and held up five fingers to indicate he wouldn't be long. She could tell he was talking to the medical examiner.

He looked puzzled when he hung up the phone. "The M E says there is nothing in the blood or urine that indicates poisoning but get this there are also no barbiturates. Now that makes me even more suspicious. We're checking fingerprints on the pill bottle and a couple of wine glasses. They lifted some from the phone and the medicine cabinet"

Karen asked, "Do you have her purse and the answer machine tape? I looked the whole apartment over and I found nothing. Oh, yes, Melanie was looking for her address book. Do you have that?"

"Yes, I have all three things and get this I want to play the tape for you." He got a small record player out of his desk and put the tape in. The first call was from Daniel Carmody confirming their date for that night. The next was from her mother just asking if she still planned to come up on Sunday.

Then a man's voice came on and he said "Margie, I sure do miss you. I wish we could get together sometime. I'm back home but it's hell. I'm afraid to leave because of the kids. Please, call me at school sometime and let me see you again."

Ed and Karen just sat and looked dumbfounded at each other. She said almost in a whisper, "That was Bill Wallace. I can't believe it. I've seen Margie for lunch every Saturday for ages. She's never mentioned seeing anyone until she started seeing Daniel Carmody."

He shook his head and said, "I was shocked, too. I heard they were an item in high school but I had never seen them together since I've been working here."

Karen was still in shock and she finally spoke, "I guess there's nothing we can do until after the funeral. We may find a clue there but I don't know what to think. The funeral is planned for Monday and as soon as I get Melanie back to Missouri we are going to do some investigating, big time!"

Ed said, "You are going to need to do the investigating because the chief has already told me to drop it. So I'll get with you later and we'll see what's going on. Okay?"

"That sounds like a plan, I know you're in a bad position. I've just got to get to the bottom of this." Karen got up to leave, and told him, "I've got to get home and get ready to go to the game. Melanie will be waiting for me."

He said, "She's lucky to have you. I'll probably see you at the game." He walked her out to the door, she told him and the sergeant goodbye and went to her car.

Chapter 19

The football game started at seven o'clock sharp with the playing of the Star Spangled Banner by the marching Tigers. Karen and Melanie were sitting five rows up in the stands close to the fifty-yard line. It was a beautiful night and there was a good crowd. Tony and Maria closed the Café to go to the games and they had their little brood with them. Even Mama came along. They needed her to help keep track of the kids. They were sitting a couple of rows down lower and Ed had sat down by them but when he saw Daniel Carmody sitting a few rows over, went to sit with him. The Distefano kids were too much for him.

The Union team came on the field first bursting through a paper sign with lots of hooping and hollering on the opposing team's side of the field. Then the Dinsmore Tigers came roaring out of their paper sign with just as much noise. They did the coin toss and the Tigers won. They chose defense and the game was on. Both teams had good reputations and it was bound to be a close, tough game.

Bill Wallace was well known as a good coach. He had a good rapport with his team and they worked hard to please him. He was very proud of Tom and Amy and they loved him. They were good kids, made good grades, went to First Methodist Church every Sunday and had never been in any trouble. Tom was playing exceptionally well this night and the Tigers were ahead by two touchdowns at the half. They had a dozen cheerleaders and Amy was as pretty as could be. It was her first year on the squad but she was good at it.

At half time the bands took turns entertaining the crowd, marching and playing. Union played tunes from the Beatles and the marching Tigers played a tribute to John Phillips Sousa. Very different but both equally excellent renditions.

When halftime was over Larry and Pamela Sloan came in and climbed up two rows to a couple of empty seats. Larry was looking bleary eyed as usual and sort of stumbling around. He was creating a little stir around him. The whole area was turning to look at him. Karen was trying not to pay attention, hoping Melanie would not see him. She had been talking to some old high school friends and seemed to be enjoying herself in spite of everything. She began to talk to the lady sitting next to her until Melanie came back from the concession stand and sat down.

All of a sudden somebody let out a whoop and when they looked in the direction of the sound, it was Larry of course. He wanted everybody to notice him and they surely were. Melanie slumped on the bench and leaned back so she would be partially hidden.

She said, "Please, God, don't let him see me. The game had started again and there was a lot of yelling all around so Larry couldn't have been heard if he tried it again. The Tigers held their lead but Tom got creamed on one of the plays and had to be taken out for a few minutes. But like a good trooper he was back in and firing the ball to his receiver. The Tigers were definitely at their best.

Just before the end of the game, a figure came running down the sidelines to the Tiger bench and grabbed Bill Wallace around his chest from behind like a bear hug. Bill's feet flew out from under him and Larry was squeezing his chest and swinging him around like a rag doll. Bill couldn't get his breath and was losing consciousness. Finally the boys on the bench saw what was happening and got up and piled on Larry. They threw him to the ground. He had his hands up like "don't hit me." Some of them started to kick him but Bill called them off. They quit kicking and picked him up by the feet and arms and hauled his butt off the field to hand him to the cops.

Chapter 20

On Friday afternoon Daniel Carmody had sent a memo to everyone in the bank telling them of Margie's death and the funeral plans. He had called the mortuary and they told him what was planned. He had sat at his desk for days unable to do much of anything. When things came up, he handled them but otherwise he was lost in a sea of grief. He had called and ordered his flowers. The president's secretary had ordered the banks floral offering. He was trying to decide whether he should call Karen and go to see her and Margie's daughter. He also wanted to talk to Ed Hawkins. He just knew Margie didn't commit suicide. They'd had a wonderful evening and they had made love on the rug in front of the fireplace before they fell asleep. He had left her about three o'clock in the morning and she was fine. He finally decided it would be best just to meet the daughter at the wake. He did call Ed, though. He asked him to meet him for breakfast in the morning at the Café so they could talk. Ed agreed that would be good and they decided on eight o'clock.

Then Ed had asked him to go to the football game, "It will be good for you, sitting at home won't help Margie or you. Give yourself a break." So he had gone even though it felt strange.

Melanie said, "What was that all about? Why would he do such a thing to Bill Wallace, one of the nicest teachers I ever had?"

Karen said, "Well, you know, your mother and Bill went steady all through high school and remained friends. I guess Larry is still carrying a grudge. He caused a scene at the country club the other night when your mother was out with Daniel Carmody. That was Daniel sitting with Ed down below us. Did you see them?"

"Oh, yes, he is a nice looking man. Mother and he were dating?," she asked, sounding surprised.

Karen answered, "Yes, she worked with him at the bank. He's the vice-president and just moved here recently. He's from Chicago. They had gone out a couple of times and that night was special but Larry managed to embarrass them in public. He was escorted from the club, too. He seems to have a habit of getting thrown out."

"Oh, my God, that's the night that she died isn't it? Do you think that was why she did what she did?"

"No way." Karen said, "I'll never believe your mother committed suicide and I intend to prove it. As soon as I get you back to Missouri and in school where you belong, I'm going to start an investigation of my own. Ed can't be involved because the chief says the case is closed but he will be helping me without the department knowing."

Melanie sighed and said, "Oh, I'm so glad you feel that way. By the way I forgot to tell you, Mr. Froder called this afternoon while you were gone. He said Mother's body would be ready for viewing by two tomorrow afternoon and that we could come then. He asked if we would like to have visitation Saturday and Sunday evening from seven to nine and I told him yes. Is that okay?"

"Of course that will be nice to have it on two nights." Melanie went on, "Good. Mr. Froder said flowers were being delivered by the dozens already."

"Yes," Karen said, "Your mother had a lot of friends. She was a truly lovely person. I haven't ordered my flowers yet but I will tomorrow. Did he say if the blanket of flowers for the casket was ready yet?"

"No, we didn't talk about that," Melanie answered, "I told him I had found the insurance policy. Did I tell you it is for one hundred thousand dollars and I am the only beneficiary?"

"That's wonderful." Karen said, "You will need that money to get started in life. You know I haven't called your grandmother yet. She's so ill, I was afraid to call so I want to run over there in the morning and see her if you will go with me." Melanie agreed that it had to be done.

By now the game was over and the crowd was up and cheering because the Tigers were victorious once again. Karen waved at Ed and Daniel as they left the stands. The two of them made their way to the car and went home to get some rest. They had a busy weekend coming up and it wasn't going to be a happy one.

After a little celebrating on the field Bill and his boys went to the locker room. Amy got changed first and waited by the truck. Several of her friends came by and wanted to know why that guy did that to her dad.

She said, "I haven't got the slightest idea. Just some nut, I guess." They asked if she wanted to go with them to Wendy's. She told them she needed to get home and would wait for her dad and brother. They went on their merry way. Bill and Tom came out soon and they all piled in the truck to go home. Bill stopped at the Quick Mart and got a six pack of beer and soda for the kids. Tom gassed up the truck while Bill was inside. He came out to the truck after he paid for it all.

When he climbed in Tom said, "What was that ruckus all about, Dad?"

Amy chimed in, "Yes, what was that all about?"

Bill hesitated and then he told them, "Well, I really don't know for sure but that was Larry Sloan. He used to be married to Margie Sloan. Margie and I went steady all through high school and I guess he was jealous. Who knows what goes through a drunk's mind?" He was quiet for a few minutes and then he said, "You know, what's funny is that he just got married to a young girl that works for him at the department store. I don't know why he would get upset over something that happened years ago." They drove the rest of the way in silence. When they got there, the kids got a soda and went straight to their rooms. Janet was in the living room watching TV and didn't speak. Bill put the drinks up and opened a beer before he went into the den and sat down in his recliner.

Janet gave him a dirty look and said, "Not going to offer me a beer?"

He said, "Sure I'll get you one." She muttered sarcastically, "I guess you won the game since you're celebrating."

"Yes, we did. We won big time. Tom played a great game and we won by eighteen points. It was a blowout. You should have been there. Your son is a great player and your daughter does a good job on the cheerleading team."

He got up and went to get her a beer. When he came back, he handed it to her and sat back down. She didn't say anything else for about an hour. By then the kids were asleep in their rooms or at least they were quiet.

Janet sat up and leaned over toward Bill and said, "You son of a bitch, I know what you've been up to lately."

He was shocked and said, "What in hell are you talking about now, Janet?"

She said, "I hired a private detective to follow you for the past three months. I just paid him off and sent him packing because you won't be able to screw around now, since your little Margie up and died."

Bill came out of his chair like a rocket and said, "You what? What are you talking about? Now I know you're nuts."

She jumped up too and grabbed a baseball bat that she had laid beside her chair. She began to hit him over and over with the bat all over his body. He couldn't get away from her and was trying to get the bat away from her but she was as big and strong as him. She slammed him in the chest and he knew immediately that some of his ribs were broken. He bent over in pain and she slammed him in the back of the neck. He went down and out.

Tom came running into the room and yelled, "Mom, what are you doing? Quit, you're going to kill him, she turned and held it out as if she would swing at him. He grabbed the bat and jerked it out of her hand.

Amy was up too and went to the phone and called 911. She told them to send an ambulance that her mother had attacked her Dad and he was laying in the floor unconscious. Janet was sitting in the chair screaming and crying like a banshee.

The ambulance was there in a few minutes and the EMT's came rushing in and started to revive Bill. Right behind them came the police. It was Detective Jeff Collins with two uniformed policemen. He asked, "Tom, what's going on here?"

"My mother tried to kill my father and I want you to arrest her."

Bill was conscious now and groaned, "No, Tom." Tom was determined. "She's not going to get away with this. She already messed with you this morning and I'm afraid she'll kill us all."

Jeff said, "Do you want to press charges? You'll have to sign for me to take her to jail."

Tom answered, "Yes, just give me the paper and I'll be glad to sign it. I'm sick of this crap. She's nuts and needs help but she won't get it so we'll just lock her up and see how she likes it."

"That's pretty tough, Tom," Jeff said.

"You don't what we've been going through here. It's like hell all the time. Yelling and raising hell all the time. Never says a decent word to any of us. Take her away, please."

They were taking Bill out to the ambulance and Tom said, "Hurry up, I want to go with my Dad. Amy get out there and go with him and I'll come in the truck."

Jeff gave him the arrest papers to sign. He had already handcuffed Janet and she was strangely silent now. Tom handed him the bat and told him to take it with him for evidence in case Dad dies. The officers took Janet out and put her in the police car. She laid down in the back seat.

Jeff was going out the door when he turned and asked, "Was she drinking."

Tom said, "No, she had a beer but she didn't even drink it. She's just mean, no excuses. Let me lock up the house and get out of here."

"Okay, just be careful driving. You're really upset, you know. We don't need any more tragedies."

Tom assured him he would take it easy. He locked the door as soon as Jeff was out of it and headed for the back door, grabbed the key off the rack and locked the back door. He went to the truck and cranked it up but he sat there a minute to clear his head and calm down. He was a good kid trying to do what's right and he was totally confused by life as he knew it.

Chapter 21

On Saturday morning Karen and Melanie slept a little later than usual. They had sat up the night before and talked for a while. They talked about Margie and then they talked about art. Karen was interested in what Melanie was painting and what she was learning. Melanie said she loved the university and the campus life but she really would like to go to the Chicago Art Institute and just specialize in her art. Karen told her that was not a bad idea but to think it over and make a wise decision. They decided to go to Union to the nursing home in the morning and see Margie's mother and break the news. After that they went to bed and they both slept soundly, being exhausted from all the excitement of the evening.

Karen had the coffee ready when Melanie got up and they both went out on the porch to drink it and play with the animals. Melanie told her how much fun it had been to ride Candy and said she wanted to ride again tomorrow morning. She knew she wouldn't have time today. She dreaded all the sadness she would have to deal with today.

Karen suggested they wear casual clothes today because they would have to be dressed up for the next three days. It was going to be another beautiful day. This fall had been so great, Karen hated to think it would end and the snows would come. She went into the kitchen got the pot and brought it out to refill their cups.

After a few minutes, she said, "Well, we might as well dress and go do the deed. Let's stop in town and get grandmother a box of candy."

Melanie asked, "Is it okay for her to have candy?"

"Oh, we'll get her the sugarless kind. They don't know what's wrong with her. It's probably just old age and senility. I bet she'll be glad to see you."

Karen got up and went in to get some breakfast ready. She warmed two bagels and got out the cream cheese. She called Melanie to come in and eat. They were finished about ten thirty and got into jeans and sweat shirts, did a little primping, put on tennis shoes and socks. Karen got her purse and keys, locked the door as they went out. Then she remembered she needed to feed Jazz and Callie.

She went back in and got the food and water for them. The phone rang and when she answered, it was Ed and he said, "You'll never guess who we've got in the jail."

She said, "No, just tell me. I was on my way out the door to go tell Margie's mother the awful news."

He said, "Oh, I don't envy you. Well, we've got Janet Wallace down here. She beat the hell out of Bill last night and put him in the hospital. Tom had her arrested and sent Jeff back with the baseball bat she had used."

Karen was stunned and said, "I can't believe it. She must be sick. I haven't seen her for months."

"Yeah, I guess so, but do you remember that stranger we saw around town not long ago?" Karen said she'd never seen him. Ed said, "Well, there was one, he came in the Café once when I was there and Tony was dying to know who he was. Well, he was a private detective Janet had hired to follow Bill. She says Bill was seeing Margie on the sly."

Karen gasped, "No, I don't believe it. Oh, my God, that message on the tape."

"Yeah, you get it now?" Ed asked. "Looks like we may have a suspect."

"Oh, I wish I had time to come down there but this is all going to have to wait until after Monday. The visitation is tonight and tomorrow night. The funeral is Monday at ten."

Ed told her, "I'll see you at the visitation. Go on now and do what you have to do."

"Oh, wait, how is Bill?"

"He was in the hospital but they ex-rayed him, taped him up and sent him home this morning." Karen said, "Good, got to go. I'll talk to you later. Bye for now."

"Bye"

She took the food and water to the animals, locked the door again, called to Melanie who was out with the horse. They got in the car and turned toward town. She stopped at the drug store, ran in, got the candy and hurried back to the car. She had left it running so she backed out and headed to the interstate. Melanie commented on the colorful leaves and said she wished they had time to paint. Karen told her maybe they could do some tomorrow morning. Melanie said, "I went into your studio yesterday and you've been doing some really good work." Karen thanked her and began to tell her more about her trip to the art colony and what the instructor had said.

They arrived at the nursing home, The Haven, and got out of the car to go in. It was a long ranch style building with several wings extending out from a main entrance. It was red brick and the wood shutters were painted white.

Karen went to the desk and asked to speak to the head nurse. When she came out, she introduced herself, "Hi, I'm Patty Kilmichael. Can I help you?" Karen told her that they had bad news for Mrs. Orson and wondered if it was okay to tell her that her only daughter had died suddenly.

The nurse seemed puzzled and said, "She's been so ill, I don't know. Let me call the doctor." She went to the phone and talked for several minutes. She hung up and said, "He says I should be prepared to give her a tranquilizer shot if she gets too upset. I'll stay with you and see how it goes."

They walked down a long hall. The building was very light and nicely decorated with pale blues and greens. Looking in the rooms as they passed Karen noticed, each room had nice furnishings and there were pretty drapes on the windows but they were pulled back to let the sunshine in. They got to Mrs.Orson's room and she was just lying there, looking at the ceiling. When she saw Melanie, she sat up and smiled.

She started to cry and said, "I'm so glad to see you. I thought I'd never see you again. Where's your mother?"

Melanie went to hug her and began to cry, too. She said, "Oh, grandma, Mommy has died and we came to tell you the awful news."

"No, you're mistaken. My Margie is too young to die."

Melanie said, "Yes, I know but she did and we don't know why."

Mrs. Orson asked, "Did somebody kill her? Somebody had to kill her. She couldn't just die for no reason!" She began to sob hysterically and the nurse moved in with a tranquilizer shot for her. She cried a little while longer and then settled down but she kept on asking "how and why." Karen showed her the box of candy she had brought. She told the nurse it was sugarless. She seemed pleased for the candy but she just couldn't quit saying, "Why, why, why?"

Melanie sat and held her hand until she fell asleep, then she kissed her on the cheek. They went out with the nurse and asked how she had been doing.

"Is she improving at all?" Karen asked.

The nurse shook her head and answered, "No, she really isn't. The doctor says he doesn't think she will but one never knows about these things. Miracles still happen and she got a tough inner strength and faith."

Melanie asked, "Will it be possible for her to go to the funeral?" "Oh, no she can't, I'm sure. She's just too weak and I'm sure the doctor wouldn't allow it. I'm worried about how she'll be when she wakes."

Karen said, "We're going to go back to Dinsmore but here's my number if you need us. She had written it on a scrap of paper from Mrs. Orson's note pad. Melanie is staying with me and we'll be at the visitation tonight and tomorrow night. Then the funeral is Monday but if you need us to come back, just call me."

They left for Dinsmore taking the road back to the interstate. Karen asked Melanie if she was hungry and she said, "No, not really. My appetite is not good these days."

Karen said, "Okay, we'll just grab a snack at home. We'll need to get ready to go to the funeral home and check on your mother at two." She decided against telling Melanie about Bill and Janet Wallace. No need for her to know just yet. They got off at the Dinsmore exit and started down the highway toward town.

Melanie said, "You know I really would like to have a Frosty from Wendy's. Would you?"

"Yeah, that does sound good, I'll go to the drive thru." When they had their Frosties, they decided to wait and eat them at home. Back on the road she turned left to go the house.

When they got to the house, they sat on the porch and ate their Frosties. Then they played with Jazz and Callie for a few minutes and went in to get changed. Melanie put on a pair of navy pants, a white shirt and leather vest. She tied her hair up in a pony tail, put on some lipstick and started out the door to the porch.

She called to Karen, "I'll be out at the barn when you get ready." Karen decided on a maroon pant suit with a white satin shell. She touched up her make up, brushed her hair and went out locking the door behind her. She got into the car and honked the horn. When Melanie came toward the car she looking so sad that Karen could hardly keep from crying. She knew this was going to be the hardest thing that Melanie ever had to do.

They both sobbed quietly as they viewed Margie's body at the funeral home. They made the final arrangements for the visitations, printing of the program and funeral. They checked the wording for the obituary that would run in tomorrow's weekly paper and left information for the minister. He had arranged to call on them later in the evening. Melanie gave Mr. Froder the insurance information and he told her, "Don't you worry about anything else and if we have any questions, we'll call you and you do the same if you think of something else we need to do."

She thanked him as they left. They were relieved to have that part of the day done but so exhausted and grief stricken that they decided to go straight back home.

Chapter 22

Tom had picked his dad up from the hospital and took him home. Amy was waiting there for them. Tom went to the fridge and got a beer for him and sodas for them. They all sat down at the kitchen table and began to discuss their situation. Bill decided the best thing he could do, was to tell the truth.

He said, "Look kids, I'm not proud of it but I did see Margie while I was gone for those few weeks."

Tom moaned, "Oh, no, Dad how could you?" Amy just looked crushed and started to cry.

Bill knew he couldn't explain it away, so he just said, "I'm sorry as I can be and I don't have any excuse, except I was just very unhappy with your mother. I've tried everything. I tried to get her to go to counseling with me or go to a psychologist. She just promised to but never did. I don't know what to do at this point."

Tom said, "We'll have her committed to some place that can help her. I don't want her back here. She'll kill us all."

Amy said, "Tom, you can't mean that!"

Tom looked very serious. "You didn't see the look in her eye when she was going to hit me. I thought sure Dad was a goner and me, too."

Bill said, "Well, I'm going to call the station and talk to Ed Hawkins and see what's going on. I ask him for advice. Then I'm going to lie down. I'm hurting in more ways than one. Can you two manage without me for a while?"

They both agreed he needed to get some rest and told him they would be fine. He went into his bed and got the phone to call Ed. He decided that he would call a lawyer for advice, too. The kids went into the den and began to watch TV. Though neither of them could concentrate on what was on because they kept thinking about what was happening to their family.

Chapter 23

Karen and Melanie got back into their casual clothes when they got home. They were at the barn when Ruth and Joseph Barry came up in the driveway. Ruth got out first and had a casserole dish in her hands and Joseph came out of the truck with a pie in hand. They all met at the back porch.

Karen said, "You didn't have to go to that trouble for us, Ruth. It does look delicious though. Melanie and I have been out all day running errands so we haven't even cooked a thing."

Ruth answered, "You've got enough to worry about, you don't need to worry 'bout cooking at a time like this." Karen introduced them to Melanie and invited them into the house as she took the dishes to the porch.

They both said, "No, we'll be going." Ruth said, "But I wanted to tell you that Monday the church ladies will be fixing lunch for family and any friends you want to invite after the funeral and burial. Just let us know how many to expect."

Melanie was overcome and choked up when she said, "Oh, that's so kind of all of you. I don't know what to say."

"Well, just don't you worry about a thing. I'm sure there will be a lot of folks bringing more food here, too. You girls won't have to cook a thing. By the way, the preacher said to tell you to call him when you get a chance. He's been trying to get in touch with you."

Karen said, "I forgot to check my messages, I was anxious to get out to take care of my animals. I'll get back to him right away."

Joseph spoke for the first time, "I'm sorry about your mother, little girl and if I can do anything for you, you just let me know." She thanked and hugged them both. They went back to their little truck, waved goodbye and backed out of the drive. Various neighbors and friends came and went all evening and the kitchen was stacked with food by eight o'clock.

Gary Oldham had been busy on the day that he went to the funeral home with a distressed church member that made him late to meet Karen and Melanie. The person he was counseling was Bill Wallace. He had come to see him between his classes that day. He told him of his problems with Janet and about how worried he was. He said he just didn't know what to do and he needed some advice. By now Gary had heard of Janet's arrest and the beating she had given Bill. He had tried to see her at the jail but she refused to see him. He wanted to talk to Bill again but when he went to the hospital they had already released him. Now he needed to talk to Melanie and make sure he conducted the funeral as she wished. While he was sitting at his desk thinking about all this, his phone rang and it was Karen. She said he'd better talk to Melanie and gave the phone to her. He told Melanie how he planned to handle things and what he planned to say. He asked about the music plans. She told him that there would be a program printed so it would be easy to follow. She and Karen both planned to speak. He asked if she needed him to come to the house and she told him that would not be necessary. So having discussed everything they both agreed they would meet at the visitation and said their goodbyes. When he hung up, he was relieved because he felt that he must go see Bill Wallace.

Chapter 24

Daniel Carmody was sitting in his apartment feeling totally broken. He couldn't move, he just sat and cried and cussed and cried some more. He was really fond of Margie and had hoped they would have a long-lasting relationship. He decided to bite the bullet and call Karen.

When she answered, she said, "Daniel it's good to hear from you. I know you are feeling lost as I am." He told her that he felt beaten.

He asked, "Do you think I could come out and see you and meet Margie's daughter? I thought I would wait 'til the visitation but I really need to talk to someone who will understand."

Karen said, "I would love for you to come out. We have a mountain of food here and I would love to share it with someone. Why don't you just come on out and we'll talk then."

He told her he would be there in thirty minutes. He barely hung up the phone before he left the apartment to get his car.

Gary Oldham called Bill Wallace's home and Tom answered. He said, "Dad's asleep right now and he hasn't been able to sleep with all the pain. I don't want to wake him right now.

Gary told him, "I really want to talk to all of you so could I come over and visit with you and Amy until Bill wakes up?"

Tom said, "Sure that will be fine. What do you want to talk about?"

"I know about the problems the whole family has been having and I want to try to help." Gary told him.

"Oh, okay, come on over. We can sure use some help. We've got to decide what to do about Mom." After he hung up the phone, he went to Amy's room and knocked on the door. "Come in."

He told her about the preacher's call and she made a face when he told her they were going to meet with him. He made a helpless gesture with his hands and said, "Well, he knows we need help so maybe he'll have some suggestions. Come and help me straighten up the house before he gets here."

Daniel was at Karen's house in no time. He came around to the front door which was unusual, because most of her guests knew to come in the back. He'd never been there before and had only met Karen once, but Margie had introduced her as her best friend in the whole world. They had been at a football game. It had been too noisy to have a decent conversation.

Karen welcomed him at the door and led him to the kitchen. "Wow," he exclaimed, "You weren't kidding about the food. I haven't been able to eat all day but this looks like a feast for the Gods."

Melanie came from her bedroom and Karen said, "Daniel, I want you to meet Margie's daughter, Melanie." She extended her hand and he took it in both of his and said, "I am devastated by all that has happened and so sorry that you have such sorrow in your young life. Your mother was a wonderful person and we had really enjoyed each other's company."

Melanie was quiet for a moment and then said, "It's been devastating for all of us. So unexpected, certainly. I thought Mother and I would have a lot of years. I wish now that I had spent more time with her."

Karen wanted to change the subject and said, "Let's sit down in the den and then we'll raid the kitchen later."

They all took a seat. Karen and Melanie on the couch and Daniel in an easy chair.

He continued the conversation, "Melanie, it was important to your mother that you get a good education so you have done the right thing. I know you're going to miss her. She loved you so much and was so proud of you and your artistic ability."

Melanie started to choke up and waited a moment to answer, "Yes, Mother and Karen are my biggest fans. They both always encouraged me to pursue art as a career. I've been thinking that I might go to the Chicago Institute of Art, though. I'd like to just specialize in my art. It's the only thing that really interests me. The other classes I take seem so unnecessary to be an artist."

He smiled. "That's something you'll have to decide but it never hurts to explore other avenues. You'll do fine, whatever you decide."

Karen told Daniel about the plans they had made for Margie's wake and funeral. Then she suggested they get in the kitchen and investigate the food. She fixed drinks for them and they all filled their plates and went back to the den. By the time they finished it was getting late and

Daniel told them, "I'm so glad I was able to see you both. I feel so much better after talking with you. I don't know if I'll ever get over this but knowing you two will help. I'm going to go now and I'll see you tomorrow evening. If I can do anything to help, please let me know."

He got up and headed for the door.

Karen grabbed his arm, turned him around and took him to the back door. She said, "My friends know to use the back door and I want you to feel free to come visit anytime."

He kissed her on the cheek and turned to Melanie. Melanie went to him, hugged him and said, "I'm so glad to meet the man in my mother's life and glad she was happy to have him."

After he had gone they just stood there a minute thinking their own private thoughts. Then Melanie said, "He seems like a very nice man. I hope he'll be all right."

Karen said, "I'm sure he will. We'll all be all right. It will take time though. You know the funeral and all the plans are really for us, the grieving ones. We need to make sure it is a celebration of Margie's life not a morbidly sad affair."

Melanie agreed. They cleaned up the kitchen, put away the food that needed refrigeration and put some things in the freezer to have later. They watched the news on TV for a little while to get the weather report for the weekend. After that they both went to their bedrooms. Karen got into her nightgown and crawled in bed. She started reading a book she had on the night stand. After a little while she got up and went to look in on Melanie. She was sound asleep and Karen thought, "Thank you, God, for giving her some peace."

Chapter 25

Ed had breakfast as usual at the Café on Saturday morning. He had slept a little later than usual and they had a full house. Tony saw him come in and shouted, "Good Morning, Ed, good to see the peace officer has arrived."

He sat at the counter. Tony brought him a cup of coffee and whispered, "Don't rush off. When I get a break, I want to talk to you."

Maria came up behind, and said, "What's the big secret. You two up to no good?"

"I'm just here to get my breakfast. Tony's always up to no good. You should know that by now. Tony, go make me an omelet and let me flirt with your pretty wife for a while."

He ordered an orange juice from Maria and when she brought it, he asked, "Have you seen Karen lately?"

"No, she hasn't been in for a day or two. I imagine she's busy with all the planning."

He said, "Well, I'll call her later and see what's going on." When his omelet was ready, Tony brought it to him. He told Maria to let him know if she needed him. The crowd was thinning out now.

He sat down and asked, "What is this about Janet Wallace being in jail?"

Ed told him, "I don't want to say too much. It's a sad situation and I'm sure the family doesn't want the gossips to get on it. That's inevitable but I don't want to be a party to it. I'll tell you this much. We're going to have a psychologist come in and interview her."

Maria called in another order and Tony had to go to work. Ed was glad to be able finish his breakfast, left the money on the counter and slipped out before Tony was able to interrogate him anymore. On his way to the station he dialed Karen's number on his cell phone.

Gary Oldham had gone to the Wallace's on Friday evening. By the time he got there, Bill was up sitting in his recliner, looking miserable.

Tom let him in and said, "Thanks for coming. We could use any help we can get."

He shook Bill's hand and said, "I just needed to see if there was anything I could do to help. I went to the jail but Janet refused to see me."

Bill said, "I'm not surprised. She's probably ashamed and then again, she may still be angry. We've got to make some kind of decision about her soon. We just can't leave her there in the jail. I feel really bad about it until my ribs ache and then I'm glad she's not here."

Tom said, "I want to have her committed to some place that can help her. I don't want her coming back here to kill us all."

Gary was shocked, "Oh, Tom, you don't really mean that. She wouldn't hurt you."

Tom was vehement, "You don't know what we've been going through. You haven't seen the hate in her eyes."

Gary turned to Amy, "How do you feel about it?"

Amy hesitated and then answered, "I really have no idea what can be done. I just want her to get better and be my mother again."

Bill told the preacher that it was time for the truth to be out. He told him about his short affair with Margie. Gary made no judgmental comments but said, "I know these things happen, especially when the home is in turmoil. It never helps but I'm sure you know it's not an unusual situation. I know you're sorry, Bill, God will certainly forgive you, if you can forgive yourself."

Bill said he understood that but his big worry was, "What can we do for Janet?"

Gary answered, "Tom may be right. She obviously needs help and won't take it voluntarily. She will hate you all at first but be grateful if she is restored to a happy family later on."

They all agreed and after a prayer, they thanked him for coming to see them. He made his way back to his car, glad to be going back to his happy little home after a busy frustrating day.

Chapter 26

When Karen answered the phone, she sounded sleepy and Ed said, "Uh, oh, caught you laying in bed. when you know, you've got a lot to do."

She told him, "We were up late last night so I thought we deserved a break today. I didn't want to wake Melanie."

"What an excuse, get up and make the coffee. I'd like to come out and talk to you both for a few minutes. Will it be okay?"

"Sure come on out. We've got a mountain of food here and need someone to eat lunch with us. Besides the day will go better if we have company."

"I hope you don't think of me as company," he said.

"No, not at all. Come around back and let yourself in. We may be in the shower or something."

Ed said, "I'm on my way as soon as I check on a few things at the station." By now Melanie was up and in the shower. Karen went to put on the coffee and the phone rang again. It was Ruth Barry. She wanted to know how many might be at the lunch after the funeral. Karen told her to plan on about thirty.

Ruth said, "Okay we'll prepare for forty so we won't be caught short on food."

"That's thinking positively, Ruth. You're a dear to be doing this. You and Joseph need to come up here and help us eat some of the food we have stacked all over the kitchen."

Ruth told her, "We might just do that so's we can visit with you girls. I'll call you first though."

They said their good byes. Karen went to take her shower and get dressed. When she was dressed in her T shirt and jeans, she came out to the kitchen and looked out to see where Melanie had gone. She could see her in the barn saddling Candy. She went out on the porch and called to her, "Do you want some breakfast?"

Melanie shook her head and came out of the barn on Candy. She rode up to the house and said, "I had some coffee. I'll wait and eat lunch. We've got so much food for lunch and dinner. I'll eat that. I feel like a ride to relax and do some thinking. Okay?"

"Sure, Honey, you go on, enjoy yourself. I'll be right here and Ed is coming out so we can talk about all that, while you're riding."

When she went in the house, she drank some orange juice and thought Melanie had a good idea with all that food to be eaten later. She got another cup of coffee and went out to the porch to wait for Ed. In a few minutes he drove up and came to the porch. She asked if he'd like a cup of coffee. He told her to sit still and he would get it himself.

He came back out, sat down and said, "Have you heard any more about Janet Wallace?"

"No, not the details. I haven't been to the Café so I haven't heard any news."

He told her all about what had happened at the Wallace home and what had happened after the police arrived.

Karen looked sad. "I can't get over the fact that Margie was seeing him. She never said a word. It surely didn't last long because we always shared everything in our lives. Not that I had anything in the romance department to share. Maybe that's why she never told me. Didn't want to hear my opinion."

Ed continued to fill her in and said, "After you get Melanie out of here, we're going to have to dig deeper into this affair."

"I know but I hope that Melanie doesn't find out what's going on. She doesn't need to have any more to worry about. Her father is enough, though she doesn't even mention him. I'm hoping she will be ready to get back to school Tuesday. Then we'll get on it big time."

Ed said, "Yes, there's really no rush now since we know that the tests showed nothing. It's going to take time to ferret it all out."

Karen changed the subject. "So what's going to happen to Janet?"

"I understand they're thinking of getting her some mental help. Maybe commitment. We have a psychologist interviewing her today and hope to run some tests on her. We're keeping her until a decision is made. Tom is adamant about not letting her come home. He says she'll kill them all."

Karen was shocked at that and says, "I can't believe he said that. Surely he doesn't mean it."

"Oh, yes, he does. He said that we didn't see the look in her eyes when she tried to attack him."

"I didn't know she tried to attack her own son."

"She would have if he hadn't been able to grab the bat away from her. She's a very angry woman and she's a big girl, you know. She wouldn't even let the preacher visit her in jail. It wasn't because she was ashamed, she said, "I don't want to see that mealy mouthed son of a bitch." I didn't tell Gary what she said, just that she didn't want to see anyone."

Karen saw Melanie heading back from her ride and said, "Ed, let's talk about all this next week after we get through the weekend and Monday. I don't want Melanie to be upset or she won't be able to get back to her schoolwork and her life. Let's have lunch now, okay?"

"Sounds good to me, let me help get it on the table."

"There's no room on the table. We have to eat in the den. But you can come in and get the ice in the glasses for the drinks. I'll get out some paper plates and we'll pig out"

They were working uncovering the dishes when Ruth and Joseph appeared at the door. "Oh, I'm so glad you came." Karen told them, "Come in here and help us eat some of this feast. You know Ed Hawkins don't you?"

They both said, "Sure." They had been married so long they spoke the same at the same time. Ed shook Joseph's hand and Ruth gave him the usual hug she had for everybody.

Ed asked, "What would you folks like to drink? We have tea and soda." They both opted for water. "It was better for you."

Melanie came in the door and spoke to everyone, got her hug from Ruth and headed to the bathroom to wash off the horsy odor. When she came out she gave Ed a hug and her drink order. They all loaded their plates and retreated to the den. Conversation was limited while they all ate.

Ed and Joseph decided to have seconds and when they got in the kitchen Joseph whispered, "Do you have any news on what really happened to Margie?"

Ed told him, "No, we haven't come to any conclusions. The chief has closed the case so I can't openly work it but Karen is going be an undercover investigator for me after Melanie leaves for school."

They rejoined the ladies and after dessert Ruth and Joseph said they needed to get home. When they were gone Ed said, he needed to get back to town, too.

He said, "I'll see you at the visitation tonight if I don't have something come up."

They both walked him to the car and thanked him for coming out. When he had pulled out of the drive Karen said, "Well, we'd better clean up the kitchen and get a little rest and relaxation so we'll be in decent shape tonight. Would you like to watch the game on TV? Your team is playing today." Melanie agreed and they went into the house after giving Jazz and Callie a little attention. She had already fed them on her way to the barn that morning.

Bill Wallace was watching the game with Tom and he said, "I'm not going to the visitations for Margie but I am going to the funeral on Monday. Will you go with me?"

"Sure, Dad, I don't see anything wrong with that. She was a friend and a beautiful lady. No reason not to go. I expect half the school will be there. Everybody remembers Melanie because of her artwork, especially since she painted that huge mural in the entrance hall. It's great!"

"Margie really loved her daughter a lot. She talked about her all the time."

Tom asked, "Do you think Mom loves us?"

Bill's heart wrenched and he told Tom, "You know she does. Something has happened to her that none of us can understand. They talk about the stigma of mental illness all the time, about how ashamed the patient is, and how that only makes it worse for them. We've got to get over our anger and get on with helping her get well."

"How can we help her when she won't even let us visit her." Bill told him that after the psychologist finished her examination, she would advise them on what kind of help was available. Amy was standing in the doorway listening to their conversation and started to cry.

Tom went and gave her a bear hug and told her, "We'll work it out. We're still a family, no matter what happens, we've got to hang together. It's the same thing Dad tells the football team. You have to hang together! Protect each other and be there when you're needed. No matter what."

Chapter 27

At five thirty Melanie and Karen began to get ready to go to the visitation. Melanie put on a long black dress that had red poppies scattered on it. She didn't wear much make up, lipstick and mascara were all she needed. The dress had a high neckline which showed off the diamond pendent she had found in the jewelry box she picked up at her mother's apartment. She slipped on black low heeled shoes because she knew it would be a long evening. Then she got a black coat sweater out in case the weather turned cooler. She tied her hair in a knot on her neck and went to the den to wait for Karen. Karen came out looking good in a navy suit with gold buttons. She had on a gold satin shell under it and metallic gold three inch heels. Karen had taken more time on her make up and hair than usual because she wanted to look her best. The whole town would probably be there.

After they complimented each other on their choice of outfits, they went out to the car for the journey to town. On the way, Karen asked Melanie if she was going to be okay. Melanie told her that if she couldn't take it, she would hide out in the powder room.

Karen said, "Maybe it won't be so bad. Everyone there will be your friends or your mother's friends so don't be intimidated by them. You don't have to worry about acting any special way. Everyone grieves in their own way. There isn't a formula for it. People still smile, and have conversations that don't talk of the dead and as they say, "Life goes on for the living." You'll do fine, just be yourself."

Melanie started to speak and then hesitantly said, "I'm so afraid my dad will show up and be drunk. You know the funeral announcement came out in the paper today and he's bound to know even though he hasn't bothered to call me. There's no getting around it, he just a jerk."

"Well, I can't deny that, but don't worry about it. If it happens there will be plenty of people to help handle him. He makes a habit of getting thrown out of places." Melanie couldn't help but laugh at that and Karen joined her. They drove all the way to town laughing hysterically. The more they laughed, the harder it was to stop.

Gary Oldham was in his office at home, working on his sermon for tomorrow and he checked his watch to see if it was time to be at the mortuary yet. He called to his wife, "Chris, what time is the sitter coming."

She came into the office and said, "She will be here in about ten minutes. Are you ready to go?"

"Yes, I was just looking over my sermon. I need to work on the funeral plan, too, but I'll do that tomorrow."

Christine was a pretty blonde, her grandparents had come from Sweden many years ago and she looked as if she came straight from Stockholm. She had on a black silk dress with a jacket and black patent shoes. Her hair was long but she had it woven into a braid, and then wound up on the back of her head. She wore a long string of synthetic pearls with matching drop earrings. The door bell rang and she went to answer, saying, "That will be the sitter. Let's go on before the kids start to fuss." He got up and followed her out, they greeted the sitter, Mrs. Adams, and told her the numbers were on the fridge and they slipped out the door before the children knew they were gone.

The parking lot at the mortuary was filled with cars when Ed drove up. He parked on the street so that he could get out easily if he got an important call. He got out after he called into the station and told them where he was. He went into the mortuary. Mr. Froder greeted him and directed him to the room where Margie lay. He signed the guest register and looked up to see Karen coming his way. The room was full of many people that he knew well and he spent the next hour shaking hands and greeting different ones. As usual the men seemed to gather in one part of the room or out in the hall and the women were clustered in another area. Melanie was sitting in a chair close to her mother's coffin and people were filing by, speaking to her, viewing Margie, making the usual inane comments like, she looks so natural or didn't they do a good job. They had dressed Margie in an aqua colored chiffon gown with a v neck that had ruffles trimming it. She had a pink rose in her hands. Her long dark hair was loosely arranged on her shoulders. She had a pearl choker around her neck and earrings to match.

Occasionally Melanie got up and went out into the hall to stretch her legs. She came rushing over to Karen and whispered, "He's here and he is drunk. I guess that's his wife with him. She must be nuts to let him come here in that shape."

Ed could see that Melanie was upset and went to see what was going on. Karen told him that Larry Sloan had just come in the door and he appeared to be drunk. Karen said, "His wife is with him, maybe that will keep him from showing his butt."

Melanie asked, "What am I going to do? I don't know if I can talk to him, I'm sooo angry with him."

Karen told her just to stay calm and everything would be all right. She told her, "Don't be confrontational. It won't help anything. You can confront him when you don't have an audience. I know you probably need to get some things off your chest but it can wait til a more appropriate time. Okay?" Melanie just nodded her head and went back to her seat by her mother.

A strange hush fell over the room when Larry and Pamela entered. Then they all realized they were staring and went back to their conversations. He approached the coffin and Melanie but Pamela backed up into a corner. She was in her usual mini skirt, but at least it was black and she had on high top black boots. Her top was tight fitting mint green and low cut enough to catch a few men gawking. Larry leaned over to kiss Melanie and she turned her cheek to him. He said something and she just nodded without speaking. He straightened up and went to the coffin. He seemed to be praying and then he began to sob loudly and scream, "Why did you do this. Why?

What was so bad?"

His screaming brought the whole room to attention. Ed and Gary quickly made their way to him and each grabbed an arm, guiding him away and out of the room. Pamela fell in behind them. They kept going until they were out the door. He was resisting but didn't stand a chance of shaking them off.

Ed turned to Pamela and said, "I'm sorry Mrs. Sloan but I think it would be a good idea to take your husband home. You be sure to do the driving so that I don't have to arrest him tonight." Pamela was speechless and just nodded her head and led them to the car. They put him in the passenger seat and shut the door with him still sobbing and screaming. They waited there until Pamela pulled out of the lot and was well on her way home.

The room was buzzing when they got back into the building. Gary saved the evening by inviting everyone to bow their heads for a moment of prayer. After that some started to leave and in a short time the room was empty and the misery for Melanie was over for that evening. Ed walked both of them to Karen's car. They thanked him profusely and invited him to lunch after church tomorrow. Karen reminded him that they still had lots of food and that more was to come. She intended to invite Gary and Christine tomorrow at the church. They hadn't seen Daniel the whole evening. They would learn later that he had come early and left before anyone else arrived. He had signed the registry though so Melanie would know he'd been there.

Karen thought, "I'll call him tomorrow and invite him to join us." They were both very glad to be back at the house and couldn't wait to get out of their clothes and into comfortable night wear. They met again in the kitchen to raid the fridge and check out some of the desserts. When they sat down in the den, Karen turned on the tube to see what was on. She found Saturday Night Live was winding down. She said to Melanie, "Considering everything, it wasn't a bad evening, you think?"

Melanie thought about it a minute and answered, "I guess not, though I could have done without Larry's episode. Mother looked so pretty, I expected her to get up and tell him to get lost." Karen was surprised to hear her joke but thought that is showed she was going to be okay. Melanie had always been a good daughter and had no guilt over her relationship with her mother. Since she had already left home, she wouldn't have that awful feeling that someone you've lost will walk in the door any minute. Karen had felt that for at least two years after her husband, Rich, had been killed.

They watched the rest of the show and then the news, and found the weather was expected to be nice for another week at least. Then they put the kitchen back in order, told each other goodnight and went to their bedrooms. Karen read a few minutes but being totally exhausted, was asleep in a few minutes. When she woke in the middle of the night the book was on her chest and the light was on. She turned it off and went right back to sleep. Melanie on the other hand, had a little trouble settling down. She couldn't get her father off her mind. She had been shocked at the youth of the new wife and the way she was dressed. She hoped he wouldn't show up tomorrow night. She put up a prayer for her precious mother and dropped off to sleep.

Chapter 28

Gary Oldham went over his sermon one more time while Christine got the children dressed. They had skipped Sunday School because they slept late. Last night had been tiring and nerve racking. They had a hard time calming down after they got home and sat up talking about the strange things that had happened. Gary said he agreed with Karen, he too, did not believe that Margie had committed suicide. There was more to the story, and he was sure of it. Christine called to him, "Come on Gary, we're ready now."

The four of them walked from the parsonage to the church and went in the back way. Christine took the children to the nursery and made her way to the sanctuary and the front pew, where she would signal Gary if he was going overtime. They had worked out a signal, she would just tap on her watch and he would know to wind down. His sermon was on forgiveness. He was an eloquent speaker and his congregation enjoyed his sermons. He didn't talk down to them but was able to reach them and affect their lives in a positive way. He saw Karen and Melanie come in while the choir was singing the first hymn. They sat in the back so that they could make a quick exit.

Karen had been up first that Sunday morning and got the coffee on as usual. When it was done, she took her cup to the porch and had a conversation with her pets. "You're such a happy boy, Jazzy, you make me feel good and you know I love you and Callie, don't you?"

Melanie said, from behind her, "Talking to animals now, huh?" She laughed and said, "Get your coffee and come out here, girl and I'll talk to you."

They hadn't talked about art for a day or two, so she asked what Melanie had been working on lately. Melanie told her about an assignment to complete an abstract and said it was difficult because she didn't think in the abstract. Karen agreed that it would be difficult for her, too. She told her about the painting she had done at the colony and what the instructor had said. Melanie was impressed, she asked, "What was he like?"

Karen told her he was very handsome and had been all over the world. She said, "I really liked him and my room mates teased me about flirting with him...or him flirting with me."

"Why, Karen, really, I can't imagine you flirting. However, I did notice a little vibe between you and Ed the other night." Karen shot back, "Now I've known Ed forever. Don't go seeing what's not there." Melanie just murmured, "Uhm, denial is a dangerous thing."

Karen got up and went in the house. She called to Melanie, "I'm going to warm a couple of bagels and we need to get ready for church." They took turns in the shower and got dressed for church. Karen chose a beige silk with a matching jacket, her brown sling back shoes and changed her purse. She already had done her make up after her shower and she brushed her hair checking to see if there was any more gray. Melanie decided to wear the grey jumper with the white turtle neck again and black flats. She put her hair in a pony tail, did her lipstick and mascara and was all set to go.

Karen was feeding the animals when Melanie came to the door. She asked, "Do we have time for another cup of coffee?" Karen answered, "Yes, we've got plenty of time. I want to make a call before we leave." She went back in the house to her bedroom and called Daniel Carmody. He must have been sitting by the phone because he answered on the first ring.

Karen asked, "Daniel, what are you doing for lunch today?"

He said he had no plans and she told him about their abundance and asked him to join them after church. He sounded relieved, "I'm so glad you called. I was dreading sitting here all alone all day. I'll surely be there. Come to think of it, I may even see you at the church. I'm not a Methodist but they'll let a Catholic in, won't they?"

"We Methodists are very liberal, we accept all who enter. I hope to see you there."

Good byes said, she hung up the phone and went back out to join Melanie who had gone to the barn to see Candy. Karen locked the door and went to the car and honked the horn. Melanie came running. Melanie said, "I left my purse in the house but that's okay. I won't need it, I guess." They backed out of the drive and made their way to town. On the way they saw Ruth and Joseph in their yard, planting a small tree.

Karen said, "Guess they're not going to church. Oh, they probably went to early service. Remind me when we get home to call and invite them to lunch."

Daniel had already taken his shower when Karen called and he went to his bedroom to get dressed. He chose his blue pin stripe, white shirt and a light blue tie. He found his Bible which he hadn't consulted recently. It was on his desk and he noticed a blue note card on one corner of the desk. It was a note from Margie, thanking him for the dinner and movie he had taken her to.

She had slipped it to him at work one day. He smiled remembering and then choked up at the thought that he would see her no more. Shaking his head to change his mood, he got his keys and went to his apartment parking lot. He got in his Lexus and pulled to the exit. Ed was driving by as he started to enter the street. He honked and waved. He wondered if Ed was going to church or on a call for a crime.

Bill Wallace and his children got up early on Sunday. Amy fixed breakfast for them and they discussed the pros and cons of going to church. In the end they decided that Amy and Tom would go but Bill would be better off at home. He still was in severe pain with every breath he took. He tried not to take too much pain medicine because it was addictive and he didn't need to add that to his problems. After breakfast Bill said he would clean up and that they should go on and get dressed. When they came out, he was in the den watching TV. They looked great, he thought. Amy in a long green skirt with a white satin blouse and Tom in a nice dark blue suit. Bill was so proud of them and he told them so, often. They told him they would be right home after church, went out to get in the pick-up and take off. They had a car which they considered Janet's, it was little Regal but the three of them preferred the pickup even in their Sunday best.

Ed got a call to a wreck on the Wal Mart parking lot and he went out to see how the patrolmen were handling it. An elderly lady had backed out into a parked car behind her. She had stepped on the accelerator instead of the brake. He wasn't needed so he just drove on by waving at the patrolmen. He called in and told them he would be at the Methodist church if he was needed and headed back to town. When he went in, he saw Karen and Melanie at the back because they had ended up running late. He slipped in beside them. A few minutes later Daniel came in and they all scooted over to let him sit down, too. Amy and Tom Wallace came in, they walked down a few pews and sat where they didn't have to disturb anyone. Ed thought what nice kids to have such a crazy mother. Janet had been giving everyone great pains at the jail. She was a very troubled woman and they would have to figure out what to do about her. He hadn't talked to the psychologist yet but would as soon as the funeral was over. If she advised it, he would get the district attorney to go to the judge and asked to have her sent somewhere for evaluation.

Gary delivered a stirring sermon that got everybody's rapt attention. He told them forgiveness was one of the cornerstones of Christianity. We ask the Lord to forgive our sins as we forgive those who sin against us. We must live by that in order to have a decent society, to live in peace and enjoy our lives as long as we are on this earth. The choir sang "What a Friend we have in Jesus." And the congregation joined in. Gary made his way to the door of the church to greet his congregation as they left the church.

Karen and Melanie were right behind Ed and Daniel. Karen told Gary what a great sermon he had preached. She asked him to bring Christine and the children out to her house for lunch. She explained about the abundance of food and told him the children would enjoy a day in the country. He promised to try and told her that he would call if they couldn't make it. They made their way to the car and found Ed and Daniel standing there.

Karen said, "Well, boys, can I interest you two in lunch at my house?"

Ed said, "What do you think we're hanging around for? Daniel told me you had invited him and I wasn't about to be left out. There's not much going on in the police department, thank goodness so I would enjoy a day with real people for a change."

Karen asked, "What do you mean? Real people. I don't know if that is a compliment or not but I guess we'll let you join us anyway. Want to follow us?" He said, "Sounds good."

Daniel spoke then, "How about a ride in a real car, Ed? I'm in my Lexus."

"Hey, that sounds great to me. I hate driving. Karen used to do all the driving when we worked together. Of course we weren't in a Lexus but the old Mercury did pretty well."

"Yes, he always pulled rank on me and made me do the driving. Of course he nagged me all the time about what a lousy driver I was."

Melanie spoke up, "Will you guys quit kidding around so we can get home. I want to take off of this get up and into my jeans." They all agreed with her. They needed to go.

When they got in Daniel's car, he asked Ed, "Would it be okay if we go by my place so I can change to jeans. You're already in comfortable clothes but I'd hate to spend a day in the country wearing a pin stripe suit."

"I'm with you. I'll call the station from your place and let them know where I'm spending the day."

When they got to the apartment, Daniel told Ed to make himself at home. Ed went to the desk to make his call. While he was sitting there, he noticed the note and picked it up and read it. Daniel came out and saw him.

Ed said, "I'm sorry to be so nosy. It's an affliction we cops have, can't be trusted with anyone's secrets. I didn't know you were seeing Margie until after all this happened." Daniel answered, "Oh, I don't have anything to hide. We had only seen each other a few times but I was really fond of her. You know that I did spend that night or part of the night with her. I was probably the last person to see her alive. Well, the last one before whoever killed her because I don't buy the suicide crap. I had planned to come see you after the funeral."

Ed told him, "The chief has shut me down, he says the case is closed. Karen and I are going to start investigating on the sly, but not until after Melanie is back at school." Daniel sighed with relief and told him that he would do anything to help. Ed patted him on the back and they went back down to the Lexus and took off for a day in the country with "real people."

Chapter 29

When Karen and Melanie got back home, they went in to change immediately. Afterwards, Melanie asked Karen for Ruth and Joseph's number so she could call them. They were glad to hear from her and said they would be up soon. Karen made tea and began to get things out of the fridge and warm what needed to be warmed. They uncovered other dishes and got out the paper plates and napkins, put plastic forks, knives and spoons out. When they had finished, it was a huge smorgasbord. Greg and his family arrived and they went to meet them in the yard.

Melanie took the children to see Candy while Karen took Greg and Christine in the back door. The three of them got drinks and went back out on the porch to watch the children and wait for the rest of the guests to arrive.

Greg said, "Melanie is doing really well, isn't she?" Karen answered, "Yes, she's a trooper. She loved her mother so much but has accepted the fact that she can't change things now. I loved her and her mother and I'm glad I could help her get through this. I want to get her back to school as soon as I can though. I don't want her to give up her dreams. Then I'm going to find out what really happened to Margie."

Greg looked shocked, "You mean it wasn't suicide?"

"I haven't believed it for a minute. Margie was as happy as she had ever been. I saw her every Saturday for lunch for years. She would have told me if there was a problem and I heard nothing but how happy she was to be on her own, to have Melanie pursuing her art studies and to have a good, interesting job."

Just then Daniel and Ed arrived. They came up to the porch and greeted everyone. Karen told them to help themselves to a drink in the kitchen. When they came back out, Ruth and Joseph drove up. Karen introduced everybody and Melanie came up with the children.

She said, "We're hungry. Is everybody ready to eat?" They all agreed it was time to start and went into the house. After they had filled their plates, Greg returned thanks. They all found a place to sit and began to eat. Melanie and the children sat in the floor and she helped them.

Christine said, "This is so nice to have someone take care of the kids so I can eat. You obviously like children, Melanie."

"Yes, I always wanted sisters and brothers but never had any. So I used to babysit a lot just to get to be with other kids."

"Well, you're very good with them," Gary said, "Our kids are usually not so quiet and well behaved."

Melanie smiled and said, "That's because I bribed them. If they are very good, I promised I would take them for a ride on Candy."

Christine asked, "What's Candy?"

"Not what, who," said Karen, "Candy is my palomino mare." When Christine looked worried she added, "It will be okay, she's very gentle and Melanie is a very good rider."

Some of the men went back for seconds and Karen went to uncover the desserts and put on the coffee. When it was finished, she invited them all to have some and she didn't have to ask twice. Melanie and the children went out on the porch to have cookies and ice cream. They shared half of it with Jazz and Callie. When the rest were through with their lunch, they came out, too. Greg went with Melanie and the kids to the barn to get Candy saddled. When she was in the saddle, Greg handed the three-year-old, Eric, to her and she took him for the promised ride.

She rode up toward the porch so he could wave at his mother and say, "Look, Mommy! I'm riding a horse."

She rode him around the yard for a while and over Eric's objections, she handed him down to Greg. Then he hoisted little Chrissie up to Melanie and she covered the same ground with her. She was very quiet and never said a word the whole time they were riding. She didn't object once to being handed back to her father.

Eric was begging to ride again so Melanie said, "Hand him to me and we're going for a real ride if it's okay."

Greg said to just be careful and away they went out to the field where she usually rode. Chrissie waved bye, bye and took her daddy's hand and pulled him back toward the house.

Joseph was entertaining them all with stories of his days working on the railroad when Greg got back. Chrissie went to sit in her mother's lap. Jazz was fascinated by the little girl and sat right beside her. Chrissie would lean over and pat Jazz on the head every once in a while and the dog loved it.

Daniel and Ed were engrossed in conversation as they walked toward the barn. Karen excused herself and followed them. When she caught up, she asked, "What are you two cooking up?"

Ed said, "Nothing really, I was just telling Daniel some of my possible theories. You know what could have happened at Margie's that night or morning that she died. Everyone assumed that she died that night but Daniel tells me he was with her until about three in the morning. He had to leave to get ready to go out of town and she was fine then."

Karen frowned and said, "You're right. After all, he told me that they didn't find her until evening, about nine that next night. The people at the bank had assumed she had left with Daniel. When her friend at the bank found out from Daniel, that she hadn't been with him. She became alarmed and they got the super to open her apartment. That's when they called 911 but of course it was too late and the police called the coroner."

Ed said, "This gives it a whole new twist. You will need to check out her apartment again when you start your investigation. I may even go there this evening and have a look. But you would know more about how things looked normally."

Karen told them, "I'm going to talk to Melanie this evening about making arrangements for her return to school. I'm anxious to get on with it and I can't do a thing until she is gone."

Daniel agreed, "There's no reason to upset her any more than necessary."

Melanie and Eric rode up so they all changed the subject and told Eric what a fine rider he was. She handed him down to Karen and he took off running to his father. Breathless, he told him how much fun it had been to ride a "real" horse. Then he asked if they could get a horse. Greg explained that they didn't have room at the parsonage but maybe they could come out and visit Karen sometimes and go riding. Karen assured him that he would be welcome anytime. He was satisfied with that and went to pet Jazz. Callie, the cat, remained in hiding. She was not fond of little people or big ones for that matter. Soon they all began to get ready to leave, Greg had evening services to prepare for and the rest of them had to go to the visitation.

Joseph and Ruth said they would see them at the mortuary. They thanked Melanie for inviting them and said how much they had enjoyed being with young folks. Karen gave Ruth the list she had made for the lunch tomorrow. Ruth said she would call her committee when she got home. Daniel and Ed got in the Lexus after they had offered their thanks . They both said they would not see them until tomorrow.

They planned to go to Daniel's apartment and talk some more but they didn't say anything about it in Melanie's presence. On the way back to town, Daniel said, "Ed, were you and Karen ever more than friends?"

"No, Karen had a very great husband and theirs was a really good marriage. I never even considered such a thing. In fact Rich and I became really good friends. We golfed together, went hunting and just hung out. I have thought about it lately though and I asked her the other day if she would go to dinner with me and she didn't say, no."

"Well, that's a good sign." When they got back to Daniel's apartment he put on the coffee and they talked until after ten o'clock. They brainstormed every imaginable thing that could have happened to Margie but came to no conclusions.

Chapter 30

The visitation that night was just as crowded as the first. Some of the same people had come back. Melanie took her seat by her mother after she said a silent prayer at the coffin. She told Karen later that she thought her face had frozen into a permanent smile. Karen conferred with Mr. Froder to make sure all the arrangements were made for the service tomorrow and the burial. He assured her that all was going to go well. All of them were relieved when Larry didn't make another appearance. At nine o'clock the lights blinked and Melanie sighed with relief.

She had done her duty. She was going to watch as they closed the casket for the last time and that was going to hurt. She braced herself for it when Mr. Froder entered the room. He took her hand and said, "Are you ready, Melanie?" She nodded her head, touched her mother's cheek and told him to close it.

Tears were streaming down her cheeks when she headed toward the door. She rushed to the car and waited for Karen to come out. By that time she had composed herself but they rode home in silence, both of them feeling the pain of their loss. They went straight to bed when they got home because they had to be up early in the morning since the funeral was at ten o'clock. It didn't take long for either of them to go to sleep because it had been a long tiring day.

Bill Wallace had gone to the jail on Sunday but Janet still refused to see him. He had appointments with both a lawyer, Jack Carter and the psychologist, Peggy Jackson, tomorrow afternoon. Sunday evening he was in the den watching TV when the kids returned from the movies.

He asked if they were going to the funeral with him tomorrow and they said they were.

He told them what he had planned for the day and how he planned to deal with their mother. He said it depended on what the psychologist told him and what the lawyer advised. They told him they trusted his judgement and whatever he did they would support him. He told them how much he loved them and appreciated their support. They took turns hugging him carefully so as not to hurt his aching ribs. Then they both went to their bedrooms. He decided to sleep in his recliner because he was more comfortable there than in the bed. He took another pain pill and soon was asleep.

Greg and Christine were enjoying a quiet time after the kids were tucked in. They agreed that it had been a most enjoyable day. Greg went to his office to look over his plan for tomorrow one more time.

Christine went to the kitchen to set the coffee pot for six a.m. She knew they needed to get up bright and early to get ready for the services. She stuck her head into Greg's office and told him that she was going on to bed and he said he would be up soon.

After Ed left, Daniel poured himself a glass of wine and toasted Margie with a silent prayer. He thought about her all the time. He had been glad to get acquainted with Ed and to know that he didn't intend to accept the suicide theory. He thought back to the afternoon and how much he had enjoyed it. Then he thought about his children and wondered how they were doing. He made a mental note to call them tomorrow night.

After watching the news he went to his bedroom and hung up the clothes he had worn to church. Then he took a shower and went to bed. He read a book he had started several days before but soon he was too sleepy to go on with it. He turned off the light and was asleep in a few minutes.

Ed went by the department on his way home from Daniel's to see what was going on. The desk sergeant told him it had been unusually quiet. He told him to leave word that he would be at Margie Sloan's funeral in the morning if he was needed. He went to his little house and got to bed right away. Sleep did not come easy because he kept mulling over all the possibilities of Margie's death. The big mystery was, "Who could have possibly wanted her dead?"

Chapter 31

Monday morning Karen was up making coffee when Melanie came into the kitchen. Karen said, "I was going to let you sleep but you look bright eyed already."

Melanie said, "Well, I got a good night's sleep so I wanted to get up early and visit with you. When can I go back to school, Karen?"

Karen was surprised, "I had planned to talk to you about that today. I thought I'd call and confirm your reservations and take you to Chicago tomorrow or the next day if you're willing to go. I'll call right now if you want me to. When would you like to go?"

Melanie told her, "I'd like to go tomorrow if it's convenient for you."

Karen made the call and arranged for her to leave at one tomorrow afternoon. That way she would be back at school before too late and her room mate would be able to pick her up. Then Melanie called her room mate, Shirley and told her the plan.

She agreed to be there for her. Shirley asked, "How are you doing?" Melanie said she was all right and anxious to get back to school.

Shirley assured her she would be waiting at the airport tomorrow evening. Melanie hung up the phone and said, "That's a relief, Thanks so much for making all these arrangements, Karen. You are so special. May I stay with you when I come back to Dinsmore?"

"You know I love having you here and you are welcome anytime. I'm going to get you a set of keys made so you can get in if I'm not here. When you come back home, we're going to have to think of getting you some kind of transportation."

Melanie said, "What about Mother's car?" Karen shook her head, "That's weird, I hadn't even thought of it. You've been here all that time and could have been driving it, though I don't know when you would have had time. We've had so much to do."

Melanie told her, "You check on it and then when I come back, I'll have a car. I want to talk to you more about the Chicago Institute of Art, too."

Karen said, "Well, that will be fine. Just get through this year and we'll check that out, too. I'm inclined to agree with you and I personally would like

96

to have you closer. Now I'm sounding like your mother but I do love you and want you to know I'm here for you."

Melanie hugged her and said, "You know I love you, too. I don't know how I would have made it this week without you. All your friends were great too."

When they got to the mortuary they were taken to the family room and Melanie was shocked to see her father sitting there alone. He stood up when she came in and he held out his arms but she didn't go to him.

He said, "I'm sorry I haven't been to see you. I don't blame you if you hate me but I'm truly sorry for embarrassing you and not being a good father."

She told him, "There's no need to worry about it. It's good to see you made it here and that you are sober for a change. Mother did deserve that you be at her funeral, at least."

He looked as if she had struck him. He spoke to Karen and held out his hand to indicate a seat for them. They moved in and sat down. The organist was playing and they were able to see the crowd of mourners being ushered into the main auditorium.

There was a rustle at the back of the family room and they turned to see Margie's mother being wheeled in by a nurse. The nurse said, "She wouldn't hear of missing this after she read it in the paper Saturday."

Melanie went to hug her grandmother and said, "I'm so glad you were able to come. I love you, Grandmother."

Mrs. Orson smiled broadly and said in her weak little voice, "I love you too, dear Melanie."

The vocalist began to sing, "The Lord's Prayer" and everything became quiet.

Gary rose and read Margie's obituary. Then he went on to tell of his personal relationship with her and how much he had enjoyed knowing her. He assured the family that she had a special place in heaven and would be waiting for them when they were ready to join her. Larry sobbed quietly this time and Melanie was crying by now. Karen was trying hard not to cry. When Greg sat down the vocalist sang Margie's favorite hymn, "Abide with Me."

Karen and Melanie had both decided that they couldn't speak without breaking down. Instead Melanie had included a poem to her mother in the program. When the service was over, they waited until the crowd thinned out and went with the nurse to get Mrs. Orson in the nursing home van. Melanie promised her she would write and when she got back in town, she would visit her. She kissed her goodbye and they went to get in the mortuary limousine for the trip to the cemetery.

Larry had followed them and stood there looking pitiful until Melanie told him to come on and get in. They rode in silence all the way. It wasn't very far to the cemetery and Karen was grateful for she was very uncomfortable. The silence was deafening. They walked to the tent and sat down in the front row to await Gary for the final graveside ceremony.

Gary read Psalms 23 and then offered a prayer for Margie and asked the Lord to comfort Melanie in her moment of sorrow. Melanie and Karen each put a rose on the coffin and started the walk back to the limousine. They stopped to hug and shake hands with friends along the way. Larry said goodbye to Melanie. He said his wife was there to pick him up. He wanted to know if he could do anything for her but she told him she would be fine. She stiffened when he hugged her and then he hurried away to get in his little Mustang with the waiting Pamela. They wasted no time getting away.

After they were in the limo, Melanie said, "That was difficult, wasn't it?" It was as if having to deal with her father was more disturbing that burying her mother at this point. Karen understood how strange it must be for her. Larry had always been so immature that fatherhood was not his big thing. He had rarely paid any attention to Melanie and she didn't mind a bit when Margie divorced him.

When they were back at the mortuary, they thanked Mr. Froder and went to get in Karen's car to go to the church. They had invited Mr. Froder but he declined because he had another family to see. Karen had told Ed and Daniel about the lunch and told them they would be welcome. When they got in the church dining hall, they were surprised to see Tony and Maria.

They both came over to hug Melanie and Karen asked, "Who is running the Café?" Tony said, "Sometimes friends come before money. We put a sign on the door and closed for the day. I brought a big tray of lasagna over before the service and they invited us to come for the lunch."

Melanie said, "That's great. I'm so glad you are here."

Tony said, "Well, we didn't make it to the cemetery because we came over to help the ladies get the lunch ready. I thought they could use a little extra help."

"You are one of a kind Tony. What a sweet thing to do."

Maria piped up, "Hey, it wasn't his idea, it was mine."

Karen apologized and said, "Well, I'm sorry. You're two of a kind and too kind."

Several more people wandered in and when Gary and his family came in he called for a moment of prayer during which he thanked all the people who had prepared the luncheon and asked for the Lord's comfort to all those in mourning.

When Karen and Melanie sat down, they were joined by Tony, Maria, Daniel and Ed. They all had a good time visiting. Melanie told them her plans and Ed winked at Karen. They stayed until after one o'clock visiting and before they left made a point of going to the kitchen and thanking the ladies who had worked so hard.

They went to the car and were glad to be on their way home. They were barely in the door when Melanie said she was going to change and ride Candy one last time before she had to go. Karen said that would be fine but they needed to talk when she got back. Melanie headed for the barn and Karen got a cup of coffee and sat on the porch and watched as she saddled up and rode off. She remembered she hadn't checked the mailbox in days and walked out to the road to see what was there.

There were a few bills and some advertisements. There was a greeting card in the mix. She opened it and read the note inside. She was shocked because it was from John, the art instructor at the colony. He gave her his sympathy and then said he really had liked her painting and would like to come see some more of her work when it was convenient. He gave her two numbers where he could be reached and asked her to contact him soon since he would be leaving the country after the Christmas holidays.

When Melanie came back from her ride, Karen told her the good news she had received. "Oh, that is so great. You deserve some recognition for your art. What do you suppose he has in mind?"

Karen said, "I have no idea but we'll see soon because I'll call him as soon as I get back from Chicago tomorrow."

"Why not now?" Karen answered, "I want to think about it on my drive so I know how I really feel about having a stranger critique my work. It's so personal to me. My paintings are like my children that I never had, except for you. I consider you my daughter now, I hope you'll treat me as your other mother."

Melanie began to cry, "I have always loved you, Karen and now even more. You've saved my life this past week. I don't know what I would have done without you." Karen patted her on the back and said, "Well, I'll get even with you. You'll have to take care of me when I get old."

Chapter 32

Bill Wallace and the kids did go to Margie's funeral but he kept his appointment with the therapist, Peggy Jackson, that afternoon. She was the one that had interviewed Janet at the jail. She told him she thought that Janet might be suffering from either bipolar disease or maybe even schizophrenia. Bill was devastated but determined to help his wife. He asked what he needed to do. She told him to talk to his lawyer and if she was needed to let him know. She printed him a copy of her diagnosis and he left for the lawyer's office.

Bill's appointment with Jack Carter, Esq. wasn't until two thirty and it was only two when he got there. The receptionist told him to have a seat and she let Jack know he was there. He only had to wait a few more minutes before she told him to go on in. Jack Carter was a man in his sixties with a monk's hair style. He had a ruddy face and was in his shirt sleeves. He had on red suspenders and you immediately thought old country lawyer when you first met him. He played that image to the hilt but he was no country anything. He had practiced law in Chicago ten years before moving to Dinsmore. He said he was tired of the rat race. He was very successful but had not married until he was thirty-nine and had a young family in a few years. He wife Emily was ten years younger than he. He decided his family was more important than being a big shot in the city. He handled all kinds of cases from divorce to neighbors fighting over fences. His oldest son, Chip, had recently joined the local police department.

He stuck out a big hand to Bill and told him to have a seat and, "Tell me what I can do for you, today." Bill explained his situation and handed him the doctors report.

Jack said, "Well, we have to get the signature of two doctors to have her committed to the state hospital in Lexington. Then I can go before the judge and have it acted upon. You need to get her a physical anyway and then we can get the doctors at that medical practice to sign the papers. You go home and call your family doctor, tell him the situation and see if he'll go to the jail to do a physical. Otherwise you'll have to get the police to take her in handcuffs and chains and that would be very humiliating for everybody.

Bill said, "We've been going to old Dr. Patterson for years and he knows

Janet real well. I feel sure he'll help out."

Jack said, "Okay, get back to me as soon as you have that handled and I'll start on my end." Bill looked so distressed that Jack said, "Look man, it's going to be okay. You don't need to feel guilty. If this is what she needs and she won't cooperate, it's the only way to proceed and get her help."

Bill nodded and said, "Yes, I know and I'm going home and call the doc right now. Thanks for telling me what I need to know. This has my whole family in an uproar and we need to have some peace." They shook hands again and Bill left the office to go home and explain it all to his kids.

Chapter 33

Melanie talked Karen into calling John Whitcomb that evening. She wanted to know what he would say. Karen called him at six o'clock and he answered on the second ring. "Hello"

"Hi, John, this is Karen Sutton. I got your note and thought I'd call to see what you had in mind."

"It's good to hear from you, Karen. I just wanted to make arrangements to come to see some more of your artwork. I'm thinking that I might be able to arrange a gallery showing for you. I just need to see more examples before I talk to my friend in Chicago."

"I would love for you to come and see what you think. I'm my own worst critic so I'm a little embarrassed to have someone as well known as you look at my work. When do you want to come?"

"Well, I have some free time this coming weekend if that would be all right. What is the motel situation there?"

"We have a Holiday Inn and it's not far from my place. Are you going to fly or drive?"

"Oh, I'll drive down in my rental. I'm still in Easton. I just started the second session."

"I didn't realize there were two. Well, I'll expect to hear from you Saturday. When you get to town, call me and I'll either meet you or just give you directions. Okay?"

"That will be great. I'll look forward to it and if anything changes I'll let you know. Thanks for calling me." They talked a few minutes longer and then said their goodbyes.

When she hung up, Melanie was standing there waiting anxiously. "When is he coming? What did he say?" She was babbling.

Karen told her the entire conversation and she jumped up and down with excitement. "Nothing will probably ever come of it. I doubt if my work will be good enough."

"You always think you're not good enough. If you could see what some of my professors call art, you would think differently. They all show at different galleries and sell their work. I haven't seen any better that yours."

"Well, you'll have to admit you're a little prejudiced. I do appreciate your confidence in me though. Now let's raid the fridge and then we need to get to bed. We'll have to leave early tomorrow. We need to be at the airport at least an hour ahead of flight time. We'll need to leave by nine or earlier."

Bill went to McDonald's drive thru and got Big Mac's and fries for three. When he got home the kids were waiting for him in the den. He yelled as he went in the door, "Anybody want some Mickey D's? If you do meet me in the kitchen right now!"

They both came in as Bill got some sodas out of the refrigerator. "This is great, Dad. I was starving." Tom said, "I thought you'd never get home. Tell us what happened."

They all sat down at the table and Bill told them what he had found out and what he planned to do for their mother.

Amy said, "That's really sad but it will be good if they can help her get well." He had passed his first hurdle by receiving Amy's okay. He already knew how Tom felt so as soon as they finished eating, he called Ed Hawkins.

Ed was at Daniel's apartment when the phone rang. It was the desk sergeant at the police station looking for him. "Hey," he said, "when Ed answered, Bill Wallace is looking for you. Thought I'd let you know so you could call him if you want to."

Ed asked him, "Did you tell him where I was?" "No, man, but I didn't figure you would want me to."

"You're right, thanks for letting me know. Did he say what he wanted?"
"Nothing."

"Okay, thanks again, I'll let you go."

After he hung up, Ed sat there wondering what he should do. He decided it could wait, at least it could wait for a little while.

Daniel had brought out two beers giving one to Ed, who said, "This hits the spot. It's been a long hard day for all of us."

Daniel looked down at the floor and when he looked up he spoke softly, "It was awful. I still can't believe that she's gone. You know I was really very fond of her."

"Well, that's one reason I wanted to come over and talk to you. Now that I know you had been seeing her. Karen and I are going to be investigating her death. We'll have to keep it quiet though, since the chief has deemed the case closed. I just wanted to talk to you about your relationship and find out if you possibly knew anything that might put some light on it. I'm not trying to pry. I just need a place to start."

103

"We'd only had a few dates but I just found her to be very smart and fun to be with. I'm afraid we didn't really know that much about our individual pasts. For instance, I didn't tell her that I was still involved in divorcing my wife in Chicago. That's one reason I hesitated to ask her out. I had no idea we would become intimate. We did though and I did spend part of the night with her on that night. I thought she was fine when I left. She said something about me not catching her cold but that was all. She knew I had business in Chicago the next day. I didn't tell her that I was finalizing my divorce."

"Did you know that soon after her divorce she had an affair with Bill Wallace?"

"God, no, I had no idea. But then it was really none of my business. How did you find out?"

"His wife is in jail for trying to kill him and she's a maniac. When we try to question her, all she wants to talk about is "that cheating son of a bitch!," so we don't know what to do with her. Her son has begged us not to let her out because he's afraid she'll kill them all."

"That is sad. What does Bill have to say? I feel sorry for his kids."

"I haven't talked to him yet. I wanted to talk to you first. But I just found out he's looking for me and I'm going to try to see him when I leave here. I want you to be thinking if there's anything that you can add. If you come up with anything, call me or Karen." He had finished his beer and he stood up to go.

Before he left, he called Bill. "Bill, Ed here. Wondered if I could come over and talk to you for a little while. Okay, see you in a few."

He walked toward the door and Daniel went with him. Daniel told him, "I'll be glad to help in any way. I'll call you if I think of anything or hear anything that might help. You know how they gossip around here. That's why I'm so surprised I'd never heard about Bill and Margie. The girls at the bank are always talking about everybody in town."

After Ed left, Daniel turned on the television and stretched out on the couch. He didn't know what was on the tube, though. He was lost in thoughts of Margie's secret affair and his own feelings for her. He hadn't been the only one keeping secrets.

Bill Wallace told his children that they'd better get to bed. They would all have to go back to school tomorrow. They didn't object because by now they were tired, too. It had been an emotional day for them. They both hugged him and Amy said, "It's going to be all right, Daddy."

He told them, "We'll have breakfast at the Café tomorrow, so be up early.

Goodnight, now."

"I hope your ribs will let you get some sleep," Tom said, "By the way we need to know what to say at school."

"You won't have to tell them anything. I'm not going to say a word, I've got my pain pills and I'll get by without anyone knowing."

He heard a car pull up outside and he went out to meet it. He figured it was Ed. He knocked on the window and Ed rolled it down. "Let me get in. I don't want to talk in the house. I'm afraid the kids will over hear us."

Ed unlocked the door and when Bill was in he asked, "What do you want to talk about?"

"I saw Janet's therapist and a lawyer today. We're going to have her committed as soon as the lawyer can get the paperwork ready for the judge. I want to have her regular doctor come to jail and give her a physical if she'll let him. If not, we'll have to get him to sign the papers without a physical. I've got to get at least two doctors to sign and I'm going to ask the therapist to appear in court. I'm hoping that will move things along faster. I'm also hoping Janet won't be required to appear. I want to save her any more embarrassment. Will you be able to hold her a few more days?"

"Yes, I don't see any problem since she has not been cooperative and won't talk to us about her reason for trying to kill you."

"I don't think she really meant to kill me. I know Tom does, but she really just lost it and did the first thing she thought of. She's very sick and I've known it, but she wouldn't consider getting any of the help I suggested."

"Bill. I've got some really personal questions to ask you. What kind of relationship did you have with Margie? Karen and I don't believe that she committed suicide. We're investigating it on the sly. Nobody in the department knows, the chief has closed the case, so this is as far as it will go, unless you had something to do with her death."

"Oh, my God, I would never have harmed her. I've loved her forever and it broke my heart when she got involved with Larry Sloan while I was away at college. They were married before I had a chance to get back with her. Right after her divorce, I had moved out of the house because Janet was giving me hell all the time. I called her just to talk. We had always stayed in touch so I called her a lot of times when I was having problems. Sometimes we just talked about what was going on in our lives though. Any way, I was staying in a motel outside of town and one night we went to Lexington to have dinner. We got kind of romantic and on the way back, I asked her to spend the night with me at the motel. That's the first time we had ever had sex, even though we dated for four years in high school. She was always a good girl but her divorce changed her. I guess it does that to a lot of people. Kind of like, what do I have to lose, my life is already a mess. That's where I was, for sure. Damned if you do and damned if you don't."

"Wow. I didn't know any of that. You sure managed to keep it quiet. That's hard to do in this town."

"Not quiet enough, because Janet hired a private detective and he got the goods on us. That's why she became so angry. Of course she had accused me of screwing every woman in town for years, so I'm really not surprised she went to such lengths to get the goods on me. But Margie was the only woman I ever got involved with and it didn't last long. I felt so bad leaving the kids to deal with Janet alone. I came on back home and didn't see Margie anymore. I didn't even get to talk to her before she died. I sure hope you can find out what happened."

"I appreciate you giving me this information and if you can think of anything that Margie said or did, that might give us a clue, you let me know. Okay?"

"Of course, I'll be glad if I can help in anyway. I'll let you know how it goes with Janet's commitment proceedings and maybe we can get her off your hands if you can get her released."

"No problem. I've got to get going, so you go on and we'll talk more, later. You take care of yourself and those kids. I want you to win this week's game." That made Bill laugh and they shook hands. He got out of the car and went back to the house.

When he went in Tom was sitting at the kitchen table with a puzzled look on his face. Bill knew he had some more questions to answer.

Chapter 34

Karen was up early as usual to make the coffee and start the day. The sun was just coming up, a big orange ball in the sky. The golden leaves shimmered with the dew drops on them. It looked like little flecks of glitter had been poured on them. She sat on the porch with her first cup of coffee, petting Jazz and Callie and telling them how much she loved them.

She heard Melanie said behind her, "The woman that talks to animals."

Karen pretended to throw the cup at her and said, "Well, I'm glad to see you're up. Are you packed?"

"Yes, I did most of it last night and I'm going to shower after I have a cup of coffee. The coffee smelled so good, that it's actually the reason I got up. I'll shower soon and get ready."

Karen said, "That sounds like a plan. Then I'll shower and we'll load up and head for the Café. Okay?"

"Fine, I'll talk to the animals while you're doing that. I'll even feed them and then I'm going out to the barn, talk to Candy and feed her, too." They both had a good laugh.

Karen thought, how good it was that she could laugh. She's going to be fine. She finished her shower and went into her closet. She decided she was tired of being dressed up and grabbed her favorite pair of jeans and a red checked shirt. She got a black coat sweater out to take with her in case it cooled off. She put on a pair of red socks and her brown loafers. She had put on her make up in the bathroom so after she brushed her hair, she was ready. She went back out to the porch.

She had just sat down when the phone rang. She looked at the clock on the way in and it was only seven o'clock. She thought, "Who could that be, so early?" It was Ed. She said, "I should have known it was you. Who else would call so early? What's going on?"

"I just wanted to let you know what I had been up to. You can be thinking about our next move while you're driving home."

"That might be dangerous. I'll lose concentration on my driving."

"Well, I can see you're in a good mood. What brought this on?"

She told him about her conversation with John Whitcomb and the plans they had made. She was still excited about it. He said, "I'm feeling a little jealous. What have you got going with this guy?"

"What have I got going with you? I wasn't aware that I had anything going with anyone, actually. But come to think of it, it's not a bad idea. She paused but got no response. "I'm just joking, I have nothing going on, except maybe my art career is going to crank up."

"I'm glad for you, Karen. You deserve a break and I'll do anything to help you. Will I get to meet this guy?"

"We'll see about it. I'll let you know what I decide. Now, what have you been up to?"

He filled her in on all of his conversations with Bill and Daniel. He told her about Bill's confession and of his plans for Janet. He said, "I intend to try to find that private detective."

"Yes, that's a good idea. He may know more than he told Janet. I'll call you as soon as I get back and we'll get together. I still have a refrigerator and freezer full of food. You can come and help me eat it. Then I'm taking the rest to the Women's Crisis Center."

"That's a plan. I'll look forward to your call. Now go on and get it over with. Talk to you later." He hung up!

She shook her head as she called to Melanie, "Ready? I'll get your bags in the car as soon as you are."

"Just a few minutes more," she said, "I'll bring them out."

She had decided to go casual, too. She had on jeans, with a blue and green, plaid flannel shirt over a navy T shirt. She had on white sneakers and her hair was in a pony tail. She checked around the room to make sure she hadn't left anything and then took the biggest bag out to Karen.

She said, "I'll bring my carry on as soon as I get my lipstick on. Will you be ready to go then?" "Yes, I hate to lose you but I'll be ready. We'll go gas up and head for the Café."

She picked up the bag and when she got down the porch steps, she pulled up the handle and rolled it the rest of the way. Melanie came out with the carry on and put it on the back seat. She had on a back pack of books and took it off to put it with the carry on. Karen returned to the house checked everything, looking in Melanie's room to see if anything was left. She went out the door, locked it, told the animals she be back soon and went to get in the car.

Melanie was nowhere in sight. Karen got behind the wheel and honked the horn. Melanie came out of the barn. She began to run and was breathless when she climbed in. "I just had to see Candy, one more time."

"I understand. She'll probably miss you, too. I don't ride her as often as you have." She backed out of the drive and headed for town once again. She stopped at the Quick Mart and went in to pay while Melanie pumped the gas. When she got back out Melanie was in the car ready to go.

Chapter 35

Ed and the two younger detectives had been sitting in the back of the Café for twenty minutes when Bill and his children came in. They sat down at a table by the window. Maria went over with coffee for Bill and water for the kids. She asked them what they were drinking and they said orange juice. Bill told her to bring him some, too. While she was gone, they decided to have pancakes and sausage. They gave her their order when she brought the orange juice. Bill was anxious to get to school, since he had been out yesterday. He would have a lot to catch up on. The team hadn't practiced yesterday because so many of them went to Margie's funeral that they canceled practice.

Tony and Maria both came to give them their breakfast. Tony sat down in the empty chair and Maria went to see about the other customers. Tony asked, "How's Janet doing? I know this is hard for all of you and if there's anything we can do to help, just let us know."

"She's not letting us see her so I really don't know but I appreciate your offer and I'll keep it in mind. Just try to keep the gossips' straight if you can. I know you hear everything in here. Janet's sick, that's all and I don't want people being mean to her."

"Okay, I'll do what I can. I'd better get back to the grill before Maria gives me the evil eye. I'll see you at the game Friday if not before. Tom, you ready to whip their butts?" Tom smiled, wiped his mouth with his napkin and said, "You know I am! Don't you dare bet against me." They all laughed and Tony got up and went back to work.

When the Wallaces were going out, Melanie and Karen were coming in. They all spoke briefly. When Karen saw Ed and his friends, she waved and they waved her on back to join them. She looked at Melanie and she nodded as if to say, "It's okay." So they joined the lawmen for breakfast.

Maria brought them coffee and asked if they knew what they wanted to eat. Karen told her to bring them the Country Breakfast, scrambled with biscuits. She said Melanie's flight wasn't serving food so she needed to fill up. Melanie blushed and said, "Karen, you make me sound like a pig."

"Oh, no, I just don't want to send you back to school undernourished. Besides the flight will go faster if you're full and can fall asleep."

Ed said, "Boy, is that a stretch. Do you call that a reason or an apology?"

She said, "Whatever works for you. Melanie knows I'm just kidding her. Don't you, Hon?" "Yes, I know. What is that thing parents say? If didn't love you, I wouldn't beat you up."

They were all still laughing when Tony and Maria brought the breakfasts over to the table. Tony asked, "What's so funny over here? Are we missing all the fun?"

Maria poked him in the ribs and he jumped like she had hurt him. "You guys saw it. She's abusing me and I need to file charges. Take her in, lock her up. Do me a favor."

She poked him again and walked away. Over her shoulder, she said, "I'm going back to work. Some people have to work around here."

Now the joke was on Tony, so he dropped it. He looked at Melanie and asked, "When are you going back to school?"

"We are on our way to Chicago right now so I can catch a flight back to Columbia and hit the books."

"That's great! Just to get you off in good shape, breakfast is on me today, for you girls. Do you need any money or anything? I'm here to help if you do."

"Tony, you are a dear. Mother had it all covered for me and I'm going to be fine. Besides, my other mother, Karen, will make sure of that. I don't know what I would have done without her. But it's surely good to know that I could call on you if I ran into trouble, so thanks a million."

She leaned over and hugged Karen. Then she got up and hugged Tony. For once, he was embarrassed and speechless. After a moment he said, "You all enjoy your meal. I'll send Maria over with more coffee."

When they had finished, Karen said, "Well, we hate to leave good company but we'd better get on the road. The plane won't wait if we're late and parking is so hard now that you can't park close to the terminal."

Ed said, "You girls be careful and don't get car jacked in the big city."

"Well, that's a comforting thought. You're just a bundle of joy today."

"Oh, I know you've got a thirty-eight in your pocket and could blow away anybody that tried to mess with you. We all know you're one tough lady."

She pretended to start to slug him and told them all, "You guys have a good day, I can't take any more of this abuse." As they left, they thanked Tony and Maria, Karen told them she'd probably see them tomorrow. They went out and got in Karen's little Toyota and headed for the "big city."

Chapter 36

After they got to school and the kids were gone to their classes, Bill had a free first period. He phoned Janet's doctor, Sam Patterson. Actually he was the family's doctor and had been for years. He knew the family very well and had delivered both of the children at the local hospital.

Bill told him the situation and asked if he would try to see her at the jail. Dr. Patterson was shocked and took a minute or two to answer. "I'll be glad to try, Bill, but what if she won't see me?"

Bill said, "Well, I'll have to get you to sign the commitment papers without seeing her. You can take my word. She is mentally ill. You weren't in the hospital when they brought me in but she hurt me. Tom is convinced she would kill us all, given the chance. I think he's wrong but I'd rather not take a chance. Besides she's needed to get help for a long time."

"I'll make a point to go today. She doesn't need to stay there in jail any longer. I'm sure it's making her sicker than ever. You can call me later this afternoon and I'll have an answer for you. Or better yet just come by the office and I'll sign the papers if they're ready."

"Okay, will do." He hung up and called the lawyer.

He asked the secretary to let him speak to Jack and when he came on the line, he said, "Jack, I have the doctor going to the jail today and I can get the therapist to sign right away. When will you have the paperwork ready?"

"My secretary is typing them up right now. I'll call the judge and see if I can get an emergency hearing tomorrow. So you come and pick up the papers as soon as you get out of school. Okay?" Bill was feeling much better and said, "I'll be there by four o'clock."

He hung up the phone and sat there thinking about how crazy life can be. Then he went to find the assistant coach, Jerry Barker. Jerry was Bill's right-hand man. He was a young black man who had proved his value many times. The kids loved him and he loved them. He had two little children of his own and a beautiful wife that was a substitute teacher.

Bill told him that he had some things to take care of after school. He asked him if he could he take over the football practice for today. Jerry said, "No problem. Do what you gotta do."

That was a relief to Bill. Bill added, "I may have to call on you more because I've got some family problems that are going to require my attention for a while. If I'm missing some times just cover for me. Okay?"

"Sure, man, that's what I'm here for. Don't you worry about it. I know you'd do the same for me."

He went back to his office and got busy preparing for his first class of the day. He had always loved history and enjoyed teaching it. As a result, his students enjoyed his classes. They would do dramatic readings of historical events and he had even been known to climb up on his desk and deliver a famous speech. The kids loved it. Since it was October, they were studying Christopher Columbus and early Americana. Next would be the Pilgrims and Thanksgiving. He didn't think the school board would appreciate him doing the witches of Salem for Halloween but he'd always been tempted. He thought he'd better wait to do that when he was ready to retire.

Karen and Melanie only stopped once on the way to Chicago. They went into a gas station to use the rest room and got some sodas. They didn't need gas, so they got back on the road. They talked all the way. Melanie told her, "You know I spent quite a bit of time in your studio. You have some great work in there. You just don't know how good you are. You've improved so much since you retired and can work more."

"Which one did you like?" "I liked them all but the one of the fall trees that you did at the colony is beautiful. I liked the seascape, too. When did you do that one?"

"Now, you caught me. Your mother and I took a trip together before she went to work at the bank. We went down to Mississippi. We went all the way to the coast and stayed at one of the casinos. We gambled until we had lost all we wanted to. Our meals and room were comped because I had made arrangements ahead of time. They were advertising in a travel magazine I read. We had a great time. All the drinks are free and the slots are great fun. I could become addicted. When you make twenty-one we'll meet in St. Louis and go to the casino on the river boat. Would you like that?"

"Hey, that would be a great way to celebrate coming of age! I'll look forward to that. You know I'll be twenty-one in February."

"Yes, I know. When you come home for the holidays we'll see if we can get Margie's car for you to take back if the weather is okay. You never can tell about our winters but anybody twenty-one should have their own transportation."

"I'd surely like that. It gets old when you don't have a car to get around in."

113

"But I want you to be sure you don't drink when you drive."

"I really rarely drink. My father has turned me against drinking. I'm afraid I'll be like him."

"Okay, that sounds like a good idea. Anyway back to our trip. When we left the casinos, we went to Florida. It's wasn't very far and it was beautiful. That's where I took a whole bunch of pictures and used them when I got back. It was fun to paint warm sunny pictures in the middle of a snowstorm."

By now they were at the exit to the airport. She was able to let Melanie and her luggage out at the door and she went to park. When she got back to the terminal so they went in the restaurant to get a soda and wait until her flight was announced. They only had to wait about thirty minutes and Karen walked with her to the security section. They hugged and said their goodbyes. Melanie promised to call when she got to her dorm room. Karen watched her until she got to her gate and then she went back to get her car and go home. She thought, "It's going to be so lonely without her."

When she got back on the interstate, she turned on the radio and tuned to the classical music she loved. She stopped once to gas up, get a soda and use the rest room half way home. She made it back at five. The light on her answer machine was blinking. It was Ed, "Call me."

She thought, "He wants to know what I came up with on my trip. I hate to tell him I still don't have a clue."

Bill Wallace went by the lawyers and picked up the papers from the secretary. He didn't bother to see Jack but hurried to the therapist and got her to sign. While he was there, he asked her if she would appear in court if the lawyer thought it was necessary. She told him she would be glad to. "I think she needs to be out of that jail. I'll be glad to help in anyway I can. Do you want me to go to the hospital with her and help get her treatment set up?"

"Oh, could you? I can't tell you how much I'd appreciate that. I know it wouldn't be wise for me to be there. She's going to be very angry with me. Besides I have no idea what to do."

"Okay, just let me know when the date is set. I can rearrange my schedule to fit it in."

"That's great! I've got to get to Dr. Patterson's now so I'll talk to you after the lawyer has things arranged." He left for the doctor's office and was grateful to find an empty parking lot. When he went in, the receptionist told him that the doctor was waiting for him and to go on in. Dr. Patterson was sitting at his desk.

He said, "Hello there, young man. You look like a whipped puppy. Maybe

I need to examine you."

"No, I'm just trying not to take too many pain pills and I'm hurting right now. Besides, I'm really so worried about my wife. How did it go?"

"Surprisingly she let me see her. I guess our good relationship all these years accounted for her trust in me. I didn't do any in depth examination. Just blood pressure, heart beat and ask her a few questions. She had a few questions for me, too. I was able to avoid any mention of commitment. I just told her we were concerned. She wanted to know if I knew when she would get out and I told her I really didn't know. That would be up to the judge when she appeared at the hearing. She seemed surprised to know she was to have a hearing."

"Yes, I'm sure she was. She has refused to talk to anyone so they haven't told her anything. Which just proves that she has a bigger problem than she thinks. So will you be willing to sign the papers?"

"Yes, just give them to me. It's very obvious that she has regressed since I saw her last. She has lost weight and that's good. I think that her weight gain bothered her more than she would admit."

Bill thanked him and got up to leave. He said, "I have to get these papers back to the lawyer so he can get on with it." He was hoping that he could still catch the lawyer.

The office door was unlocked but the secretary was gone so he knocked on the door. "Come on in." Jack was on the phone and waved to him to sit.

When he hung up, he said, "I've got great news if you've got signed papers. Judge Watson is willing to clear his morning calendar to get this thing taken care of. I explained the importance of the situation. He had already heard of the problem with Janet when he and the district attorney had lunch one day last week."

"Here are the signed papers. The psychologist will appear if you need her. She's going to go up with Janet to the hospital and get her treatment started."

"Sounds like we're in good shape then. I don't think we need the therapist in the court since the judge is being so cooperative. Give me the papers and you go home and get some rest. You look like hell."

"You're the second person to tell me that. First the doc and now the lawyer. Guess I'd better get my butt to the house. I can tell you this. I'll sleep better tonight, especially after I take a pain pill or two. I haven't taken any all day because I wanted to keep a clear head. Thanks for getting this done so quickly. I'm sure someday Janet will appreciate it, too. I'll call you tomorrow or you can call me at the school if you need me." He shook Jack's hand and turned to leave. Going to his car, he delivered up a silent prayer of gratitude.

Chapter 37

Karen had called Ed soon after she got home. She told him to come on out when he could get away. Then she got the food out and some paper plates and utensils. The animals were at the open back door so she went out to give them some attention. She sat on the steps with Callie in her lap and Jazz by her side taking turns to pet them both. In a few minutes she got up and told them to come with her. She went to the barn to see about Candy. She got the brush and began to brush her. Candy loved to be brushed but she loved to be ridden even more. Karen decided to saddle her up and have a ride. It had been two weeks since she had ridden her. When she got on, she took off thru her pasture and then on to neighbors land with Jazz running along behind them, sometimes he even ran ahead of them. Barking all the way. She had been riding about thirty minutes when she heard a horn honking.

She headed back to the house. She rode up in the yard right to the porch where Ed was sitting. She said, "Want to go for a ride?"

He smiled and said, "I'm afraid horses and I don't get along. It's a good thing we don't have mounted police here in Dinsmore."

"Well, my goodness, I can't believe a big old, strong policeman is afraid of a horse."

He tried to sound tough and said, "I didn't say I was afraid. I'm not afraid of a damn thing except women. They scare me to death."

"I noticed that, Mr. Bachelor, why are you here then?" He frowned at her and said, "You know, I carry a thirty-eight."

"Gosh, now you're scaring me."

"Would you get off that horse, woman, and get me something to eat?"

"Now the cave man comes out in you."

She turned the horse and headed for the barn, laughing all the way. Jazzy decided to stay by the porch and bark at Ed. He said, "What's the matter with you, dog?" He went up and sat down by him. When he patted him on the head he wiggled all over the place.

Karen put the horse up for the night, making sure she had hay and food. Then she walked back to the house. Callie had been in the barn and she followed Karen to the house. "Okay, Ed. let's go in and put on our feed bag now."

She went into the bath room to wash up and when she came back out, Ed was pouring soda into their glasses. They filled their plates and decided to go on the porch and eat at the umbrella table out there. The evening sun was going down and the weather was cooler but it was pleasant to be outside. They discussed their day between bites but didn't get much said until they finished eating. By that time it was getting much cooler and almost dark. They decided to have dessert in the den.

Bill told his children all that he had accomplished that day and then he asked how their day had been. Tom said, "Some smart ass asked me how I liked my mom being in jail. I ask him how he'd like to join her? I told him, "maybe after I beat the hell out of you, we could both go and check it out." He got out my way after that." Bill just shook his head and smiled.

Amy told them nobody really said anything to her but there was a lot of whispering and snickering when she walked into some of her classes. "I pretended not to notice. They're just some stupid kids that don't know any better. Nobody mentioned it at cheerleading practice and they all acted the same as usual. I'm not worried about what other people think. It's our problem and nobody else's business."

Bill told them that they would just have to put up with some people's stupidity. Eventually they would get their mother back and life would be different. He said, "Until that day we'll have to pull together. We'll take turns cooking and cleaning. We have to keep this place neat and clean or she will pitch a fit when she comes home…I didn't mean that! I meant that she always kept everything so nice and we don't want to mess it up."

The kids both laughed at him and Tom said, "Sure, Dad, we know what you mean."

Amy said, "Okay, I'll take my turn first and do the dishes after you two cook. What kind of frozen dinners are we going to have?"

Bill said, "We're not cooking or washing dishes tonight. We're going out to eat. What will it be?" They both said, "Wendy's" and away they went. Out to their favorite mode of transportation, the pick-up. They were all feeling much better. Bill had taken his pain pills, so he told Tom he'd better drive. Amy sat in the middle between her two favorite men.

Chapter 38

Ed and Karen talked until after ten o'clock. They decided that she should question Daniel and Bill again sometime, just to see if they might have recalled something of interest. She was going to the apartment and go over it with a fine tooth comb. Ed would call Larry Sloan in to be interviewed or go to see him at his home. He was going to see if Bill had a name for the private detective that Janet hired. Maybe she wrote him a check or had his card somewhere. There had been a stranger hanging around the Café a few days ago. He didn't seem to want to be known. Tony had tried to talk to him but he didn't have any luck. He said that he had watched him after he left the Café. He wanted to see what he was driving but he was walking. He had followed two postal workers to the post office. They had been talking about Larry Sloan being drunk at the country club. One of them said there was a rumor was that Daniel Carmody had knocked him on his butt. It wasn't true but the rumor went all over town. Nothing new to report.

When they had exhausted that subject, Ed asked, "When is your new boyfriend coming to see you?"

"You jerk. I don't have a boyfriend. In the first place, I'm too old for a "boyfriend" and if I had a man friend, I wouldn't tell you. You'd go to the Café and tell Tony, he would start asking me personal questions. Then you'd tell everyone at the station and they would have it all over town that I was sleeping with someone. I'd have to leave town because my reputation would be ruined."

"Good God, I didn't know you had such an imagination. But now that you mention it, is he going to stay with you?" He dodged, as if she had tried to hit him.

"No, I don't have overnight male guests unless they're relatives and I don't have any relatives. None that I know of anyway. I've outlived them all."

"You are a real clown, aren't you? What do you mean, you don't have any relatives? Everybody has relatives. Some of us would like to forget them but they're a fact of life."

"No kidding, my parents were both only children of only children. Dad's parents immigrated from Russia. They were laborers and couldn't afford to have a bunch of kids. Mom's were from Ireland and you know how they were treated when they came over. Now they're all cops like you and me. Even Irish Catholics couldn't afford kids. My folks did want more but they just didn't get their wish. They never found out why. People just accepted things in those days. Didn't have in vitro or fertility drugs. I never knew Rich's family. They weren't close. He never would talk about his brother. They had some kind of disagreement and never had anything to do with each other. It's sad but true. Rich moved here from Wyoming when he was sixteen. He had lived on his own since he was fourteen. He stayed with a family here in town until he made enough to get his own place. He was one of a kind. I met him at a dance at the Community Center and it was love at first sight. Why did you get me talking about all this?"

"You and Rich never had any children either, did you?"

"Well, I got pregnant once but it only lasted three months. The doctor said I shouldn't try again and advised me to have a hysterectomy. I put it off until it became absolutely necessary and became an emergency operation."

"What made you decide to be a cop?"

"I knew that I wasn't going to be able to just be a housewife and police work had always interested me. You know, solving mysteries and all. Rich didn't object to me working. We had a great marriage. He wasn't the domineering sort and he enjoyed hearing about our escapades at the station. You know that, after all, he was your best friend."

"I didn't know anything about his past. He never talked about old times, only about today and maybe tomorrow. He seemed to enjoy life and was always good for a laugh."

"Do you realize this is the first time we have talked about Rich since he died? That's been five years now."

"I don't know why, but to talk about him would acknowledge his death. I just didn't want to think of him as dead. We had such good times. I still miss him."

"I have never woken once, without him being in my first thoughts. I really loved that man and he was gone too soon. Why do you think bad things happen to good people?"

"I don't know but it sure seems to work that way. Just like Margie dying so young and healthy."

"Yes, she was the best friend I ever had. We've just got to figure out what happened to her."

"Somebody out there knows what happened. I hope we don't have a nut on the loose."

"I'm going to be busy getting ready for John's visit but next week I promise to get on with it."

"You will go to her apartment before that I hope. Things might need to be taken care of there."

"Oh, her rent was paid for the rest of the year. I want to find out what to do about her car so Melanie can have it after the holidays. Do you know how that works? We need to look for a will, too. I assume that if she had one, a lawyer would have contacted someone. Don't you suppose?"

"You thinking Larry might know something? Who was her divorce attorney?"

"It was Jack Carter, I'll call him tomorrow and see what he knows."

The phone rang and Karen went to answer it. It was a little before nine on the kitchen clock. She answered and heard, "It's me, Melanie, I'm here at last. I'm sorry I didn't call earlier but I really haven't been here long. The flight on Ozark was delayed by rain so I got in late but Shirley was there. She's such a good friend to wait so long and not be mad. So how was your trip back?"

"It was just fine. I got back about five and came home and rode Candy. Ed came out to help me eat some more of this food. I'm taking the rest of it to the Crisis Center tomorrow."

"I'm glad you got home okay. I'm worn out so I'm going to bed soon. I'll call you again soon or you can call me. I love you Karen, you take good care of yourself. I'll be looking forward to hearing about John's visit."

"Okay, you go to bed and I think I'll do the same. Come to think of it, I'm kind of tired myself. Ed and I have been talking for hours and the time got away. Goodnight, sweetie."

"Goodnight."

Karen hung up the phone and went back to Ed. He said, "I didn't realize how late it was. I've got to go home. I hope I haven't been a nuisance."

"You are most welcome anytime. You know that. I enjoyed talking to you. We haven't talked like that since I retired. It was good, and I've enjoyed it. Would you like to take some of this food?"

"Well, I might like some of that apple pie, if you can spare it."

She got a plastic container to fill with apple pie. Then she said, "Now here, go home."

He kissed her on the cheek, turned away quickly and went to get in his car. He tooted the horn as he backed out of the drive. She turned off the porch light, Jazz and Callie had already gone to the barn. She locked the door and went to turn on the television news. Afterward she watched a little of Leno, then went to her bedroom to read some more of her novel. She was asleep in ten minutes.

Chapter 39

Wednesday morning Tony opened the Café as usual at six in the morning. He was looking out the door at the beautiful fall day. The weather had been so unusually nice for so long, he was just wondering how much longer it could last. Ed Hawkins and Jeff Collins were his first customers of the day.

He opened the door when he saw them drive up and park. " Welcome to the members of the bachelors club."

Jeff high fived him as they came in. He said, "Good Morning, old married man."

"What can I get you two after I get your coffee?"

"Where's your gorgeous wife? I'd rather have her get my order," Jeff asked.

"Oh, she'll be out in a bit. She had to stop for some supplies on her way." He brought three cups of coffee to their table and sat down. "Since you want my wife to wait on you, I'll just sit with you til she gets here."

Ed asked, "What's the story today, you surely have some gossip to share with us."

"Not really, it's been kind of quiet in the gossip department. There has been some talk about Janet but I really don't know much about that situation. Do you?"

"Nothing that I'm at liberty to tell you. I do understand that she'll have a hearing today but she won't have to appear. Her lawyer will take care of matters."

"That's good, I hope they can get her out of there. That's got to be bad for a mother and for the kids."

Ed changed to a more general subject, "Who's going to win the football game this week. They're playing Conway. Do you know anything about that team?"

"No, but Tom told me not to bet against him. He's a great kid. I hope he can get a scholarship to play in college."

"You're right about that. The Wallaces can be proud of both their kids. What did you think of Melanie Sloan?"

"That's a beautiful girl. Just like her mother was and just as nice. I miss seeing Margie. She used to come in at least once a day."

"She's going to be missed by a lot of us. It's a dirty shame."

Jeff chimed in, "Why do you think she committed suicide, Ed? I can't imagine what would have caused her to do that."

"I don't think she did commit suicide. But that's between you, me and the gate post. The chief has issued his orders. The case is closed. The end. My butt will be in a crack if he thinks I don't agree with him, so you keep it to yourself."

Tony is really curious now and he leans in asking, "What do you think happened then?"

"I don't know Tony. I don't want my feelings to get around but if you overhear anything, you let me know. I'm looking for that private detective that you saw in here."

"You mean that stranger I told you about? What makes you think he's a private detective?"

"I've got reasons, that's all that matters. I need to contact him and find out what he was up to. If he shows back up, you let me know right away. Now go get my breakfast, you nosy so and so."

Tony got up chuckling, "Okay, okay, I'm gone. I just heard Maria come in the back door anyway. She'll be on my case if she sees me sitting around. Wonder where everybody is this morning. I never get to sit still that long." Maria came from the back putting on her apron. She came right over with the coffee pot and asked if they had ordered yet. They gave her their order and she called it into Tony.

Larry Sloan came in and sat down at the counter. He looked sober and was nicely dressed in a dark brown suit with a blue shirt and a darker blue tie. Maria took him a cup of coffee and said, "Good Morning, Larry. How's the world treating you today?" He muttered, "It would be a lot better if I didn't have to go to work this morning."

"What can I get you?"

"I'll have pancakes and bacon. I guess I'll have some orange juice, too."

"I'll be right back with the orange juice. Tony, we need some pancakes with bacon here."

She picked up the orders for Ed and Jeff and took them to their table. She told them she would be back with more coffee for them. Then she took Larry's orange juice to him.

He asked her, "Has Melanie been in?"

She considered her answer for a minute, then said, "Well, yes, she was here with Karen yesterday morning. They were leaving for Chicago so Melanie could catch a plane back to school."

He just shook his head and said, "Damn, I wish I could have talked to her. I don't know why she won't have anything to do with me. Well, I do know but I don't know what to do about it." Maria thought, "Sober up.," But she didn't say a word.

Tony said, "Pick up on the pancakes and bacon." That saved her. She brought his order, refilled his coffee and headed for another customer that had come in. While she was getting that person's order, the farm crew arrived. There were six of them this day. They pushed two tables together and Maria went to get the coffee for them.

After Ed and Jeff got back to the station they checked to see if any calls had come in. It was a quiet day in Dinsmore, so far. Ed asked the jailer how Janet was doing and he said, "The same as usual."

He sat down and called Jack Carter. The secretary put Jack on the phone and he said, "What can I do for you, Ed?"

"I was wondering what time you expect to have Janet Wallace's hearing. I'd like to be prepared for transporting her."

"We're scheduled for nine thirty and as soon as I finish which will be minutes, I'll call you and give you a heads up."

"Okay, is anybody going with her?"

"I understand the therapist that saw her there in the jail plans to go get her situated. I'm sure she'll follow the sheriff's vehicle."

"Okay, I'm going to go ahead and call the sheriff and have him on standby. I wasn't sure who would be responsible for transportation."

"It falls to the county so you're off the hook after that. I need to go now. Talk to you later."

Ed was left holding a dead phone.

Chapter 40

Karen was in her studio painting a large canvas she had stretched early that morning. She had gone through her photos and chosen one of the Florida shots. The Pensacola beach. She was mixing the pretty aqua and turquoise colors of the ocean. Then she mixed the sand colors for the dunes and put out some burnt sienna and yellow ochre for the sea oats. She had piled on a lot of paint with a painting knife and was working fast and furious. She stopped occasionally and stepped back to survey her progress. She went to kitchen and refilled her coffee cup, came back and sat down to think about her next move. When she felt that the painting was complete she still had a pallette full of paint so she got a smaller canvas and did a quick floral in the same pallette knife technique. She liked using the knife to paint because it assured that the results would be impressionistic. No chance of being overly realistic.

Her paintings ran the gamut of super realism to impressionism but she really preferred the impressionism and she felt that they would do better in the gallery setting. She thought to herself, "I'm now thinking of painting for the gallery and I don't think that's wise of me. I'll lose my spontaneity and become too stiff and studied."

She planned to start using bigger brushes, too. But most of all she was going to paint to please herself and hope that the gallery goers will like her work, too. Then looking around her studio at all the canvases, at least twenty large ones, she said out loud, "If not, my friends will be getting large paintings for Christmas and birthdays from now on."

The phone rang and it was Ed. She said, "Gosh, I'm glad you called. I have been reduced to talking to my self."

He wanted to bring her up to speed on Janet's situation. She told him how bad she felt for the family. She said, "You know I planned to take some of this food to the Crisis Center but I think I'll wait til school is out and take some that I froze to Bill and his kids. It's going to be hard for him to keep up with everything at home and coaching. He has a lot on his hands."

Ed said he thought that was a great idea, "I'm sure Bill will appreciate it. You'd better call first. He and Tom have football practice after school and I'm sure Amy waits for them to go home."

"Good idea," Karen said, "Now get off this phone so I can get back to my painting."

"Oh, yeah, got to get ready for the boyfriend." She hung up on him. He sat at his desk and thought, "That's twice in one day."

Chapter 41

Larry Sloan had opened the doors of the store at nine o'clock sharp. Customers were waiting outside because they were having a big sale. The clerks were all at their stations and he said, "Good Morning." to each as he passed on his way to his office which was his sanctuary. Pamela didn't come to work until ten o'clock so he had a few minutes to himself. He was going to meet with his assistant manager at ten thirty and he wasn't looking forward to it. She had been criticizing everything he did lately and he was really tired of her attitude. He thought about the bottle he had in the bottom drawer of his desk but thought he'd better wait until after their meeting. She might be trying to torpedo him and he didn't want to give her any more ammunition. He recently found out she had managed to become friends with the owner's wife. They had worked on some committee together and gotten cozy. That was making him paranoid.

Pamela came in a little before ten, she closed the door to his office and went over and sat on his lap. She gave him a long kiss on the lips. He slapped her on the butt, and said, "You'd better get off my lap and out there to your desk."

She looked hurt and said, "You sure are acting weird lately. Before we got married, you couldn't keep your hands off me. Now you don't even like to kiss me."

"That's not true, I've just got a lot on my mind. I've got a meeting with Rebecca after a while."

"I know what you've got on your mind. It's your poor little ex wife Margie. You still love her and not me."

"Don't be silly, that's not it at all, you're just jealous of everybody I ever knew."

That really made her mad and she flounced out of the office. When he went out to go to the meeting with Rebecca, she looked like she'd been crying. He pretended not to notice and told her to be sure to take his messages but not to interrupt the meeting. She gave him a dirty look and when he turned his back, she gave him the finger.

Rebecca Magee was in her office thinking about the meeting that she was to have with Larry at ten thirty. She was wishing she could avoid it but once in awhile they had to discuss the plans for the store. She thought to herself, "I may be the assistant manager, but I've really been the manager of the Regal Department Store for six months. He's been out to lunch, on his ass drunk, most of the time. I'm going to have to see what he's up to before I decide what I want to do. So meet we must and meet we will. Then we'll see."

There was a knock on her office door and she said, "Come, in." Larry entered and she smiled broadly and said, "Have a seat, I'm so glad we could get together. I've got some plans I want to get your input on."

Chapter 42

The hearing for Janet Wallace was over swiftly. Jack Carter presented the case, handed the papers to the judge, he signed them and handed them back. With the bang of the gavel, Janet Wallace was on her way to the Wayne County Institute of Mental Health for an indefinite length of time.

Jack went into the hall, got to an empty office and used the phone to call Ed at the station. He told him to call the sheriff and get the show on the road. Then he called Peggy Jackson, the psychologist, and suggested she go on down to the jail and wait for the sheriff. She could follow them to the hospital in case Janet gave him trouble. He might need her to tranquilize her. She said she would do that, but thought it unnecessary. Then he called Bill, "It's over Bill and your wife will be transported soon by the sheriff. You can rest easier now that she's at least out of jail and getting some much needed help."

"Thanks so much, Jack, I can't tell you much that means to me. Maybe I'll be able to sleep now."

"You're entirely welcome. I'll be sending you a bill." He hung up the phone and headed out of the courthouse. Bill was sitting at his desk holding a dead phone.

Karen quit working on her painting about two o'clock, had a sandwich and a soda. Then she went to take a shower and wash her hair. She put on her jeans and a flannel shirt. Decided a little blush and lipstick would be sufficient today. She just shook her head to arrange her short hair. She went outside to sit with the animals and enjoy the beautiful weather for a few minutes. She sat thinking of what she must do before winter sat in. This mild weather was not meant to last much longer. When she went back in the house, she began to pack a cardboard box with containers of food. A chicken casserole, some lima beans, half a cake and a pie to take to the Crisis Center. She packed another box with a foil pan of lasagna, half a loaf of garlic bread, a fruit salad and a pie that she got out of the freezer for Bill Wallace and his family. She took the first box to the car and then came back to get the other, got it, her keys and purse. She locked up the house, put the box in the back seat and got in. When she backed out of the drive, she stopped at the mailbox and got the mail. She skimmed through several pieces and recognized one from John Whitcomb.

She decided to read it before going on to town. It was a short note saying he was looking forward to seeing her on Saturday and would call her when he got into town. She smiled, thinking she was looking forward to seeing him, too. But I've got to get some more work ready and it's Wednesday evening already. She went to the Crisis Center first and dropped off her box of food. Women from different churches took turns volunteering there and they were very appreciative.

After football practice, Bill and Tom both showered and changed clothes in the gym. Amy had finished cheerleading practice and was sitting on the back of the pickup. She was doing her homework so she wouldn't have to do it at home. She heard somebody say, "Hi, Amy." and looked up. It was Karen Sutton. "Oh, Hi, Mrs. Sutton, what are you doing here?"

"Actually, I'm looking for the Wallace family. Do you happen to know them?"

Amy smiled shyly. "I might but I hope we're not in trouble. Aren't you a cop?"

"Honey, I retired a year ago and I'd never arrest you anyway. We've just had so much food brought to the house and I thought I'd share. Melanie stayed with me after Margie died and people wanted to feed us. I'll never be able to eat it all and she's back at school. Anyway, I knew your mother was in the hospital and I thought you'd be able to use it. I went by your house. When nobody was home, I realized Bill and Tom had practice here, so here I am. You won't have to cook tonight because I brought you a box full."

Bill and Tom came up to the truck. Bill said, "Hi there, Karen. What are you up to?"

Amy interrupted, "She brought us some food. Isn't that great?"

Karen explained her reasons for delivering food again. Bill said, "That was nice of you to think of us."

"Ed told me that Janet was going in the hospital so I thought you could use a break if you are doing your own cooking."

"Yes, I guess everybody will know eventually but that's okay. It's best that she get some help. Actually we are all taking turns with the cooking and cleaning. That's the plan, anyway."

She went to the car and got the box to give him. She said, "Well, none of you will have to cook tonight. Where do you want this?"

He took the box and put in the back of the truck, took her hand and shook it, and thanked her again. "Coming to the game tomorrow night?"

"I've got company coming Saturday but I'm going to try to make it. I really enjoy watching you, Tom."

He hadn't said a word, feeling embarrassed by the conversation about his mother. Now he said, "I really love to play. I'm glad you like to come to the games. Dad works really hard to have a good team. Dinsmore supports our team and that makes it more fun for all of us."

"Well, I've got to get back home. I'm working on a painting, and I want to finish it tonight."

"Okay, thanks again."

They are got in their respective vehicles to go to their homes. Bill hadn't even cranked the engine before Amy said, "Why didn't you tell me that Mother was going into the hospital?"

"Honey, I told you I'd hired the lawyer. I didn't know when he would get the court order. He called me this morning here at school. The sheriff had to take her because of the court order. I haven't seen you all day. I told Tom because I saw him at practice."

"Oh, okay, I was just shocked when she knew and I didn't. Now will we be able to see her?"

"That will be entirely up to her. If she doesn't want to, we can't make her. I'm sure she will eventually. Let's go home and get some of this food on the table. I'm starving." He cranked the engine and dropped the subject like a brick.

Chapter 43

Daniel had failed to call his children when he had intended. So much had happened since his divorce was finalized. He had a decent day at work and felt like it was time to see how they were doing.

His daughter, Allison, was a medical student at Harvard. She was twenty-two and had graduated from high school when she was sixteen. She was a resident at a Boston hospital now. She wanted to be a pediatrician. She had always wished for a sister but they hadn't had any more children after David, who was now twenty, was born.

David was a theater major at University of Illinois, Northwestern. He was never an A student but he was in all the school stage productions. Summers he studied his craft with amateur theaters. He did all of it, building sets, lighting and some bit parts in the plays. Daniel hadn't seen either of his children for six months.

He called Allison first. She lived with two other girls in a rented house in Brockton, a suburb of Boston. The phone rang three times and he thought he would get an answer machine but a girl came on the phone. He said, "Allison?" She said, "No, this is Cindy her room mate, let me get her."

In a minute or two Allison said, "Hello, this is Allison." Daniel said, "This is your Dad."

"Oh, Hi Dad, how are you? I've been thinking of you but didn't know how to reach you. Well, that's not really true. I could have called the bank. You know how it is, you think of it and then put it off. I heard from Mother, that the divorce is final. She's still not facing facts but she'll be okay. I'm blathering on and haven't let you say a word."

"I've enjoyed listening to you. Sounds like you're happy and I'm glad to hear your voice. I was wondering what you're planning for the holidays."

"I haven't made any plans. I know Mother will expect us to be with her. We can be with you, too. What have you got in mind?"

"I thought the three of us might go to Colorado on a skiing vacation."

"That sounds great. Just make it for after Christmas day and we'll be okay with Mother."

"Okay, I'm going to call David in a few minutes and when I get the plan

I'll either write or call."

"I love you, Daddy."

"I love you, too, little girl. Bye for now."

"Bye." He hung up the phone and dialed David's number. He got a busy signal, so went to pour himself a glass of wine to have while he waited.

Karen was in her studio finishing up the seascape painting. She hadn't signed it but was leaning on a stool, studying it and trying to decide if it was finished. She got her box of photos to see what she would do next. She decided on the farm scene she had photographed on the way to Easton. She stretched another large canvas and signed the one she had just finished.

She decided to have a snack and watch some television before bedtime. She got a beer and cheddar cheese out of the fridge, opened a box of crackers and went in the den to relax. The phone rang. She looked at the clock. It was after nine, kind of late for her to be getting a call. She picked up the phone and immediately heard, "I hear you don't think Margie committed suicide. Who the hell do you think you are? Keep your mouth shut or it will be shut…Permanently." They hung up.

She just sat there dumbfounded. She thought, "I haven't been talking to anyone. Who would do such a thing? Does somebody think it's a joke? No…" She hadn't even been able to tell if it was male or female. They had disguised their voice. Who had she talked to? She was racking her brain. They hadn't frightened her but had angered her. Now she'd never be able to sleep. She called Ed.

Daniel finally got through to David. "Hi, David, it's Dad."

"Dad! How are you doing? It's been ages."

"Yeah, I know. I've missed you and your sister. How have you been?"

"I'm fine. I'm having a ball. I've got great room mates and I like living in the dorm. There's always something going on. You know me, got to have action."

"Oh, I know that for sure. I was wondering what you and Allison had planned for the holidays. I know you'll have to spend Christmas with your mother but after that I'd like for the three of us to go skiing in Colorado."

"That sounds great, have you talked to Allison?"

"Yes, she's up for it. I'll get the reservations and get back to you both. I'll either write or call."

"Okay, Dad, this is so great. I've missed you, too and it will be fun to be with you and Allison."

"I'll be talking to you later, okay? Bye for now."

133

"Bye, Dad, take care." He hung up the phone, feeling much better than he had in days. He went to his computer and began to check out skiing vacation packages on the Internet.

Chapter 44

Ed had been exhausted after dealing with Janet and her reaction to the fact that she was being transferred the Wayne County Mental Health Institute. When the sheriff went to her cell and to get her, she thought she was getting out of jail to go home. They didn't want to put leg irons on her but she was acting so crazy they had to restrain her some way. She resisted getting in the car. Then she started yelling and screaming. Thank goodness, the car was behind the station and no civilians saw or heard. The psychologist went out and talked to her and got her calmed down a little. They finally got on the road. The sheriff came by on his way back to his department and told them that when he left, she seemed okay. She told them that "at least it's better than jail" but she'd like to get her hands on Bill Wallace. The whole department had broken up over that one.

Ed said, "I guess she doesn't remember that's what put her where she is."

When the phone rang he had just come out of the shower. He groaned because he thought it was the department calling him back to work. He answers gruffly, "Ed here, who is it?"

"It's me Karen. Were you asleep?"

"Hell, no, I thought you were the department calling me in. What's up?"

"Oh, I'm sorry to be calling you so late but I just got a strange phone call. A threatening phone call."

"What do you mean, threatening?" She told him exactly what had happened and how it made her feel.

She said, "Who could know what I've been thinking? I didn't think I had talked about it to anybody but you."

"Somehow this makes me think that Tony Distefano has been talking out of turn."

"He's always eavesdropping at the Café. You know that. I can't think of anybody else except Jeff and he knows better."

"Okay, so who'd Tony tell? That's the question. Who would give a damn that I didn't think it was suicide.?"

"That's the sixty four-dollar question. It does make me think we're onto something, though."

"That's true so maybe it's a good thing."

"No, it's not a good thing. I don't like you being threatened at all. Out there in the country, all by yourself. It's dangerous, damned dangerous. I don't like it at all."

"I'll be all right. I've got a thirty-eight and Jazzy. They won't bother me."

"Oh, yeah, Jazzy would lick them to death. You make sure you lock up tight and we'll do some checking and see if we can come up with a suspect. Can you meet me at the Café in the morning?"

"No, I've got to get ready for John's visit. I've got a painting I want to finish."

"Well, hell, I'll talk to Tony and see if he has shot off his mouth to anybody and I'll check on you tomorrow evening. I'll probably call you in the morning and make sure you're okay."

"Now I'm sorry I called you. You'll just stew over it. I hate to accuse Tony. Hey, I just remembered the game is Friday night. Are you going?"

"If I don't have to work. Want to meet me there?"

"Yeah, I would like to. I don't have anybody to go with any more."

"Well, I've got to get to bed. Janet Wallace about did us all in today. I'm one tired puppy. You take care. Do like I said, check the doors and windows before you go to bed. Okay?"

"Yeah, yeah, yeah, I will. I'll see you at the game. Meet me at the gate. Good night."

"Ga'night." He hung up the phone and sat down on the bed. He was worried and curious. Then he was angry. He was thinking he was going to whip somebody's ass. He laid down across the bed and went to sleep in his wet towel. He woke about three a.m., freezing cold. He threw the towel across the room and got under the covers.

Bill Wallace had a lot of explaining to do when he got home Wednesday evening. Why the sheriff had taken Janet to the hospital, why she was still under arrest, when they could see her . He answered as much as he could, explaining that he didn't know a lot of the details himself. Finally, he said, "Enough of this, lets see what Karen brought us to eat."

Tom went to his room and when he came out he was in shorts and sweatshirt. He announced, "I'm going for a run. I don't feel like eating right now."

"Okay, whatever you want to do.," Bill said, "I would think you're worn out after that practice I put you through." He didn't answer, just went out the door.

Bill looked at Amy and asked, "Do you know what's eating him?"

"No, he's been in a really bad mood lately. I thought he'd be happy that mother was out of the house but he's been kind of sad. Did you notice that he cried at Margie's funeral? Tom never cries. I was shocked. We didn't know her that well. You're the one that knew her."

"No, I didn't know that he was upset. I guess I've had so much on my mind. I wasn't paying attention. Between my ribs killing me and dealing with your mother, I've been preoccupied."

Amy had the food was all laid out on the table by now. Bill said, "Let's eat, I'll see if I can talk to him later."

"I'm going to take mine into my room so I can finish my homework."

"Okay, I'll be in the den. You really ought to give yourself a break, but do whatever you want. I'm beginning to think you and Tom are both mad at me."

"No, Daddy, I'm not mad, I'm kind of sad, too. I'm worried about Mother, I'll bet she's scared."

"Yeah, I'm sure she is but they'll help her and get her back to us in better shape." He thought to himself, "I hope and pray."

Amy and Bill were both in bed before Tom slipped into the house and to his bed. Bill had laid awake worrying about where he was. He heard him come in but didn't get up to confront him, just breathed a sigh of relief, knowing he was safely at home.

Chapter 45

Karen was up even earlier than usual. She couldn't get the strange phone call off her mind. It was too early to call Ed so she got her coffee and went into her studio. She turned on her stereo and listened to broadway show tunes while she sketched the picture she was going to paint. At six o'clock, she called Ed. When he answered, she said, "I hope you were up."

"Yes, I am getting ready to go to the Café. Why don't you change your mind and meet me?"

"That's why I called. I realized I actually had two days before I have to be ready so as soon as I can dress, I'll see you there."

"Okay, hurry up."

"Soon." She went to put on her sweats and ran a brush through her hair, skipped the make up, put on blush and lipstick. When she went to get her keys she remembered she had to feed her pets. She went out on the porch and poured their food into the bowls and got them some water. She locked the door and went to her car.

When she got to the Café, Ed was in the back at their regular table. Maria brought her a cup of coffee and asked, "Going to eat today?" Karen said, "I'll just have a doughnut. Will you have one, Ed?"

"Yeah, bring us each a doughnut, Maria."

"Did you talk to Tony?," she asked, when Maria was gone. "Not yet. He's really busy and I want to wait until it clears out a little."

Maria brought the doughnuts and went back to get the coffee pot and make the rounds. Karen leaned across the table and said, "You know I got to thinking that you had talked to Bill Wallace. Did you tell him what we were thinking?"

"Yes, I did but he wouldn't be calling you. I mean, I don't think he would be calling you. I didn't think he would be seeing Margie, either, though."

"You never really know what people are capable of. Do you?"

"Well, you let me know if you get any more calls. We can't really do anything until next week so unless you get another call, I'm just going to leave it alone. Then you can go to Margie's apartment and see if you can spot anything that is out of place. You'd know better than anybody."

"That makes sense. Let me know if you get a chance to talk to Tony."

Maria came to the table and said, "Ed, Jeff in on the phone. Wants to talk to you." She filled the cups and went back to pick up an order.

When Ed came back, he said, "I've got to get to work. Jeff says some woman called and said there's a stalker in their neighborhood. I doubt if it's true but got to check it out anyway. This is one of those women that is always calling us about some dumb thing."

"Okay, I've got to go anyway. Want to get back to my painting. I'll see you at the game tomorrow night."

Ed left in a big hurry. He tried to act unconcerned but he knew that he couldn't assume that the lady in question was just upset for nothing. Karen was finishing her coffee when she looked up and Larry Sloan was standing there looking angry.

She said, "Good Morning." He said, "What's the idea of keeping my daughter away from me."

"I had nothing to do with your daughter not seeing you. I think you can take responsibility for that. You manage to show your ass every time she sees you. Besides her mother had just died. She didn't need to be upset by you."

"You don't know what I do!" His voice was rising.

"You're on the verge of doing it again, right now. Tone it down. If you want to talk to me, sit down and talk like a grown man."

Tony came over to the table and said, "Hi, Larry, can I get you something?"

He whirled around and growled, "No, I don't want a damn thing from you."

"Well, then maybe you had better take off. Don't you need to get to work?" Tony reached out to pick up Ed's coffee cup and when he looked down, Larry hit him in the side of the head. Tony looked shocked, but he straightened up and hit Larry in the stomach as hard as he could.

Maria called 911. Larry was doubled over with pain but when he raised up he grabbed a chair and started to hit Tony with it. Karen grabbed the chair leg from behind and it made Larry lose his balance. He fell backwards onto the floor and Tony stood over him with his foot on his chest. He said, "Get up you bastard and I'll knock your head off. Thanks, Karen, that was a good move."

Ed came running back in the door, saying, "What the hell is going on here?" Tony said, "Just a little misunderstanding. You can arrest this bastard. I'm filing charges."

Ed told Larry, "Get up and lean on the table so I can frisk you." Larry was suddenly speechless and did as he was told. Ed handcuffed him and marched him out the door.

He said as he was leaving, "Come to the station as soon as you can, to the sign the papers."

Karen asked Tony, "Are you okay? I'm sorry that had to happen. He's such a fool."

"Nah., don't feel bad. I haven't had a good fight in a long time. He didn't hurt me, just caught me by surprise. I didn't think he was that stupid."

"Well, I think I'll get back out to peace and quiet of the country. City life is just too exciting."

Tony walked her to the door. He asked, "You going to the game tomorrow night?" "Sure am, I'll see you there. I know you're going."

Chapter 46

Daniel had his first decent day at work since Margie's death. He had a meeting with the president of the bank, Patton Smith, they discussed some loans that were going to come before the board on Friday. Then the mayor, Grover Patterson, came by to talk about some city business. In the afternoon, he got on the Internet and checked on skiing vacations. He printed out some information to take home and study. He talked to a couple of farmers about loans for the next planting season. Then he talked to a friend at the home bank in Chicago, just to find out what was happening up there.

He called Ed about four o'clock and asked him what he was doing for supper. They made plans to meet at the Café at six. Ed said, "After we eat, I'll take you to my favorite bar out on the highway and we'll shoot a little pool. Daniel said he was up for that.

When Karen got home, she sat on the porch and petted Jazz and Callie for a few minutes. Then she went to the barn to see about Candy and make sure she had plenty of feed. She was surprised to find Candy locked in her stall. She was never locked up unless the vet was coming to treat her or there some other reason to keep her up. She had five acres to run in if she wished to. Karen let her out and walked with her to the back door of the barn. She slapped her on the rump and she took off running across the field. Karen went back in and climbed to the loft where the hay was stored and looked around. Seeing nothing out of place, she came back down. The hair was standing on the back of her neck. She had an eerie feeling that someone or something was there but she didn't see anything. She went back to the house, unlocked the door and went into her studio to work on her painting. Then she stopped and went back to lock the door. She never kept the door locked when she was at home but suddenly felt uneasy and decided to exercise caution. While she was in the kitchen she got a soda from the fridge and went back to her painting.

She decided to use a limited palette on this painting. She chose yellow ochre, indian red, and viridian green. She used broad strokes and filled the sky with pale yellow, mixing titanium white with the yellow ochre. Working fast she painted a line of trees on the horizon. She added the little white house with the picket fence and the big maples with red and yellow trees. Then the cedars with their dark greens. The foreground was ochre and red mixed to represent the sage grasses of fall. She worked for four hours without taking a break. Then she sat on her stool and surveyed the results. At this point it was a very impressionistic work. Now she would decide whether to leave it as it was or to go back and try for more realism. She opted for impressionism.

She decided that she had worked long enough for a while and went to the den to turn on Oprah. She went in the kitchen and made a ham sandwich, got some chips and put it on a paper plate. She sat in the den and watched television for a couple of hours. Then she got up and went to her desk and got a yellow legal pad to write on. She sat back down in her recliner. She listed all the people that knew Margie. Then beside each name she put their relationship to her, her feelings, if known, about each of them and any animosity that she might have seen or heard about.

Then she went to her computer to check her email. She had a mailbox full. She scrolled thru it, deleting some, reading some. She emailed Melanie to tell her what she had been doing. Promised to email or call after John had been there. She started another search for poisons that could go undetected after death. No luck. Then she decided to see if she could find any information on John Whitcomb. She searched his name but found there were many and she didn't remember, if she knew, where he really lived. He had spoken about his travels but had never really mentioned home. Then she searched "art by whitcomb," "whitcomb art," "whitcomb gallery" and just "artists." Nothing came up that she thought would be him. She decided she would just wait, use her cop experience and interrogate him when he got there. She smiled thinking, "I sure am looking forward to this visit. Ed's really going to be aggravated if I don't let him meet John."

Bill called Peggy Jackson, after he got to school. He wanted to find out how it had gone with Janet. He felt good after their conversation. She told him that once Janet knew exactly what was going on, she settled down. Peggy had talked to the doctor that would be in charge of her treatment and was convinced that he would be able to help her. She said they planned to just let her hang loose for a couple of days. Having been jailed for so long they felt she needed to have a little freedom to check out her surroundings. They said she didn't seem to be dangerous and that she would be watched and kept on medication. He made a mental note to be sure to tell the kids the good news tonight. When he hung up, he began to get ready for his first class. He still had time so he got on the computer to check on the weather for tomorrow night. It looked like it would be cool but dry and that was good news, too. Things are finally looking up for Bill Wallace, he thought.

Chapter 47

At six o'clock, Daniel was in the Café sitting at the counter talking to Tony and drinking coffee. Ed didn't get there until after six thirty. He apologized for being late. He told Daniel, "I hope you don't mind, I invited Jeff Collins, my partner to join us. Figured we could have a pool tournament." They both had to laugh at that.

When Jeff came, in Ed introduced him and the three of them got a table. Maria came over with water for all and asked for their drink order. They all said the water would be good. They read their menus, and when Maria came back, Ed ordered lasagna and a salad, Daniel got spaghetti and meatballs with a salad and Jeff ordered a cheeseburger and fries.

Ed was telling them about arresting Larry and taking him to jail for slugging Tony. Maria brought the salads and said, "That was a mess wasn't it. He didn't really hurt Tony that much, just made him angry. He was afraid Larry was going to hurt Karen. Is he still in jail?"

"No, we let him cool his heels in a holding cell for a couple of hours. When Tony came in, he just said, "If he'll apologize for what he did, I won't press charges. I don't want the fool to lose his job." So we let him out after he agreed that he owed Tony an apology. They shook after he made good on it. That guy needs to get some help, he's definitely out of control. Do you know anyone in a twelve-step program that could get him to a meeting?"

Daniel answered, "They tell me the person with the problem has to want to get help. That they have to hit bottom. Then when they're in enough trouble, they'll go. Sometimes a judge will order them to go. Maybe Tony should have filed charges."

"I'll remember that the next time I arrest him. I'm sure it will happen again. It's a wonder, but he doesn't have a DUI. I notice he has his little wife doing the driving though. Not a bad idea."

Tony and Maria delivered their food and they got busy eating. Tony brought a pitcher of water over and refilled their glasses. It was his excuse to make his usual inquiries. He wasted no time. "What are you guys up to tonight?"

Ed told him, "We're going out to the "Town Hall" to shoot a little pool.

Want to join us?"

"I wish I could but by the time I get this place cleaned, I'm too tired to do anything but flop on the couch. That's not easy to do with five monsters running around either. Besides it wouldn't be fair to Maria and Mom. They need me there to help get them all to bed. It's a major production."

Daniel said, "I can see you now, reading bedtime stories and tucking them in."

"Hey, I don't read them stories. I make up my own horror stories and scare them to sleep."

Ed said, "I'm sure you do, some father you are."

Maria called, "Tony, I have an order I need pronto. Get yourself back to the grill."

"Yes, dear. He held out his hands in despair." When they were finished, they paid their bills and got in their cars to go have some fun.

The place was crowded but they got a table in a few minutes. They each ordered a beer and began to play. First Ed played Daniel while Jeff waited to play the winner. Ed won the first game and when Jeff got up, he said to Ed quietly, "Did you see who's back there in the corner? He's with some woman."

Bill Wallace was sitting in a back booth with a blond that they didn't recognize. They decided not to let him know they saw him since it was obvious he didn't want to be seen.

Ed muttered, "Maybe Janet had good reason to beat the shit out of him. People never cease to surprise me. After all the years I've dealt with the scum, you'd think I'd know better."

Jeff told him, "Hey, don't let it get you down. We don't know what he's had to put up with."

Daniel put in his two cents, "Yeah, I know I was ready to tear my hair out before I finally decided to get out of my marriage. Comes a time when it's no good to even try. I never did step out on her though until I took Margie out. I had already sued for divorce. It was finalized, the day Margie died. I had never told her I had been married and she had never asked."

Ed said, "Yeah, I guess I shouldn't talk since I've never been married and don't have any experience dealing with a woman except Karen and we both had homes to go to. Her husband was my best friend. I never even considered making a move on her when he was alive. But I'll tell you and you better keep it under your hats. I think a lot of her and I'm going to ask her out after this weekend."

Jeff asked, "What are you waiting for? What's the weekend got to do with it?"

"Well, actually she is meeting me at the football game tomorrow night but I wouldn't call it a date. Just friends going to the game."

Daniel said, "That still doesn't answer what this weekend has to do with it."

"Oh, she's got some guy coming for the weekend to look at her artwork. Does that sound like a line or what? Look at her artwork, that's a switch, hope she doesn't look at his artwork."

Jeff snickered and said, "You sound jealous, man. You sound like a guy that's got it bad."

Ed said, "Oh, hell, I knew I shouldn't have said anything. I drink one beer and get loose lips." Embarrassed he said, "Okay, it's my turn to play Jeff now. Quit the gabbing and get serious about this game. Daniel, get us another beer."

They didn't go home til midnight when the place was starting to close. The three of them went out and got in their cars and headed back to Dinsmore. It had been a good night but they were going to hate themselves in the morning.

Bill had slipped out the backdoor of the Town Hall while the guys weren't looking. At least he thought they weren't looking. His lady friend went back to work as a waitress after he left. She had taken a break to sit with him. It happened that she was one of Janet's few friends. Bill had wanted to have a beer and talk to somebody that knew Janet. He went out there where he thought he wouldn't be noticed. He didn't know that he had been seen. His actions made the situation seem more indiscreet than it was. Appearances mean a lot in a little town. When he got home, Amy was alone in the house.

She looked upset and Bill asked her, "What's wrong, you by yourself? Where's Tom?"

"I don't know and I didn't know where you were either. What's going on here?"

"Nothings going on, I just went to have a beer and talk to friends. I didn't think it would cause trouble."

"Well, it would have been nice if the two of you had told me. I've been sitting here for hours, worrying about what had happened to you. Isn't Tom with you?"

"No, I have no idea where he is. I guess I'd better go look for him."

Just then Tom came in the door and said, "You don't need to go look for me, I'm right here. Where have you been?"

"Since I'm the adult in this house, I don't think I need to report in but since you are just seventeen, I think you should. What have you been doing?"

"Well, I went out to run and I ran into some of the guys. I went with them to get a beer at the Town Hall."

"Oh, I see. When did you start drinking beer and how did you manage to buy it?"

"One of the guys was twenty-one. He bought it and brought it out to the parking lot. That's where we drank it."

"I'm really disappointed to hear that, Tom. You've not only broke training but you broke the law."

"Well, I noticed your truck was at the Town Hall. What were you doing?"

"I was having a beer or two with friends. I am of age."

"Yeah, well, the guy that bought the beer was Chris White. Remember him? He played ball on your team four years ago. He said he saw you sitting with a woman in the back of the place."

"That was your mother's friend Sandra, it didn't mean a thing. She wanted to know how Janet was. She had tried to visit her in jail and she wouldn't see her either. Okay?"

"I don't know if it's okay or not. It didn't look good."

Amy finally got a word in, "Both of you can quit arguing, I'm the one that got left sitting here wondering what was going on. It had better not happen again or I'll go live with Grandmother Wallace. I'm tired of all this mess."

Bill had cooled down by now and he said, "I'm really sorry, kids. I had planned to come home and tell you some good news for a change. I talked to Peggy Jackson and she said that your mother was fine when she left her at the hospital. She thinks she'll do just fine as long as they can keep her on her medication and counsel her."

Amy said, "That is good news but I wish you had stayed home long enough to tell me before you snuck off to have your beer. I'm going to bed now, before I say more than I want to. I think you both stink. Goodnight." She left the room. Tom didn't say a word, he just turned around and went to his room. Bill sat down and put his head in his hands.

Chapter 48

Karen slept a little later than usual on Friday morning. She got up to make her coffee and when it was brewed, she took it outside to the porch. Jazz and Callie were there waiting for her. She sat on the steps and petted them both. She said, "It's a pretty day, isn't it kiddies? Guess I'd better get you something to eat." They wagged and purred as if to answer.

When she finished her coffee, she filled their bowls and they got busy. She went back into the house, put on her jeans, a sweatshirt and her boots. Then she went to the barn and saddled Candy. She rode for a while on her land and then rode up to the Barry's house. They weren't outside so she tied Candy to the fence and went to the back door. Ruth came to the door and said, "Well, come in here, girl, and have some breakfast with us."

Karen told her, "I didn't come for breakfast. I figured you two had eaten hours ago."

Joseph said, "Oh, we sleep late now. Since we're old folks, we need more rest. But once we get started we can get a lot done in a day." He was laughing at himself.

Ruth said to Karen, "Yes, it doesn't hurt to sleep late. One reason we sleep late is we stay up too late watching television. How have you been doing, Honey?"

"I've been fine. I've been painting a lot and I've got to get home and try to do one more or start one more. I've got a guy coming tomorrow to look at all my work. He might arrange a gallery showing for me in Chicago if he likes it well enough."

Ruth got excited and said, "Where did you find this guy? My heavens, that would be wonderful. I sure hope it works out for you."

Karen told them about meeting John at the art colony and about her plans for the weekend. She said she planned to give him a tour of Dinsmore and that should last about fifteen minutes. Joseph liked that, he had a great booming laugh and always slapped his knee when he began laughing. It made Karen feel better every time he did it. By this time Ruth had put a plate of sausage, scrambled eggs and biscuits on the table. She put a big jar of strawberry preserves right by her plate and poured her a cup of coffee.

Karen said, "Gosh, this is too much. I'll have to take a nap when I get home after this meal." She stayed and visited after they finished eating and tried to help with the clean up but Ruth would have none of it. So she climbed back on Candy and went home.

When she got back to the house, Ed was sitting on her back porch. He said, "Woman, what are you thinking? You've been gone a long time and your back door is wide open. I was getting worried but everything looked okay so I decided just to wait."

She dismounted and said, "Well, I'm sorry I was just enjoying my ride so much I didn't even think of locking up."

He snickered, "Really. I went to the barn and when I saw Candy gone, I knew that you two were out there somewhere."

"Okay, just trying to give me a hard time, I see."

"There wasn't much happening at the department so I slipped off. I've got my radio on if they start looking for me, I'll hear it. I just had to come out and tell you about my night out with the boys." He told her about seeing Bill and a lady in a booth. Said he was really surprised to see him out like that and it made him wonder about Janet's temper tantrums.

Then he said, "I'll be damned if I didn't see Tom Wallace in the parking lot with a bunch of boys. It looked like a bunch of under age kids had somebody getting them beer to drink in the parking lot. I pretended not to see him and watched across the road until they left. They were driving okay and I followed them until they dropped Tom off at his house."

"Don't you think you should have confronted him? I mean that he of all people shouldn't be drinking. He could lose his chance for a scholarship, not to mention his life."

"Well, I figured the kid had enough problems, but I just didn't want to embarrass him. I intend to talk to him when I can get him by himself. He's a good kid. He'll be all right."

"Okay, you're right. Why don't you come on in and I'll get you something to drink?"

"No, I've got to get back to town but I just had to tell you about my night."

"What's the matter with the phone?"

"I can't see you over the phone," he said it before he thought and he looked embarrassed. Karen pretended not to notice and just acted like it was a big joke but she was surprised. She was also sort of pleased. She playfully slapped at him and he got up to go to his car.

She got back on Candy and told him that she'd see him tonight. He said,

"Why don't you let me come out and pick you up? There's no need for you to drive. Then I can check things out when I bring you home and make sure your okay."

"That's not really necessary but if you want to, it's fine. What time do you want me ready?"

"I'll be here by six fifteen so we can get a good seat. See you then." As he drove off, he thought, "That was pretty slick, Eddy old boy. Got yourself a date and she don't even know it."

As she rode off, she was thinking, "That was pretty slick, Eddy old boy, asked me for a date and didn't even know it. She put Candy out to pasture.

Chapter 49

Daniel went to the Café to have breakfast before work. He wasn't used to drinking much and had a little bit of a hangover. He thought a good breakfast might help. He had a board meeting today and wanted to be in good shape.

By now business was brisk and Tony just yelled and ask, "What will you have this day, Daniel? The Country Breakfast, over easy, sausage, hash browns, biscuits and orange juice?" Daniel nodded in agreement.

Maria brought him a cup of coffee. She said, "Good Morning, Daniel. Did you have a good time last night?"

He said, "How did you know I was out last night?"

"Oh, Tony was feeling sorry for himself. He said all the guys were going to shoot pool and he couldn't go."

"Well, he didn't miss that much. You tell him a lot of guys would like to stay home with a pretty girl like you."

"Thank you, kind sir. I will certainly tell him that." She went off for her coffee pot rounds.

Tony brought him his breakfast and said, "What's the idea of flirting with my wife? You should have told her to let me go the next time."

"The way my head feels this morning, you'd be wise not to go."

"That explains the big breakfast. Bet you had a big time."

"We did but I wouldn't be able to make a habit of it. I'm getting too old for the night life."

Maria brought the orange juice Tony had forgotten. She informed Tony that he had orders to cook. He went back to work and she did, too. He finished his meal, paid the bill and went out to walk to work. It was another beautiful fall day and walking felt good.

Larry Sloan was in his office early Friday morning. He and Pamela had been arguing for days. He was disgusted with the whole marriage but didn't know what to do about it. He was thinking the bottle in the bottom drawer might help but decided that he'd wait a while. There was a knock on his door. He said, "Come in."

Rebecca entered looking perturbed. "We have a problem in the Women's Department," she announced.

"Okay, what is the problem? People problems, merchandise problems, your panties in a wad problem. What problem?"

"You're very funny. There's no one to work there. Seems that two people have the flu. I'm thinking it's the blue flu."

"Why do you think that? People who work here don't get sick?"

"I don't know why you're being such a smart ass. I had a run in with both of these employees yesterday and I think they're trying to get even."

"Oh, now the truth comes out. You've been harassing the help and they don't like it."

"Since I can't get a decent response out of you, I guess I'll have to call Mr. Regal and see if he can help me."

"That's a great idea and while you're at it, tell him I'm gone, too. Tell him I've got the blu flu and just left for California. I'm going to become a beach bum and forget I ever saw you, him or this store."

She just stood there looking shocked as he reached down, pulled out the drawer, got his pint of Old Charter out and turned it up. He took a big swig while she stared with her mouth open. She turned and left.

He grabbed his briefcase, put a couple of pictures in it, got his desk set that Margie had given him years before and left the building with his bottle in his coat pocket. He waved at the clerks he saw on his way out. He went to his Mustang, put the top down and left town.

When Pamela came back to the office, she noticed his desk was a little bare. She went to find Rebecca. On the way she stopped in the break room and her friend, Alicia, who worked at the Clinique counter, was there. Alicia said, "What are you doing here."

"I work here. Where else would I be? What's the matter with you?"

"Your husband just quit and left the building in a huff. You didn't know?"

"You're kidding me aren't you. Tell me the truth."

"Pamela, I am not kidding you. He quit and he left. He and Rebecca had some kind of run in."

Rebecca came in the room and said, "Pamela, your husband just quit. Do you plan to do the same?"

"No, I mean I don't think so. I don't know what's going on. I didn't know he was going to quit. We've been fighting all week. He got in a fight at the Café last week and I got mad at him because they had him arrested."

"Well, if you want to stay employed here, I need you to go work in the Women's Department today. It may become permanent since you don't have anyone to be a secretary to. Can you do that?"

151

"I guess I'll have to, if you put it that way. I don't know what else to do. Will somebody help me learn the job?"

"Yes, Mrs. Mackey has been here forever and she'll help you. I've got her in there, right now. I had to open the store. He just walked out guzzling his whiskey on the way. He's such a pain in the ass."

Pamela said, "You noticed that, too? I will go on down to see what I can do. Don't hold his stupidity against me. I'm going to get rid of him. I've had enough." She turned and left the room.

Bill was on his way to school with his kids when they met Larry Sloan driving down the street with his top down. He had suitcases piled in his back seat and waved at them like he was in a parade or something. Bill was thinking, "I wonder what he's up to now. What a guy! Must be going on vacation or something."

Chapter 50

Neither of the kids had much to say that morning. They all ate cereal for breakfast in silence. He tried to talk to them but they just grunted in response. He finally gave up and let them pout. He figured they'd get over. After all they were going to want something and who else could they get it from? He dropped them at the door to the school and went to unload some supplies he had for the locker room. He was excited about the game tonight. It was the best team they had played all season. It would be a good test of his team, especially for Tom. It would be a chance for him to show his stuff. A couple of college scouts were supposed to be there. He hadn't told Tom because he didn't want him to be nervous. After he parked the truck, he went to his office as usual to prepare for his day. He was giving a test to his classes today so it would be easy for him, hard for his students. But of course he would have to spend the weekend grading test papers.

Karen decided the farm house painting was finished after she worked a few more hours. She signed it and went back to her photos. She knew she didn't have time to finish another but she could start one anyway. She had a canvas stretched and she decided to do another seascape but this one would be a night scene with the moon shining on the water. She would use some prussian blue with naples yellow and work in some titanium for the breaking waves. She would add a couple walking on the beach in the moonlight. A romantic scene she was thinking. I'm feeling strangely romantic, I guess. She blocked in the colors to see how they were going to work. She was using a lot of thinner until she had it worked out. She usually did a sketch but she was just doing this one free hand. She wanted it to be really loose and impressionistic. She'd worked a couple of hours and went in the kitchen to warm a cup of coffee in the microwave. She looked at the clock and it was already four.

She took the coffee to the bedroom. She picked out some black slacks from the closet and got a red and white sweater from the drawer. She laid them on the bed and chose a pair of black loafers. While sipping her coffee and surveying her selections, decided they were good and headed for the shower. She washed her hair with lavender shampoo and then used a lavender bath scrub. After she rinsed off, she wrapped a towel around herself and blow dried her hair. She didn't spend a lot of time on her hair. Just let it do its own thing. She put on her make up and got dressed. By now it was after five.

She went into the kitchen and made herself a sandwich, got some chips and went to watch the new on the television. She forgot the beer she had put on the table and went back to get it. She was still watching the news when Ed knocked at the back door. She could see him through the glass and told him to, "Come on in, Ed."

He did and he said, "Hey, we need to get going if you're ready."

She told him, "Just let me run and brush my teeth right quick. I'll be right back. When she was through, she redid her lipstick, took a look in the mirror and thought, "Not bad for an old broad."

When she came out, Ed said, "You look nice tonight. But then you always look nice. Are you ready?"

"Yes and thank you. I try. I was just thinking I wasn't bad for an old broad."

"You don't know what old is. I'm the old guy here." They went out, she locked the door, gave Jazz a pat on the head and Callie got hers, too. Then she followed Ed to the car. He was in his own car tonight, a big blue Cadillac. She said, "Ooh, we're going in style tonight. You obviously do not expect to be called back to work." He opened the door for her and answered, "I threatened their lives if they called me."

The stands were filling up when they got there but they found good seats close to the fifty-yard line. They saw Daniel come in and waved for him to come sit with them. Ed asked her if she wanted anything from the concession stand and she said, "No, I'm fine. You get something if you want it."

He said, "I'm going to get a hot dog and a drink. I didn't have time to eat supper."

"Busy day at the department?"

"No, I just goofed around and ran out of time."

Daniel sat down and said, "I'm glad to see you two. How are you doing?"

They both said, "Fine." Ed said, "I'm going to the concession stand. Do you want something,

Daniel?" "Yes, I do but I'll go with you. How about you, Karen?"

Ed said, "I already got her order. Nothing."

They took off after they laid their coats on their seats. Karen was watching Tom practice his passing and thinking what a fine-looking boy he was when Rebecca Magee came walking by. She stopped when she saw Karen. Karen knew her but had never really talked to her before so she was surprised when she stopped to speak. Rebecca said, "Did you hear about Larry?"

"No, what now?" "He's gone. He left the store in a huff. Took all his personal possessions and Pamela hasn't seen him since. He left a note at their apartment. Gone to California, get a divorce. I won't be back. Is that nuts or what?"

"Sounds just like him to me."

"I guess so. Mr. Regal was shocked. I don't think Pamela cared. She said they had been arguing for days."

"Well, too bad. Here come my friends so I'll talk to you later." Rebecca got the message and moved on. Karen wondered why Rebecca seemed to be alone. Ed and Daniel sat down just as the Lexington Arrows came thru their paper sign. Their band was playing and the fans were yelling. Then the Dinsmore Bulldogs came out of the other sign. They all stood while the Dinsmore band played the Star Spangled Banner. The ref blew his whistle and Dinsmore got the coin toss and chose to play offense. Tom hit his receiver on the first pass for thirty yards. The crowd went wild.

John Whitcomb had finished teaching his last class at the colony at three o'clock. He gave out the awards and made his little exit speech. He told Ann that he was headed to Dinsmore to see Karen Sloan. Ann seemed surprised.

"Actually," he said, "I was impressed with her artwork and I want to see more of it. It was a shame she couldn't finish the week. If she's got more work that good, I think I know a gallery in Chicago that could use some of her paintings."

Ann said, "That's great. She was a nice lady and seemed to enjoy being here. You tell her that I want her to come back next year."

He went to his cabin and finished packing, loaded his rented car and drove to the main office. He went in and Ann gave him a check for his two weeks of work.

She said, "I hope you'll come back again sometime. You did a great job and I never heard one complaint. Travel safely and tell Karen hello for me."

He took her extended hand and kissed her on the cheek before he went to start on his journey. He waved from the car as he pulled away and Ann returned to the office to close the books for the season and wait for spring to open the camp again. She would return to her home in Chicago to start preparations for the holidays.

He left the colony headed for Dinsmore and Karen. He was feeling euphoric and didn't know why but he liked the feeling. It was five o'clock by now. He had already called the Holiday Inn and confirmed his reservation, so he didn't have to hurry. He would make it to Dinsmore by nine or ten. He'd wait to eat when he got into town and wouldn't call Karen until morning.

Pamela Sloan was sitting in her apartment feeling sorry for herself. Most of Larry's clothes were gone and she was abandoned. She still had a job and her college major had been marketing, so selling women's wear wasn't a bad deal. Maybe she could move up and become a department manager. Mr. Regal was to be in the store on Monday to check on the conditions since Larry's sudden departure. She was hoping he hadn't done anything too stupid since it might reflect badly on her. She had become increasingly unhappy with Larry and she wasn't heart broken, just angry at the way he left. The rent on the apartment was paid until November. She would have to check the bank to see if he had cleaned it out. She decided to get her little Neon and go to the ATM to find out the balance. If there was anything there, she would make a big withdrawal so that he couldn't get it all. She put on some jeans, a T shirt and jacket and went out to take care of business. Larry Sloan wasn't going to destroy her as he had Margie.

It was half time at the game and Dinsmore was ahead by two touchdowns. The bands were performing their great routines with flags flying and dancers doing extremely intricate routines.

Karen told Ed what Rebecca had said. He looked pleased and she said, "Why are you grinning?

"I wanted to question the fool. He was on my list of suspects. I never suspected him at all. He's just too stupid to pull off the perfect murder. I'm grinning because I won't have to deal with him any more."

"Okay, but you know all crooks are stupid to some extent. They always screw up or we hope they do. Of course, I think he still loved Margie, but he just wasn't able to be a decent husband. His drinking habit ruined their marriage."

"Well, don't worry about it. If he turns out to be a real suspect, we'll find him and bring him back. I'll bet he didn't burn all his bridges behind him. He can be found if need be."

Daniel wanted to know what they were talking about and Karen started to tell him the story.

Ed said, "Hey, I'm going back to the concession stand. What do you two want?" They gave him their orders and he left while they were discussing the latest "Larry news."

On his way down the steps someone grabbed his arm. He stopped and was going to cuss the guy out when he realized it was an old friend. "Perry Neal,

I haven't seen you in a long time. You here to scope out Tom Wallace?"

Perry was one of the scouts that Bill had expected. He answered, "Yes, I've been hearing a lot about that kid and it looks like it's all true."

Ed sat down and told him, he agreed. "Great kid. He deserves good things."

Perry said, "Well, I'll bet he'll get 'em but there will be a lot of competition. I saw another recruiter in the stands. He went to sit on the opposing side. What have you been up to?"

"Just the same old, same old. I love to come to these games. The kids are really outstanding players and Bill Wallace is a great coach."

"Yeah, I'm surprised he hasn't gone on to coach in college."

"I'll bet he does when Tom get's a scholarship. He's really worked with him over the years and of course Tom took to it like a duck to water." He slapped Perry on the back and said, "Good talking to you, man. Don't be such a stranger. I've got to go get some drinks for my friends and get back to the game. I'll see you around."

"Sure, I'm going to come by the station sometime and see what's going on. Take care now." Ed hurried to get the drinks for all of them and just as he got back, Dinsmore scored another touchdown. Everybody was on their feet. He looked down at the bench and Bill was hugging his son and the team had surrounded them.

Tony and Maria didn't get to go to the game because one of their children had the chicken pox and was very sick. They knew they were going to have a few weeks of dabbing calamine lotion by the time it had affected all five children. Mama was worn out from caring for them so they all decided to stay home and watch some movies.

The phone rang and Tony went to answer it, "Hello."

"Hi, Tony," the little voice said, "This is Pamela Sloan. Did you happen to see Larry today?"

"Hi, Pamela. No, he hasn't been in since our little run in. Why?"

"He quit his job, cleaned out his closet and disappeared."

"Oh, my God, the man has lost his mind. How are you doing?"

"I'm fine, but I just went to the ATM and there was only a little more than two hundred dollars left in the account. I got all I could out because he'll probably try to get it, too."

"I'm sorry you got left holding the bag."

"Oh, I'll be all right. We haven't been getting along and I was really sick of him. I still have my job. I just thought he might have told somebody, you know, where he was going. Come Monday, I'm going to file for a divorce."

"I don't blame you a bit. You let me know if I can help you and I'll ask around tomorrow to see if anyone knows where he is."

"Thanks a lot, Tony. I'll let you go now. Bye." He told her, "Bye." Maria was right on him, wanting to know what and who it was. He began to tell her the news. Tony loved a good story. He was sure to take this news and run with it.

Larry Sloan was pulling into a Motel 6 in Joplin, Missouri. He had been driving for twelve hours with a few stops for a beer and bathroom. He had gone to Wendy's drive thru and got a burger and fries. He munched that on the road. He wasn't drunk but he was unusually happy. He felt as if the weight of the world had been lifted off his back. He had hated his job for a long time and was scared to quit. Desperation and disgust had forced him to act. Now he was relieved that he had done the deed. He did feel bad about Pamela but he would get a job and send her some money. He hoped she would take his advice and file for divorce. They both knew it wasn't working. After he checked in, he went to his room and collapsed on the big bed. He didn't even undress. He slept the sleep of the dead for the first time in months.

Meanwhile John Whitcomb was checking in at the Holiday Inn in Dinsmore, Illinois. When he came through town, he saw the lights of a football field. He had picked up a chicken combo at Wendy's and after he took off his jacket and turned on the television in his room, he sat down to eat. It was nine thirty and he thought, "Too late to call Karen now." After he ate, he undressed and hung up his clothes. Then he went to take a shower. The news was on when he was finished. He watched it and then some of Letterman before he fell asleep. He dreamed about Karen. She was in a painting walking toward him. He was not in the painting and she vanished just as he reached for her. He woke for a minute, turned off the light and the television. He went back to sleep immediately. He had asked the desk clerk for a seven o'clock wake up call.

Dinsmore won the ball game by three touch downs. Tom had excelled at his quarterback position and his receiver had held on tight. Bill was delighted even when they dumped the water on him. The fans had stayed for the entire game and cheered them onto victory. They went to the locker room, high fiving all the way. The big guys picked Tom up and carried him on their shoulders half way. Bill delivered his congratulatory speech in the locker room and they all began to shower and dress. Tom was gone when Bill was ready to leave so he went on to the truck where Amy was waiting.

He looked around and asked her, "Where's Tom?" "I don't know. I haven't seen him. I thought he was with you. He must have caught a ride with his friends. He's acting so weird lately. I can't stand him."

"Oh, he's just growing up. Thinks he's bigger than he is, though. I'm going to have to give him an attitude adjustment."

"Yeah, Dad, he's six inches taller than you, you know."

"I know that but I control the purse strings and I don't intend to wrestle him."

They both laughed at that and he said to his pretty daughter, "How'd you like to go get a burger with your old man?" He put his arm around her waist and walked her around to the passenger side of the truck. He unlocked it and made a sweeping motion with his arm saying,

"Have a seat in my chariot, Missy." Then he got in, cranked up the truck and away they went to get their burgers.

Bill had hoped to see Tom at Wendy's but he wasn't there. Everybody he saw congratulated him on the great game and he was glad when their order was ready and he could sit down. Amy was proud of her Dad and glad to be with him, without Tom, by herself for a change.

When the game was over Ed, Karen and Daniel let the crowd thin out before they made way to their vehicles.

Daniel walked with them to the Caddy and said, "Wow, you do have something besides that old Mercury.

"Yeah, but I guarantee you this won't get the fast take off, we had that old Merc especially modified, it will run the wheels off anything trying to escape from us. Do you remember those movies with Robert Mitchum, the moonshiners outrunning the cops in Tennessee or Kentucky? We have reversed the situation here."

"Okay, I'll quit making fun of your Merc. I can tell you are attached to it."

"Well, I like my Caddy, too. But it's for special occasions. It's not often that I get to pick up a pretty lady."

Karen had been listening to all this man-talk about cars and letting them rattle on. Now she said, "What do you pick up?"

They said their goodbyes and Ed opened the door for Karen. When he had climbed in, he said, "Would you like to go somewhere for a bite to eat or a drink? We could drive over to Lexington."

She said, "Oh, I'd like a rain check. I really need to get home and get ready for tomorrow."

He sounded disappointed when he said, "Oh, that's right. I forgot you were expecting company. We'll do it another time. Okay?"

"Sure, I'd love to, another time."

He took her home, kept the door locked until he could open for her, being the perfect gentleman. He walked her to the door.

She asked if he'd like to come in but he said, "I'll go on and let you get ready for tomorrow. I'll check with you on Sunday. Think you'll go to church?"

"I don't know how long John will stay but we'll see. Thanks for taking me to the game. It was really fun."

"I enjoyed it, too. We'll do it again if you're willing. He took her hand and kissed her on the cheek. Good night, Karen."

"Good night." She unlocked her door and went in locking it behind her and waving at him, still standing on the porch.

He gave the dog a pat on the head and went back to his Caddy. He sat there a minute, thinking, "Why the hell didn't I really kiss her? I really wanted to but I don't know how she feels about me. If she only knew how long I've wished she gave me a little hope for more than friendship. Maybe she does know. We'll see."

When Ed got to his house, he went in and undressed right away. Grabbed a beer and some chips, went in his bedroom, turned on the television and climbed in the bed to watch Letterman and eat his snack in bed. He lay there thinking about the old times when Rich was living and they would go off for hunting and fishing on weekends. Karen never seemed to mind. She always liked to use the time to paint or visit with Margie and Melanie. Sometimes she went with them and she would spend the time taking photographs. Those were the good old days.

Then he thought about poor Margie and wondered if they'd ever find out what really happened. What did Larry leaving town mean? He wanted to sleep later than five a.m. for once. Well, he wasn't going to solve anything tonight. As he was falling asleep, he was hoping and praying they wouldn't call from the station, and they didn't. He rolled over and started to snore.

Daniel had gone to his apartment and after he got ready for bed, he put a tv dinner in the microwave. He went into the living room, turned on the television and watched the news. He went into the kitchen when the microwave shut off and sat at the table to eat his oriental chicken.

He got a glass of wine and went back to the living room. He tried to find an old movie to watch, but couldn't, so he turned on his computer and went to the site he had been searching for skiing vacations. He read his email and found one from each of the children. They were the usual, doing fine, hope you are fine, been really busy and so on. He wrote one email about his efforts to find a vacation for the three of them, told them he was fine and glad that they were. He sent it to them both.

After a while he decided he was tired and went to his bedroom. He lay in bed thinking of Margie and then deliberately made himself change his mind. He began to think of the past evening and how much he enjoyed being with Ed and Karen. He thought, "I think Ed is in love with Karen and she acts like she doesn't have a clue." Then he thought what Karen had told him about poor little Pamela and how Larry had deserted her. She wasn't any older than his daughter and he would sure hate to have her treated like that. He was glad that she had higher ideals and educational goals. He fell asleep feeling better than he had in some time.

Bill and Amy got home about ten o'clock and Tom was still not there. Bill was worried but knew it would not be a good idea to go looking for him. He tried not to let Amy know what he was thinking. She gave him a hug and a kiss and went off to her room. He heard the shower start up.

He got a beer and went to the den to watch television. He watched the news, the last of Leno and then watched football on ESPN until he fell asleep in his chair. His ribs were healing nicely and he could rest now. He wanted to be there when Tom came in. He woke at three in the morning and Tom hadn't come in. He figured that he was okay or he would have heard, so he went on to his room, undressed and went to bed. He thought of Janet, then he thought of Margie, and he thought about Amy. He wondered what she would do when she was grown. He wondered if Tom realized that it was important for him to stay out of trouble. If he didn't, his scholarship opportunities would be in jeopardy. He finally fell asleep again but didn't rest well because Tom wasn't at home.

Karen went right to her bedroom when she got in the house and took off her clothes to hang them up. She put on pajamas because the house was a little cool. She went in the kitchen got a bottle of water and went to the living room to watch the news. She decided to go to bed and read after the news went off. She got in bed with her book. She started to read but then laid the book on her chest and thought, "I really had a good time tonight. Ed was so nice to me. He used to be so tough when we worked together but now he's so nice. I thought he was going to kiss me when we got to the door. I think I might have liked it, too. Funny, I have never even considered a thing like that since Rich died. Why would I be thinking that now? I'm too old for this foolishness. Ed even acts like he's jealous of John coming to see me. How weird! I've got to quit thinking about this. It's probably my overactive imagination." She started reading again and before long was fast asleep. She woke up in the morning with the lights still on and her book on the floor.

Chapter 51

Saturday morning John got up at seven when the office called. He washed up, brushed his teeth and got dressed in a red flannel shirt, levis, and boots. He opened the door to go but went back to put on a jacket because it seemed cooler this morning. He went to the motel dining room and order scrambled eggs with ham, coffee and tomato juice. He went back outside and got a Chicago paper out of the machine. When he got back to his table, his coffee and juice were there. He read the front page, turned to the sports section before the waitress brought his food.

He asked the waitress how to go into the town. He was turned around from coming in after dark. She gave him directions, so after he ate and paid the bill, he got in his car and drove into town. He went down the main street and turned around to go back to the motel. He thought it was a pretty little town and the maple trees were fantastic. The colorful sights wouldn't last much longer because there would probably be a hard freeze soon.

When he got back to the motel, he figured it would be okay to call Karen now. She'd surely be up and he was anxious to see her and her paintings. The phone rang three times and he got scared that he was waking her.

She answered on the third ring, "Hello." He said, "I sure hope I didn't wake you. This is John and I was wondering when I could come over."

"Oh, no, you didn't wake me, I was out feeding the animals. You can come anytime, whenever you're ready."

"I'm ready. Can you give me directions? I'm at the Holiday Inn."

"It's really easy then, because I live on that same road. It's about two miles from the interstate on the right. Look for an oversize white mailbox with Sutton on it. I have a vine growing on it. The flowers have died but the vine is still there."

"I drove into town earlier so I guess I drove right by it. I was so interested in looking at the trees I didn't pay attention to the houses."

"Well, the house is quite far off the road. The drive is before the mailbox. Will I see you soon?"

"Yes, I'll be right there."

"Okay, see you soon."

"Goodbye." He picked up his briefcase and went out to his car.

Karen had really been up for hours. She wanted everything to be just right when John got there. She had showered and dressed in her usual jeans, put on a yellow shirt and a denim vest with her boots. She had a bagel and cream cheese with her coffee and went to check in the studio and see if all was in order. Then she went outdoors to play with her pets. She threw the frisbee for Jazz and all the while Callie was going 'round and 'round her legs. Then she saw Candy coming to the fence and went to her. She patted her on the nose and said, "How's my Candy Cane, today?" She gave her a sugar cube from her pocket and went back to the house.

That's when the phone rang. She went back outside to wait for John on the porch. When she heard a car in the drive, she got up and walked out to meet him. She noticed he was carrying a briefcase. She was surprised because that really made it look like business. She had just thought of it as a visit not business. She greeted him with a handshake and introduced the pets who had tagged along to check out the new visitor. Then she led him to the back door and into her kitchen.

"Would you like a cup of coffee or a cold drink, John?"

"I'd love a cup of coffee."

"Well, have a seat here at the table or would you rather go in the living room?"

"This is fine. I love kitchens and this one is so homey and pleasant."

"Well, how did your weeks at the art colony go? Were you pleased with the outcome?"

"It was fine. Turned out a lot of good work, really. I'm anxious to see yours."

"In a little bit, I'm really a little nervous about showing you. I've never had a professional critique other than yours at the colony. Would you like a bagel?"

"No, I had a big breakfast. Are you trying to stall me?," he smiled at her.

She put his coffee on the table with the cream and sugar. Then she got hers and said, "Yes, I guess I am. Like I say, I'm kind of skeptical about showing my work. I've never had much confidence in it since I am self taught for the most part."

"Nothing wrong with that. I'm not going to rip you apart, I guarantee I'll be kind but honest. Tell me what you've been doing since you got home."

She told him about Melanie and Margie. All the things that they had to take care and how many legalities were still up in the air. The two round trips to Chicago. The funeral and the sadness. She told him about Melanie and how much she meant to her. About her wanting to change schools. She was talking a lot, trying to put off the inevitable. Now she asked his opinion of the Art Institute.

He said, "If she's sure that she wants to make art her life and she doesn't like the academics, it's probably a good plan. Of course, it also depends on how talented she is. Sometimes it requires more ambition and drive than talent, though. It's like any of the arts, acting, music or whatever. It's sometimes a hard life and you have to be willing to do odd jobs to survive and keep pushing your artistic abilities. It's like selling your soul sometimes."

"Wow, that makes it sound difficult. I think she's very talented but I'll let you look at some of her work that I have stored here. I have always loved my art and I loved teaching Melanie. I just never thought of making it my life. I loved being a cop, too."

"Well, you've put me off long enough, now let's have a look." She gave up and showed him to her studio.

Ed slept until seven in the morning. He didn't have to work this Saturday. The first thought in his mind was of Karen. "Wonder what this John guy is like. Wish I had an excuse to call her."

He told himself, "I am being totally ridiculous." He got dressed in khakis, a red flannel shirt and put on some high top suede brogans.

He phoned Daniel and said, "This is Ed, how about meeting me at the Café for breakfast?"

"Hey, that sounds good. I don't have a thing planned for today and the weather is so great, it's a shame to waste it staying inside. What time?"

"I'm on my way there in a few minutes. Take your time. I'll be there. See ya."

Daniel smiled as he hung up the phone and thought, "Ed doesn't waste words when he's hungry." He put on his favorite outfit for a Saturday, Army fatigues he bought at a surplus store and work boots. He got a leather jacket out of the closet to take with him in case it was cold. He went down to the parking garage and got in his Lexus and headed for the Café.

When he went in the Café, he didn't see Ed right away so he went on to the table where they usually sat. There was a half full cup of coffee there so he assumed Ed had been there. Maria came over with a cup of coffee for him. He asked, "Is Ed here?"

She said, "Oh, yeah, he is helping Tony unload a heavy box full of cooking oil out back. He's been hauling it around for days. He got a good price if he'd buy the whole case but it was too heavy for one person to handle."

"Well, I'll wait to order until he gets back. But you can bring me an orange juice."

"I didn't hardly recognize you when you came in. Never saw you in anything but a suit and tie."

"Yes, it feels good to get out of the suit and tie. We missed you guys at the football game."

"Well, we have a couple of sick kids at home and Mama does well to handle them in the daytime but it would be too much to leave her with them at night."

Tony came in from the back room door and spoke to Daniel. "Hi there, Daniel."

Tony said, "How are you doing? I've been makin' Ed do manual labor back there."

"So I heard. Guess I'm lucky I didn't get here earlier."

"Ed says I missed a good game last night. I sure hated that we couldn't make it."

"Yeah, your wife told me the circumstances. Sorry about that."

"Well, it's kind of good that I was there because Pamela Sloan called me looking for Larry. Of course I wasn't any help to her but I feel sorry for her. He just about cleaned out their bank account before he left."

"That's a shame. She doesn't deserve that kind of treatment. Where did he go?"

"Nobody knows, at least nobody that I've talked to, knows." Maria called him to get some orders out and he finally went back to work.

Ed had gone to wash his hands and was back. He sat down and said, "Don't ever tell Tony Distefano anything you don't want broadcast. That man loves gossip. Sometimes he helps me when I'm trying to find someone I need to question. He knows everything that goes on in this town."

"I got that message, no more than I come in here. Are you ready to order?"

"Maria, we're ready when you are." They both ordered the Country Breakfast. By now it was past ten o'clock so they were having brunch."

Ed said, "How would you like to go out to my hunting camp today? I want to go check on it and see if I need to make any repairs before hunting season."

"I'd like that. I haven't gone hunting since I was a kid. My dad used to take me and my sister. He even took us to Montana once. Now that is some beautiful country and good hunting."

Ed said, "I do well to get away right here. When I retire, I plan to do some traveling. I don't know if I'll go hunting but I'd like to see some more of America. We'll go right after we finish here."

Chapter 52

Bill and Amy got up at the same time. It was eight o'clock. He went to Tom's room and it had not been used last night. Bill fixed some breakfast for the two of them. Eggs and bacon. Amy made the toast. She poured them each a glass of milk. They weren't talking. They were worrying. Neither one wanted to say it out loud. They were about finished eating when Tom walked in the door as if he stayed out all night all the time.

Bill stood up and yelled at him, "Where the hell have you been?"

"I spent the night at a friend's house. You don't know him. Don't get riled because I'm just fine. I know what you're going to say. I should have called you. I just forgot and then it was too late."

"You won't be spending any more nights with friends, because you are grounded. You will not be allowed to leave that school with anybody but me until further notice."

Tom acted like he didn't even hear him and went on to his room. Amy just shook her head and said, "This family is falling apart. I don't know what can happen next."

Bill went outside to cool off. He sat in a lawn chair for a while and thought about what he had to do. When he finally realized that he was freezing, he went back in and got his briefcase, took it to his bedroom and started grading papers. His mind was definitely not on his work. He was going to need help with this problem. He heard the back door slam and went to see what was going on. Tom was in his sweats running down the drive. He turned and ran down the street toward town. Bill thought, "I should go get him but what good will it do? Maybe a run will help clear his head. He's sure not thinking clearly these days. Amy's right, this family is falling apart."

Chapter 53

Karen and John were in her studio and she was putting another painting on one of her easels. She had shown him several and he would just keep on looking and telling her to let him see another.

Finally he said, "This is great work! You have a genius for color harmony and sweeping strokes. You paint feelings and they are good feelings. You use strong brush work but soften the lines which are enhanced by your use of lights and darks. You know contrast but not hard and edgy, soft and dramatic at the same time. Do you understand? Am I making sense?"

He smiled at the stunned look on her face. She said, "Well, I understand but I didn't expect you to like it this much. You're overwhelming me with your compliments. I don't want you to just flatter me. This is serious to me. I want you to give me you an honest critique."

"I assure you I am being totally honest, and I wouldn't change a thing. This is your expression, who would I be, to tell you how to express yourself? You are a very warm, lovely person and it is reflected in your art. There are enough ugly depressing works out there. This world needs some good feelings. That's what they'll get when they look at your work and buy it for their homes and businesses."

"Who's going to buy art from a little old lady in Dinsmore, Illinois? You've got to be kidding. I do well to sell a painting or two to my friends occasionally."

"You're right. That's why you need a show at a gallery in Chicago, Los Angeles or New York. Wherever there's a gallery that wants to sell great art. Let's go back in the kitchen and have another cup of coffee and talk about this."

Ed and Daniel drove about forty miles north before they turned onto a state road. Then they took a right and drove another three miles to a little country store. Ed was driving.because he had told Daniel the roads were too rough and rocky to take the Lexus. They went in the store and got some sodas.

Ed knew the old man behind the counter. He said, "Hank, this is my friend Daniel, I'm taking him out to the deer camp."

Hank said, "Glad to meet ya' Daniel. Welcome to the best huntin' in the state."

Ed bought two cigars and handed one to Daniel. Daniel said, "What do you expect me to do with this? I haven't smoked a cigar since college."

"It's about time you tried it again but I'm not going to hold your head if it makes you sick. So let me light you up, Mr. Banker."

"Ed, I think you're starting to be a bad influence on me. Who would have thought, the law officer was being a bad influence."

"Nah, I'm just showing you how to let your hair down and have some fun."

"I'm up for that, God knows, I could use a little fun. It's been a while."

"Let's head for the camp now. Wait til you see it."

"I can't wait. I'm sure it's luxurious, huh?"

They got back in the Merc and went down a gravel road about five miles to a shack in a grove of trees. Lots of trees and lots of deer stands. Ed said, "Let's get out and have a look around."

They went inside and Daniel said, "This is really roughing it." There were some folded cots leaning against the wall, a table that was made from an old door on wooden horses. It was just one room about four hundred feet square. There was a Coleman lantern hanging from the ceiling.

Ed wasn't paying attention so Daniel said, "Ed, what do you do about food out here?"

"We bring it in ice chests and some of us bring Coleman stoves. We've got a kerosene heater but we can't leave anything here or vandals will get it. That's one reason we keep it so primitive. Nobody wants anything that's here. We bring bottled water and other drinks. No alchohol. Alchohol and guns don't mix. We have a great time. Five or six of us at a time. Nobody bathes for days. We eat good and play cards when we're not out on the deer stand. I love it. There's no pressure, no worries, no phones, it's great."

"Where do I sign up?"

"Hey, you'll come as my guest if you want to. We'll be out here as soon as the season opens. It's my vacation every year. I used to come with Karen's husband before he died. I've missed having a buddy to run with." They went outside and walked around to the back and Daniel saw the outhouse.

"All the comforts of home. Does it have a Sears catalogue?"

"Yeah, you have to bring you own Charmin. They walked further out into the woods and saw a doe with her little one. The squirrels were skittering all around.

Then Ed said, "Think we better head back out now? They might be sending out the search party soon."

They went back to the car, out to the highway and made it back to Dinsmore before dark. They didn't realize how long they'd been gone. When they were driving back into town, Ed noticed Tom Wallace, in sweats, running down the drive into the cemetery .

Daniel said, "That's a strange place to run."

"Well, I guess you don't run into much traffic there."

Daniel looked kind of sad and Ed said, "I'm sorry, that was a dumb thing to say."

Daniel said, "No, it's okay, I just thought of Margie being buried out there. I need to come and bring her some flowers."

"I know you really liked her a lot, didn't you? How long did you know her?"

"Not nearly long enough but I thought we might have something going for us."

"I know how you feel. It's hard to find somebody you can really relate to. Since I've never even been close to getting married, I know. Of course most women don't want to be married to a cop. So I've been married to my job for almost thirty years."

"That's a long time, when are you going to give it up?"

"I don't know if I can. It would be too lonely and boring not to have a place to go. You know something to do every day. I'd probably just curl up and die."

"I get the feeling you've got more than a friendly interest in Karen, don't you?"

"Yeah, I guess I do but I don't think she feels the same. We've been friends so long and her husband was my best friend all those years. It's hard to switch gears but I do wish I had nerve enough to tell her how I feel."

"Hey, tell her, you chicken, haven't you heard the saying, she might kill you, but she can't eat you?"

Ed was groaning, when they pulled up to the Café and said, "Man, get out of my car. Your advice could get me in big trouble. I'm going to check on things at the station and I'll see you later."

Chapter 54

When Tom came back from his run, Bill was still grading papers. He heard him come in and go to his room. Amy had gone shopping with the next door neighbor and her daughter, so they were alone in the house. Bill wondered if he should go talk to him or to leave him alone for now.

He thought he heard voices but the television wasn't on.

He walked over to his door and realized it was Tom on the phone. He carefully lifted the receiver on the extension in his bedroom. Tom was talking to a girl. He didn't recognize the voice but he'd never known Tom to have a girl friend or anyway not one he talked to on the phone. He was too wrapped up in his studies and football. He only dated when there was a dance or homecoming or some other special occasion. The girls all chased him but he just didn't have time for them. Bill was glad because he didn't want him to make the same mistakes he had. He was much too interested in girls and let that interest cause him to marry early in his life. He felt he would have gone further in his coaching career if he had waited on marriage and family.

He listened for only a few minutes, feeling guilty for doing it. Tom said, "I know I shouldn't go there but I can't help it. I feel so guilty and I'm so sorry."

Bill hung the phone up and thought, "My God, he is feeling guilty about his mother. I need to make arrangements for us to see her soon so they'll know she's okay. The poor kids don't understand."

He decided not to push it with Tom for now. He would see if they would go to church with him in the morning. Maybe that would help. He'd take them out to lunch after and try to have a good Sunday. His own conscience was killing him and it was hard to come down on Tom when he had not behaved like a good father should. He wondered if his kids would ever respect him again.

Amy came in all excited about her shopping trip and had to show him what she had bought right away. Then she went into Tom's room and Bill heard him telling her, "That's really neat, Amy. Did you see any of the other kids at the shopping center?" That was all it took to get Amy telling about the entire afternoon and Tom listened patiently. He really loved his little sister. Bill was feeling better and went back to grading papers.

Chapter 55

Karen and John talked for hours. He showed her a catalogue from a gallery in Chicago that he had a working relationship with. He told her that he would like to arrange a meeting for her and see what they could work out. He knew from experience how to get a good contract and he would help her plan an opening show.

She was in a state of shock but she didn't let onto him. She was thinking, "I don't have any idea how these things work. I've only gone to a couple of gallery openings. One in St. Louis and one in Chicago. I didn't know the artists either time, just happened to be visiting and decided to go see what other artists were doing."

He's talking and talking and she is only hearing bits and pieces. She can't comprehend it all. She finally says, "Stop, I can't absorb any more. I'm just not able to really believe all this. Let's take a break and I'll take you out to an Italian supper in town."

"That sounds like fun. Do I need to change?"

"No, we're both fine. It's very informal and simple hometown style, but they serve delicious Italian dishes. Of course they do hamburgers, too. But I recommend the Italian. It's my treat. I don't want to cook. I paint much better than I cook, I assure you."

"Well, let's go. I'll drive. You navigate." They got in his car and on the road to town and the Café. When they pulled up, it looked crowded but she knew they'd get a table very quickly. They sat at the bar and Maria brought them water and Karen introduced John. She told Maria to bring them some coffee and they'd order when they got a table.

Tony looked up from the grill and said, "Hi there, Karen, how ya' doin'?" She answered, "I'm fine, Tony, good to see you working." He shook his head and went back to work.

She told John about Tony and Maria's big family and how much Tony liked to talk. She said, "By Monday, it will be all over town that I was in here with some new guy."

"Well, nothing like a little gossip to further one's reputation, huh?"

She didn't answer, just asked him, "How long can you stay?"

"Oh, I'll leave in the morning. I've got to get to Chicago. That's why I wanted to see you on my way. I'll be calling you from there after I talk to the gallery owner."

"What are you going to tell them?"

"I'm going to see when you can have a showing there."

Maria came to take them to a table. She led the way and he helped Karen to her seat as she said, "Do you really think I'm ready?"

"You will have plenty of time to do some more work. You'll need about thirty paintings of different sizes to show. It will probably take a few months to set it up."

"Oh, my, let's look at the menu and think about eating, instead of art. I'm feeling queasy and I don't know if it's because I'm starving or scared."

"You'll do fine. Don't be such a pessimist. I know right now I want to check out their ravioli."

"It's my favorite. Let's have a salad, too. You can order for both of us."

Maria came to get their order. She came back right away with their salads, the special garlic bread in a basket and a separate bowl of crumbled blue cheese, that she knew Karen loved. She sat a basket with a variety of dressings in the middle of the table, too.

Karen had her back to the entrance so she didn't see that Ed and Jeff had come in. She heard them. Or rather she heard Tony, as he hollered, "Hey, Ed, Jeff, how ya' doin' tonight?"

Jeff answered, "Fine." Ed answered, "Hungry."

They headed for Ed's favorite table. It had just been cleared, as if it magically became available because he walked in. When Ed came by her, he stopped and said, "Hello there, Karen, how are you tonight."

Jeff said, "Hi, Karen."

She said, "Hello, you two. I'd like to meet my friend, John Whitcomb. This is Ed Hawkins."

Ed held out his hand, shook and said, "Glad to meet you, John." John said, "Yes, nice to meet you."

"And this is Jeff Collins," he shook John's extended hand and said, "Pleased to meet you."

John said, "Glad to meet you, too. I"m guessing you are friends of Karen. I'm here to check out her artwork and I'm quite impressed."

Karen was blushing as she explained, "They are my friends but they don't know anything about my artwork. I used to work with these two. They're the local lawmen, so you'd better watch your step."

Jeff said, "Oh, heck, why did you have to tell him. Actually Ed's not on duty but I am. He came by the station and offered to buy my supper. I wasn't going to pass up a chance like that."

Ed mumbled, "Well, let's sit down and order or I'm liable to change my mind. Let these people enjoy their meal. Enjoy your visit, John. See you later, Karen."

They moved on and Maria went to them with coffee cups in hand. Tony brought the ravioli order to their table and stood there waiting to be introduced.

Just for fun Karen took her time before she said, "John, this is Tony, the head chef in this establishment."

Tony stuck out his hand and asked, "You visiting our fair city?"

"Yes, I'm here to see Karen's paintings."

"He's a famous artist, Tony." Tony looked surprised and said, "Welcome, I hope you enjoy your visit." Not knowing what else to say he turned and went back to his work. Maria came by to see if they needed anything and they were preparing to eat. John said, "Karen is so right. This is fantastic."

She thanked him and said, "Enjoy and let me know if you need anything."

They did very little talking while they ate and when they were finished, Karen asked, "How about dessert?"

"No, I couldn't. That was a large serving and I'm stuffed."

"Okay, we might find a dessert at my house if you change your mind." She left the money on the table as they got up to leave. She didn't want to make a big deal of paying for John's supper.

They went out to get in his car. He opened the door for her and went around to get in himself. He said, "Where to now?"

She told him how to get back to her house. When they got back she invited him in again. They went into her living room and sat down to talk some more about her art. A little later he said, "It's getting late and I need to get an early start in the morning. I'm going to go now and I'll probably be getting back in touch Monday night or Tuesday. I'll be flying out of Chicago on Wednesday."

"I have certainly enjoyed having you here today. I'm so pleased with what you have told me, I'll be forever grateful. I hope you'll visit again."

"I will definitely come back to help you get ready for your show. I know the setup and you are going to need help the first time around."

"That sounds great, you are too kind. Please drive carefully and I'll look forward to hearing from you." They were going toward the back door. She opened it and walked with him to his car. They shook hands, then she hugged him and he got in the car. She waved as he pulled away and went back toward house. She sat on the porch with the animals for a few minutes and went on in. She locked the door and turned out the light in the kitchen. She watched television for a few minutes before she went to her bed and her book.

When John got ready for bed, he turned on the TV but didn't pay much attention. He was thinking about what a lovely woman Karen was. He thought, "It's a shame that I'm such a vagabond and don't want to be tied down or I'd try to pursue more than her paintings."

He decided that she was probably too smart to get involved with someone like him, anyway. When he went to sleep, he did have that same dream about Karen in spite of himself.

Chapter 56

Gary Oldham was in his office at home working on his sermon. Christine was getting the little ones bathed and to bed. He was thinking of the football game on Friday night and how the crowd cheered for their team. He thought he could relate it to being on God's team and cheering for his side. He put his thoughts on paper and then sat there thinking it over. He wanted to give it some punch, to knock his congregation out of their complacency. He prayed, "I'm asking you for help, Lord. Give me a knock out line to use."

He sat quietly waiting and it came to him. He made some more notes and left the office with a smile on his face.

Christine came down the stair and sighed, "At last. They are down and I am done."

He motioned for her to sit beside him. When she did as asked, he put his arm around her and pulled her to him. He kissed her hard and long. She sat back and said. "My, aren't you feeling foxy?"

"I was just thinking how much I love you and thought I'd show you." She squeezed his hand and told him, "I believe you and I'm just mad about you, too." They both got up from the couch, turned out the lights and went up the stairs to their bedroom.

Sunday morning Karen was in her kitchen making coffee at seven o'clock when the phone rang. It was Ed. He asked, "Is your guest still there?"

"No, he was going to leave for Chicago early this morning. Why?"

"I was wondering if you're going to church. If you are, I'd like to go with you."

"Gosh, I'd love for you to. Aren't you afraid the roof will cave in?"

"Okay, so I don't go often but I thought it was such a great day. I have the luxury of another day off." He paused, embarrassed because he sounded so stupid. "I thought maybe we could go together."

"Sure, how about I pick you up? I can drive, just like old times."

"Sounds great! I'll be looking for you. About ten thirty?"

"Fine, I'll see you then." She hung up the phone. He sat there on his bed thinking, " I'm really getting desperate, inviting her to church. I really just want to see her and I can't think of another way. What a wimp I'm becoming."

Karen chose to wear a red suit. It wasn't new, but she hadn't worn it for a long time. She had put on her make up and brushed her hair after her shower. She decided on a white silk shell instead of the long sleeve one she usually wore with the suit. Then she couldn't decide, black heels or red heels? She decided she felt like being flamboyant and chose the red. She giggled and thought, "Flamboyant for me is wearing red shoes. Wow, I am so with it."

She went to the kitchen and poured another cup of coffee. She still had plenty of time but she hadn't fed the dogs yet so she got their food and took it out to them. She gave them each a pat but they were more interested in eating right now. She went back into the house and sat at the table drinking her coffee and thinking about John's exciting visit. She hoped he was serious but she wondered if he was just being flattering. "Well, we'll see.," she said to herself, "She talks to animals and now she's talking to herself. A sure sign of senility setting in." She got up to go to her car, locked the door and was soon on the road to Ed's place.

Bill Wallace got up early and after the coffee was made he called the hospital to make arrangements to see Janet. He asked them to see if she would agree and call him back as soon as they could. He woke up the kids and said, " I've made pancakes for breakfast so come and get 'em." They were not happy to be awake so early but pancakes were their favorite breakfast. So soon they were sitting at the table ready and waiting to be served. Bill did his fancy work with the spatula, flipping them in the air and onto the plate. He had the maple syrup and melted butter on the table. He gave them each two pancakes and by the time he had four more done, their plates were empty, waiting for more.

He said, "Hey, when does the cook get to eat?" He made four more and the phone rang. He said, "Amy, it's your turn to cook."

He went to his bedroom to answer. It was the physciatrist who was treating Janet at the hospital. He said, "I just talked to your wife and she said she would like to see all of you this afternoon. I thought maybe you didn't care to see her since I hadn't heard from you earlier."

Bill explained, "She wouldn't see us at the jail so I was just waiting to see how she did in your care. I'm glad she's willing to see us, though. Do you think she is going to try to get me to bring her home?"

"No, she understands that she needs more therapy. I don't think you'll have any problem. We have a nice garden for patients and their families to visit when the weather in nice. You can come at three o'clock. Visiting hours are three to five. Okay?"

"We'll see you then. Thank you."

"Okay, I'll try to get with you while you're here to let you know how we're treating her. Goodbye for now."

"Yes, sir. Goodbye." He went back to the kitchen and Amy had his pancakes ready. He warmed them in the microwave and told them about their mother. Then he asked, "Will you go to church with me this morning and then we'll drive up there and see her. Okay?" They both agreed immediately. He thought to himself that maybe this would make Tom feel better. They all went to their rooms after the kitchen was cleaned up.

The phone rang again and Bill picked up in his bedroom. It was Gary Oldham, he said, "Bill I need a favor." Bill said, "Sure." The conversation was very short. Bill hung up after he said, "I'll see you there."

When they gathered in the kitchen again, they were in their Sunday best. Amy in a pretty blue jumper over a lighter blue blouse, Tom in khakis and a red sweater over a white shirt and tie. Bill had on his favorite pin striped dark blue suit, starched white shirt and red tie.

He said, "Are we a good lookin' bunch or what? I hope you kids know how proud I am of you." Amy hugged him and Tom just looked embarrassed. They all climbed in the pickup and took off.

He told them on the way that they'd go out to eat after church. "So don't go off with anybody so we can get to the hospital on time." When they parked in front of the church, they saw Ed and Karen going in.

Karen had honked the horn when she got to Ed's place. He came right out, looking very handsome in a camel sport coat, with dark brown pants and a cream-colored shirt and green tie.

She told him, "You are looking good." He answered, "And you, too. The lady in red. I like it. Looks great with your blond hair."

She smiled and said, "The gray is creeping into the blond these days but thank goodness it's not too noticeable, yet."

On the way to the church he told her about his day with Daniel in the woods. He said, "I think it was culture shock for Daniel but he seemed to enjoy himself."

Karen said, "Well, he's a big city boy and country club type."

"No, he's really a down to earth guy and I enjoy spending time with him. Not as much as I enjoy you but when you're not available and out with your boyfriends, he'll have to do."

"You are the silliest thing I ever knew. I'm sure he'd be glad to know that."

"Seriously, I haven't had a buddy since Rich and Daniel seemed interested in our rustic hunting camp. I hope he'll go with me when the season opens. Now, tell me about John's visit. How did it go?"

"He was most flattering. He says my work is worthy of a gallery showing in Chicago."

"Do you believe him?"

"He's on his way to make arrangements for it now."

"That's great, I hope it happens, you deserve it. If I can do anything to help, let me know."

"He said there would be contracts and stuff, so I'm probably going to need a lawyer to look it over before I sign. Not that I don't trust him because he's used to dealing with galleries. He's really quite well known."

"Maybe you will be famous someday and I can say I knew her when."

"Always the funny man. Tell me more about what you and Daniel did."

"That was all, we had breakfast and drove the forty miles there and then back. By the way, we did see something I found funny, no, it wasn't funny it was strange. Tom Wallace was running in the cemetery. Don't you find that strange?"

"Well, it's not somewhere I would go to run, but I don't see any harm in it. They do live in that area. Did he see you?"

"No, I don't think so. You know I'm just naturally suspicious of anything out of the ordinary. Just a cop quirk. Can't help myself."

They were at the church and Karen pulled the car into the parking lot. Ed got out first and opened the door for her. They had plenty of time and talked to several people on their way in. The seats in the back were filled. That's where Ed would have preferred to sit but they had to go in closer to the front.

The sanctuary was buzzing with quiet conversations until the organist began to play. Then it became very quiet. Gary Oldham, the preacher in his black robe, came out and took his seat and the choir director took his place in front of the choir. They sang a rendition of "His Eye is on the Sparrow" that was really stirring. The Sunday School Superintendent made a report on Sunday School Attendance. Then the lay preacher came to the lectern and made some announcements about church activities for the coming week even though they were all in the bulletin. He asked the congregation to join him in prayer. Then everybody sang "The Old Rugged Cross," just two stanzas.

The preacher began his sermon by reading scripture and then he told them that he had been thinking about how everybody supported football. Some people wouldn't think of missing a game.

He said, "I've been wondering how I could get my congregation to be that loyal. How I could get them to be on the Lord's team." He spoke for several more minutes and then he started to wind down.

He said, "I want you to think of me as the Lord's recruiter and I'm picking you for his team and I'm passing the ball to you ."

Just as he spoke those words, he stepped back, he had a football in his hand and he threw it out over the congregation. There was a loud gasp and Bill Wallace stood up, caught the ball and quickly sat down. The preacher sat down, he had made his point.

The choir director got up immediately and said, "Join us in singing page three fifty one, "What a Friend we have in Jesus," everyone please stand." The organist played the offertory and then the invitational. One of the church leaders said the closing prayer while the preacher made his way to the entrance to greet his "team." He got a lot of comment that morning and he loved it. He told them, "You have to shake things up sometimes."

When Bill came out, he thanked him and said, "I knew if anybody could catch it, you could."

On the way out of the church, Ed said, "How about I take you to lunch at the Holiday Inn."

"That sounds good. I'm awfully hungry though."

"Well, if that's the case, we'll do the buffet."

They each shook Gary's hand and told him it was a great sermon. Then they went to get in Karen's car. They spoke to several more people on the way to the car. Ed opened Karen's door and went around to the passenger side.

He said, "Take me to food, woman." She did just that. It was crowded but they were seated in a few minutes and the waitress brought water and menus.

She asked, "What would you like to drink," they both ordered the cops favorite, coffee. They were quiet as they read the menu. Karen said she'd like the shrimp scampi and a salad, so when the waitress returned, Ed ordered for Karen. Then he ordered the grilled chicken dinner with a salad for himself. The conversation was about mundane things like the weather, the sermon, the plans for their week and when they were both wondering what to talk about next, the food came. It was a welcome diversion. Then they could talk about the food.

There they were, two old friends struggling to keep up the conversation. For the first time ever, they were uncomfortable in each others presence. It seemed like the moments of silence were deafening and neither of them knew why.

When they were finished and had decided against dessert, Ed paid the bill and they made their way back to the car. Karen asked, "What are you doing the rest of the day?"

Ed said, "I'd like to go to your place and see those paintings you've been showing to John."

She was surprised because he had never seemed interested before and she told him, "Sure, we can do that. I didn't know you were interested or I would have shown you before."

"Oh, I don't know a thing about art but I'd like to see what you do. I just never gave it much thought. I knew you painted but I thought it was just a hobby, not a serious vocation."

As she turned into her driveway she said, "Well, come on in and I'll give you a private showing."

Chapter 57

The Wallaces went to Wendy's after church. He told the kids to order anything they wanted, which they did. Then he ordered his and paid the cashier. They took their trays to a table and sat down to eat. Tom asked how Bill knew to catch that ball and he told him about the phone call before they left. Both of the kids thought that was a neat trick he played on everybody.

Bill said, "The preacher was trying to stir things up and get people excited about their church and their spiritual life."

Amy asked, "Do you think Mother will be glad to see us?"

"Yes, I think she will. The doctor said he thought it would be good for her and that she gave her permission for the visit. We must not mention her coming home, though. She's not ready."

Tom said, "I don't want her coming home until she's the old Mom. I mean the mom she used to be when I was little." Amy and Bill agreed with him. Finished with lunch, they started on their way to see Janet for the first time in almost three weeks. The sun was shining brightly and they all felt good about the day.

Daniel had slept late and when he got up and made his first cup of coffee, he sat in the living room and watched "CBS Sunday Morning." They always had a piece about art on the show and this time it was about the artist John Whitcomb teaching at the Art Colony in Easton. He thought, "That's the guy that was visiting Karen this weekend. I didn't know he was that well known."

They had shots of the workshops and his paintings. It was the second week's class so there were none of Karen or her room mates. There was a lady named Ann Neal that was the director of the camp and she explained the operation. Bill Guice was the reporter, so he put a humorous spin on it and tried his hand at an abstract painting. Of course it turned out looking like a poor imitation of Jackson Pollack. Then they interviewed John at a gallery in Chicago and he told them he was always looking for new American artists to promote and that he had been in Dinsmore talking to one recently. Bill ended the interview saying, he would let everyone know when he had his first gallery opening. He looked like he had been rolling in the paint.

When the show ended, Daniel decided to get on the Internet and finalize some ski trip plans. He wanted to go right after Christmas. He found a package to Steamboat Springs but he wanted to talk to his kids before he booked. He decided to email them first, so they'd have the information when he called them. The sun was shining so brightly, he decided it was too pretty to sit in his apartment so he dressed and went out for a walk. His apartment was not far from downtown so he walked there. Of course, nothing was open, the drug store would open at noon. It was far too early for that. He walked to the end of the business district and kept on until he had reached the City Cemetery. He realized he had been drawn to visit Margie's graveside. There was no stone yet, just a simple marker. The flowers that were left were wilted and dried. But there was a fresh pink rose laying there. He looked around to see if it had somehow blown from another grave but there were no other roses in the area. He thought, "I need to talk to Karen about a stone for Margie."

He squatted down and stayed there a few minutes, not praying but thinking how much he missed her. He said, "I didn't know you long, but I will love you long." He went off wondering where the rose came from and vowing to come back soon and bring some more flowers for her.

When Karen opened the door, she said, "Come on in, Ed. Would you like something to drink?"

He was still on the porch petting Jazz, "No, maybe later. Take me to your studio, my dear."

He was smiling, joking as usual. She went to her bedroom to kick off her shoes and jacket. Then she said, "Come on and I'll give you a private viewing."

He was thinking, "I wish it was in your bedroom instead of your studio." But he followed her to the studio. He said, "It looks like you have been busy." Paintings were all over the place. Big paintings in every color imaginable. He was speechless for once.

He hesitated before he said, "No wonder he wanted to see this. It's great. Even I can see that. You really are good!"

"I can tell you had your doubts."

"Well, as I said, I don't know anything about art, but I know I like this."

"I hope other people will, if I get to show in a gallery."

She went to a stack of paintings in back of another bunch and pulled out a big one. It was of him and Rich in their hunting garb. She had done it years before and never shown it to anyone else. He looked shocked and then sad. "God, those were great days. I've got to have that one, would you sell it to me?"

"No, I won't sell this one, it means too much. But I'll give it to you if you really want it."

"I really want it. I don't have a thing on my walls but I sure will put this up. You can't just give it away, though."

"Ed, you're my friend and I want you to have it."

He moved closer to her and suddenly pulled her to him and kissed her hard on the lips. She broke away and looked at him like he'd lost his mind. He said, "I'm sorry but I've wanted to do that for so long, I couldn't help it."

"What are you talking about? Wanted to do it for so long? You never even tried before."

"Rich was my best friend. I couldn't when he was alive and I was afraid after he died. I didn't want you to reject me and I didn't want to risk our friendship."

She punched him on the arm and said, "I had decided that you just didn't think of me as any more than a friend, you dummy. I have loved you for a long time and figured we'd always be "just friends."

Then she grabbed him and planted a hard kiss on his lips. She didn't let go for a long time. He backed up and looked at her like she had hit him.

He shook his head and said, "Boy, have I been a fool. But it's never too late, is it?" Then she hugged him and said, "Never."

Chapter 58

The Wallace family got to the Wayne County Mental Health Institute at two forty five and signed in at the guard station. They were asked to empty their pockets and Amy's purse was searched. They looked all over the truck and directed them to the main building. They went to the main desk and told the attendant that they were there to see Janet Wallace. She told them to have a seat and she would let them know when they could meet her in the recreation room.

They were all nervous but anxious to see how she was doing, hoping she would be glad to see them.

After about fifteen minutes a lady in pink scrubs came thru the swinging doors and said, "Mr. Wallace?"

Bill put up his hand, because there were several other people there by now.

She said, "I'm Alice, you and the children can come with me."

She started back through the doors and they followed. She led them to a big sunny room with one whole wall of windows. There were ping pong tables and lots of game tables where patients were playing cards and checkers and other board games. Some were just sitting alone, staring off into space.

Bill spotted Janet first and pointed to her to show the kids. She was sitting a big overstuffed chair looking out at the gardens. The chairs were grouped in a circular pattern for easy conversation purposes.

Alice led the way and when they got to her, said, "Janet, your family is here to see you."

She turned and jumped to her feet. She hugged Amy first, then Tom and lastly Bill. She almost squealed, "I'm so glad to see all of you. I'd begun to think that I'd never see you again."

They took turns telling her how glad they were to see her and how much they'd missed her.

"Did you really miss me? I figured you were glad I was gone."

Bill hung his head and said, "No, we weren't glad at all. We just hope you're getting the help you needed so we can be a family again."

"I know now how awful I was to treat you the way I did. Not just you, Bill, but you kids, too. They're treating me with some kind of medication that regulates my moods."

She looked so sad they all hugged her again. Then she asked, "Don't you want to go out and sit in the garden to talk? It's so pretty out there. I spend a lot of time walking for exercise."

Tom said, "Mom, you have lost a lot of weight haven't you. You look great." She did look great. Her hair was piled up and held with a comb. She had on make up and even though she had the hospital scrubs, they looked neat. She told them she had lost twenty-five pounds and wanted to lose ten more.

She went to the door and rang a bell. An attendant near the entrance looked at her, nodded her head and released the lock. They all went out to the gardens. It was beautifully landscaped and there were lots of benches. There were tables with umbrellas and paths that wound throughout.

They all walked around for a while and then chose a bench to sit on. Tom sat down on the ground in front of the other three on the bench. They talked about school and football and church. Tom told her about his dad catching the football.

That made her say, "Gary's getting downright theatrical. Guess he wanted to wake folks up, huh?" Amy told her about Karen bringing them all that food.

Janet said, "That was really nice of her."

She was a little embarrassed that someone had to bring them food because she wasn't there. At five o'clock a bell rang and they got up to go inside as the attendants came out to make sure everyone came in.

Janet said, "I wish I could go home with you. But I promised my doctor that I would not beg you to take me with you. He says I need to stay at least ninety days to make sure the medication is going to continue to work."

Bill said, "Well, now that we know it's okay, we'll be back next week and try to come every weekend. Do you need anything? We can bring it with us next week."

"No, except you could leave me some money with the front desk so I'll have some to get a cold drink or snack sometimes. You can't give it to me but they'll keep it for me and I can get it as I need to."

"Sure, that's no problem. Can you make phone calls yet?"

"Only if I get permission."

"Well, if you think of anything, you just call or have them call and we'll bring it."

He pulled her to him and kissed her for the first time in months. She gave him a big smile. The kids each kissed her cheek and hugged her. When they were inside, she followed them to the swinging doors and told them, "I'll see you next week."

They nodded in agreement and went out to the desk to give them some money for Janet. The attendant gave Bill a manila envelope to put the money in and he wrote her name on it. He watched her place in a little safe and thanked her. He turned to find the kids were already gone to the truck. The three of them rode home in much better spirits. They talked a lot and then listened to the music on the radio. Now they knew she would soon be well and coming back home with them.

Chapter 59

Daniel got back to his apartment and heard the phone ringing as he unlocked the door. He hurried to answer it. It was his daughter, "Hello."

"Hi Dad, it's Allison. I just had a minute and thought I'd check on you. How are you?"

"I'm fine, Honey. It's so good to hear your voice."

"Good," she said, "I'm glad to hear that. I wanted to let you know my good news. I've been accepted at University of Chicago Hospital, Comer Children's Hospital, to finish my residency. Isn't that great? I'll be home again."

"Oh, that is the best news I've heard lately. When will you be back?"

"I'll finish here sometime in December and I'll be home for Christmas and go to work there in January."

"Make your start date after the fourth. I'm booking our trip for the twenty seventh to the fourth. Okay?" "That sounds great! Have you told David yet?"

"No, but why don't you tell him when you call him. I know you're going to have to tell him. He'll be so glad to have you close. So will your mother."

"Yes, I'm hoping to be able to see if I can help her, too. I've learned a lot about her disease and maybe I can convince her to get the right medication."

"That's good. Do you talk to her very much?"

"I call her about once a week, I know she's lonely and misses us. I don't want her to get too depressed."

"You're a good daughter. I'm a lucky man to have such great kids."

"We're lucky, too, Dad. I'm going to hang up and call David now, so you take it easy and I'll talk to you soon. I love you."

"And I love you, bye now." He sat back and gave a sigh of relief. It would be so good to have her within a three hours drive and with David at Northwestern, he will get to see them more often."

He thought, "My life is good because I do have great kids and good new friends. I need to remember that I'm really lucky to have it so good and be grateful."

It was eight in the evening in San Diego, California and Larry Sloan was just waking up in his Motel 6 room. He had been there about a week and had a job at a curb market. He worked the eleven to seven graveyard shift. He took the first thing he could find so he wouldn't go broke. Now he needed to find a cheaper way to sleep. He figured he could survive on the food he scrounged from the market if he could just find a room somewhere. Then he would look for a better job in the daytime. So today he was going to get the Sunday paper and look for a room. He needed a beer, too. He wasn't drinking as much because he still didn't think he had a problem. He did drink a beer or two in the cooler where the camera couldn't see him.

Escaping the department store, Rebecca, and Pamela had been a big such a big relief that he was able to control his drinking for now. He thought about Pamela, Margie and most of all, Melanie, but not enough to call them. He just wanted to start his life over without any ties. Eventually he would write to Pamela so she could send him divorce papers or whatever she did. First he would get a box at Mailboxes, Etc. so he couldn't be found at home. It was a plan, he thought, a good plan. Someday he would include Melanie in his plans but not now, she wasn't ready and neither was he. It was just too hurtful for both of them.

Chapter 60

After Ed made his pronouncement, Karen was in shock. When she regained her wits. She said, "Well, you've seen it all now. Here's the painting of you and Rich. I want you to have it."

"I feel bad taking it and not paying you. Are you sure you don't want to keep it?"

"You saw where I had it stored. I would never hang it so it belongs to you. Let's go make some coffee and sit at the kitchen table. I may find a little dessert in there."

He took the painting to the car and sat down on her back porch to pet Jazz and Callie. She called to him, "You're going to get cat and dog hair all over your coat. Come on in the coffee is ready."

Taking his coat off and hanging on the back of the chair, he said, "That sure looks good." She had placed two plates of pineapple upside down cake on the table with two cups of coffee.

She asked, "Do you want some ice cream?"

"No thanks, this is enough calories. When did you bake this?"

"Actually, I baked it Friday to have while John was here but we never got around to eating any of it."

"Oh, yeah, your boyfriend. Do you know how jealous I was of him being here with you?"

"I knew you didn't like the idea. You didn't hide it too well."

"Don't you understand? I'm crazy about you? This old bachelor has loved you for years and never could get up the nerve to tell you. I was afraid you'd shoot me with that thirty-eight."

"You are such a nut. I love you, too, Ed. It feels so good to say that. I love you, Ed."

"What are we going to do about it? Now that it's out in the open? You want to get married?"

"My God, is that what you call a proposal? Let's not move so fast. I'm still trying to get my mind around this."

"Okay, I'll give you a couple of days to give me an answer. I won't push. I'll give you time but I really am serious. I just want you to know that. After all we aren't getting any younger. At least I'm not, I know you're younger than me. Does that bother you?"

"No, you're in very good shape for an "old guy." I want you to be around for a long time."

They went on talking for hours and finally Karen said, "I'd better get you back to your place, don't you think?"

"Well, I'd like to spend the night but I guess I'd better get home. It's back to the grindstone tomorrow."

"I'm going to Margie's apartment tomorrow and see what I can find." They got their jackets and went out the door. She locked up and turned around. Ed took her in his arms and kissed her again and she kissed him back. Then she took him home and let him out after another kiss or two.

Chapter 61

Monday morning Tony opened up at six a.m. as usual. Ed Hawkins was out front in his car waiting and came in immediately. "Hey there, Ed, how ya' doin'? You're up bright and early. Got to get to work early or something?"

"No, couldn't sleep. Had a bad night."

"What's the matter, too much weekend?"

"No, had a great weekend. Just couldn't sleep. Got the coffee made?"

"Yeah, I'll get you some right now."

He came back with two cups and sat down with Ed. "So what's going on at the police department?"

"I don't know. I've been off for two days. It was great!"

"Whad ya do? Go huntin'?"

"No, I did take Daniel up to the hunting camp though. Checked it out because it won't be long before the season opens."

Two customers came in and Tony got up to go wait on them. Ed didn't recognize them. Probably just passing through, he thought. Maria came in from the back and said, "Good Morning, Ed."

He answered, "Good Morning, Maria. How are the chicken pox kids doing?"

"One got over it and two more got it. Poor Mama, she's got her hands full. I feel guilty leaving her to contend with it. She's so much better at it than I am though. She entertains them to keep their minds off the itch. I got the other two shots so maybe they won't get it."

Bill Wallace came in with his kids and he spoke to everyone. Ed thought, "He seems to be in a better mood today."

Bill sat down with the kids and told them what to order for him. Then he got up and came over to Ed. He sat down and said, "We went to see Janet yesterday and she's doing real good. I thought you'd want to know since you had a hand in getting her there."

"Hey, man, I know that is good news for you and the kids. I'm glad to hear it. Say, that was some neat trick you and the preacher played yesterday."

"Yeah, that was a trip. I was scared to death that I wouldn't catch it."

"It was a great catch. Everybody gasped when he threw it. The preacher's got a pretty good arm, too."

"Well, we've got to get to school so I'll get back to my table. I just wanted to thank you for taking care of Janet while you had her. I know it wasn't easy."

"Hey, you're welcome. You know "Serve and Protect" is the word."

Maria came over after she served Bill's table and asked, "Are you eating today, Ed?"

"Yeah, but I'm going to wait for Jeff or somebody to come in. I don't have to get to work yet."

Tony served up omelets to the two guys at the counter, refilled their coffee cups and came over to Ed. He sat down and leaned in close to Ed.

"Those two guys are talking about going out to Karen's to look at her artwork. They asked me if I knew her."

He said it so quietly, Ed could hardly hear him. Ed said, "Oh, I knew that guy looked familiar. One of them is that guy that was at Karen's Saturday, looking at her paintings. I'll bet she didn't expect him back so soon. You know, you met him, too." Tony slapped his forehead and said, "Oh, yeah, he looks different, somehow."

It was seven by now so he said, "Tony, let me use your phone in the office."

"Sure go on back, you know where it is." He got to the phone and called Karen's number.

When she answered, he said, "Good Morning, darlin', it's Ed. That guy John is here at Tony's having breakfast with another fellow. Did you know they were coming? Tony overheard them talking about you and he got all flustered. I don't know what he thought but he came over to tell me like it was a crime or something. I didn't recognize John. I'd only seen him once before for a minute. I had my mind on other things."

"Yes, he called me last night after I got home from your place. They must have left Chicago at three in the morning. They are going to mess up my plans for going to Margie's. Maybe they won't take long. I wanted to talk to you about that. You know, going to Margie's. What do you think of taking Daniel with me? He was there last, as far as we know. He would know what it had looked like that night. What do you think?"

"I think that would be fine. Just don't touch things or wear gloves if you do. Just be careful in case there are some clues there. I want you to know that I didn't sleep a damn bit last night, thinking about you. I'm like a lovesick teenager."

"Can anybody hear you? You know how Tony likes to eavesdrop."

"No, I'm in his office alone. I love you, Lady."

"I love you, too. You crazy man. I'll call you when those guys leave town. You take care of yourself. Now go to work."

"Okay, bye." He went back out and Jeff Collins was sitting at the table looking puzzled. He asked, "Who were you talking to?"

Ed told him, "I'll tell you later."

Maria came over with the coffee pot and said, "Ready to order now?."

Chapter 62

Pamela Sloan had to get to work earlier these days. She had to be there by eight thirty to be ready to work at nine when Rebecca opened the store. Mr. Regal had been pleased that she took the job in Woman's Wear. He told her if she did well, he would see that she got a promotion and a raise. She could tell he felt bad about what Larry had done to her but he didn't embarrass her by talking about it. Rebecca had been really nice to her so things were okay. When she saved enough money, she would file for divorce. Another Regal employee, Leah Oliver, was going to move in with her so they could share the rent. At least she did have furniture and it was paid for. Larry had paid for her car, too. So her only bills were rent, utilities and food. Sharing the rent would help a lot. Rebecca had told her to tone down her dress style now that she worked out on the floor. She was nice about it, so Pamela didn't mind. She had bought some more conservative clothes with her store discount.

Karen had gone out to see about Candy when she fed the cat and dog. She fed her and talked to her, promising they would go for a ride later on today. The weather was getting much colder now. It would be Halloween on Wednesday so everybody had pumpkins out on their porches and candy was selling well at the local Wal Mart. She would need to pick up some when she went grocery shopping. Candy liked candy corn, that's how she got her name. When she was a colt, Karen had used it to get her to come to her. You weren't supposed to feed them candy but she liked it so much. She didn't give it to her every time. When she had gone back in the house, Ed had called. She was thrilled when he said he loved her. She was feeling like a lovesick teenager, too. She thought, "I don't care, I like feeling this way."

She got her second cup of coffee and went out to the porch to wait for John and his friend. Jazz and Callie were thrilled to get her attention and they wiggled and wagged all over while she sat on the steps. She couldn't believe John was back so soon. He might have some good news, she hoped.

She heard a car pull into the driveway and went out to meet them. It wasn't John, but it was Joseph and Ruth Barry. They both got out of their truck and went to get something out of the bed. Ruth got a basket of apples and Joseph got a huge pumpkin. "Hi there, dear, we thought maybe you would like some

195

apples. We have picked more than we can use and Joseph says you need to make a jack o' lantern for your porch. All those kiddies will be out here Wednesday night to get their treats."

Karen said, "That's so sweet of you to think of me. I love apples and I'll paint a face on the pumpkin. The kids will like that. Don't you think?"

Joseph said, "Honey, you fix it any way you want to. I'm going to sit this heavy thing right on your porch. If you want it out front, you'll have to use a wheelbarrow."

She answered, "No, I'll leave it right there. Everybody comes to the back and on Halloween I'll have the back porch light on."

Another car pulled in the driveway and Joseph said, "Oh my, you've got company and we're blocking the way."

Karen told him, "No, it's okay." She motioned for John to park over on the grass and went to greet him and his passenger. He did as she directed and when he was parked, both men climbed out of their car. John walked up and took Karen's hand and said, "Karen, I want you to meet Harry Rose, he owns "The Rose Art Gallery" and I'd like for him to see your artwork."

"It's nice to meet you, Mr. Rose, welcome to Dinsmore."

"Let's get right to Harry and Karen. Okay? I hope that we're going to be friends. John was so enthusiastic about your work and I needed some time off. That's what made us get up at three o'clock this morning."

"Okay, Harry, I'm glad you're here and you too, John. I was shocked when you said you were coming back already."

She started walking back to where Ruth and Joseph were standing. They were taking it all in and wondering what was going on. There were handshakes all around as Karen introduced them and told the Barrys why the gentlemen were here.

Joseph said, "My goodness, you have business to take care of and we need to get out of the way."

Ruth said, "Yes, it's nice to meet you and we'll go and let you get on with your business."

They started toward their truck and Karen walked with them. She said, "I am going to ride Candy after they leave and I'll ride down and tell you all about it. It's very exciting." They each hugged her and got back in their truck and backed out of the drive.

John and Harry were on the back porch petting the animals when she turned to go to them. She thought, "Good sign, I don't trust anyone who doesn't like animals."

Then she spoke to them, "Well, come on in the house and I'll get you a cup of coffee. I'll bet you need one after your early drive." They told her that they had visited the Café and had breakfast with plenty of coffee.

"We just want to see your paintings, right now." She took them to her studio and began to put an assortment of paintings on the easel. She would leave them up until Harry would say, "Okay, let's see another."

He didn't comment until she had shown him all of them. He said, "This is exceptional work and I'm so happy John found you. We need this kind of work in our gallery. It will appeal to the people who like realism and those who like impressionism because it can be viewed in either way. You know the eye of the beholder thing. I know that sounds crazy but it's true."

Karen was speechless for a minute. She hadn't expected him to be so complimentary. She still was having trouble believing all of this praise. She said, "What do you mean, our gallery?"

"Oh, I mean John and me, he didn't tell you he's my partner? He's a silent partner in "The Rose Gallery."

John spoke up, "I didn't think it was necessary. I wanted to be the art instructor, not the gallery owner to Karen."

"Well, I'm ready to talk business now and have that cup of coffee," Harry told them and turned to head back to the kitchen. Karen and John followed him and she got the cups from the cabinet and filled them. The sugar and creamer were still on the table. The men were already sitting at the table and Karen joined them.

John reached inside his coat and produced some folded papers. "These are copies of our contract and the instructions for galley showing. I want you to read these and then we'll answer any questions you might have."

Harry said, "Yes, we want you to feel comfortable with our gallery operation. It's geared to promote the artist and the gallery at the same time. But our main interest is introducing new American artists to the world of art buyers and collectors."

Karen asked, "Do you want me to read these right now?"

John answered, "Yes, they're not complicated, you won't need a lawyer, we keep it simple. Artists don't like to be tied down and constrained too much. Besides they're not very good at following rules."

She started reading them. The first one was a contract which gave them exclusivity to the artist's work, the second was a list of instruction on how to prepare to ship or deliver the work and how many would be necessary. At least thirty paintings would be required. The third was how the gallery opening honoring the artist would be arranged and held. It only took her a few minutes to read.

Her only question was, "How soon do I need to be ready?"

Harry said, "We were thinking sometime in January would be a good way to start off the new year. What do you think? Could you be ready by then?"

"Yes, of course. That's great, I wouldn't feel rushed and could get some more work done. I have about twenty right now. Will you want to see them before I deliver them?"

Harry spoke up, "No, I think it obvious we can trust your judgement. You have a great eye, you know about the third eye?"

"Yes, the eye which makes it possible to critique art without bias, especially your own art." John and Harry looked at each other and smiled.

John said, "She's definitely got the right stuff."

Karen said, "I'd like to sign up right now. I'm thrilled at the thought of being exposed to the huge city of Chicago and having a chance to paint to my hearts content. That is if I sell anything." They both told her there was no doubt she would sell. They would help her by correctly pricing her work, making her money but keeping the gallery profitable, too. She signed the contract and handed it to John.

He said, "You keep the other two sheets and I'll mail you a copy of the contract." Then he smiled and said, "You need to get to work now and we need to get back to Chicago. I've got a plane to catch on Wednesday, you know. We've got some other business to take care of before I go back to San Diego."

Karen said, "That's the first time you mentioned San Diego. Is that where you live?"

"Yes, it's my favorite place in the world. I have a small place in Taos, too. I don't get there as often these days. I moved from there to San Diego. Did I tell you we have a gallery there too?"

"No, you two are into this in a big way, aren't you? I had no idea what I was getting into when I met you at the colony." She smiled at him and went on, "I was so disappointed when I had to leave and I'm so grateful that you remembered me."

"You're not easy to forget, Karen. I'm glad I found you and proud to be of some assistance." She blushed at that remark but avoided further comment and went on to tell them, "I won't be able to start immediately. You know, the reason I had to leave the colony was that one of my dearest friends was found dead. So as an ex cop, I'm going to investigate her death. They said she committed suicide and I just know it's not true and I intend to prove it."

Harry said, "I didn't know you were an ex cop! John, why didn't you mention that? What a gimmick for advertising. The ex cop showing her art work at "The Rose Gallery!"

John looked at him like he'd lost his mind and said, "I don't think so, let's not get carried away."

"Oh, no, please don't run with that. It's no big deal, you know how little Dinsmore is and there isn't much crime so being a cop here would be a joke in Chicago. It might rate a small mention but very small."

John got up and said, "Well, Harry, we'd better get back on the road now. We've taken up enough of Karen's time."

Harry reached over to shake Karen's hand. "It's been so good to meet you and I've enjoyed your hospitality."

She said, "It's been my pleasure." Karen walked with them all the way to their car, "I'm sorry you have to rush off. I really appreciate you coming all the way down here to see me. Please come back soon."

John got in the driver's seat and said, "Oh, we'll be back for sure, you can count on it." When Harry was in the car, they backed from the drive. Karen waved, John honked the horn and they were gone.

Chapter 63

Ed and Jeff had their breakfast together at the Café and later went to the station to see what was going on. There wasn't much to do since it was so early. Patrolmen were out directing traffic at the schools and investigating fender benders but there was nothing for a detective to detect.

Ed started on some paper work he had been avoiding and after a few minutes he called Daniel and asked him to meet him for lunch. He said, "Let's just go to the Holiday Inn for a change. I've got something I want to tell you. And I need your advice."

Daniel said, "Good Lord, you've got my curiosity aroused now. How do you expect me to keep my mind on my work when you're being so mysterious?" he paused, "Really I hope it's nothing serious, nothing wrong, I mean."

"No, I just need to talk to an impartial listener and you fit the bill for this one."

"Okay, I'll see you at eleven thirty at the Inn." They disconnected and went back to their previous chores.

The desk sergeant called Ed and said, "A Fax just came in wanting information on Larry Sloan, seems he's trying to be bonded for a job in San Diego, California. When did he move there?"

Ed told him, "Just Fax them back that he has no record with us. We never really arrested him and there's no need to mess things up for him. He's obviously trying to start over. He's been gone a couple of weeks. You are obviously not keeping up with the local gossip. Good for you."

He continued, "Let's give the boy a break even though he is a first class jerk, I'm glad he's gone and want him to stay gone." The sergeant said, "Okay, I'll do it right now."

Daniel was at his desk when Pamela Sloan came into his office. His secretary hadn't said who was coming in so he was sort of surprised to see her. He greeted her, "Good Morning, Pamela, how are you? It's good to see you."

"I'm fine now that I'm back on my own. I wanted to talk to you about a bank account. You see, Larry almost cleaned out our joint account and I want to open a new one that he can't get into. Is that possible?"

"Sure no problem. It will just be in your name. You can even use your maiden name if you want to. Then there would be no connection at all."

"That's good because I'm seeing a lawyer today about a divorce or maybe an annulment since we weren't married very long."

"Okay, you just go out there to my secretary and she'll set it up for you. If I can help you anytime, feel free to call me or come by. You know, I have a daughter about your age and I hope people would help her if she needed it."

"I appreciate that so much. Larry has a daughter my age too. I'm hoping I can meet her sometime. I was too embarrassed when she was here for her mother's funeral."

"Well, she and I got acquainted. I was seeing Margie before she died. So when Melanie comes back to town, I'll see that you two get together. She's a really nice girl."

"Thanks, Mr. Carmody. You've been a big help. I'll see you later." She turned and left the office. She went to take care of her business. She was going to see Jack Carter later in the day.

Shortly before lunch time Daniel went to his car and drove to the florist that was close to the cemetery. He bought a pot of daisies and got back in his car, drove to the cemetery and placed them on Margie's grave. There was another fresh pink rose on it. He was puzzled but thought, "Someone else is thinking of you, Margie."

He stood there a few minutes and turned to go. He thought he had seen another man leaving the cemetery on foot but when he got back in his car, no one was in sight. He went out to the highway and the Holiday Inn to meet Ed.

Ed's car was already parked out front and he parked and went into the table where Ed was sitting. Ed stood up and shook hands. He said, "Thanks for meeting me, friend. I just had to talk to somebody who would understand me."

"What the hell is going on with you, Ed? Are you in some kind of trouble?"

Ed laughed so loud that Daniel looked around to see if anyone was watching them. "Well, you might call it trouble. I was with Karen yesterday. We went to church and came here to eat lunch. Then we went back to her house and she showed me her etchings," he laughed at the old joke, but Daniel just looked confused. Ed went on, "I mean her paintings. We talked and talked and I finally told her."

Daniel said, "What?"

"I told her I loved her, man, I told her I had loved her forever!"

"Well, it's about time. You old fool!"

"That's what I feel like, an old fool."

The waitress came to take their order. They said they would do the buffet. She gave them their water and got their drink order. They went to the buffet and filled their plates. When they were seated again, Daniel asked, "Well, what did she say or do or what?"

"Get this, she said she loves me too. Do you believe it?"

"Well, hell yes, I believe it. It's been obvious to everyone except you two. We knew it was something more than friendship."

"She'll kill me for telling you. I already asked her to marry me."

"Boy, you do move fast, once you get moving. What did she say?"

"She'll think about it."

"Oh, man. Are you worried?"

"No, I think she'll go for it. I understand that she needs to catch her breath. After all she didn't expect it, after all this time. I've had plenty of chances before but I couldn't get Rich out of my mind. I was just really scared that it would make her mad. I didn't want to lose her, even if it stayed just friendship."

"I'm damn proud of you and I wish you both the best." By now their food was getting cold and the waitress was staring at them.

Daniel said, "She's probably thinking we should eat and let someone else get the table. They began to eat and Ed said, "Don't worry about her, I'll leave her a good tip."

Before they finished Ed told him, "Karen is going to ask you to go to Margie's apartment with her. She thinks maybe you'll notice if anything doesn't look like it did when you were there."

Daniel said, "Well, I'll be glad to go but I was only there once so I don't know how much help I'll be."

"You never know about those things. Strange things can show up where you least expect them. The only reason I'm telling you is that you can put in a good word for me if it comes up but don't tell her that I talked to you unless she brings it up."

"No problem, but I doubt if she will. Don't you?"

"I don't know, depends on how well she feels she knows you. You know kind of the unbiased opinion. She's aware that you and I have become friends so, who knows?" They finished their meals and got up to leave.

Ed left the waitress a five-dollar tip and she smiled broadly then and thanked them. He paid for both of them at the cashier's desk. They got in their cars and went back to work.

Chapter 64

After John and Harry were gone, Karen put on her boots and went to keep her promise to Candy. She rode in the fields in back of her place for about thirty minutes and then went out to the road and down to the Barrys. They were in the backyard picking more apples. They waved at her and Ruth came up to the house. Karen climbed down and said, "Don't quit, I'll come and help you." She tied Candy to the fence.

Ruth went over and to give Candy an apple asking, "It's okay if I give her this, isn't it?"

"Sure, she'll love it. I've already spoiled her with candy corn."

Ruth said, "We've picked enough today. John, come on in." She turned to Karen, "Let's go in and we'll have some of the apple pie I baked this morning. It may still be warm and we'll put ice cream on it."

Joseph was coming in the door right behind them and asked, "Well, when are you going to tell us what those two men wanted with you. Were they policemen?"

"I never thought about that. You probably thought it was something about police work. It was about my painting, my artwork, they own a gallery in Chicago and I'm going to have a big opening show there in January. Isn't that wonderful?"

Ruth got so excited she had to sit down for a minute, fanning herself with a hand, she squealed, "Oh, that is grand, will we be invited?"

Joseph said, "Now Ruth, you shouldn't ask her that. She may not want old fogies at her art show."

Karen said, "You two will be at the top of my list, talk about old fogies, you know I'm no spring chicken. Imagine starting a new career at my age."

Joseph slapped his knee and said, "Yeah, you're just another Grandma Moses."

Karen pretended she was going to hit him and Ruth told her, "You ought to do it, he's downright ornery." She had placed three plates with big slices of apple pie ala mode on the table and they all sat down.

They both wanted to know more about the gallery and she told them all the details. They talked about the weather getting colder now and how they dreaded winter more every year. Then they asked her if she had heard from Melanie and if she knew any more about Margie's death. She told them her plans to go to the apartment and said she was glad they mentioned Melanie. She had been so busy, she had forgotten to call her. She was there a couple of hours and then said she needed to get back home. She climbed on Candy and rode back to the barn. After she had her unsaddled, she sent her out back to graze and run free. Soon it would be too cold for her to be out as much.

Nothing of any consequence happened in the police department that afternoon. Ed had caught up on all his paperwork, or at least most of it. He got up from his desk at five o'clock and announced to anyone who cared, "I'm leaving. Don't call me unless it's a murder."

He got his jacket and left the building. Jeff said, "He must be sick. He never leaves at five unless he's going on a case."

Chapter 65

Daniel was back in his office going over some loan papers when his secretary said, "There's a Karen Sutton on the phone. Can you speak to her?"

"Sure, put her on. Hi, Karen, what can I do for you?"

"I just wondered if it would be possible for you to meet me at Margie's apartment after work. I want to go through and see if there's anything out of place. I also need to search for a will and the papers and keys for her car."

"I'll be glad to. Ed had told me you might call me. As for the will, I imagine it's in her safety deposit box here at the bank or with her lawyer. If her lawyer had it, he would have contacted somebody, I think. Anyway what time?"

"I'm going over now and you just come when you leave for the day if you don't mind. I really will appreciate it. I want to call Melanie tonight and I'd like to have something to tell her."

"Sounds good. I'll see you there."

As soon as she hung up the phone, Karen got on a jacket, locked up the house and went to Margie's place. She still had a key and the apartment rent was paid so she didn't have to check with anybody to get in. She parked beside Margie's car and looked in the windows and on the outside to see what was inside and if there was any damage done to it. Then she took the elevator up to the apartment.

She felt a shiver go down her spine. It seemed eerie to go in alone because she felt so sure that it was a murder scene. She went to the desk found a small key but no papers. She didn't know how Melanie had found those insurance papers. She thought to herself, "I should have called her first. She knew where to look."

She went into Margie's bedroom where the bed was not mussed. But the coverlet was pulled back as if she had prepared to go to bed. She looked in the closet and under the bed. That's where she found the small safe that the little key would open. In it she found the car insurance and title, the keys to her safety deposit box, the lease for her apartment and another diamond pendent in a little velvet bag. Karen thought it must have been another piece that her grandmother had left her. Either it was very valuable or had a special significance.

The door chime sounded and she went to see who was there. She let Daniel in and he looked very uncomfortable as he sat down in one of the chairs. "I really don't know what I can do here."

Karen agreed, "I feel the same way but I've just got to try. I'll never believe that Margie committed suicide."

"Here's what happened that night," Daniel started, "We came in here and she told me to light the gas logs while she changed. She came out of the bedroom and went to the kitchen to get us a glass of wine. We laid in here on that rug by the fireplace and got romantic. Yes, we had sex to answer your next question. We fell asleep right there and at three o'clock I got up and went home. I had to leave early the next morning for Chicago."

"What did she do when you got ready to leave?"

"She got up and walked me to the door. Kissed me goodbye, said she hoped I didn't catch her cold and that was the last time I saw her. Did the cops get the wine glasses or the bottle?"

"I don't know, I guess I'd better check the kitchen next." She went to the kitchen, didn't see a wine bottle, looked in the trash can and found the bottle. "Daniel, did you two finish the bottle of wine?"

"No, she opened a new one. We only drank a glass apiece. I know she didn't finish it. When I left, she was sleepy and said she was going to bed."

Karen got out her gloves and picked up the bottle. She found a paper bag in the pantry and put the bottle in it. "We'll get Ed to check it for fingerprints." She read the notes on the refrigerator door. Then she checked the trash cans in the bedroom and the bathroom. She looked in the medicine cabinet and saw nothing but some aspirin, ibuprofen, a thermometer, eye drops and some skin creams. Then she went to Melanie's room. It was almost bare because after all Melanie had taken her all her things to college. She checked the drawers and looked in the closet and only the summer clothes were there.

Daniel was just following her around and didn't say a word until he said, "Hey, I forgot to tell you that I was watching the television yesterday morning and saw a piece about John Whitcomb and the workshop at Easton. It was real interesting. He really is well known. Mentioned he liked promoting American artists and that he had been in Dinsmore."

She said, "Oh, I wish I had seen that. Ed and I went to church. John was back here today with his partner, Harry. He got Harry so excited that they got up at three in the morning and drove down with a contract for me to sign. It's a done deal. I'm having a show in January."

Daniel said, "That is just great. I'm so happy for you. Does Ed know?"

"No, I haven't talked to him. Why do you ask?"

Daniel thought fast and said, "Oh, I just figured he would be interested and I know you talk to him once in awhile."

"Well, he knew they were here and called to tell me they were at the Café this morning and got Tony all excited, about strangers looking for me. I haven't talked to him since then."

She was looking around the room as she talked and then she went back to Margie's bedroom and checked some drawers but found nothing. She went through the closet and all of Margie's pockets, looked in all her purses for the umpteenth time. She turned to Daniel and said, "There's not a prescription in this place. I'm sure the detectives took those sleeping pills, but you said she was sleepy. Why would she go take a bath and follow that with sleeping pills?"

He said, "I'd bet my life that she didn't take any pills. She might have decided to take a bath because she was still half dressed and probably wanted to put on her night clothes."

Karen's mumbling now, "Nobody takes sleeping pills and gets in the bathtub. A bath makes you sleepy."

Daniel just shakes his head and goes back to the living room and sits down and begins to cry. Karen, sorry she asked him to do this said, "Oh, Daniel, I'm so sorry, I shouldn't have done this to you."

He shakes his head again and tells her, "It's okay. It's the first time I've cried in a while and I need to. It just builds up every so often. I just can't believe it has really happened." He just sat there a few minutes and Karens sat down across from him.

She said, "Well, I've surely not accomplished a thing here."

Daniel didn't speak for a while and then he told her about his trip to the cemetery. "You know a funny thing is going on there. I went by the other day and there was a pink rose, a fresh pink rose on her grave. Then today, on my way to meet Ed, I stopped and got a pot of daisies and took them to her grave. There was another fresh pink rose. When I went into the cemetery, I thought I saw a man or it looked like a man leaving the cemetery. He was gone when I drove back out to the street."

"That is weird, the rose I mean. Did you think it was from the guy you saw leaving?"

"No, not really. It was just funny that I didn't see him after that."

Karen got up and started to walk away. Trying to figure out what to do next but curious about the lunch date, she asked, "What did you meet Ed for?"

"We just went to lunch at the Holiday Inn and talked."

"What did you two have to talk about?"

"Are you writing a book or something?" He grinned mischievously at her puzzled look.

She answered, "No, I was just curious. Ed doesn't usually go to lunch at the Holiday Inn."

"Well, he did today. Want to know what we talked about? Don't cha?" He teased her.

"No, I'm sorry. I guess I'm being nosy. I'm just naturally nosy, like Tony."

He said, "That's why we didn't go to the Café. Tony is nosy. We talked about you, and Ed. He's nuts about you, you know."

Now she was blushing, "Oh, my God, I can't believe he told you that. He's lost his mind."

Daniel is roaring with laughter now, "A man does strange things when he's in love. He says he wants to marry you and I'm to put in a good word for him." At this point she collapsed into the chair.

He's still laughing when she says, "It's not funny. I am totally embarrassed. Quit laughing! You think we're too old to be in love?"

"No way, I think it's great. And I'm here to tell you that you'd better say, "Yes" because I want to be the best man."

"I am going to kill him as soon as I leave here. You can be a pall bearer." She was smiling when she said it, but she said, "I'm definitely going to find Ed Hawkins tonight."

"Don't be too hard on him. He's in pain, he's so afraid you'll turn him down."

"Let's go, I'm through here. I can't think what else to do. All I've got it one wine bottle."

"Okay, but I'm going to follow you and save Ed from your wrath."

"Hey, I'm not really going to kill him, not yet anyway. Living with me, may do it. But I'm going to go find and tell him,"Yes." How do you like that?"

He jumped up and grabbed her and hugged her. He said, "I think that's super! I won't say a word to anybody. I know you guys will want to do it your way. This is the best news I've heard lately."

They went out of the apartment and Karen locked it up. She thanked Daniel for helping her and they went down to their cars. She drove straight to Ed's house but he wasn't home, so she turned around and went back to see if he was at the Café, but he wasn't there either. She didn't know where else to go so she went to her house and there he was, sitting on the back porch with the animals.

Chapter 66

Pamela Sloan had kept her appointment with Jack Carter that afternoon. She told him about her situation and ask him what she needed to do. He said, "Well, if he told you to get a divorce, we need to find out where he is."

She told him that she would ask Ed Hawkins to see if he could locate him. "After you find him, we'll do a no fault divorce. It's cheaper and faster. You'll want your maiden name back. I'm sure." She agreed and told him she would get back to him when she found Larry.

He said, "If you can't find him, we'll have to run ads saying you are suing for divorce and so on." She thanked him and went home to her apartment, feeling much better. Her new room mate was moving in when she got there. Things were working out for her and she would not be anxious to get married again, not for a long time, she promised herself. "I'm going to be somebody, on my own."

The Wallace family came home from school in good spirits. It was Tom's turn to cook and he cooked the spaghetti, opened the Ragu and warmed it. Got a loaf of garlic bread from the freezer and put in the oven. Amy set the table and put ice in the glasses. After it was all ready, they sat down together and joined hands. Bill returned thanks for family, for Mother feeling better, for all their blessings and especially for the cook. Tom just grinned.

They took turns telling about their day and Bill was truly grateful that it looked like things were working out. He said, "It's my turn to clean up. After that let's all watch Monday night football."

They both said they would join him as soon as they had their homework done. He agreed so when they had finished eating, the kids headed for their rooms. Bill cleared the table and did the dishes. He went into the living room to relax and get ready to watch the game. He was feeling quite good and thinking about how well things were going.

Then Tom came in and said, "I've finished my homework and I'm going for a run. I'll be back in time to watch the game with you."

Bill thought it was strange that after they had practiced for two hours he should want to go run. He figured it was best not to argue the point and said, "Okay, son, be careful out there." He watched him go out the door and thought, "I wish I knew what's bugging him. Wonder if it's a girl."

Karen got out of her car and walked up to Ed. She said, "I just left Daniel. He was laughing his butt off."

Ed looked surprised, "Why?"

"Because he told me that you two had lunch today at the Holiday Inn."

"So?"

"He says you want to get married to me."

"Oh, my God, he didn't say that."

"Oh, yes, he wants to be the best man."

"I'm sorry if he embarrassed you."

"Yeah, he acts like old people can't be in love."

"Well, he's wrong" He reached up and pulled her onto his lap and kissed her."

"You know you're nuts, don't you? We're both nuts." She kissed him back.

"Will you marry me, Karen and put me out of my misery?"

"Okay, if you put it that way, I guess I will."

He jumped up and almost dropped her, he hugged her and twirled her around right there in the backyard. He said, "I am the happiest man in the world. When?"

"We'll have to talk about it. Would you like to come in the house now?"

"Oh, yeah, let's go talk about it." They didn't talk much that night. They didn't even eat. Ed spent the night. They woke up the next morning still in each others arms…and the next morning…and the next morning.

Chapter 67

Wednesday morning the Café was crowded. Tony and Maria were so busy they didn't even see Ed and Karen come in. Jeff Collins was already at the table and he looked up surprised to see the two of them together. He said, "I went by your place and you weren't at home. You sure got out early. Did you get called out on a case?"

Ed just grinned and said, "Yeah, I was on a case. Can't talk about it, right now."

Jeff looked puzzled, "Okay, we'll talk later I guess. I am your partner, you know." Then he turned to Karen, "How are you, Karen. You run into Ed here?"

"I'm fine, Jeff.," She said and turned away avoiding him. She looked over at Maria, who waved and went to get the coffee she knew they wanted.

Maria came over and said, "Happy Halloween." She asked if they were eating and they ordered the Country Breakfasts.

Jeff said, "Wow, we're hungry this morning!" They both were smiling and he began to think maybe he was out of place. "What the hell is going on with you two?"

Together they answered, "Nothing." That made him even more curious.

Karen changed the subject, "Have you got your candy ready for tonight?"

Jeff answered, "I won't be at home. I'm sure we'll have to be on duty in case the Halloween vandals are at work."

Maria and Tony brought their breakfast platters over and Tony said, "I haven't seen you guys for a couple of days. What have you been up to?"

Ed looked at Karen and said, "Boy, you can't get lost in this town. You're gone one day here and it's like you've been put on the missing list."

Tony wasn't satisfied, he went on, "What's going on? You on a new case or something? Is it those two guys that were in here talking about Karen?"

Now they began to laugh hysterically. Everyone looked puzzled as if they missed the joke. Karen explained, "No, those two guys were here to see my artwork. Let us eat our breakfast and then I'll tell you all about it." At this point, Jeff was really feeling like the fifth wheel, the two old partners seemed to be shutting him out.

He stood up and said, "I'm going on to the station, I'll see you later." And he left without another word. The Distefanos went back to work. The place was filling up again.

Ed smiled at Karen and said, "We're never going to be able to keep this a secret, you know. I don't want to wait to get married. Do you think we can go to the courthouse today and get the license?"

"Okay, that sounds good but first I want you to take that wine bottle and get it dusted. Then I'll meet you at the courthouse. Let's plan to get married on Sunday after church, okay? "

"Well, I rather do it tomorrow but I guess I've waited this long, I can wait a few more days."

"I'll ask Maria to be my matron of honor, do you want Daniel to be your best man?"

"Yes, since he played cupid, it seems only right. Is it okay to tell everybody?"

"I guess so, you can't keep a secret around here anyway."

Suddenly to her surprise, Ed stood up and said, "Ladies and gentlemen, I'd like to make an announcement. I have asked this beautiful lady to marry me and she has accepted." Everybody cheered and applauded and Karen just sat there dumbfounded and beet red.

Ed pulled her to her feet and kissed her right in front of everybody. Then the place went wild. They were whistling, and cheering like they were at a football game.

Tony and Maria came over and hugged them both, whispering congratulations. They wanted to know when and Karen said, "Sunday after church if it's okay with the preacher. I want you to stand up with me, Maria. Can you do that?"

"Oh my, I'd be honored. I'll have to go shopping for a special dress."

"We'll go together. I'll need one, too."

Tony said, "Another excuse to go shopping. Maria never passes up a chance. Get used to it, Ed."

Ed said, "I'm going to ask Daniel to be my best man because he had a hand in this romance. If it wasn't for that, I'd ask you, Tony."

"That's okay, man… Want me to be the ring bearer?" More laughter! The next few minutes were spent shaking hands and accepting congratulations from people they didn't even know. They just happened to be eating there when Ed made his big announcement.

When they finally sat down, they decided to meet at the courthouse at one o'clock. Ed said, "I'll have to go to work after that but I'll see you this evening at your house, okay?"

He got up to go and leaned over and kissed her again. She said, "I never expected a shy guy like you to be so public. I'm still in shock."

He grinned and said, "You ain't seen nothin' yet, Baby." He turned and left like he was being chased.

Maria came over and sat down with Karen. She asked, "How long has this be going on?"

"It hasn't been going on. We've just always been friends. He and my Rich were such good friends, too. Ed was afraid to make a move until Daniel encouraged him. I just assumed he was a confirmed bachelor and we'd stay friends. I'm surely happy he finally told me because I've loved him for a long time."

Maria asked, "When do you want to go shopping?"

"I've got to get some other things done but we can plan to go tomorrow if it's okay. Sometime after you finish with the lunch crowd. Okay?"

"Great! I'll get back to work now, Tony's giving me dirty looks."

Karen sat there a few minutes, digesting the events of the last forty eight hours. She mentally went over the things she wanted to do today and decided to go to the grocery store first. "Got to get my candy for the trick or treaters." She thought, "Then maybe I can calm down and think straight."

She got back in her car and after she had her groceries, went home. She sat on the back porch awhile and talked to her animals. "We're going to have a man around the house soon, my little pets, won't that be nice?" She unlocked the door and went in to get their food. Then she went to the barn to get Candy saddled and went for a ride to clear her head. It was a beautiful, crisp morning, the sky was gray-blue and the sage was like a golden blanket reaching to the horizon and the line of deep green cedars that surrounded her land. She had planted the cedars as little tiny sprigs. Now they were sixteen feet tall. There was an occasional maple with gorgeous orange and red leaves. She was thinking. "I've got to paint this, today. It can't wait. I need to get it right now." So after Candy was back out in the field, Karen was in her studio working furiously, painting the picture of her morning ride. She worked for about two hours and then took a break. She got a cup of coffee and went back in the studio to sit and study the almost finished product. She decided it would need more work but not today.

It was still early but she wanted to fix something special for supper. Ed would be coming out this evening. She was in the kitchen when the phone rang. She hurried to answer, hoping it was Ed. There was a pause and then an ominous voice said, "You're still nosing around at Margies and I'm warning you to stop it!"

She asked, "Who is this? What are you watching me for?" There was a dial tone. She stood there, puzzled and disturbed. "I'll tell Ed when he gets here. Probably just some crank that is trying to scare me. He obviously doesn't know me very well."

She went back to the kitchen and her meal preparations. She fixed stuffed pork chops and scalloped potatoes. Then she got the salad ready and put everything in the fridge to have it ready to cook later. She made some apple dumplings with the apples that the Barrys had given her. While she was at it, she made some extra for the freezer.

The phone rang again and she answered with some trepidation. It was Daniel. He said, "Well, Ed called me and told me the news. I'm so happy for you both, and it's the best news I've heard in a long time. So have you called the preacher yet?"

She screamed, "Oh, my God, I have to go. I'm supposed to be meeting Ed at the courthouse right now. I'll talk to you later."

She rushed out of the house and into her car. She broke the speed limit getting to town and when she got to the courthouse saw Ed standing there. She pulled to the curb, got out and ran up to him breathless. She asked, "Have you been waiting long?"

He said, "About thirty minutes. I thought you'd stood me up." He was serious, she took his hand and told him she was sorry. The time got away from her and told him that there was no way she would stand him up.

They went in the courthouse and got the marriage license. The young lady who waited on them was a stranger to them and they were glad. No one was there to ask silly questions. It was strictly business. When they left the office, she stopped and kissed him. He looked embarrassed. He said, "Wow, you're getting to be downright brazen hussy. And I love it." Then he kissed her. When they went back out to their cars, they decided to go to the Café for lunch. Then they would go pick out the rings.

Since the lunch hour was over by now, the place didn't have many customers. They sat at their favorite table and Maria came over with their coffee. Ed told her they would have a couple of burgers, no fries. Karen had told him what she was fixing for supper so they wouldn't need to eat much. She told him about Daniel's call and that he reminded her to call Gary. She decided not to tell him about the other call yet. Tony brought their burgers over and sat down with them.

He said, "You'd better have a lot of candy, ready tonight. I'm bringing my gang out there. They finally got over the chicken pox."

Ed said, "I forgot that is tonight. I'll bet anything, I get called out. This town will look like a toilet paper city in the morning."

Karen said, "Maybe Jeff will take the calls."

He answered, "It will take both of us, if it is like last year. At least it won't start til after dark." When they were through eating, Ed paid the bill and they went to their cars. Karen got in and Ed leaned in the window to kiss her. He said, "Can I spend the night again?"

"I'd be disappointed if you didn't. We're adults, I don't see anything wrong with it, we've waited long enough. After all we have the license."

He said, "I'll have to go by my place and get some more clothes. Then I'll be out there."

"Okay, I'll see you then." He kissed her again and went to his car. She drove away feeling like she was the luckiest lady in the world.

When she got home, she was surprised to see she'd left the door open. The animals were on the porch as usual. When she went into the kitchen, she could tell someone had been there. There was an empty plate and soda can on the table. A note under the can said, "Thanks for lunch."

She went through the house and nothing was disturbed. She looked in all the closets and under the bed, in the pantry and the bathrooms. She went into her studio. Someone had made a big black X across the painting she had been working on. She thought about calling Ed but decided it could wait until he came out. She didn't want to ruin his day. She got her camera and photographed the table with the note and then took one of the painting. She left the table as it was and decided she would like to have the meal in the dining room any way.

She sat down at her desk and made some notes about what she needed to do before Sunday. The first thing right now, was to call the preacher. Christine answered the phone, because she had called the parsonage. "Hello, Christine, this is Karen Sutton. Is Gary at home by any chance?"

"No, he's making calls at the hospital right now. Do you want me to have him call you?"

"Yes, that will be fine. Ed Hawkins and I want Gary to marry us Sunday after church."

"Oh, what a surprise! That's just great. I'm so happy for you. I'm sure it will be okay but we'll need to do something special for your wedding. Are you going to have a reception?"

"I haven't even thought about anything like that. We just want to get married."

"Well, you just leave it to me. I'll get some ladies together and we'll have a small reception for you. Not much, just cake and punch. So don't worry about it at all. We will love doing it."

"That is so nice of you. I just never thought about it and I certainly don't want to be a lot of trouble."

"I'll bet you haven't told Ruth Barry yet, have you?"

"No, I haven't had a chance. We just decided yesterday and I haven't seen the Barrys since."

"I knew it, because if she knew she would have already been here planning. She thinks the world of you and she's going to be delighted. You must go tell her or she'll be disappointed."

"Okay, I'll do that as soon as I hang up. Thanks so much."

She decided to walk to the Barrys this time. She hadn't had time to walk lately. This time she locked the door as she left. The Barrys were out picking apples again and waved as she came up their drive. She went to them and said, "I've come to help you pick apples. You've got quite a crop here. I made some dumplings with mine this morning."

"You don't have to help. We'll go in and get something to drink. We don't see you often enough."

"No, I really want to help. I have something to tell you."

"Oh, about those men looking at your paintings? Is that what you want to tell us?"

"No, well, yes and no. They did like them but what I want to tell you is…I'm getting married."

"Married? Who to? When? What are you talking about?" Ruth was sputtering.

Joseph said, "Now, Ruth, if you'd be quiet, the girl might tell you."

Ruth giggled and Karen told them, "I'm marrying Ed Hawkins on Sunday after church."

Ruth hugged her and said what everyone was saying, "I'm so happy for you."

Joseph hugged her then and whispered, "Me, too."

They wouldn't hear of picking apples now, they had to go to the house and have a cold drink.

After she had visited for an hour or more, she walked back to the house. Ruth was already on the phone with Christine before she left. She was feeling so loved and happy she was afraid it might be a dream and she'd wake soon.

Chapter 68

Bill cut football practice a little short on this day because the kids all had parties to go to. He had stopped to get candy on the way home, too. Amy was going to a party at the church. Tom had plans with his friends since Bill hadn't kept the curfew as he had threatened. He wasn't sharing what they would be doing. Bill was afraid to ask but he figured one plan would include a large toilet tissue purchase. He fixed a light supper of sandwiches and chips, on paper plates to avoid dishwashing. He opened some sodas and called the kids to eat. They came in already dressed in their costumes.

Tom was a farmer, he was not going to do anything too drastic, just put on his overalls, a plaid flannel shirt and a filthy old cap. Amy was dressed in an old formal and had on a tiara. Bill said to Tom, "You look more like a red neck than a farmer."

Tom's reply was, "That's okay. All I care about is staying warm. It's getting cold out there."

Amy asked, "What do you think of my costume?"

Tom said, "Oh, we already know you're a princess."

Bill told her, "You look very pretty. I hope you have a good time. Do I need to take you to the church?"

"No, Dad, Sara's mom is going to take us, she's a chaperon so she'll bring me home, too."

"Okay, sounds like I've got the night off, except for the trick or treaters."

When Gary Oldham came home from his visitation chores, Christine was anxious to tell him about Karen and Ed's news. He smiled and said, "That is good news. They've been friends and co-workers for years. I need to call my secretary and tell her to make sure it's in the church bulletin. Do you think we need to order extra flowers?"

"I don't think Karen really wants a lot of fuss. They are having Maria Distefano and Daniel Carmody stand up with them. I forced the reception idea on her and when Ruth Barry heard, she was on the phone immediately. The reception is taken care of now. You won't need a big act this week because you'll have a wedding to perform. How do you like that?"

"I love it and I'm going to write a new sermon for the occasion. I'll use the one I've already done, later on."

When Karen got home from visiting the Barrys it was after four o'clock. She decided to call Melanie and tell her the news. When Melanie answered Karen said, "Hi there, it's Karen, how are you doing?" "I'm fine, Karen. How are you?"

"I called to tell some good news for a change. First, I'm going to have a gallery opening in Chicago in January and second, Ed and I are getting married on Sunday."

"Oh, my gosh. You can't mean it. When did this all come about? I mean I knew you were friends but I had no idea."

"I've always thought he didn't have any romantic ideas about me. He was such a confirmed bachelor. But he finally told me he had been in love with me for years but didn't think I had gotten over Rich. He said he even loved me when Rich was living, but they were good friends He wouldn't have done anything to spoil the friendship or our marriage."

"I wish I could be there. I'm going to hate missing it? Why are you doing it so fast?"

"There's no reason to wait and we're not getting any younger. Once we both knew we were in love, he proposed and I accepted. We got the license today. We're getting married after church and they are having a reception for us. Isn't that wonderful?"

"Oh, and soon you're going to have a gallery opening. That is so great. You deserve happiness, Karen. I'm so glad for you. I wanted to tell you my plans, too. I'm really thinking about applying to go to the Institute in the spring or the first of the year, if I can get in. I may be living in Chicago when you have your opening and I can help."

"That would be good. Let me know how that goes."

"I will and you send me pictures of the wedding, Okay?"

"Sure, I will. I'm going to hang up now and get supper on the table. I have to get ready for the trick or treaters. I'll bet you have parties to go to, don't you?"

"Yes, I do. It should be fun. We're going as Raggedy Ann and Andy. You call me soon, okay? I love you…and Ed, too."

"Bye, now, I love you, too, Melanie."

Chapter 69

Larry Sloan had started a new job on Monday. The convenience store where he had been working was hiring manager trainees and he applied and got the job. His only experience was in retail so it was natural for him to take a retail position. Mr. Regal had given him good references in spite of the way he had left. He had been a good employee until his drinking became worse about five years before. Now he had found a twelve-step program and was attending on a regular basis. It would have been to embarrassing to go to meetings in Dinsmore. He knew the people there had grown to hate him but he finally had to admit that it was his fault and that he did have a problem.

He had sent Pamela a letter with his mailing address and told her to mail him the papers when she applied for a divorce. He apologized for treating her so badly, but he just couldn't take Dinsmore any more. He said, he thought a lot of her but shouldn't have married her. She was much too young and should marry somebody who would treat her better. He told her that he was not drinking these days and that he was fine. He hoped she was fine, too.

Larry had been living in one room with a hot plate. He had done most of his eating at work when he was cashiering. Now he was going from store to store in his training and learning the operation. He was getting much better money and would get more when he completed the training, so he planned to get a decent apartment, soon. San Diego was beautiful and he loved the sunshine, especially in his Mustang with the top down.

He had made some friends at his meetings but wasn't revealing much about his past. Occasionally they would go out to eat before a meeting or go for coffee after, so he was trying to live like a normal human being.

Pamela Sloan had put in a full day at "The Regal Department Store" and was bone tired when she got to her apartment complex. Her room mate hadn't come in yet. On the way to her apartment, she stopped by the mailboxes. There were some bills, a letter from Jack Carter and one from Larry. She was shocked to see that he had written. She went and sat on a bench by the swimming pool and opened it. She was relieved to know that he was not going to give her any problem in the divorce proceedings. She was surprised that he wasn't drinking, if you could believe him. His apology seemed sincere and she agreed whole heartedly that they should not have married. No need to cry over spilt milk though. She would have to go see the lawyer tomorrow if he could see her on the lunch hour.

When she opened the lawyer's letter, it said the papers were ready whenever she wanted to pick them up. If she had found her husband, she could mail them to him with a stamped envelope and she would be divorced soon after that. She was very happy with that news.

There were little kids wandering around the apartment grounds in costumes. She realized, she had forgotten to get candy. She hurried back to her car and to the closest store to get some candy.

When she got back, her room mate, Leah, had come in. When she saw the candy, she said, "Oh, I'm glad you thought to get some. Did you see all those cute little kids out there?"

"Yes, I was ready to come in when I saw them and had to run to the store. I had forgotten all about it."

"What frozen dinners are we going to eat tonight? It's my turn to cook."

Pamela said, "You choose, I'm so tired and hungry, I could eat the box."

Chapter 70

Ed called Karen at five thirty and told her, "I just got things tied up here and I'm coming out there after I go to get some clothes. Do you need anything from town?"

"No, just come on, I'm keeping supper warm in the oven. I'm anxious to see you. When are you going to call this home? We are going to live here aren't we? I couldn't bear to live in town and leave my animals."

He sighed and said, "I didn't want to presume, but that will make me very happy. I've always liked your place. I'll sell mine and put the money in our joint account. How's that sound?"

"That sounds wonderful, now get onto your errands and come home. I've got lots of things to tell you."

"Okay, I'll be right there. Bye for now." She said, "Bye."

She had the back door open but the screen hooked. There was a knock on the door and three little ghosts were standing there with their bags, saying "Trick or Treat.." She went to give them their candy. They were just the start of many to come.

She went out to sit on the porch to wait for the kids and Ed. Jazz was happy to be having company but Callie was hiding under the chair. When Ed drove up she went to meet him and they kissed and hugged and then they kissed and hugged some more. He was holding a hanging bag with several changes of clothing.

She put the meal on the dining table while he hung up his clothes. Before they sat down, she put a bowl of candy out on the porch so they could eat undisturbed. Ed oohed and aahed over the meal. She was very pleased that he liked her cooking. They decided to forgo dessert, until later. He helped her clear the table and she put the dishes in the sink. She said, "Let's go out on the porch before it gets dark and cold. The kids are going to keep coming anyway. I'll take care of the dishes later."

He put his arm around her waist and they went out to meet all the little hob goblins. After a while a big ghost and a smaller witch with five even smaller ghosts came around the corner of the house. They all yelled, "Trick or treat!" It was Tony, Maria and their kids having a great time.

Ed and Karen were delighted when they recognized their voices and Ed asked, "Who's running the Café?"

Tony, the big ghost said, "Hey, we close that place when we have something important to do."

Maria, the witch sat down on the steps and said, "I don't know but I think working would be easier."

The kids were running around with Jazz and he was loving it. Karen said, "Sit down, Tony. Would either of you like a soda or something?"

Tony said, "No, we really need to go on and get this over with before dark, if possible."

Maria said, "Besides, Mama is at home dealing with the other kids coming to our house. She's tired after of day of these kids so we need to give her a break." Then she said, "Karen, want to meet at two tomorrow to go shopping?"

"That sounds good, we need to get that taken care of. We might need to get alterations done."

Tony said, "Not to worry about that. Mama can do that. Maria always has to have her things altered. Her butt is so close to the sidewalk." Maria smacked him on the back but she had to laugh, as did, all of them.

When they left, Jazz came up on the porch, looking sad because he didn't have anybody to play with. But it wasn't long before some more children were there holding out their bags to receive donations. It was ten o'clock before they stopped showing up. They went inside and left the door open so they would hear if more arrived.

Karen got the apple dumplings out and put a dollop of ice cream on them. She said, "Let's go into the den and watch Leno or Letterman."

"This looks so good but you're going to have to ease up on the rich food or I'll become a blimp in no time."

"Yes, I know, I will, too. Consider this a rare treat and I'll bring it down a notch after this." They went into the den and watched television for an hour. Then they both went to the bedroom. She decided to wait until morning to tell about the eerie events of the day. She had cleaned off the kitchen table earlier.

Chapter 71

Thursday morning at breakfast, she told Ed about the phone call, the note and the painting. He was livid at the thought that someone was threatening her. He asked, "Why didn't you call me?"

"I just thought we would deal with it without involving the department. We don't want the chief to know I've been snooping, do we?"

"Yeah, you're right about that. I'm glad you saved the plate and can in a bag. Can you print out a picture of that painting?"

"Yes, I'll do it while you're getting showered and ready for work. Will you be able to get the prints on the bottle and maybe the DNA on the top? Daniel said they only drank two glasses of it and the whole bottle was empty and in the trash. I'm surprised the investigators didn't find it."

"I was supposed to be the investigator, so it was my negligence. I was blown away by seeing her. I'm afraid I didn't do my job."

"I'm sorry. I can understand how you felt. But I mean, can you do all that now without the chief smelling a rat?"

"I'm really good at going around him. He's always been too quick to jump to conclusions so I've had to do this before, many times."

He went to shower and she hooked up her camera and started to print out the picture of the painting with a big X on it. After he was dressed in his khakis and white shirt with his yellow wind breaker. He came into the den where she was on the computer and kissed her for a long time before he went out to his car.

She walked out with him. She went to clean up the kitchen, left in a mess the night before. After her shower, she put on a black dress that buttoned down the front and the lingerie she would be wearing Sunday. She did not like trying on clothes but she definitely wanted something new for her wedding day. She put on black flats with black panty hose.

She went out to feed her animals before deciding to go to town and eat lunch at the Café. She hoped maybe Ed would be there too, but he never came in. After lunch, she waited for Maria.

When the lunch crowd was gone they went to shop for their dresses at The Regal. She was hoping they would find what they liked there, so they could get it over with quickly. Maria felt the same way, because she needed to get back to work.

Pamela Sloan called the lawyer, Jack Carter, on her morning break and the secretary put her right through. She told him about the letter from Larry. He told her again, as his letter said, the papers were all ready, she could read them and if they were right, she could mail them to Larry. His secretary would have the papers so all she had to do was get them from her. She told him she would be by on her lunch hour.

He said, "Good, if Larry gets them back quickly, you'll be out of this marriage in no time. Just let me know when you get them back." She thanked him and hung up the phone.

When she went back to her department, Karen and Maria walked over to her. Maria said, "Hi, Pamela, we need to get dresses for an informal wedding. Do you think you can help us?"

She said, "Sure, who's getting married."

"Have you met Karen Sutton? This is Karen and she's getting married to Ed Hawkins."

Karen said, "It's nice to meet you, Pamela. I hope you can find something suitable for me."

"I"m sure I can. Congratulations on your engagement. You were good friends with Margie weren't you?"

"Yes, and I'd give anything if she could be here for this. She always said Ed was in love with me, but I thought she was crazy."

"Well, she obviously knew what she was talking about. Let's see what we can find for you. Maria, you are going to need to get yours in the petite department but I can help you there, too."

Karen told her she would like something soft and kind of silky, with long sleeves. They went to look at the rack that had dresses suitable for the mother of the bride. Karen looked confused, because she saw the sign over the display that said "Mother of the Bride."

Pamela said, "Don't be insulted. These are just semi formal styles that are really suitable for anyone, any age, to wear to a wedding. It's just a place to start, so I can find out what styles you like."

It definitely was not as easy as Karen had hoped. She tried on what seemed like dozens. Pamela kept giving her more to try on, finally she gave her one that looked awful on the hanger, but when she put it on, it was perfect. It was mid calf length crepe material, it had a scoop neck and was sleeveless but it had a jacket with a jacquard woven design. The long sleeves on the jacket were finished with a ruffle and tied narrow ribbons that fluttered from the ruffles. It was a deep jade green, very feminine and she felt good in it. She also looked good in it.

They went on to find Maria something and she didn't have to try on as many as Karen. She found a purple two piece that she loved. The contrasting color of the two outfits was important and pleasing to the artist in Karen. They went to find shoes and Karen chose a silver metallic mule with 3 inch heels. She didn't want to be taller than Ed. Maria chose gold ones that were similar to Karen's.

Karen asked, "Pamela, I'm going to ask you to do something that you'll probably think ridiculous, but if I send Ed in here tomorrow. Could you help him? I mean just get him to a good salesperson that will guide him. You know what I'm wearing, so you could tell them if we will look good together."

"I don't think that's ridiculous at all. We'll want both of you to look your best, and I'll be glad to help."

"He may not even agree to come, but I'm going to try to get him to. I know he doesn't wear suits often and I'm sure what he has is well worn. By the way, I'd like to invite you to the wedding. It's to be right after church, Sunday. We didn't decide to get married until Monday so there was no time for invitations."

Maria said, "Yes, Pamela, you should come. They are having a reception afterwards and you could get acquainted with more people there. I understand you don't know a lot of folks. Larry didn't seem to take you out much."

Pamela finished her sentence, "And when he did, he made an ass of himself and embarrassed me. He's doing well now and so am I. I appreciate the invitation and I'll try to make it. I also want to thank you for coming to me for your outfits. You're both going to look swell."

They went to Karen's car and back to the Café. Karen let Maria out and told her, "I'll see you later. I'm glad I don't need alterations so Mama won't have to worry about me."

Maria told her, "Thanks for taking me, I enjoyed it." Karen headed for home, happy to have that chore finished. Now she could get back to her painting.

Chapter 72

Daniel had just finished going over a loan application for a customer who wanted to start a new business in Dinsmore. He was thinking about what he would do for the evening and decided to call Ed. The desk sergeant said "Ed is out on a call right now but I'll have him call you when I talk to him."

"Okay, thanks." He dialed the phone again and Karen answered, "Hello."

Daniel said, "Hi, Karen, I was trying to find Ed but he was out, so I thought I'd call you for a heads up, I want to take you two to the club tonight for dinner a little private celebration. Just the three of us, how does that sound to you?"

"It sounds wonderful, but I don't know how Ed will feel. He's not exactly the country club type, you know. You'd better check with him first but I'll keep my fingers crossed because I'd love to go."

"You just go ahead and plan to be ready at seven, I'll pick you both up and be your chauffeur. I'll talk him into it. I'll tell him that you want to go, that will be the closer. The man's crazy about you."

"The feeling is mutual, you know. But don't you use me to get your way. I don't want to marry an angry cop."

"No problem, I'll see you at seven. Bye for now."

"Okay. Bye."

She went to her closet to see what she was going to wear and checked on Ed's to see if he had anything suitable. Surprised, she saw that he had brought the outfit he had worn Sunday. "That will do very well," she thought. "I hope he'll wear a better suit for the wedding but if he doesn't, it's okay. I'm not interested in his dress habits, anyway."

Pamela had gone to the lawyer's office and picked up the divorce papers on her lunch hour and mailed them at the post office on her way back to work. She hadn't had time to eat so she was already starving at three o'clock. She was feeling good after her big sale to Karen and Maria. When she took her break, she called Leah at her counter. She said, "I feel like celebrating tonight, I got my divorce papers in the mail and I made a big sale. So I want to take you and me to the country club tonight, treats on me."

"Oh, I don't know if I have anything to wear but I've always wanted to go there. I never dated anybody that rich, unfortunately."

"I still have Larry's membership, he put me on his list so we're in like flint. If you get home before me, go ahead and get ready. I'll want to shower before we go. Plan to leave about seven thirty. Got to go, Rebecca's coming my way. Bye."

Ed called Daniel about four and Daniel told him the plan. He objected for a few minutes but Daniel told him, "Listen here, your fiancee wants to go, I want to celebrate and you're just going to have to put up with us for one night."

Ed said, "Okay, okay, you have twisted my arm enough. Karen already knows, I take it."

"Yes, I called her so she'd know not to cook and to get done up for the big evening."

"You're scaring me to death, now. I've never been to that place unless it was police work. I'm kind of uncouth, you know. I may embarrass you and Karen."

"We'll just have to take our chances. I'll be picking you both up at her place at seven. Be there!"

"Okay, see you then." He hung up the phone, shaking his head in disgust.

Jeff asked, "What's the matter?" Ed told him the plans for his evening. Jeff began to howl with laughter.

Ed yelled, "It's not that damn funny." Then Jeff began to cluck like a chicken. Ed faked a left hook at him and said, "I am not hen pecked." Everybody in the department joined Jeff in clucking.

Ed just got his coat and left the building.

As soon as he was gone. Jeff said, "How are we coming on the wedding gift? Have we got enough money to go shopping?" Having heard all the noise, the chief, Bradley Stone, stepped out of his office and said, "Who do I pay? I want to be in on this."

Cameron spoke up, "I'm taking up the funds, chief. We want to buy them a golf cart. They can use it out on the farm and Ed loves to play golf."

The chief said, "That's a great idea, here's a hundred bucks, hope you can raise enough. There are a lot of good used ones, so check that out. Anyway, if you come up short, let me know. Maybe I can raise a little more."

He went back in his office and they all stood there in shock. Jeff said, quietly, "The old boy does have a heart, after all. Let's go shopping tomorrow. We don't have much time. They're getting married on Sunday and I want to drive them away in the golf cart. We need to get it, decorate it and then hide it until Sunday."

227

One of the patrolmen in the back of the room said, "I know right where we can get a good one. I may be able to get him to give us a special deal."

Jeff replied, "Then you are definitely going shopping with me tomorrow." Ed had already invited all of them to the wedding. They were totally surprised to hear the old bachelor was really going to get married.

When Ed left work, he went by the florist and got a dozen yellow roses in a blue vase. He went "home" to Karen. She had just climbed out of the shower when he came in the door with the flowers. She was wrapped in a towel and he had a big grin on his face as he handed her the flowers. She began to cry. He said, "My God, what's the matter. You don't like them?"

She was blubbering and said, "No, I love them and I love you for getting them for me. I'm just so happy! That's why I'm crying."

"Well, you could'a fooled me. I thought I'd done something wrong."

She put the flowers on the dining room table and went to him. She hugged him and kissed him for a long time.

He said, "You'd better quit that or I'll have to take that towel off and we won't be able to get ready for our date."

She said, "We've got plenty of time." She took his hand and pulled him into the bedroom saying, "I have missed you today."

When Daniel drove up to the door of the country club, the valet opened the doors for them and he gave him the keys. They went in then and the maitre de said, "Good evening, Mr. Carmody, it's nice to see you."

Daniel said, "Hello, nice to see you too, I think you have a table for me and my guests."

"Yes, right this way." He led them to the table and seated Karen. He turned and snapped his fingers and a waiter appeared with a bottle of champagne in a cooler. He opened the bottle and poured them each a glass of the bubbly.

He asked, "Will there be anything else, Mr. Carmody?"

"Not right now, we'll need to read the menus for a few minutes. Thank you."

After he removed himself, Daniel said, "A toast to the happy couple!" They clicked glasses and sipped their champagne while they looked at the menus.

Ed said, "You are a VIP here, huh? I thought they were going to kiss your ring."

Karen poked him in the ribs and Daniel said, "Oh, they just go out of their way when they know the cops are in the house." Then he added, "I'd like to order for all of us if you don't mind. I know what's best on the menu and I want you to have it. Okay?" They both agreed, since they had no idea what to order.

They had another glass of champagne after he ordered. Daniel was facing the entrance and he said, "There's Pamela Sloan. Gosh, she looks so different, I can't believe it. She has a new position at the Regal now."

Karen said, "I know, she helped me and Maria with our shopping today. She's very nice and very knowledgeable about fashion."

Ed said, "Well, I can't believe that, when I saw her at the football game, she looked like a streetwalker."

Karen poked him again and Daniel just shook his head. He said, "Ed, you've just got to learn to say what you think." Ed became very quiet and Daniel went on, "She's just a kid. She makes me think of my daughter. I'd bet money that Larry wanted her to dress like that. You know what a sleazy guy he was. Now that he's out of the picture and she has her new job, she can be herself."

When Pamela saw them, she came over and said, "Hello, Daniel. Hi there, Karen. How are you all this evening? I'd like you to meet my room mate, Leah Oliver."

They all said, "Hello, it's nice to meet you."

Karen said, "Pamela, I'd like you to meet my future husband, Ed Hawkins."

Ed and Daniel had already stood up when the girls walked up. Ed shook each of the girl's hands.

Karen went on, "This is the man I told you would be in tomorrow to shop for a suitable outfit for our wedding. So now that you've met him, you'll recognize him tomorrow."

Ed looked at her like she'd lost her mind but didn't say a word. For once, he was speechless.

Pamela said, "It was so nice to see all of you and I'll be looking for you tomorrow, Mr. Hawkins."

They went to their table and both of them had drinks with umbrellas in them waiting when they sat down. Karen said, "They are so cute. Some girls would be afraid to come here alone. Well, I mean some of us old fashioned girls."

Ed answered, "Yes, I know that but I want to know something else." He leaned over to Karen, and grumbling he said, "What's this about me going shopping? A girl is going to wait on me?"

"No, she's just going to advise the clerk who does wait on you. I just want you to look your best on Sunday. It's just this once and I'll never ask you to shop again. I promise."

"And I told the guys at the department that I wasn't hen pecked." Ed was still mumbling.

Karen looked surprised and asked, "What is heaven's name, are you talking about?"

She sounded upset and he said, "Oh, it's nothing, you know how the guys like to kid around. I said something about pleasing you, and they all started clucking like a bunch of damn fool chickens."

Karen and Daniel both laughed until they cried. Ed just sat there looking at them like they were crazy. Then he began to laugh, too.

The waiter brought them each a shrimp cocktail and when they had finished that there was a garden salad. Before the salad was gone, he brought filet mignons, with twice-baked potatoes and a vegetable medley.

There wasn't much conversation while they ate, other than an occasional, "This is so good."

Karen groaned when he brought some slices of cheesecake covered with strawberries and of course the coffee came with it. She said, "Daniel, we don't deserve such a great evening but I'm surely glad you invited us. It has been grand."

He said, "Oh, it's not over yet."

They had just finished their dessert and were on a second cup of coffee when a violinist appeared and played "Claire de lune" because Karen had mentioned it was one of her favorites. Then he played, "Send in the Clowns." Daniel said, "That one was for Ed."

Ed and Karen were both visibly embarrassed but they enjoyed it, all the same. The three of them discussed the plans for Sunday and when Daniel got up, the happy couple did, too.

Once outside, the valet brought the Lexus and they were back at home before eleven. Karen invited Daniel in but he declined saying, "Workday tomorrow, got to get my beauty sleep. I'll probably see you at the game tomorrow night. It's in Lexington this week. Call me if you want to go together."

When they went in the house, they went to bed and made love for the second time that day. They were sound asleep when they were waked up by Jazz barking loudly on the back porch. Ed got up, grabbed his gun from the holster hanging on the door knob. He went to the back without turning on the lights.

A dark car was backing out of the driveway and by the time he got out of the house it was gone from sight. He could hear the gears shift and could tell from the sound that it was a souped up engine. When he went in Karen was warming a cup of coffee in the microwave. He said, "Aren't you sleepy?"

I won't be able to settle down now, this is beginning to worry me, not really worry, I guess. More like pissing me off."

"Now, that sounds more like the old Karen."

He began to warm himself a cup of coffee, too. He said, "I wanted to tell you what I did today any way. Just didn't have time with all that was going on."

She said, "Tell me what?"

"I boxed up all that stuff that you had collected at Margie's and shipped it off to a friend of mine in the FBI. He can run the tests and the fingerprints check much easier than I can. He knows about the chief's feelings so he'll keep it quiet until I call him. It might take a while but there's really no hurry. I don't think we've got a serial killer here."

She said, "You are so smart. It'll be interesting to see what they come up with. Then she asked, "Got any idea who that was outside? Somebody just turning around? I hope."

"It might have been just that, but would Jazz bark at a car. I think he must have been out of the car for Jazz to bark like that."

"Yeah, he probably woke Jazz up and scared him. He scared Jazz, I mean. He never barks unless he's playing."

"It was probably a kid to get scared off that easy. He was driving a souped up car. You could hear a mile away."

"Maybe but you know, somebody sure doesn't want me checking on Margie's apartment."

"Yes, I know and that does worry me but I hope you'll be careful and for Pete's sakes don't leave the door unlocked after this."

"Okay, let's go back to bed. You need to get your beauty sleep. Be time to go to work before you know it."

Chapter 73

It was Friday, always a big day for the Wallaces. They were up early to get to school because the game was out of town this time. They had to take a change of clothes to school with them in order to leave from there. Tom and Bill would be going on the bus with the team. Amy and the other cheer leaders would go on the bus with the band. They just had some toast and orange juice and got in the truck. Bill let the kids out and went to park around in back of the school. He went to his office and got on the computer to print out some plays he had worked on all week.

His phone rang and it was Janet calling from the hospital. She said, "I was just wondering if you were coming up this weekend. I really enjoyed your visit last week."

He answered, "Yes, we are planning on it. I know you must miss the kids." There was a long pause and Bill said, "Are you still there?"

She was almost whispering, "Bill, I miss you, too. I'm so sorry about what I did to you. I didn't want to mention it in front of the kids, when you were here."

He said, "Oh, I probably deserved it, I wasn't exactly the kind of husband you deserve."

She didn't try to deny that remark but went on, "I hope you can forgive me."

"I'm just glad you're getting better and when you come home, we'll get some family counseling and get things right again. Okay?"

"That sounds good. I'll do it this time. I've got to go now. My times up. See you Sunday."

He said, "See Ya." And hung up the phone. He thought, "God help me, I don't know if I can do this again." He just sat there trying to figure out what he was going to do. "What can I do that won't destroy all of us." He was asking himself. Then it was time for his first class.

He was giving a test on the circumstances of the witch trials in Salem. He thought, "This may get me fired but the kids loved reading about it and really got into comparing it to the Civil Rights era and lynching in the south. It made them use their minds and he felt that was what a teacher should do. Make them think, that is.

Chapter 74

Daniel had a meeting first thing Friday morning with the Mayor of Dinsmore and a committee that was planning the Christmas parade. There were a dozen business owners on the committee. Today they were to divide up into teams. Each team was supposed to draft some more citizens to be on each team. Mayor Clint Baker chaired the meeting. It was very informal. Everybody was getting coffee and visiting with each other. The mayor called the meeting to order and they all sat down. He said, "I am going to name our teams and their duties today. You will have co-chairpersons on each team and each team will be responsible for getting more team members from the community."

He began to call out the names…"Tony and Maria. You will be in charge of publicity.

Rebecca Magee and Pamela Sloan will be in charge of the beauty contest.

Daniel Carmody, you and Grant Cullen will be in charge of the floats." Grant owned the local drugstore. "Marty Thompson and Rachel Brent you will be on the street decoration's committee." Marty managed the Wal Mart and Rachel was the local florist. "Todd Wood and Jeb Morris will be in charge of concession stands." Todd managed Mc Donalds and Jeb managed Wendys. "Sam Catron and Jane Lewis you will be in charge of the craft booths." Sam owned the downtown gas station and Jane had a beauty shop. "My wife Lynn and I will be coordinators and help out wherever we are needed. Now, do we have any questions?"

There was only one question. Tony asked, "When will we meet again and do we have a budget for each committee?"

The mayor answered, "The next meeting will be two weeks from now. You should have selected your complete teams by then. I will meet with each team. We will decide what kind of money the team will need to complete their task. In the meantime you each should meet with your team and get a handle on what you plan and how much it will cost. In other words you need a budget to present to the city council and the chamber of commerce." He didn't waste words, "If that is all, this meeting is closed."

Tony went over to Daniel and said, "Wow, that was short and sweet. You going to the game tonight?"

"Yes, I think so. I'm not sure I know how to get there but I'll find out and see how the rest of the day goes. I'm going to get back to work now, since we got through so quickly. I've got several things that need to be wrapped up before the weekend."

"Yeah, I need to get back and give Maria a break, too. See you later."

Chapter 75

Karen had the coffee made when Ed came out dressed for work. He was running late, but he sat down to drink a cup with her. He said, "I don't have time to eat but why don't you meet me at the Café about nine thirty? We'll have breakfast then."

Karen said, "You're spoiling me. I love it and I love you, so much. Why did we wait so long to do this?"

He said, "Are you going to still feel that way when I retire and I'm hanging around all day?"

She said, "No problem, you can help me with my art career if it pans out. We'll go to Chicago and San Diego and anywhere we wish."

"Hey, you've got it all worked out, haven't you?"

"Yeah, I'm always thinkin' and I'm thinkin' you'd better get to work or the chief will have you retiring early."

He got up and came around to her side of the table, he turned her chin up and kissed her as he said, "See you at nine thirty." She went to the porch with him and waved as he left. Then she fed the animals and sat down on the steps to have a little talk with them. They wagged and purred and she talked, "Let's go out and see how Candy is today." They all walked out to the barn.

When Ed got to work, the place was near empty. He went back out to the desk sergeant and asked, "Where the hell is everybody? Was there some kind of disaster or something?"

Sarg said, "No, I guess they're just out patrolling or trolling this morning. A couple of them said they had to run an errand for the chief, another said we were out of coffee and went to Wal Mart. I don't know where the rest went."

"Okay, I'm going back and do some paper work and then I'm going to meet Karen. I have a feeling I'm going to have to buy a suit today. I don't wear suits but I'm going to buy one today."

The sarg laughed and said, "It's crazy what a man will do for love." Ed pretended he didn't hear him and went back to his desk.

Tony and Maria had a busy morning at the Café. The weather was getting colder and more farmers were coming into town to loaf around, drinking coffee. Some of them did eat but most just drank coffee. Tony had to take off to go to the parade meeting and that left Maria alone. She managed okay but he wished she had called Jennie to come in and help her. Jennie Brown was their part time help. When her children were in school, they could call on her anytime. Fridays were always busy. A lot of people got paid and liked to eat out. In football season they closed early on Friday evening because Tony wouldn't think of missing a game. They would close even earlier today because the game was out of town. They had a baby sitter coming so they could take Mama but leave the children at home.

Karen came in a little after nine and saw Ed wasn't there yet so she sat at the counter. She said, "Where's Tony?"

Maria brought her a cup of coffee and said, "Tony had to go to a parade committee meeting."

Karen said, "It doesn't seem possible that it's that time already."

"Yeah, but it is. The mayor told me that he's making me and Tony do the publicity. You want to help us?"

"They'll probably have me decorating or painting something but I'll be glad to help wherever I can."

"Well, we'll probably be asking for help. Publicity is a pretty big job."

"Maria, the funniest thing happened to me awhile ago. I went by the cemetery to put a couple of roses on Margie's grave. There was a fresh pink rose there. Daniel had told me that every time he went there was always a fresh pink rose there. What does that make you think?"

"Oh, I don't know. Maybe she had a secret admirer or another boyfriend."

"Yeah, but we had lunch every Saturday for years and she never mentioned anyone."

"I said, secret, you know, I mean she never told you or anyone else."

The door opened and Ed came in. He came up behind her and put his arms around her and kissed her on the neck. She said, "I was afraid you got tied up and couldn't make it."

"No, I told the chief I had some things I needed to do and he said to take my time. He may be suffering from a fatal illness."

"You are so mean. Even when he's trying to be nice to you."

"Come on back here to my table and let's get Tony to cook us an omelet and some biscuits. "Okay, where's Tony?"

Maria told him, "Tony's not here but omelet and biscuits are coming up. Here's your coffee." They went to the back and sat down.

Karen said, "So I hope you're going to go to the Regal and get a new suit."

"I already knew that was coming. I will go but I won't like it. Don't you want to come with me?"

"No, I want to be surprised when you get dressed on Sunday. I know you'll be handsome no matter what. I just want Sunday to be special and we'll get somebody to take pictures with my digital so we can print them out."

"Honey, I am so glad that you're marrying me. I'm very glad we're doing it at church but I will be so glad when we are married and can just enjoy being together all the time. You know 'til death do us part."

Maria brought the omelets over to the table and went back to get the coffee pot just as Tony came in the door. He said, "What did you do? Run everybody off except Karen and Ed?"

She said, "Nobody would stay when they found out you weren't here. Doesn't that make you feel special?"

He said, "Well, we may as well enjoy the break, it's Friday and the lunch crowd will be a killer. Jennie is coming in at eleven."

She said, "Good." As she poured the coffee and sat down with her own cup. "Now tell me about this wedding, what took you so long? And now you're in a big hurry."

Ed said, "Once I make up my mind, there's no way I'm waiting, she might change hers."

"Did Karen tell you about what happened at the cemetery?"

Karen cringed, and said, "No, I didn't tell him. Why don't you?"

She did and Ed just shrugged his shoulders. He said, "Very interesting but so what? Somebody feels bad about her dying. A lot of us feel bad about her death."

Two customers came in and Maria went back to work. Ed said quietly, "I really do think that rose thing is strange but I didn't want to let onto her. You know Tony will tell everyone he sees. I might start making a run by there every once in awhile and see what I can see."

They ate their omelets and then Ed said, "I've got to go buy a suit. I'll see you later, Love."

"Okay, I'll be waiting. Don't forget the game tonight is in Lexington so we'll need to leave early."

"I'll be home in plenty of time. Let's just eat sandwiches tonight."

"Okay, see you then." Karen went home to work on the painting with the X on it and decide what she would start next. Talking about Christmas parades had her realizing she needed to paint a lot more in order to have enough paintings by January.

When Ed walked into the Women's Department, Pamela went to meet him. "Hi, Mr. Hawkins, are you here to get your suit?"

"Yes, are you going to take me to the man with the plan?"

"Yes, Sam Brown is very knowledgeable and will help you. Come on, I'll introduce you. You probably know him anyway."

"Why has he been in trouble with the law? I'm just kidding, I guess I do know him. I know of most people in town."

"I keep forgetting you're a policeman. What should I call you?"

"I'm a detective but we don't have to be formal. Ed will do just fine. But I do need to ask you something. I want to get in touch with Larry to ask him some questions. He's not in trouble or anything. I just want to talk to him. Do you know how to reach him?"

"Yes, he sent me his address and I'll get it for you before you leave. Here we are. Sam, this is Detective Hawkins and he needs a suit. He's getting married on Sunday. I promised him that you would take good care of him."

Sam stuck out his hand, Ed shook it and said, "Okay, let's get this over with."

Chapter 76

When Ed had come home that evening, he had a suit in a black garment bag. Karen met him at the door and gave him a big kiss. She was already dressed for the game in jeans and sweatshirt. She had her heavy coat and a blanket on the kitchen chair. She reached for the bag and said, "Oh, good, you got your suit. May I see it?"

Ed held it away from her and said, "Oh, no you don't, you can't see it until Sunday. You wanted to be surprised."

He went to the bedroom to hang his new suit in the closet and get ready to go to the game.

He called to Karen, "Daniel is picking us up to go with him. I hope that's okay with you."

She replied, "Sure, he's a good driver. We can sit in the back and make out."

"Woman, you are becoming downright lecherous and I love it." He got into his jeans and a flannel shirt and boots. He got a heavy coat out and carried it to the kitchen. They sat down and had a ham and cheese sandwich with a beer.

He said, "Pamela was a big help today. You know she's really a sweet kid. She gave me Larry's address so I can get in touch with him by mail. She says he's quit drinking, that's according to him, and he has a new job."

"Why do you want to contact him?"

"I want to get his fingerprints to run on the computer when I get the information back from the FBI. I'll get Daniel's and Bill's, too. I need to compare them all. We already have Daniel's story but we need to find out what Bill was doing that night. Just need to cover all the bases."

"Yes, that's a good idea. We also have to find out who Janet's private detective was."

"We can ask Bill when we interview him. Rather you can ask him, because you will have to do the interview. We still can't let the chief get wind of this."

They heard Daniel honking his horn and grabbed their coats, locked up and got in the back seat. Ed said, "To the game, James."

There was a huge crowd at the football game. Daniel was glad that Karen and Ed had agreed to ride with him. They always got the good seats. There was no score for a long time and then the Lexington team fumbled the ball and Dinsmore recovered to score soon after. Lexington came right back and scored. The crowd roared. Dinsmore didn't make much yardage on their next possession so when the Lexington passed the ball, the receiver ran sixty yards for another touchdown. They didn't make the point after though because Dinsmore blocked their kick. Dinsmore's team was behind by one touchdown in the last minute of the fourth quarter. Tom Wallace threw a "Hail Mary" pass and his receiver caught it. He made it to the end zone still on his feet. The kicker made the point after and the crowd went absolutely wild. They were yelling Tom, Tom and the team was carrying Tom off the field on their shoulders. Then some of them picked up Bill. He was beaming with pride and when they put him down, Amy ran to hug him and all the cheerleaders joined her. The Wallace family would be celebrating tonight.

Pamela had been in the apartment fixing supper when Leah came home. Leah said, "How nice. It's great to have supper waiting. I had to go to the drug store on the way home. The druggist wanted to know if I was going to the game. Do you think we could go?"

"I think that's a great idea. I thought it was going to be a boring night. Dinsmore has a great team and their games are exciting. Besides it's a perfect night for football. Not too cold, just right. Let's eat and then we'll change and get going. The games in Lexington, you know."

"Okay, what can I do to help with supper?"

"It's almost ready. You can do the salad while I finish up." After they ate, they changed to warm, casual clothes and went to Pamela's car. Her car was the newest of the two. They pulled onto the interstate and just as they started to enter the right lane, a white Toyota veered from the left and sideswiped Pamela's little Neon sending her into the ditch. The Neon came to a halt when it hit the embankment.

The girls both sat there in a daze for a few seconds. Pamela was crying and asked, "Leah are you okay."

"Yes, I'm fine. What's wrong with you?"

"I'm not hurt but this is the pits. Let's get out of here before this thing blows up or something."

Leah started laughing hysterically, "I don't think it's going to blow up." They both started laughing as they climbed out. The driver of the other car came down into the ditch.

He thought they were crying. He started saying, "I'm so sorry, I thought

I was past you when I started to pull over."

Pamela screamed, "Well, obviously you weren't!"

He asked, "Are you all right?"

Leah said, "We're fine, just pissed at you. With all that road out there you don't expect anybody to run you off into a ditch."

A highway patrol car pulled up and parked with his blue lights flashing. He came down to the group and asked, "What happened here? Is anybody injured?"

Pamela said, "No, we're fine. Just upset. Sure ruined my plans for the evening."

"Well, I'll go call for a wrecker and then you can give me the details."

The Toyota driver said, "No doubt about it, Sir. It was my fault. I misjudged and pulled over too soon and sideswiped her. My car doesn't need towing. It's fine. Just a little dent."

The patrolman said, "Well, this one will need towing with that front end smashed and the radiator steaming."

When the tow truck pulled up, they had Pamela's car out quickly and told her they would have it at the Fast Gas station. The patrolman said, "I'll take you girls into town." To the other driver he said, "You follow us. Don't try to run because I've got your tag. Let me see your license." After he had written the information on a ticket, he took the arm of each girl and escorted them to his patrol car.

When they got to the station, they exchanged names and numbers and took turns calling their insurance companies. The young man apologized again and said, "I'm Nathan Morris, my dad is the manager of Wendy's and I go to college in Easton. I live here though and won't be hard to find if I can do anything to help."

The trooper came over to them and handed Nathan his ticket. He asked if the girls wanted a ride home. Nathan spoke up and said, "I'll take them if they're not afraid to ride with me."

Pamela thanked the patrolman for all his help and asked his name. "I'm Stuart Brent. My wife is the florist in town. I'm sorry we all had to meet this way. Just give me a call if I can help. I will be seeing you in court, young man."

He got in his car and went back toward the interstate. They were getting ready to leave after Pamela made arrangements for her car. It would remain at the station until the adjuster could come by. Then he would send it for repairs. Jeff Collins pulled into the station in an unmarked police car. He got out and went over to the little group. He said, "Hi, Nathan, what's going on here?"

Nathan told him, "Well, I screwed up and ran these pretty girls off into a ditch."

"That was a stupid thing to do. Is everybody okay?"

Pamela said, "We're not hurt. Just my feelings because my little Neon is a wreck and now we've missed the football game."

Nathan said, "That's where I was going, too. We can still make most of the game if you want to go with me."

Jeff interrupted, "Hey, I'm off duty now. I wanted to see the game, too. Climb in my car. I'll put the old blue light on and we'll be there in no time."

Pamela asked, "Won't you get in trouble for doing that? I mean it's not an emergency."

"Who's going to tell? We'll be there before anyone knows. We'll have to do it if we're to make it before halftime."

Nathan turned to the girls and asked, "Well, what do you think? Go to the game or go home?"

The girls both smiled and Leah said, "What the hell, let's go, Pamela. We need a little excitement."

They didn't take the interstate because they knew Stuart Brent was out there patrolling. They went on the two lane state highway. They were there in thirty minutes. It was half time, the attendants had left the ticket stand so they didn't even have to pay. They went in and found some seats quickly. Jeff asked, "Do you girls want something from the concession stand? I need a cold drink"

Pamela said, "I'd rather have black coffee, it's cold up here." Leah said, "Me, too."

Jeff said, "Come on, Nathan, you can help me get it. The game's going to start up again, soon."

On their way to the stand, Jeff said, "That's a hell of a way to meet girls, Nathan. They're cute, too."

Nathan said, "Yeah, I like that Leah. She a looker, of course Pamela is too."

Jeff said, "Well, I'm glad because I like Pamela. I think she's still married though. I hear she's getting a divorce."

"I can see the gossip mill is still at work in Dinsmore," Nathan replied, "I hope I can get Leah's number later."

As they worked their way through the concession stand line, Jeff said,

"Well, if you get one you'll have the other, I think they are room mates and they both work at the Regal."

Nathan looked surprised, "You keep tabs on everybody, don't you? Is that part of your job or are you just nosy?"

"Nah., I get all my information from Tony Distefano, he's the mouth of Dinsmore. I'm telling you the truth. Don't ever say anything to Tony, unless you want it to be common knowledge."

They got their drinks and some popcorn and headed back to the stands and the girls.

Ed, Karen and Daniel were sitting up higher in the stands near the fifty-yard line. Ed leaned over to Karen and said, "Look down there. Jeff is with Pamela Sloan and some other couple. I thought she was still married."

Daniel looked and said, "Yes, she is, but she has filed for divorce."

Karen said, "The other boy is Nathan Morris, I don't know the girl. Do you, Daniel?"

"No, I don't recognize her either, maybe she goes to college with Nathan. I do know him, nice kid."

Ed said, "You two don't have very good memories. We just met the other girl at the club last night. I don't remember her name though. She's Pamela's room mate. Remember?"

They had lost interest because the teams were back on the field. When the game was over Jeff and his group got out to his car quickly. He said, "I saw Ed Hawkins in the stands and if he sees me in this patrol car, he'll have my ass. Let's get out of here pronto."

Nathan said, "I thought you said it was okay."

"I said it was okay but I should have added, if I don't get caught by my partner." They went back to Dinsmore the same way they came and he dropped them all at the station. Nathan had said that he would take the girls home so Jeff wouldn't be seen with all of them in the car. Pamela had invited them to the apartment for a drink. She emphasized soft drink and Jeff said, "I'll see you there."

When they were all assembled in the apartment, they joked about their exciting evening. They watched the Late, Late Show and during a commercial, Jeff said, "Pamela, I've got a wedding to go to on Sunday. It's after the church service. Would you like to go with me?"

"Hey, I'd like that. I sold all of them their wedding clothes, except Daniel. I imagine he had plenty of appropriate suits to wear. Karen invited me to come."

Nathan said, "Hey, that's my church. Is the congregation going to stay for the wedding?"

"I guess those who want to, will stay." Jeff answered, "Why?"

Nathan said, "I thought maybe Leah would like to go with me."

Jeff said, "That sounds like a plan. How about it, Leah?" She answered, "Sure, I'd love to go."

Jeff said, "Good deal. I'll pick you all up in my real car on Sunday at ten thirty if that's okay. It's a four-door sedan so there's plenty of room. Let me tell you all something. You've got to promise not to breathe a word to anyone."

They all said, "What?" He told them of the plan the police department had to give them a golf cart for a wedding gift.

He said, "We found a good deal on a used one. But that's not all. When they come out of the reception, I'm going to drive them home in it. We've got it all decorated with ribbons and tin cans and the works. Ed Hawkins is going to have a fit."

Pamela said, "Yeah, he is a little straight laced. I'll bet you're right about him having a fit. He'll probably be a good sport though. He seems like a nice man and Karen is just great. What's the story on them anyway?"

Forgetting the television show, Jeff spent the next hour telling them about Ed and Karen's history. When he had finished his opus, Nathan said, "Hey, man, I need to get back to my car and home. My folks are going to be wondering where I've gone and if they heard I was in a wreck, they'll be frantic."

"Okay, we'll go, it's getting late anyway and these girls have to work tomorrow. I'll see you Sunday. I really enjoyed the evening, thanks for the drinks."

Pamela said, "You're welcome, we enjoyed it, too. You are the first guests we've had in our little apartment."

Leah said, "Yeah, and thanks for the exciting ride. I don't think I want to do that again. Don't let him turn on that light on the way to your car, Nathan. Somebody might tell your folks, you've been arrested."

Chapter 77

When Daniel got off the interstate to go to Karen's house, they met Jeff in the patrol car turning into the Fast Gas station. Ed said, "What is that boy up to now? Isn't that the kid that was at the game?"

Karen said, "Yes, he must have given him a ride."

The three of them had stopped at an all-night truck stop and had coffee and hot apple pie, ala mode. They had talked for an hour or more. Nobody had to work on Saturday so there was no hurry to get home. Besides it was fun to watch everybody coming in from the game. Even the Dinsmore school busses stopped and sent the restaurant help scrambling to wait on all of them. Of course they were all very noisy but really quite well behaved. They had several chaperons to see to that.

Coach Wallace was with the team. When he passed by their booth, Ed and Daniel both stood up and shook hands with Bill and Tom and some of the other team members that stopped with them. When the two men sat back down, Karen said, "They're going to start calling us the three musketeers. Ed, we need to find Daniel a girlfriend, got anybody that we can hook up with him?"

Daniel snorted, "Hey, I'm not ready for another girlfriend and when I am, I'll do my own hooking. Well, that's not a very good thing to say. I'll find my own girlfriend, thank you, Ms Karen. When did you become a yenta?"

"I'm just looking out for my friend, but if that's the way you want it, I'll butt out." She pretended to be hurt.

Ed said, "That reminds me, have you ever met the lady that's the new manager at the Regal?

Her name is Rebecca Magee, and she's a looker. You bringing anybody to church Sunday?"

"No, I'm going to come alone, thank you. Boy, have you two formed a new dating bureau? Yes, I do know who Rebecca Magee is, and she is a looker, but she's never applied for a loan so I haven't met her. I did see her at the parade committee meeting though, just didn't hang around long enough to meet anybody. I had to get back to the bank. Fridays are always very busy."

Karen said, "I really don't know her but I did talk to her at last weeks game for a minute and she is very nice and very good looking." Daniel just shook his head and changed the conversation quickly.

When the Wallaces got back to Dinsmore and home, they were all exhausted. Before they went to bed, Bill told Amy and Tom about talking to their mother that morning. He told them that he had promised they would visit on Sunday and he asked, "Is that all right with you kids?" They both said, "Yes."

Amy added, "Mother needs us to support her and we need her to get well so she can come back home."

Bill said, "You're right. You go on to bed now and I'll see you in the morning." He hugged and kissed them both. He whispered in Tom's ear, "Great game, son." He went to unwind and watch some television and they went to their rooms. He was grateful for the peace and quiet. It had been a long day.

Chapter 78

The crowd at the Café was always came in later on Saturdays and Tony was glad because he was usually sleepy and grouchy. He had to have several cups of coffee to feel like dealing with the public. Maria always came in later, too and it was probably best since Tony was not easy to be with, in his present state of mind.

At eight o'clock Daniel Carmody was the first customer of the day and Tony took him a cup of coffee as soon as he sat down at the counter. Tony asked, "You taking anybody to the wedding tomorrow?"

Daniel was stunned and said, "What is this? A conspiracy? People asking me if I have a date for the wedding? Who needs a date to go to a wedding? Tell me about it."

"Hey, man, I was just asking. Thought maybe you were, didn't mean to upset you. You know you beat me out for being best man so I'm the one that ought to be upset." He was smiling when he said it.

Daniel returned, "I didn't know there was a contest, excuse me." He was smiling, too. He continued, "Ed and I have become good friends. We're kind of like the odd couple but he's such a likable joe. He's been good for me. You know getting over Margie's death and all. And that Karen is just a joy, she's so nice and I am so happy for them. It's unusual to see two people at their age, so in love. I think it's great."

Pamela Sloan and Leah Oliver came into the Café together. They sat down at a table and Maria went to get their order. She put glasses of water down and the silver ware wrapped in napkins. She said, "Good Morning, Ladies. What can I get for you?"

Pamela said, "Good Morning, Maria, I'd like an orange juice and a sausage biscuit, please."

Leah said, "Hi, Maria, I'll have the same and some jelly, please."

"Okay, be right back with the juice." On the way back, she said, "Two biscuits and sausage, Tony."

She took the orange juice over to the table and said, "Didn't I see you girls at the game last night."

Pamela answered, "Yes, wasn't that a good game?"

Tony came to the table and put two plates with sausage biscuits down and said, "That was a great game. That Tom Wallace is a terrific quarterback."

Leah said, "He sure is and Amy is so cute. They're a great family. I envy them."

Tony said, "Well, they have their share of problems."

Maria poked him and said, "We have another customer. Let's see what he wants."

Tony knew he had just been shut down and he went back to the grill. Maria went to wait on the customer. Leah and Pamela just looked at each other, puzzled by that exchange. Pamela said, "Looks like everybody has their problems."

Daniel was walking when he left the Café. It was cold but the sun was shining brightly so he had decided he needed the exercise. He walked for a long time and came to the florist's shop. He got three red roses and asked the florist to tie them with a ribbon. Then he walked onto the cemetery. He hadn't intended to go there but when he got so close, he couldn't resist the urge. He went to her grave and there was another, new pink rose. He shook his head and placed his flowers on the grave.

He said, "I miss you, Margie and I hope you're at peace. It's still a mystery to all of us why you died, but maybe we're not supposed to know." He walked back out and started toward his apartment building. On the way, having a lot time to think, he thought of a plan to blow his friends away if he could bring it off.

He had to pass the Regal on the way. He went in and pretended to look at the appliances.

He thought, "I do need to get the happy couple a gift so might as well get it here." He had no idea what they could possibly need so he ended up with a fifty-dollar gift certificate.

As he paid, he asked if the manager was in. The girl who was waiting on him, looked downright frightened. He hastened to tell her, "Oh, nothing's wrong, I just want to speak to her."

She turned and picked up the store phone. When she turned back around, she said, "Ms Magee said to come on up to her office." She gave him directions and he proceeded to the office.

Her secretary said, "Go on in, Mr. Carmody." When he went in Rebecca was seated at her desk looking very puzzled.

He smiled and said, "Ms Magee, I am Daniel Carmody. I work at the

Dinsmore bank."

She interrupted him, "I assure you, Mr. Carmody, I know who you are, but what can I do for you? Have you had a problem with our staff?"

He smiled   again and told her, "No, no problem whatsoever. Let me tell you my situation."

He went on to explain, talking very fast. It seemed that all his friends were interested getting him a girlfriend. One of them had mentioned how attractive she was and he already knew that because he had seen her at the parade meeting.

He was talking faster and she held up her hand to stop him, "And this is all leading where?" She was both amused and confused by this man who seemed to have a problem.

He sighed and said, "I am best man at a wedding tomorrow. Ed Hawkins and Karen Sutton are getting married right after church. I just wondered if you would be willing to go with me?"

By now she was laughing, "Am I to understand that this is a date or is it your way of getting even with your friends?"

He nodded. "Well, it's a little bit of both, I must admit. But I would certainly be honored to have a date with you." He was totally embarrassed by now and he said, "I'll understand if you have me thrown out. I know it is probably the stupidest thing you've ever heard."

She thought a minute and said, "No, I love it. It is the most unusual way I've ever been asked out but I would love to go with you. What time will you pick me up?"

He stood there in shock for a moment, then he asked, "Where do you live?"

She told him the Gardenside apartments and he said, "Oh, my God, that's where I live."

"Well," she said, "Then what time will I meet you in the parking garage? Or would you like to come to my apartment?"

He answered, "Give me your apartment number and I'll pick you up there at ten fifteen, church doesn't start until eleven but I want to be there in plenty of time. I can't stand walking in late."

"I'll be ready. It's B-10, just ring the bell."

He said, "I'll see you then, thanks a lot." and hurried out of her office. He got out of the store as fast as he could.

She sat at her desk smiling and thinking, "What a handsome guy. How did I get so lucky? This should be very interesting." Never one to pass up a chance for a new relationship, she'd had many bad experiences with jerks but always got rid of them in a hurry. She thought, "This one may be a keeper." She went out into the store to get a new dress for the occasion. Her secretary waited until she was out of earshot and called her friend, Lynn, the mayor's wife to tell her, "Lynn, you know that handsome Daniel Carmody? He was just in talking to Rebecca for thirty minutes or so. What do you suppose is going on there? I heard he was dating Margie Sloan before she died."

The gossip mill was off and running, but Daniel's secret would not come out before the wedding. Even Dinsmore gossip didn't travel that fast.

Chapter 79

The phone woke Karen on Saturday morning. It was Ruth Barry inviting her to breakfast. She said, "Well, Ed is here. Is it all right if I bring him?"

Ruth was quick to answer, "Of course, we need to get to know him. I want to talk to you about the arrangements, you know make sure I haven't overlooked anything."

Karen asked, "What time do you want us?"

"Honey, you just come as soon as you're able. I won't start the eggs until you're here. Everything else is in the warming oven."

"Okay, we'll be there soon."

Ed came out of the bedroom scratching his head, "Be where, soon?"

Karen kissed him and told him the plan. She suggested he dress and to be sure not to mention that he had spent the night. "Oh, don't want them to think you're a wanton woman, huh?"

She pinched his cheek and told him, "That's right, what they don't know won't hurt them but knowing might. So get dressed and let's go. When we finish there, I want to get back to a painting I'm working on and you can get lost for a while or watch football or whatever."

"She's ordering me around already and the ink is not dry on the license. What have I done?"

When they got there, the Barrys came out to greet them at the car. Then they went in and had a bountiful breakfast, scrambled eggs, sausage patties, bacon, and biscuits with gravy. They were stuffed after that and Ed said, "I may have to take a nap after that delicious meal, Mrs. Barry."

She said, "Now, Ed, I'm Ruth and he's Joseph, we don't stand on formality around here. Karen is our dearest friend and I know you will be, too." Then she started to talk to Karen about the arrangements at the church.

Joseph said, "These women are going to be talking about all that fancy stuff. Why don't you come out here and help me pick some more of those damn apples." Ed followed him out the door.

Karen was at the back door a couple of hours later calling them to come in. When the men got to the house, she said, "It's been a lovely morning but I need to get home and feed my animals. I've got a painting I want to work on, too."

Ed added, "Yes, this was just great. I need to go clean out my house and get it ready to sell."

Ruth said, "Oh, my, I'm so glad to hear that. We were so afraid we would lose Karen. You'll like it out here, Ed."

"I know, and I wouldn't think of making Karen move to town."

As was their habit, they walked them to the car and waved them off as they left. Ed said, "Think we'll be that contented when we're their age?"

Karen leaned over and kissed his cheek and said, "No doubt about it, no doubt about it. Tomorrow we start our new life." When he turned into the drive, he pulled her to him and kissed her, a very long passionate kiss.

She loved it and said, "You want to try that again?"

Rebecca went to see Pamela and watched as she finished up a sale. Pamela was thinking, "Why is she watching me. I hope I'm not doing anything wrong."

She said to her customer, "Thank you for shopping at Regal and I hope you'll be happy with that outfit."

The customer said, "Oh, thank you, you were very helpful."

When the customer had gone, Rebecca stepped over to Pamela and said, "You have a good eye for fashion and I need a new dress or something to wear to a wedding."

Pamela asked, "What wedding are you going to?"

"Karen Sutton and Ed somebody."

"Leah and I are going to that, too. They must be a very popular couple. I sold Karen her outfit and her bridesmaid's, too. Then I introduced Ed to Sam in men's wear and he sold him a suit. He wouldn't buy until I approved. He was so cute. Obviously not into suits. He's a cop you know, and she's an ex cop."

Rebecca said, "Well, I have come to the right person for help then. What do you suggest?"

Pamela thought a moment and asked, "You thinking suit or dress? I'm wearing a suit, I think that will always work and it's easy to mix and match. You get more bang for your buck."

Rebecca said, "That's true, let's see something in a light weight fabric. Maybe wine color but I really have an open mind on color. No red, though I have a red suit."

Pamela showed her several and she went to the fitting room. She wasn't impressed with any that she tried and then Pamela brought her a pretty, rose-colored suit trimmed in satin piping, with a satin shell blouse in the same color. She said, "This is it, definitely. It's dressier that the others. I felt like a lawyer or something in those others. Just put it on my charge and I'll pick it up when I leave this evening."

Pamela said, "I'm glad we were able to find something you liked, Rebecca, and I'm flattered that you asked my opinion."

"Well, why wouldn't I? You're the best in this store and you should know it."

Pamela thanked her and went back to work with another customer that was "just looking." She was feeling much better about her life and her career. Everything was beginning to look up.

Chapter 80

Sunday morning the bride and groom were up early sitting at the kitchen table eating bagels and cream cheese. Karen had almost finished her painting the day before and Ed had moved the rest of his clothes. He was going to wait on the furniture until Karen could pick out what she wanted. The only thing he cared about was his roll top desk. That he had to have moved. They were both excited and nervous.

They talked about what they had accomplished on Saturday and what they would do tomorrow but avoided talking about today.

Finally Karen said, "Well, I'm going to take my shower so I'll be out of your way. You know there's another bathroom but it's so small I never use it. That's in the spare room where we'll make you an office if you'd like."

He said, "No problem, I'll have another cup of coffee and finish reading the paper while you shower and do your make up."

She stopped to kiss him on her way and went to see about getting done up for her wedding. While she was in the shower, the phone rang so Ed answered, "Hi, Ed, it's Daniel. I want to know if I can pick you and Karen up and take you to the church. That will keep your buddies from messing with your car."

Ed said, "Well, that's not a bad idea at all. What time will you be here?" Daniel said, "Ten thirty should give us plenty of time. Okay?"

Ed answered, "We'll be ready."

When he hung up, Daniel gave high five to heaven, he said, "Thank You, Lord!"

Jeff Collins had called him last night and asked him to pick up Ed and Karen. He had told Daniel about their plans. He loved the idea and assured Jeff he would take care of it. He had planned to just walk into the church with Rebecca on his arm but this would work just as well. He could imagine their surprise when he drove up with Rebecca in the passenger seat.

When Karen was out of the bathroom, Ed took his turn. She went in to put on her best lingerie and her new dress. She had done her make up and hair in the bathroom. She took one last look in the mirror and decided she was ready. She went out on the porch and fed the animals. She could see Candy out in the field and knew she was content.

The phone rang and she went in to answer it. "Hello, Karen, it's Melanie. Are you excited?"

Karen answered, "I'm a nervous wreck. I'll be glad when it's over. That's what Ed keeps saying. We are so happy though, I wish you were here."

Melanie said, "Oh, I wish I were too. You'll send me pictures, won't you?"

"Yes, I sure will, but I hope you'll be home for Thanksgiving. Do you think you can make it?"

"Well, I don't know. You would have to pick me up in Chicago and that's a lot of trouble."

"I don't mind at all. We'll check out the "Rose Gallery" while we're there. When do you get out of school?"

Melanie replied, "I'll finish up Tuesday afternoon. I was wondering if I could possibly get Mother's car to come back in. What do you think?"

"Well, I don't know but I can't think of any reason not to. We'll have to check with the insurance man and so forth. I'll talk to the lawyer in the meantime. I haven't had time to go to the bank and check her safety deposit box but I have the key. We're hoping to find a will somewhere."

"Okay, I need to go now but I'll get back with you about dates and all. You have a wonderful wedding day. I love you, Karen. You'll have to tell Ed that he's my daddy now because you're like my mother."

"That's a lovely thing to say, I'm sure he'll love you as much as I do. You take care and we'll talk later. Bye for now."

When she hung up the phone, Ed was standing in the door way in a great looking gray pin stripe suit with a burgundy tie. She said, "Who is this handsome man in my house. The Lord has surely blessed me by sending you."

"You are really full of it, Karen, my love. But don't stop. You're almost making me feel decent in this monkey suit."

"What are you talking about? It looks great and you look great."

"You look beautiful. Have I told you that I'm nuts about you?"

"Yes, but I love hearing it. That was Melanie on the phone. She said to tell you that you'll have to be her daddy because I am like her mother, now."

"That will be okay with me, she's a great kid. Speaking of phones, Daniel called and he's picking us up at ten thirty."

"Okay, we're going to have to get him a chauffeur's license if he keeps this up. I think he just likes to drive that Lexus."

"It works for me. We can make out in the back seat again."

They heard the horn honking and knew the time was getting close. She hugged him and kissed him, then wiped the lipstick off his mouth. She picked up her purse, and her camera, gave him the key to lock up and they went out to the Lexus. They both paused for a moment and then realizing they must look stupid, just standing there, staring, they moved forward slowly, to get in the car.

Daniel was in hysterics, he was laughing so hard. Ed spoke first, "Okay so what's the joke."

Daniel sobered up and said, "This is no joke. I want you to meet Rebecca Magee, she has agreed to be my date for your wedding. Rebecca, meet the bride, Karen and the groom, Ed."

Ed was speechless but Karen spoke up, "It's so nice to see you again, Rebecca."

Rebecca said, "Yes, it's nice to see both of you. Congratulations, I feel lucky to get to be at your wedding." Still not able to come up with a wise crack, Ed just said, "We'd better get on with it, Daniel. I sure don't want to be late to my wedding.

Chapter 81

Daniel let Ed and the ladies out in front of the church and he went to park on the church lot. When he got back, they went in together, to seats near the back, as Ed was directing them. He didn't want to make a big entrance. He and Karen had given Daniel the simple gold bands they had bought the same day they got the license.

When Tony and Maria came in they scooted over so that they could all sit together. They were surprised to see Jeff come in with Pamela, Nathan and Leah. Ed whispered, "They were all together at the game last night." Karen just nodded.

Tony leaned over to Ed and said, "Are you nervous, Ed. Want to change your mind?" Ed smiled and said, "No way." Maria was poking Tony in the ribs, to shut him up. He just grinned at her.

The organist played "Little Fugue in G Minor" by Bach. The only way they knew what the music was that it was printed in the program. The choir entered and then the preacher came in and sat down. One of the lay ministers got up and made the announcements. The preacher came to the lectern and led the congregation in a prayer first and then a responsive reading. He sat down again and the choir sang "How Can I Keep From Singing."

The preacher rose again, offered another prayer and began by reading scripture passages. He began to talk of the sanctity of marriage. He spoke of many biblical references and it was a very good sermon but Karen and Ed didn't know a thing he said. The organist played for the offertory and the dedication of the offerings. The congregation sang with the choir, "Amazing Grace."

The preacher said, "Before I close the service I would like to announce that as soon as we are finished here I will have the pleasure of marrying two of Dinsmore's finest citizens and Dinsmore United Methodist Churches finest members. You are invited by the bride and groom, Karen Sutton and Ed Hawkins, to attend if you wish to do so. The Woman's Society has planned a reception to be held in the Fellowship Hall immediately after the wedding. Now let us pray."

As soon as he finished the prayer and the organist began to play he went out to the foyer to greet his congregation as they left. There were still many people left in the church and Ed said, "Karen it looks like we're going to have quite an audience."

She said, "Yes, I see." Just then, little Ruth Barry appeared and handed a beautiful bouquet of yellow and white roses to Karen and a yellow rose with a ribbon streamer to Maria. Karen was on the verge of tears when she got up and hugged Ruth. "I never even thought of flowers," she said.

Ruth replied, "I knew you wouldn't and I wanted to do something special for you. I've told the organist to play the wedding march when you and your groom walk to the altar and then after he pronounces you married, Amy Wallace is going to sing, "The Lord's Prayer." Is that all right?"

"I can't believe you thought of all this. It just never entered my mind. Thank you so much."

The preacher came back to where they were and said, "Are we ready to start, folks?"

Ed said, "Yes, let's get this over with before I have a heart attack."

The preacher said, "Why don't you and Maria, come on down with me now, Daniel? Then when the organist begins to play, Karen and Ed can come down. We will be well on the way to getting it over with, Ed."

Ed managed a smile and Karen said, "Thanks a lot, Gary."

So the preacher walked in front as Daniel held out his elbow to Maria and they followed. As soon as they arrived at the altar, the organist began, "The Wedding March" and Ed stood, holding his elbow for Karen, thinking "I'm glad Daniel knew what to do."

They made it to the altar, the music stopped and the preacher started, "We are gathered here today to join Karen Marie Sutton and Edward Dean Hawkins in holy matrimony." That's the last thing either of them heard until Gary said, "Repeat after me."

They repeated after him and then exchanged the wedding bands that Daniel handed them. When Gary said, "I now pronounce you, man and wife. They kissed briefly and turned to go. They waited while Amy Wallace sang the "Lord's Prayer." After that Gary said, "I'd want to introduce Mr. and Mrs. Hawkins."

The congregation applauded them. The organist played "William Tell Overture" as they made their way out of the church. When Daniel came out, Karen asked him to get her camera from the car and act as the photographer. He said he would be glad to do that and went to get it. When he was back, they made their way to the Fellowship Hall and formed a line at the door to greet their guests.

It was a long time before they could go into the hall and see the wedding cake that Ruth Barry had made with her own hands and the flowers that the Women's Society had picked from their own gardens. Karen couldn't believe they were able to find so many flowers still blooming. Many of them were camellias which were beautiful this time of year and there were all colors of fall chrysanthemums.

They had a stereo system playing romantic music and Ruth came to the newlyweds and asked if they would cut the cake so that they could begin to serve. They agreed and went to do it.

Daniel had been taking pictures of everybody and he followed to take one now of them and the cake cutting. He said, "Before you cut the cake just pose for me. You can put your arm around her waist, Ed."

Ed said, "Oh, thank you for allowing me to do that, Daniel." There was a ripple of laughter.

Then Daniel said, "Now would you kiss for the camera, please." They both looked horrified.

He said, "Come on now, we've got to have a picture of you kissing."

Ed looked at Karen and she looked as if she didn't mind so he kissed her. He said, "H'm, that was so good, think I'll do it again." And he did.

The crowd roared with laughter and applauded. His face turned beet red. Ruth handed them the knife and they cut the cake and gave each other a bite for the photographer. Ruth handed them each a cup of punch and they clinked cups at the photographer's request. Ed said, "Okay, now Tony would you take one of the four of us?"

After Tony did as he was asked, Ed said, "Now enough of the pictures. Let everybody have some cake and punch. Isn't that right, Ruth?"

She smiled and nodded and their guests started to line up for the refreshments. Gary and Christine had come in and came to shake their hands and congratulate them. Ed and Karen both told him how much they appreciated all they had done for this day. He told them it had been a real pleasure. Ed gave him a check and Gary said, "I'm not taking money for performing this marriage. I'll see that it goes into the church coffers."

Ed said, "Well, I have another for the Women's Society." Gary told him to give it to Ruth later.

While Ed and Karen were occupied with the preacher, as per the plan, Daniel slipped out to meet Jeff and his cohorts in the parking lot. They had the golf cart pulled up close to the door but far enough back that it couldn't be spotted immediately. Daniel said to Jeff, "I'll give you a heads up when they get ready to leave. They'll think I'm going to get my car. All the cops had bags of rice. Big one pound bags of rice and could hardly wait for the couple to exit. Daniel told them he didn't think it would be long because Ed had smiled about as long as he could.

Daniel went back into the hall and found his date. He apologized for neglecting her and promised he would ask her out again, if she would accept. She assured him that she understood, he had a lot to do for his friends. She thought it they very charming.

"Well, that's not how I would describe Ed but you're right about Karen. Don't they look happy? They're such great people, and I'm really happy for them."

As the afternoon wore on Ed was easing toward the door, little by little. The preacher found them again and they talked about how beautifully Amy had sung. They asked where she was and he told them that they had gone to visit Janet. They asked where his children were and he said, "We got a sitter so that we could enjoy this event. They tend to go a little wild at things like this." So polite conversation was running out and Ed was looking for Daniel to save the day.

Daniel spotted him looking around and knew it was time to let them go. He came over to them and said, "Whenever you're ready, we'll go. Okay?"

'Ed said, "Karen are you ready to go now?" She nodded and said, "Thanks again, Gary."

She looked for Ruth but she was involved in conversation with some of the guests. Karen said, "Please tell the ladies how much I appreciated this beautiful reception. I'll write a note to them later." Gary said he would do that and Daniel headed out the door.

Jeff pulled the cart up to the door when Ed and Karen walked out. They both did double takes which Daniel got on the camera. There was a roar of laughter as the crowd joined them in the parking lot. Daniel came to tell them that he was sorry but the Lexus wouldn't start and they would have let Jeff take them home on the new golf cart the police department had bought for them.

When the shock wore off, being good sports, they climbed in the cart beside Jeff. Karen had to sit on Ed's lap and the rice was raining on them as they rode off. Daniel told Rebecca that they would follow behind them to keep someone from running over them and one of the cops got in his car and turned on the blue lights and siren as he led the way down the road.

As it happened, many others got into their cars and followed. It became a convoy and it took almost an hour to get home. As they got to the driveway, Karen said, "I'm changing the name on that mailbox tomorrow. She kissed him for umpteenth time and when Jeff finally stopped, she thanked him for the ride of a lifetime.

Jeff said, "Well, I knew you had a horse to ride so I thought Ed would need something to keep up with you."

She asked, "Is it really ours?"

Jeff said, "Of course, I wouldn't kid about a thing like that."

Cars were driving by honking their horns and waving. Ed and Karen stood there waving back and smiling from ear to ear. A car pulled up and Jeff said, "There's my date and our friends. I'll see you later. By the way the chief said not to come to work next week. He said you might need a little time to recuperate."

Ed asked, "Are you serious?" Jeff answered, "As serious as a heart attack. We love you, Man."

He took off after that dodging, like Ed might hit him.

When Jeff and his group had gone, Daniel pulled in the driveway. He was laughing when he got out of the car. He said, "We got you good didn't we?"

Ed just glared at him, feigning anger. Karen said, "You are a trickster, Daniel Carmody and it was a great surprise. I've never laughed so much."

When Daniel got closer, he said quietly so Rebecca wouldn't hear, "Did you notice that I am quite capable of getting a good-looking date?"

Karen answered, "Yes, I never doubted it for a minute. Why don't you get her and come in the house for a bit."

He said, "I'll see if she won't mind. I've really neglected her with all the other stuff I had to do." He went to the car and opened the door and said, "They would like us to come in. Would you mind?"

Rebecca started getting out of the car saying, "Why no, I'd like to get to know them better."

Ed unlocked the door. Everybody had a pat for Jazz and they started into the house for the first time as married folks. Ed stopped and turned around, he picked Karen up and carried her over the threshold while she screamed, "Have you lost your mind?"

Then he put her back on her feet and let Rebecca and Daniel come in. Daniel produced a bottle of champagne and the gift certificate. "I met Rebecca while I was getting your wedding gift." Rebecca just smiled thinking about the meeting yesterday. She said, "I love your house, Karen.

Daniel tells me that you're an artist. Could I see some of your work?"

Karen said, "Sure, come on back to my studio. It's a mess but there's no sense in pretending it's ever clean and neat because it isn't. When I'm out there, I don't worry about neat and clean."

Daniel was following them, he said, "Do you realize that I've never seen your work?"

"Well, I'm sorry, Daniel. We've always had something else going on when you've been here."

He said, "This is great stuff, Karen. I had no idea what you could do."

Ed said, "Yeah, she's going to take care of us in our old age. Did she tell you? She has an opening at a Chicago gallery in January?"

Rebecca said, "No wonder, this is really nice work. I love art and wish I could do it. I tried it in college but had no talent."

Karen said, "Melanie is going to be better than me, after she finishes school."

Ed said, "Well, you're the one who taught her, aren't you?"

"Yes, but she took to it, like a duck to water."

Daniel explained, "Melanie is Margie's daughter. Karen is like her mother now that Margie is gone." It was obvious that Daniel had told Rebecca about him and Margie.

After she had shown them several canvases, they all went into the living room.

Karen asked, "Can I get you something to drink?"

Daniel said, "Let's pop the cork on that champagne and we'll have a toast. Then we've got to go and let you old married folk's play house."

Karen said, "Okay, we'll have to drink it from water glasses with ice cubes."

He said, "Sounds good to me." He followed her to the kitchen and opened the bottle with a loud pop.

Rebecca and Ed joined them and when the glasses were filled, Daniel made a toast, "I wish the best of everything to the most deserving couple I've ever known." They all clicked the glasses and drank the bubbly. There were hugs all around, goodbyes, thanks, and more hugs.

Daniel and Rebecca got in the Lexus and left. Karen and Ed stood by their new golf cart and waved to them as they left. Ed got Karen to get on the golf cart and did wheelies in the driveway while Jazz ran in circles around them. As they walked into the house the first snow of the year began to fall. Karen said, "Oh, now we're going to be snowbound. Won't that be great?" Karen was the only person in Illinois that thought that a snow storm would be "great."

Chapter 82

Bill and the kids made it to the hospital by three o'clock to visit with Janet. She was waiting in the recreation room and when attendant led them, she got up and came to meet them. There were hugs for all of them and then they went outside.

Janet got a sweater from the chair as she said, "It's chilly out today, are you going to be warm enough?" "Yeah, we're fine." Bill said.

"I was afraid you weren't going to make it. You were later than last week."

"It took longer to check in this time for some reason. We started late because we stayed after church for Karen and Ed's wedding. Amy sang and her song was last."

Janet was excited and said, "That's wonderful, I mean that they got married and that Amy sang. When did they decide to marry? I didn't think Ed would ever marry. He's been a bachelor so long."

Bill told her what he knew, "I guess they had been spending more time together lately and just got to be more than friends and once they knew the feeling was mutual, they wasted no time."

Tom wasn't having anything to say so Bill said, "Tom, why don't you tell your Mom what you've been up to. Tom told Janet about his touchdown passes at the game and that Amy had been selected to be freshman representative for homecoming queen court. He said proudly, "I'm going to be her escort."

Amy then told her that all the girls wanted Tom to be their escort, now they were all jealous because he was going to escort her. Janet said, "Well, that is so nice, I'm so proud of both of you. When is the homecoming?"

"The week before Thanksgiving, whenever that is, I don't know the date," Tom replied.

She said, "I hope I can be there because it will so nice to see both of you out there on the field. I'm so proud of both of you."

"What have you been doing, Bill?," she asked, "I mean how are your classes going? I already know the football is doing fine."

Bill said, "My classes are doing fine. I gave them a test on the trials of the witches of Salem. I hope the school board doesn't fire me for it." He chuckled and said, "I was just trying to keep them interested in history. The kids found more parallels to present day incidents than I even thought about."

"That sounds like good teaching to me, getting them interested enough to think out of the box."

Amy said, "Mom, we brought you a couple of outfits, shoes, socks and underwear, just so you could change once in a while. The doctor said they might take some of you on a field trip one day."

Janet said, "Oh, I don't know if I want to be seen out with these nuts." She was smiling, but they figured she probably meant it.

Bill said, "Don't worry they won't take the nuts out." He smiled, too, hoping that he hadn't said the wrong thing. Everybody was quiet for a long time.

Finally Janet said, "Look, we may as well talk about my illness, because it is a fact. I know now that I was out of control when I went off on you, Bill. I was mad at all of you for a while after I got here, but the doctors have explained that I have an illness that can be controlled by medication. It will control my mood swings, and my paranoia. In addition I have been able to lose weight which really makes me feel better about my looks. I'm really sorry that I treated all of you so badly and I promise when I come home things will be different."

Bill said, "We know that and we're looking forward to having you at home."

Then Janet said, "Now tell me about the wedding. What was Karen wearing and who stood up with them? Just tell me all about it. I love weddings and I need to hear about something happy."

They began to tell her all that had happened at the wedding, they kept interrupting each other talking excitedly. They all laughed when they told her about the golf cart gift. They told her about forming a convoy and honking horns all the way to Karen's place. Then they had left the convoy and got on the highway to come to the hospital.

When visitors' hours were over, they had to leave, but she was still smiling as she waved goodbye. Bill thought, "She is getting better but what about me? How am I doing? How am I going to handle it when she comes back?"

Chapter 83

After their visit to Karen and Ed's, Daniel drove Rebecca back to her apartment. He had asked if she would like to go somewhere for lunch but she said, "Why don't we go back to my place and I'll fix us a sandwich or something. I'd really like to get out of these clothes and relax."

He said, "That sounds good if you're sure it won't be too much trouble. Should I stop and pick up something?"

"No, I have some sesame rolls and some cold cuts. We can make our own and we'll just use paper plates and pretend we're on a picnic. I've got beer and soft drinks and chips, so I think that will do, don't you?"

"It's sounding better all the time. I want to tell you I really appreciate you going with me."

"It was my pleasure. They're such nice people and I'm happy to have been able to get better acquainted with them."

When he had parked at the complex, he said, "If it's all right, I'm going to run up to my place and change to jeans. I'd like to get out of this garb, too."

"You go right ahead, and I see you at my place in a few minutes."

He was thinking, "I'm feeling good about this girl, she's a looker and sharp. I think I'll have to see more of her."

When he had changed to his jeans and a T-shirt, he put on his boots and went back to Rebecca's place. She opened the door when he knocked and said, "You look a lot more comfortable. Come on in and make yourself at home while I get the stuff out."

"No, let me help. What can I do?"

"You can open a couple of beers. The glasses are in the second door on the left."

"Okay, I think I can manage that. By the way you look more comfortable, too. That suit you had on was really pretty, though. I was very proud to be your escort."

"Why, thank you, kind sir. I was just thinking how funny it was, when you came to my office yesterday. I thought you were an irate customer and I was thinking, "Oh, damn, what am I going to do about this?" The last thing I thought was that you just wanted a date. That was truly unique. I've never had an invitation quite like that before. I was so intrigued, I didn't dare say no. I really did not know who you were or what you did until the parade meeting. You haven't been here long, have you?"

"Well, I'm sure glad you didn't think I was an escapee from the funny farm. I don't usually act so impulsive but it seemed like a good idea at the time. You were a good sport to go along with me. I transferred here about six months ago from Chicago. I'm a vice president, loan officer at the Dinsmore bank. How long have you lived here?"

"Let's sit down and eat this gourmet meal I've fixed. Then I'll tell you all about me. Come on in the living room we can sit in the floor at the coffee table. I'm going to turn on the television to get the football scores right quick."

"You're a football fan? Do you ever go to the Dinsmore High games?"

"Well, I really haven't made a lot of friends here yet and I don't like going places alone but I did go to the one last Friday with a lady from work. She kept telling me how great they were and I wasn't disappointed. It was a great game. I saw Karen there and that's when I told her about Larry. I had heard that she was Margie's friend. My job has become my obsession, I'm afraid. I'm going to have to break out a little more often."

"Well, I'm inviting you right now, to go with me this coming Friday night to the Dinsmore High football game. They have a great quarterback that makes their games more exciting."

"Hey, I'd love to go. I saw that quarterback in action. He is great. Just let me know what time to be ready."

"I'll call and remind you later this week. If you have your scores now. It's still your turn to tell me more about you."

"There's really not much to tell. I moved here from St. Louis. I have always worked in retail. That is what I got my degree in. You know merchandising and so forth. I'm single and as I said, obsessed with my career. I haven't been dating anyone. So there's no history that I care to share. I hope that will be satisfactory with you. I'm kind of a private person. I'm not going be too active in the parade business. I have reasons for not wanting my name in the paper. I'm not a fugitive from justice but as I say, I have my reasons."

"Well, I'm sorry. I didn't mean to be pushy. I could get with Tony about it but he's the most nosy person in town and he'd wonder why and start asking questions. I mean about keeping you out of the paper. You know he and Maria are doing the publicity."

"Okay, I'll consider myself warned. I've never gone to the Café, so I don't know them."

"You must be one of the only people in this town that has not gone there. It's the main meeting place. They do have a great menu and I've never had a bad meal there. They are really nice people. It's just a known fact that Tony's got a big mouth. He doesn't mean any harm but sometimes gossip can be so destructive. We ride him about it all the time, but he doesn't get the message."

"Hey, this conversation about me is getting to be downright depressing. Let's change the subject. Tell me about this Margie that you mentioned earlier. Is she the reason you divorced your wife?"

"No, I didn't know Margie when I decided to divorce my wife. She died before I could even tell her about my divorce. We had only dated a few times. I went to Chicago to finalize my divorce and when I got back, she had died. They said it was suicide but I don't believe it."

Now she was embarrassed and said, "I'm so sorry. I didn't realize…"

He went on to explain, " I didn't divorce my wife for another woman. She is bipolar and won't get help or take her medication. I simply couldn't deal with her moods and wild behavior anymore. I warned her and warned her. She was killing my love, but she just kept on, so I did what was good for me. Fortunately my kids understood because she has been this way for years and they have escaped to college. They still visit her but they don't live with her either."

"I'm so sorry about Margie. What do you think happened?"

"I really have no idea but I'll never believe it was suicide. The chief of police won't let Ed investigate it. He says the case is closed but Karen is checking it out. She was a cop at one time and she can do it without causing problems for Ed."

"Wow, we seem to have such depressing stories. Let's see what's on the boob tube to lighten up this party. Oh, there's America's Funniest Videos, that should give us a laugh."

They sat on the couch and watched television until after nine and Daniel said, "I'd better get back to my place, I'm expecting a call from my daughter tonight. We're planning a ski vacation in December and she's supposed to let me know her schedule."

"Okay, thanks for the fun day. I'll look forward to the football game on Friday." He kissed her on the cheek and went back to his apartment. Allison wasn't going to call him but he thought he'd better leave. Didn't want to wear out his welcome. He couldn't believe they had told such private information about themselves. He guessed it was better to get all the bad stuff out of the way though. He definitely wanted to see more of Rebecca Magee.

Chapter 84

Jeff, Nathan and their dates went to the girl's apartment after the wedding and ordered Pizza. They watched the end of the Packers versus the Colts football game, eating pizza and drinking beer the guys had picked up at the Quick Stop. Pamela figured they knew she was married so she told them about her impending divorce and about the letter from Larry.

Jeff said, "I'm sure glad to hear he's not drinking. He was a nice guy when he was sober but he had seemed to be drunk most of the time in the past year."

Pamela said, "Yeah, I think he must have been drunk when he married me." She giggled but she didn't look like she really felt it was funny. Then to change the subject, she said, "Now, Nathan, just what are you going to do about my little Neon?"

Nathan looked embarrassed and said, "I'm sure my insurance will take care of it. I'm really sorry I smashed it up. I'll make sure they do right by you."

Leah said, "You'd better or we'll come looking for you, with Jeff and his handcuffs."

Jeff said, "But just think, if he hadn't run over you, we wouldn't have met. This has turned out to be a fun weekend for me." They all agreed that he was right. When the game was over, Jeff said, "We'd better get going, Nathan. I have to be at work bright and early. With Ed off duty, I'm going to have more to do."

"Yes, good idea. I've got to get back to school. It's been fun and I hope we can all get together again. I won't be back until Thanksgiving. Maybe we can do something then." They picked up their coats and started toward the door.

Following them, Pamela said, "I hope you'll call me, Jeff. I had a really good time. Thanks for taking me to the wedding."

"I sure will and thank you for going with me."

Leah said, "And thank you, Nathan. Maybe we'll see you Thanksgiving." The boys went out to the car and high fived each other on the way down the stairs.

Pamela and Leah were doing the same thing when they got back inside the apartment.

Chapter 85

Monday morning Karen got up, made the coffee and took a cup out to the porch. It was chilly but she had on her warm robe. She sat on the steps, so that Callie could sit on her lap while she was petting Jazz. Ed came to the door and just stood watching her, for a few minutes.

Then he said, "I see you are always an early riser."

She turned and said, "Good morning, sunshine. I hope I didn't wake you when I got up."

"No, I usually get up early, too." He smiled, "But something kept me up late last night. Seems a wild woman came into my bedroom and ravaged me."

She said, "Oh, you wish. Want to go back to bed?"

"No, I need to eat breakfast to get my strength back. Do you want to go to the Café to eat?"

"Let's go to the Holiday Inn for a change. I don't want to hear Tony's jokes today."

"It's a deal. Come on in and put on your jeans, I'm starving. You realize we forgot to eat last night?"

"Okay, I'll be right there after I feed these guys. I need to go check on Candy, too. I've been neglecting her lately. I think I'll ride her today."

"I'll go shave and get ready while you do your chores."

When she came back from feeding Candy and turning her out to pasture, he was already dressed and sitting on the porch. She said, "I'm sorry. I took too long with her but I'll be ready in a jiffy." She leaned over and kissed him on her way into the house.

She was back out in fifteen minutes and they were off to the Inn to have their breakfast. After they were seated and had ordered, Ed said, "It was really nice of the chief to give me the time off. If I had known, I would have taken you on a honeymoon trip."

"We'll do something later. I'm enjoying just having you around. Later on maybe we can go to the city or down to Mississippi. Did you know that Margie and I went to the Mississippi coast to gamble?"

"No, I didn't know you liked to gamble. I've never been to a casino in my life. I do like playing poker when we go to deer camp, though."

"Well, we can go anywhere we want to after you retire. I'm sure you won't get too much more vacation this year."

"Probably not with the holidays coming up. It's always busy when the weather gets bad. There are more wrecks, shoplifters and drunks for some reason. I thought you said we were going to be snowbound today."

"Wrong again, it was just a little flurry I guess. That reminds me, Melanie was asking about getting Margie's car when she comes home for Thanksgiving, and driving back to Columbia. I'm thinking that with the weather so uncertain at this time of year, it might not be a good idea."

"You're right. Maybe you can talk her into waiting until later."

"She's talking seriously about quitting school in Missouri and going to the Art Institute in Chicago. She can take the car then. That is, if the weather isn't bad."

Their breakfast order came and they concentrated on eating for a while. When they were finished Ed asked, "Well, what do you want to do now? We could go to my place and see what you want to move and what you want to sell. I'll sell the kitchen appliances with the house. I need to go list it, too. Do you want to do that?"

"That sounds like a good plan to me. Let's go." Ed put the money for their breakfast on the table and they went to run their errands.

Chapter 86

Daniel was at his desk and he had several loans to review. So many of the local farmers had applied for loans to get them through the winter months. He didn't have his mind on work though. His mind kept wandering to the weekend, the wedding and Rebecca. He started to call his secretary and then thought better of it and called the florist, himself. He ordered a vase with three roses sent to Rebecca at her work. He told them to just put "Thanks for Sunday" on the card, no name. Then he went back to work and tried to concentrate.

He looked up and saw Ed and Karen coming in the bank. He watched them from his office and finally they looked his way and waved. He waved back and motioned for them to come to his office. When they came in, he asked, "What are you two up to?"

Ed said, "We're opening our joint account. We're going to keep our separate accounts and have a joint one, too. Don't you think that's wise?"

Daniel thought a minute before he offered, "It is if it works for you. Whatever prevents disagreements about money. Nothing ruins a marriage faster. Sit down and I'll get the paper work for you."

Karen asked, "Don't you have more important work to do?" He smiled and said, "Hey, what's more important than helping my friends get off to a good start."

Ed told him, "I just went to the realtor and put my place on the market. Next we're going to meet the movers to move some of my junk out to Karen's."

Daniel asked, "When do you start calling it, our place instead of Karen's?" "When my junk is there, I guess."

Karen said, "When I change the name on the mailbox. I'm going to do that today."

They finished up their business and went on their way. Later they got some local movers to load the few pieces they had chosen. They followed the van back to Karen's. While Ed showed them where to unload, Karen went to get ready to ride Candy. The movers put Ed's big desk in the guest room with his television and an old recliner that was still in good shape. He had them store the rest in the barn for the time being. When they had finished, he paid them and went back into the house.

He decided to check with his friend at the FBI and see if they had any hits on the fingerprints. He was on the phone when Karen came out in her jeans and boots, ready to ride Candy. She waved at him as she went out to the barn.

After Candy was saddled and Karen had hoisted herself up on her back, they rode off into the pasture and on over into neighboring pastures. When she started back to the barn, she saw Ed standing on the porch. She rode on up to the house and asked, "You want to ride her?"

He answered, "No, I'm afraid she doesn't want me riding her. I've only been on a horse once and it didn't go well."

"I was thinking I would buy you a horse and we'd ride together."

He said, "Save your money. The only riding we'll do together is on that golf cart."

She went to let Candy go out to the pasture and when she got back to the house, Ed said, "I want to tell you the news Sam Fortune had for me."

"Who's Sam Fortune?"

"He's my friend at the FBI in Chicago. He said there are several different sets of prints on the bottle and they haven't lifted the DNA from the top of it yet, if there is any. He also said that the fingerprints on the plate and can from your table match one set from the bottle. How about that?"

"So that means somebody, who was in Margie's place, was also here that day. One set of the fingerprints on the bottle would be Margie's. Daniel didn't touch it, so other people were in Margie's apartment and touched that bottle."

"What makes you think there might be DNA on the bottle top?"

"Because Daniel said they only had one glass apiece and the bottle was empty. There was no other glass, so I thought, maybe whoever drank the rest, drank right from the bottle."

"That's kind of reaching, don't you think? They may have poured it down the sink."

"Yes, you're right. I am reaching, because I just can't figure it out. Even if I can't prove it, I'll never believe Margie committed suicide."

"Well, I'll call him back in a few days and see what else he can find out."

"I'm going out and paint the mailbox. Then I'm going to paint our name on it."

"Okay, want some help?"

"No, you need to get your office arranged like you want it. Did you bring a phone to put in there?"

"Yes, I'll get it plugged in and then I need to hook up my computer. I want to write to Larry Sloan and see if I can get his fingerprints. It's really just for the process of elimination. He probably was never in Margie's new apartment. By the way, have you ever talked to the manager of the apartment complex?"

"No, I need to do that. They might have seen somebody coming or going. I have never seen him or her. Margie never did mention who the manager was. I'll check it out tomorrow."

"I'll go with you this time. I know who it is. His name is Ben Malone. Let's think about a way to get his finger prints, too. I want you to interview Bill Wallace and somehow manage to get his finger prints."

"Why don't you just get them to come into the station?"

"The case is closed, don't forget. I'm not supposed to be involved."

"Oh, that's true. Then what will you do with the prints?"

"Send them to Chicago. Sam can compare with the others I sent him. Who knows? It's a long shot but what choice do we have? Now go paint your mailbox…I'll get on with my office and then we'll go have some fun."

She sprayed the mailbox with white paint. When it was dry, she picked up the palette from her studio and lettered "Hawkins" on it. Then she decorated it with flowers and hearts. She stood back and admired her work and thought, "Ed is going to have a fit, when he sees this work of art."

Ed came out to where she was standing and said, "Now that doesn't look like a cop lives here." He hugged her and said, "I don't want anyone to know a cop lives here, just a pair of love birds, thus the hearts and flowers."

She kissed him and said, "You've got it, mister. Now what are we going to do? You said we'd go and have some fun."

"Let's go to dinner and a movie in Lexington."

"Okay, We'll need to shower and change, but it's early, so let's go in and get ready." While she was in the shower, she was suddenly surprised by Ed joining her.

"Thought maybe you'd like me to wash your back," he said, "It's early and we have plenty of time, don't we? Remember, I said we'd have some fun, this is my idea of fun." Karen answered, "I certainly can't argue with that."

Chapter 87

At eleven o'clock Monday morning, Rebecca called both Pamela and Leah to her office. When they got there, they had worried looks on their faces. Pamela spoke to the secretary, "Do you know why Rebecca wants to see us?"

She shrugged her shoulders, "I don't, but you can both go in. I told her you were here."

They entered with trepidation. She smiled, when she saw how worried they looked, "Hey, I just wanted to invite the two of you to go to lunch with me. I thought it would be fun to discuss our dates for the wedding."

Leah sighed and said, "Thank goodness, I was trying all the way here to think what I had done."

Pamela said, "Me, too."

Rebecca said sternly, "You should not assume that I'm an ogre. I really think you are both doing a great job. Larry always tried to make everybody think I was the bad guy so he could look like the good guy. It will take a while to overcome that impression. Maybe you girls can help me in that regard. Now do you want to go to lunch me or not?"

"Sure, what time?," Leah asked.

"Let's leave right now and get in before it gets crowded," Rebecca said. "Meet me at the entrance.

They went to get their purses and coats, checked their make up and met her in a few minutes.

One of the stock clerks had Rebecca's car out front and they all got in the big Buick. She announced, "We're going to the club for lunch and Mr. Regal is meeting us there later."

Leah and Pamela looked at each other in shock. Leah said, "Oh, my gosh, I don't think I've ever even met him."

Pamela assured her, "I have and he's a very nice man. What does he want to see us for, Rebecca?"

"Oh, you'll see soon enough. Tell me about your dates for the wedding. How did you know them?"

It was obvious, she wasn't going to tell them any more so they took turns telling her about the wreck, the football game and all the fun they had. They told her about Jeff's relationship to Ed. Then how he had told them about the wedding and invited all of them to go.

She told them about the strange way she had been invited. They all broke up when they heard about Daniel's unusual way of meeting her. They agreed that it had worked out quite well.

Arriving at the club, the valet took the car and they entered. After they were seated, the waiter came and took their orders. He brought their soft drinks back and they continued their conversation until he brought their orders. They each had ordered salads of one sort or another.

When Mr. Regal arrived at their table, he came from another area of the room. He had been there observing the three of them for some time, while he had his lunch with some other businessmen.

He shook hands with each of them before he sat down. He inquired about their perspective on their jobs and asked for their input, if they had any opinions. They both told him they liked their present positions but did hope to advance. He said, "Well, that's the point of my meeting you here. I wanted to treat you to a nice lunch and to tell you that I'm making you each the head of your department at Rebecca's request. That is, if you're willing to accept and of course Rebecca will remain as manager. We will announce these changes at a store meeting and in the local paper."

Pamela said, "Am I to be over the entire department, not just Women's Wear?" He answered, "That's right."

Leah then asked, "What about me?"

"You will be manager of your particular department for now." He added, "We'll discuss more responsibility later. We'll see how you perform in this position for six months. Okay? "

She answered, shyly, "Yes, sir, it's perfect."

He rose and said, "Okay, ladies, I will go now and let you get back to taking care of my business." They all smiled broadly and thanked him again.

When he had gone, they went to get the car and hurry back to work, so they could prove their worth. Pamela and Leah were both wondering how much of this would show up in their paychecks but didn't dare ask. The conversation went back to the new beaus and the plans they had for the future.

Chapter 88

Daniel had gone to lunch at the Café and found Jeff sitting alone at the cop's favorite table.

He went back to him and said, "Okay, if I join you, Jeff?"

"Sure, how are you doing today? Make any big loans?"

Daniel answered, "It's been a pretty slow day and I'm glad since we had such a busy weekend. What about you, had anything in the crime department today?"

"I've been at loose ends with Ed out. I'm so used to him making the decisions."

"I didn't know he had the time off. That's great! I had the idea he was going to work as usual."

"The chief said to tell him not to come in this week."

"I'm glad to hear that," he turned, "hey, Tony how about some service here. I'm starving."

Tony called for Maria, "You've got a hungry man out here, Maria. Better shake a leg." He ducked when she threw a sponge at him. Maria came to the table with a glass of water and said, "I'm sorry, I was in the office working on the books and didn't realize you had come in."

"No problem, just get me a burger and fries and I'll be happy."

She went to give his order to Tony and whispered, "Now, I'm busy back there, so you take it to him. Okay?"

"Yes, dear, sorry I bothered you." Seemed there was a little anger in the air at the Café today.

Presently, Tony brought Daniel's order to the table and sat down with them. He said, "I am in the dog house today."

Jeff sputtered, almost choking on his first bite. He observed, "I noticed a little static in the air. Knowing you, I'd say you probably deserve it."

"Yeah, you're right. I messed up the checkbook and now Maria has to straighten it out. I usually let her take care of all the check writing but I gave a big one to a vendor and didn't write it in, messed up and had some bounced checks. She's steamed."

Daniel said, "Maybe I can help you out and get the charges removed.

Maybe she'll cool off then, huh?"

"Man, if you can do that, your lunch is on me, today. Can I tell her?"

"Yeah, but wait til we're gone. I don't want to get in the middle of a family quarrel."

Jeff spoke up, "I was kind of hoping the guy that got the hot check would press charges and I could take Tony in, to the can."

The two of them snickered but Tony said, "Oh, no, he knew it was an error. We've been doing business with them for years. I won't be writing any more checks, though."

Daniel asked, "Have you seen Ed or Karen today?"

Tony shook his head, "Not today, they're on their honeymoon, Man. Didn't expect to see them for a while." He went to wait on a couple that had just come in.

Daniel turned to Jeff and asked, "How did your date with Pamela go? She's a nice girl, isn't she?"

"Yeah, I was impressed. She had Nathan and me over, after the wedding. We had pizza, watched the football game on television and drank some beer. It was fun. I think Nathan really liked Leah, too. Did you hear about how they met?"

"No, how was that?"

Tony was back and began to get excited to hear a new bit of gossip. Jeff gave him a dirty look but went on to tell the story of the wreck, the football game and the rest of the evening. Daniel asked, "What about Pamela's car. Is it totaled?"

"I really don't know, I probably ought to go check on it. It's at the station waiting for the adjuster."

Daniel got up and said, "Well, I've got to get back to work. I'll see you guys later."

Jeff stood and said, "Yeah, they'll be sending somebody to look for me if I don't get back to the department."

Tony shook Daniel's hand and said, "Thanks, Daniel, I'll appreciate if you can help me with my little problem." Daniel said, "Problem solved."

Chapter 89

The Wallaces got to school early Monday morning. They had stopped at the Quick Stop and bought milk and doughnuts. The three of them sat in Bill's office to eat and while they were there, the phone rang. Bill answered and it was Janet.

She told him that the doctor said she could come home on leave next weekend if Bill could pick her up. He told her to have the doctor call him because he had the game on Friday night and it's homecoming. He would need to pick her up on Thursday evening if that was possible. She said, "I'll tell him in a few minutes. I sure enjoyed the visit this weekend. Thanks for coming. I love you, Bill. Tell the kids. I love them, too."

Bill didn't respond. He started to, but choked on the words. He just said, "Okay, I will."

He hung up the phone without even saying goodbye. The kids were both looking at him. They thought something bad had happened, because he looked so grim. Finally he managed a smile and told them that their mother would be home on leave this weekend.

He said, "I guess she'll get to see you get crowned homecoming queen."

Amy protested, "Daddy, I haven't been selected, not yet, anyway. I'm lucky to be in the court. They're not going to pick a freshman."

Tom said, "Oh, you don't know, they might."

Bill told them, "You'd better get to your classes now and let me get my day planned. I didn't do a thing over the weekend to prepare. It's going to be an extemporaneous class today."

Tom answered, "Those are the best classes. Everybody gets involved and it's more fun."

Bill murmured under his breath, "I hope you're right."

They went on to class and he sat staring into space, wondering what he was going to do about Janet and their marriage. They would just have to go to counseling and see what happened. There was no real hurry since Margie was gone, he had no one to go to, no one to even talk to, no hope, except for the kids. He thanked God every day for his great kids.

Chapter 90

Ed and Karen had driven to a nice restaurant in Lexington for dinner and drinks. Ed had on his new suit and Karen was in her red dress, with her sterling necklace and earrings. She had on her red heels and a black shawl. Ed had told her how great she looked and she said, "Don't we make a handsome couple?" He agreed. The waiter got their drink order, a beer for Ed and a glass of wine for Karen. Ed suggested steak and she said, "Make mine medium rare, with a baked potato and bleu cheese dressing on the salad."

He said, "Well, you sure know what you want, don't you."

She answered, "I picked you, didn't I?"

He smiled and said, "Here I thought it was my idea." They enjoyed each others company so much, it was hard for them to believe that they were really married and would always be together. After their dinner, they went to the movies at the local cinema and saw a comedy with Robin Williams.

On the way home, Ed said, "Tomorrow we'll go check out the apartment manager, and then after school, to check with Bill Wallace. Then how about we drive up to Chicago on Wednesday or Thursday, see Sam Fortune, go to your gallery, take in a play or something and spend the night in a hotel?"

"Wow, you planned that itinerary in a hurry but I love it. We've never gone on a trip together and I love staying in fancy hotels."

"Hey, I didn't say a fancy hotel but I guess I could manage fancy for my bride. After all, we are on our honeymoon, Right?"

"You are so right, my handsome husband and don't you forget it. Have I told you that I love you?"

"Yeah, but it's okay for you to repeat it occasionally."

"We can take the golf cart up to see the Barrys and I'll get them to feed the animals for a day. They are always good about doing that for me. We'll have to be back Friday for the game. It's homecoming and I love seeing the girls in the ceremony."

"We'll be back. I still have some things I want to do at my old place, before I have to go back to work. We need to go see about Margie's safety deposit box, too. See if she had a will or some information about a lawyer. I feel like she would have taken care of things like that for Melanie's sake."

"You're right, I think so, too. Look, we're home already and there's Jazz to meet us. Thanks for the great evening, Hon."

He parked the car and when he turned off the engine, he pulled her to him and kissed her. "You are most welcome. I love you so much, Lady." They went to the house hand in hand.

Chapter 91

On Tuesday Pamela got the divorce papers back from Larry, signed, sealed and delivered. On her lunch hour she took them to the lawyer's office and left them with his secretary, Mary Sue Collins. She told Mary Sue to be sure to tell Jack that she wanted her maiden name Dixon back. She asked that he call after he had gone to court and let her know when it was final.

She went back to work feeling on top of the world. Now she needed to check on her car and see what the garage had to say. She decided to call the insurance adjuster on her break and see what he had to tell her.

As she was going back into the store, Jeff Collins pulled up beside her and honked his horn. She waved and he pulled to the curb, rolling down the window, said, "Where you headed?"

She told him, "I'm going to work." She was in front of the store at the time.

He said, "Can I call you this evening?"

She nodded and said, "Sure." and she went on into the store.

He drove onto the station thinking, "She didn't seem to be all that thrilled that I wanted to call her."

She really was hoping he would though, just didn't want to seem over anxious. Later on when Pamela spoke to the insurance adjuster, he told her that Nathan's insurance was taking care of her car repairs. It was just a broken radiator and dented fender. It didn't damage the frame so it would be fixed in about a week. He asked if she had been injured.

She could have had a rental car if she wanted one but she decided she didn't need it since she and Leah worked the same hours. Leah didn't mind giving her a ride until the car was repaired. They were both going in early every day, learning their new jobs and responsibilities. Rebecca was helping them get the hang of it. They were both surprised at how nice Rebecca was, once you got to know her.

Karen was on the porch having her first cup of coffee with Jazz and Callie when Ed got up. He came out with his coffee and they sat on the steps. It was cold but sunny and Karen loved the early morning outside before the dew evaporated. Jazz couldn't get used to Ed being there so he wouldn't leave him alone. He was always placing his head in Ed's lap, like, "Pet me, please."

Callie was happy to sit on Karen's lap.

Karen said, "Come with me to see about Candy." They walked to the barn and Candy was happy to see them. Karen used the comb on her for a little while and Ed just stood there watching her, so relaxed around that huge animal.

Karen said, "Are you afraid of Candy."

He looked insulted but said, "I just don't know anything about horses and they're so big. I'm fascinated at how you don't seem to be afraid of her at all."

"She loves me. She wouldn't kick me. I've had her since she was a colt. Sometime you'll have to try riding. It's wonderful to be up there galloping across the field."

"Well, I'll leave you to that experience. I'll stick to the golf cart, thank you." Karen slapped Candy on the rear and sent her to graze in the pasture. Then they walked back to the house and went in to fix breakfast.

After they had finished, they went outdoors again, got the golf cart and rode down to the Barrys. Nobody was around so they knocked on the back door. Ruth came to the door and squealed, "Look who's here, Joseph, the newlyweds are out and about.

Karen said, "Yes, we're here to ask a favor. I need you to feed the animals on Thursday morning. We'll be back later in the day but they need to eat in the morning."

"Why we'll be glad to do that. May I ask where are you going?"

"We're going to Chicago and see some sights. We thought it would be fun to see a play and spend the night while Ed is off work."

"Well, good for you. You just go have a good time and we'll take care of those little guys. Now let's have a cup of coffee."

Joseph said, "Sit down here and tell me what you've been doing this week. I saw the movers at your place. Did you sell your house, Ed.?"

"No, not yet but it's on the market. I still need to sell some of the furnishings. I'll run an ad in the weekly and see if I can sell them. I'll donate whatever is left to Goodwill."

Ruth spoke up, "The Women's Society is having a yard sale next week if you want to donate to it."

"If you can get someone to move it, you can have it all except the kitchen appliances. I'll give you a key and you can take it all. That will be much simpler for me."

"Oh, that's wonderful. We'll move it tomorrow. We're raising money to cook Thanksgiving dinner for the poor and homeless. We plan to deliver meals to the senior shut ins, too. That will help a lot. Then we'll give what's left to the Goodwill."

"I like that idea, glad to have my old stuff do some good."

Karen said, "We've got some errands to run, so we'd better go now. Thanks for the coffee, next time it's at our house. I need to fix dinner for you two now that I'm back to cooking."

They got on the cart and headed for home. Jazz ran out to meet them and Karen let him climb on for a ride.

Prepared to do some investigating, they decided that they didn't need to change. They didn't want to look official, just curious.

Margie's apartment building was first on the list. The manager was in his apartment. When he answered the door, Ed said, "I'm Ed Hawkins and this is my wife, Karen." He extended his hand. He shook and said, "Ben Malone. What can I do for you?"

"We were friends of Margie Sloan and we got to wondering if you'd seen any of the people that visited in her apartment." Ed asked. Malone said, "I don't think I ever noticed anyone, why do you want to know? She committed suicide, didn't she?"

Ed said, "Well, that's what the cops decided but we have our doubts and my wife received some threatening phone calls after she visited the apartment. It sort of makes one think that someone has something to hide."

Malone looked a little angry and said, "Well, I doubt if that had anything to do with what happened here."

Ed continued, "You haven't seen anyone, huh?"

"I don't see many of the people who live here unless they have a problem."

Ed gave him his notebook and asked him to write down his telephone number in case he wanted to talk to him again. Malone took it and the pen Ed offered and wrote his number. Ed went on to explain, "This way we won't have to bother you again."

Malone said, "Her rent was paid until the first of the year. Do you think her daughter will keep the apartment?"

Karen had remained silent while the two men talked but now she spoke, "I doubt if she will but we'll let you know when she comes home for the holidays. She'll be staying with us."

They both thanked him and went back to their car and heading for the high school. On the way Karen told Ed, "You know it may be my imagination but that guy sounded a lot like the one on the phone. Did you notice the New England accent?"

Chapter 92

Bill had finished his last class of the day and was in his office by the gym, when Ed and Karen came in. "Hi, Bill, how are you doing?" Ed inquired just to be friendly.

Bill looked surprised to see them and said, "Why I'm just fine. How about you two newlyweds?"

Karen said, "We're doing great. I sure did love Amy singing at the wedding and I want to pay her." She gave Bill her notebook and said, "Would you write your address in here so I can mail it to her. I want to send a card with it."

Bill shook his head and said, "No, you don't need to pay her, she was glad to do it."

Karen insisted, "I know that but I want to, so please give me your mailing address."

He did as she asked and she tucked the notebook back in her purse.

"Bill, I hate to ask, but I know you had been seeing Margie at one time. I just wondered when you saw her last. I'm still not convinced that she committed suicide. I thought she might have told you if she was seeing anybody else. You know, if Larry had threatened her or even something that she might have said about her feelings." She paused, then continued, "Did she say anything that would explain her actions that night?"

Bill looked puzzled and answered, "I didn't realize there was any doubt about her death."

Karen hastened to add, "No, there's no official question, but my own doubts trouble me. You know, her and I were very close for years and she never seemed unhappy. At least not since her divorce. She seemed really happy as a matter of fact."

Bill looked at Ed and said, "Then you're not here as a cop?"

Ed said, "No, I'm just with Karen. She's been worried about this for weeks and so I told her to talk to some people who knew Margie and make peace with it."

Bill said, "Yeah, that makes sense. It's upset me, too. I never thought Margie would do a thing like that either. But there's nothing I can tell you.

When she found out that I had gone back home, she refused to see me at all."

Karen said, "Well, I appreciate you talking to me. We'll go now, I know you have a team to work out. I hope you win the game this week, especially since it's homecoming."

Bill said, "I hope so for the kid's sake. Amy is in the homecoming court and Tom is escorting her. By the way Janet is coming home on leave. I've got to pick her up Thursday evening and bring her home so I guess she'll be at the game unless she too embarrassed."

"Oh, I hope she'll come to the game. It will mean so much to Amy. You tell her to sit with us and we'll make her feel comfortable if we can."

Bill's face lighted up when he heard that and he offered, "I'll tell you what, I'll save you seats on the fifty-yard line if you'll sit with her. Just don't let her know I planned it. Okay?"

Karen agreed immediately, "That's a deal, we'll see you then." They exchanged goodbyes and went back to their car.

Ed squeezed Karen's hand and said, "You are so slick. Once a cop, always a cop. Now we've got both our prints for Sam."

On the way home, Karen said, "Ed, stop at the florists so I can pick up some flowers for Margie's grave and we'll go by there."

He pulled up in front of the shop while Karen ran in and came back out with three red roses. They went to the cemetery and walked over to the grave. There was a fresh pink rose and many others that had dried up. Karen picked up the dead ones and knelt down to place hers gently on the barren earth. She spoke softly, "We are taking care of things, Margie. May you rest in peace."

She looked up at Ed, "I've got to talk to Melanie about a headstone for her soon."

They decided to go to the Café to eat supper and hear the latest gossip. When they went in, Tony yelled, "Well, look who has surfaced. The honeymooners."

Karen blushed and looked around to see how many others were there. She grumbled, as if angry, "You've got a big mouth, Tony."

Ed said, "You sure know how to make enemies of your friends, Tony."

"I knew nobody else was here or I wouldn't have said that. Sorry, Karen."

She shook her fist at him and said, "Oh, just shut up and get me a cup of coffee."

Maria came out of the backroom office and said, "You can hit him for me, too, Karen."

Tony was just amused at the two ladies and said, "I'll swear, Ed, I can't stay out of the doghouse, no matter how hard I try."

"I don't think you're trying hard enough. As a matter of fact I think you may be under the doghouse if you don't shut up and get us that coffee. We haven't had any coffee for a long time and you know a cop has got to have his coffee."

They sat at the counter for a while, just visiting with Maria and Tony. Then they got up and went to the back table to eat the burger and fries they had ordered.

While they were eating, Jeff came in and sat down with them. He said, "I just talked to Pamela and she's going to the game with me Friday night. I guess we'll take Leah, too. The guy that she went with is back at school. Did you know about him hitting Pamela's car on the interstate?"

Karen said, "No, was anybody hurt?"

Ed asked, "Did you investigate the wreck?"

"No, a highway patrolman did that and gave him a ticket. He got a tow for the car and I found them at the Fast Gas. We all got to talking and decided to go to the game together. Her car is still in the shop."

"So did you have a good time on your date? You know she's married, don't you?"

"Not for very much longer. She gave the lawyers the papers Larry signed and she'll soon be Pamela Dixon again. She's really a nice girl and I did enjoy being with her. She's kind of quiet and shy. I think those sleazy outfits she used to wear, were Larry's idea, actually."

Karen said, "I'm sure you're right. He thought of her as his trophy wife, just wanted to irritate Margie and her friends."

Ed said, "Well, we need to go home. We're going to Chicago tomorrow and kick up our heels, so we need to get to bed early."

Jeff said, "Oh, I'd love to see you kicking up your heels. Take care and come back safe, I've missed you this week. Nobody to rag me."

Ed got up, went to Maria at the cash register to pay the tab. The night air was cold and they hurried to the car. Winter was definitely on it's way and they were hoping the good weather would last for their trip.

Chapter 93

Rebecca had called Daniel to thank him for the flowers and he asked her to go to dinner at the club on Wednesday evening. She accepted, so now he was at her door to pick her up. When she came to the door, she looked beautiful. She was in a teal crepe dress that had a draped effect one side and ended with a slit at the bottom. She had on black mules with four inch heels. Her black hair was pulled back in a chignon on the nape of her neck showing off drop gold loops on her ears and a wide gold choker above a low-cut neckline.

He told her, "You look great, I'll be the most envied man at the club tonight."

She said, "Why, thank you, kind sir. That's a great compliment and you're looking good, too." He was dressed in his best dark blue pinstripe with a white shirt and red tie.

When they got to the Lexus, he opened the door for her. As he got in on the driver's side, she said, "I'm so glad you called. I've been working so hard all week and I needed a break."

They discussed their jobs for a few minutes and were soon at the club. The valet took the keys after he opened the door for Rebecca and they went in.

The maitre' de met them and said, "Good evening, Miss Magee and Mr. Carmody, so nice to see you."

He led them to a table in the corner of the room and motioned for the waiter. Daniel asked Rebecca what she would like to drink. When the waiter came, he ordered a Chablis for each of them. He told her about bringing Ed and Karen there for dinner and surprising them with the violinist.

She said, "That was nice of you. How long have you been friends with them?"

"Well, not very long but they are both such great people that it's easy to be their friend."

She told him about her lunch with Pamela and Leah the other day and the result of their visit with Mr. Regal."

He said, " I'm so glad to hear he did that for Pamela. She is a deserving girl who had a rough start in Dinsmore. I don't know Leah but she must be equally deserving. Mr. Regal doesn't pass out promotions without good reason. I guess you are aware of that though."

"Yes, he is a very nice man but he does expect his employees to perform their jobs well and truly believes that the customer is always right. They must be treated as if they are very important, because of course they are."

When Ed and Karen got home, she got on the Internet and looked for tickets to plays in Chicago on Wednesday night. She asked Ed if he had a preference, and he answered, "I'll go to whatever you want to see."

She said, "Well, then we're going to see the road company of "Fiddler on the Roof" tomorrow night at eight o'clock, the tickets will be at the window."

"Okay, but the first thing we'll go see Sam Fortune and give him those pages from our notebooks."

Karen asked him, "After that, can we go to the Rose Gallery and see what it's like?"

Ed answered, "Fine with me. Sometime we'll eat. By the way, where do you want to stay?"

Karen said, "Oh, I guess I'd better check with the Downtown Mariotte and make our reservations."

She went back on the Internet and took care of their reservations with her credit card. When she was through with that, Ed was in watching television. She made some microwave popcorn and got two beers and went to join him. He smiled and said, "This a great life, I've never had it so good. I should have proposed to you three years ago."

Karen sat down beside him, kissed him on the cheek and told him, "That would not have worked. I was still a cop and your partner. One of us would have been fired or separated. This is good, we've got plenty of years left and we can make the most of them." They stayed up to watch the news and then went to their bedroom where television was not allowed.

When Daniel and Rebecca had finished their dinner and he was driving her home, he said, "I enjoyed the evening. I hope you did. I'd like to take you to the football game Friday night if you're interested. They're just high school games but I enjoy them. Dinsmore has a great team and it's always fun to go cheer them on. We could get Karen and Ed to go with us, if you'd like."

She said, "I already told you I wanted to go. Did you forget? It would be fun to go with the Hawkins. They seem like a lot of fun and she's so talented."

"No, I didn't forget. I was just double checking."

She smiled at him and he thought, "My God, she is so gorgeous."

When he walked her to the door, she invited him in but he said, "I'd better get to my place. I'm expecting a call from my daughter. I'll pick you up on Friday about six fifteen if that's okay."

She said, "Well, pick me up at the Regal then, because we're open late on Friday but I can leave a little early. I'll take some jeans and a shirt to work so I can change and I'll just wait for you in front of the store. Is that okay?" He agreed and then he stood there wondering if he dare kiss her.

She made the first move and he gave her a long lingering kiss. He liked her response but he was a little embarrassed. He couldn't think of anything else to say except, "Goodnight, and thanks again for the nice evening."

He had watched until she had unlocked her door, and was inside, to go on to his apartment. He wasn't expecting a call. He just didn't want to over react and become involved in a relationship yet. He wanted to get to know her better, not to appear needy. He wondered if he was over thinking himself. But he thought again, "Better safe, than sorry. I won't be able to use that ruse again."

Inside her apartment she was thinking, "I really like that guy. He's such a gentleman. I hope we can get to know each other better. I don't know how to read him though. He's so nice but he seems a little stand offish. Maybe he's not over the lady who died. Well, at least he did ask me out again so maybe I have a chance."

She laughed out loud at herself for thinking about him in such a serious way. She went into her living room and out of habit turned on television but didn't really watch it. She got the journal that she had kept for ten years and wrote about her evening. She was still thinking about the evening when she was in bed.

She dreamed about Daniel that night, a very romantic dream. When she woke, she was startled, because he had impressed her enough to appear in her dreams.

Chapter 94

Karen and Ed were up early preparing to go on their trip. Karen fed the animals and made the coffee while Ed showered. When he was finished, he put the notebooks and other information about their investigation in his briefcase. He took his coffee and went out to play in the cold with Jazz while Karen had her shower and dressed. For their travel, they both opted for jeans and jackets, taking the clothes for the theater and dining in hanging bags. They had packed the other necessities the night before. Karen got a cup of coffee after she was dressed and joined Ed.

She said, "How about stopping at the Café for breakfast, before we leave?"

He answered, "Sounds good, are you ready to go?" She nodded . After they put their things in Ed's big Cadillac they went into town.

Tony had just opened the Café when they pulled up in front. He had their coffee on the counter before they got in the door. "Glad to see you this morning," he said. They both greeted him and sat down at the counter.

He was cooking their order when Daniel came in. He slipped up behind Karen, holding his finger to his lips and put his arms around her in a bear hug.

She said, "You're not fooling me, Daniel, I recognize your after shave."

He backed up and exclaimed, "Oh, I must be overdoing it, if it's that obvious."

"No, it's just a unique aroma and you're the only man I knows who wears it. It must be expensive or more men would use it, because it smells great."

Ed quipped, "Well, if it's that good, I'll have to get some, won't I?"

Daniel got right back at him, saying, "No, it won't do any good. It depends on who wears it. Smells different on different men."

Karen said, "Oh, sit down. Enough talk about after shave, this is not a very manly conversation. I wish I'd never mentioned it."

Then he asked what they were doing out so early and they replied that it seemed early for a banker, too. He confessed he was walking for the exercise, had been eating a lot of rich food and didn't want to gain weight.

Karen said, "Sounds to me like the man is staying in shape for a lady, maybe."

He smiled at that and confessed, "Well, I did have a nice evening with Rebecca Magee, last night."

Ed said, "Does evening mean you stayed over?"

Daniel acted as if he was shocked, "No, of course not, would I do a thing like that?" He went on to assure them, "No, I'm really serious, it was a nice evening. She's a beautiful lady but I'm not interested in starting anything more than friendship right now."

Tony had lingered when he brought Daniel's coffee before he went back to get Karen and Ed's breakfast orders. They all were aware that he was eavesdropping as usual and Daniel wanted to be sure he heard the entire conversation.

Tony asked, "Are you having breakfast, Daniel?"

"Yes, fix me one of the same as theirs.," Daniel answered.

Then when Tony was gone, he asked, "What are you two up to today?"

Ed said, "We are on our way to Chicago to have a little fun."

Daniel said, "That's great. I was glad to hear that the chief gave you the week off."

Karen said, "By the way, thank you for the gift certificate. We really appreciated that. I'll get around to thank you notes eventually when Ed goes back to work. We've just been enjoying ourselves this week."

He said, "I'm so glad that you have been able to. You both deserve all the best. I thought the wedding was wonderful and the golf cart ride was hilarious. Jeff got such a kick out of doing that."

Tony said, "How did you like the convoy we formed?"

Karen said, "It was a great end for a great day. Everybody went out of their way to make it even more special."

They were finished with their breakfast and after they had said their goodbyes, they got in the car to go to interstate fifty five and headed for Chicago. Karen tuned the radio to her favorite classical music but low enough for conversation because they always had a lot to talk about.

Halfway there Ed pulled into a truck stop for a break. They had a soda and gassed up while they were there. They got to the city at about ten a.m. and after they checked in at the Downtown Mariette, they took a cab to the FBI offices.

Ed had called Sam the day before and made arrangements to see him. When he came out of the office, he said, "Let's go down to Starbucks and talk there. I don't want to have these people asking questions about my visitors. I'm doing this all under the radar screen."

He was a little short fellow, with a sturdy build that made him look like a boxer. He had a full head of bright red hair. He was so muscular, he looked like he might burst out of his conservative brown suit.

Ed introduced Karen to him. He shook her hand with a firm grip and said smiling broadly, "Well, it took you long enough to get married, but you certainly got better than you deserve."

Karen said, "It's nice to meet you, Sam. I think I did all right, too."

Sam just nodded his head. When they got to the coffee shop, they all got lattes and sat down in a booth. Ed explained the reasons they were so determined to find out what happened to Margie. He gave him the note paper they had gotten from Bill and Ben.

Ed said, "I don't know if these will turn up in your system but they may match some of those from the bottle and the dish I sent you. Just make sure you don't contact me at the police department. You can call the house and tell Karen. She's an ex cop so she'll understand."

Karen said, "We're not trying to prove murder or anything like it. We do want to prove she didn't commit suicide. Her daughter means a lot to me and it's been very upsetting for her to lose her mother, but thinking she took her own life makes it even worse."

When they finished the meeting with Sam, they all shook hands and made plans to meet again or to talk on the phone. Karen told him, "I'll probably be back here next week to pick up Margie's daughter at the airport. So if you need anything else just let us know and I'll bring it then."

Sam agreed and they parted company. Sam went back to work. Ed and Karen got a cab to find some lunch. They decided to get some good Chicago barbeque at Carson's. They enjoyed the change of pace in the big city and the lunch was delicious. Ed said, "I'm so full, I could use a nap but we'd better go find the gallery first."

He hailed a cab that took them to "The Rose Gallery," where Karen would be showing. Harry Rose saw them enter and came to greet them. He was smiling and said, "It's so good to see you again. I'm glad you'll have a chance to see how we display our artwork here."

Karen said, "I'd like you to meet my husband, Ed Hawkins. We just got married this last Sunday."

Harry said, "Well, that is great. Are you honeymooning here in Chicago?"

Ed explained, "We're just here for the day. We really didn't have time for a honeymoon. We'll take a real trip later next year after Karen has her show. She wanted to have a look at the gallery. I'm going to have to quit taking up so much of her time so she can get back to her painting."

Harry said to Karen, "Well, I know it will be a busy time with the holidays and all but you have a very good start on them, don't you?"

Karen answered, "Oh, yes, I'll be ready, don't worry about that. This is a great opportunity for me and I won't let you down."

He said, "Well, let me show you around the gallery."

It was a big two story building with lots of glass and the natural light was good for the paintings. They had many examples of sculpture and pottery in addition to the paintings which ran the gamut from extreme realism to abstract. Karen could see that her work would fit in very well.

They spent about an hour with Harry on the gallery tour. He offered to take them to dinner but they explained their plans for the evening. They needed to get back to their hotel in order to get ready.

They got another cab back to the hotel. By now it was after four and they had been up and going for a long time. They decided a nap was in order. They had a beautiful room that looked out over the city but they closed the drapes to darken the room and they both fell asleep on the bed.

When they woke up, it was already six o'clock. They took a shower together and went back to the bed for a brief interlude. When they got up, they dressed in the same clothes they had worn for their wedding and decided to walk to the theater.

Ed told her, "You know that I've never been to the theater, don't you?"

She was totally surprised and said, "I had no idea. I didn't think to ask you, but I always think theater when I'm in any big city. I sure hope you enjoy it because I love it."

He said, "If you like it, I will. I've heard the music from this one and I like it. Actually, I'm looking forward to it. I figure you're never too old to learn a new trick."

Karen took his hand and squeezed it, she leaned into him and said, "You are so good to me, I guess that's why I love you. You're so easy going."

"You used to think I was a grumpy old man. I was really a tortured old man, so much in love and afraid to tell you. Really stupid, huh?"

"Not stupid, just careful. I wasn't too receptive because I didn't have a clue. I had no idea how you felt. You managed to hide it so well. Did you think Rich would come back and haunt you if you asked me out?"

"I guess that I did. I felt like I would be betraying my best friend because even though he was gone, you were his wife after all."

"Well, I believe that if it's possible, he's up there looking down, pleased that we're together."

"Knowing Rich, you're probably right."

They were at the theater now. They had to stand in line for a little while and then they went in. They had excellent seats and thoroughly enjoyed the show. Theodore Bikel was wonderful and the music was just great. When the show ended the audience gave the cast a standing ovation.

When they were back on the street they went to Petterino's, an extremely nice restaurant. They were seated and ordered drinks, wine for Karen, scotch and soda for Ed. They had prime rib with vegetables. Then they had cheesecake for dessert.

Ed said, "We've got to watch it or we're going to get fat, eating like this."

"I'll fix light meals the rest of the week."

Afterwards, it was quite late so they took a cab back to the hotel. They watched television for a few minutes before they both fell asleep until eight o'clock in the morning. Karen was shocked when she woke up and the television was still on. Ed woke, too and said, "Wow, I think I died after all that food, I wasn't able to stay awake."

In spite of all the talk about eating too much, he called room service and ordered coffee and bagels with cream cheese. It came in about thirty minutes with fruit and some raspberry preserves, beautiful silver service and china on an elegantly set table.

When the waiter had gone, Karen said, "I think I could get used to this kind of life."

Ed replied, "Don't get too used to it. Not on a cop's pay."

"Hey, you're going to have a famous artist for a wife."

He got her right back, "You know artists' don't get rich until they're dead."

"Well, we'll just see about that. I might make you eat those words."

"Okay, I'm sorry. I have more faith in you than that. I hope you're right, anyway. I'd like to be a kept man. But until that happens, how do you feel about heading back to our dull life in Dinsmore?"

She laughed at him and said, "I'm ready when you are. I thought you might want to go back to bed."

"I'd rather wait until I get you back home, but if you insist."

He picked her up and threw her on the bed. Afterwards, they had showered and got back into their travel clothes, checked out of the hotel, called for the Cadillac and started back to Dinsmore.

Chapter 95

Bill Wallace left school early on Thursday to pick up Janet at the hospital. He left Jerry, the assistant coach, in charge of football practice and arranged for him to give Amy and Tom a ride home. Amy wanted to go with him but he convinced her to stay for cheerleader practice. She had to meet with the other girls in the homecoming court. Besides he wanted to have some time alone with Janet, so they could talk without the kids present.

At the hospital, Janet was already waiting with her overnight bag. She had put on make up and looked better than she had in years. He hugged her and signed the necessary papers to take her home for a few days.

It only took a couple of hours to drive back to Dinsmore. Bill asked, "Well, how have you been doing this week?"

She answered, "I'm really doing fine, I don't see why they're keeping me so long. My medication is working and I'm feeling like a new woman."

He asked, "What do you mean by that, a new woman?"

"I mean, I'm not angry, I'm not depressed, I've taken off the weight so I feel better about my looks. I'm anxious to get back to normal relations with you."

He cringed, hoping she didn't notice, "I don't know if I'm ready for that. You know, you might have killed me if Tom hadn't stepped in. I do want us to be able to have a nice weekend for the kid's sake, though. I mean, no arguments and yelling. That's why I wanted this time alone with you."

"I can't blame you for feeling a little hesitant but I thought you had forgiven me."

"I have forgiven you, I just don't know if I can be a real husband to you anymore. I don't want to give you the wrong impression. I want you to get well but I'm not sure I can keep up the pretense of being happily married."

"Did you tell my doctor how you felt? I mean maybe I shouldn't have taken this leave if you feel that way."

"I wanted you to come home so the kids could have some time with you, away from the hospital. They have really missed you a lot. Besides Amy is in the homecoming court tomorrow night and she'll want you there."

"I don't know if I can face those people again. I mean they all know where

I've been and what I did to get there."

He decided not to have secrets anymore and told her, "I've arranged for you to sit with Karen and Ed and you'll be fine. People don't think that much about a person having a breakdown these days. It happens to the best of us. Don't let it bother you, just hold your head up. At least you have done something to improve and that's more than a lot of folks can say."

"I guess you're right. Are you still willing to go to family counseling when I get discharged?"

"Yes, I'm willing, but I don't want you to get your hopes up. I'm trying to be as honest as I can with you. I just don't know if I can keep on trying to have a decent relationship with you and keep my own sanity."

She began to cry softly, and he was almost sorry he had said anything, but he went on, "Please don't be sad. I didn't mean to hurt your feelings. I just want to be sure you know how I feel so that we don't get in a fight or anything with the kids in the middle. I want us to have a good weekend. We'll go out and have some fun and try to act like a normal family."

He reached over and patted her knee and said, "Don't cry, it's going to be all right. You'll see."

She wiped her eyes and replied, "I'm okay, I know you're doing your best and I appreciate it. I'll try to be a decent wife and mother." She giggled then and said, "Maybe I can do it for the weekend anyway."

They began to laugh and before long they were back in Dinsmore. When they went in the house, Amy and Tom were waiting with open arms. Amy had even fixed a nice dinner for them and it was a "happy" family that sat down to dinner. Bill asked the Lord's blessing on the family and the meal.

Chapter 96

On Friday morning Tony opened the Café early as usual and his first customer was Jeff Collins. Tony took him a cup of coffee and sat down to talk. "What's going on in the Dinsmore crime scene these days?"

Jeff said, "Nothing, thank goodness. Two little old ladies decided to crash at the corner of Elm and Main yesterday. Of course they each blamed it on the other. It was funny to listen to them rattle on. I just told them to call their insurance companies, that it looks as though they were equally guilty."

"Have you seen Ed or Karen lately? They were in the other day on their way to Chicago for a day or two, but they haven't been in since then."

"No, I haven't seen them since the first of the week, but I'll see them tonight at the game, I'm sure."

"Yeah, this is a big night, be a bigger crowd because of the homecoming. It's going to be colder, too. Be tough for those little girls in their formals. It might even snow."

"I hope not, then we'll have more wrecks for sure. I always dread the snow." Another couple of customers came in and Tony went to wait on them.

Jeff was finishing his coffee when Daniel came in. "Well, you're out mighty early for a banker."

Daniel said, "I've been walking and running early for a few days. Trying to keep my girlish figure."

"Yeah, got to look good for that new gal in your life, huh?"

"Well, look who's talking. I hear you've got a new special person in your life, too."

"Yeah, if you can call a couple of football games special, I guess so. I really do like Pamela. She's a very nice person and fun to be with. I like her room mate Leah, too. I'm taking them both to the game tonight."

"Well, how about that? Taking two girls out, that should be interesting."

"You're a dirty old man, just like Ed. Always coming up with a different twist on things. I just didn't want to leave Leah out in the cold. It is just a football game after all."

"Well, good for you. I'm taking Rebecca, myself. Should be a good game and the girls will like the half time with the homecoming activities."

Tony brought Daniel a cup of coffee and got his breakfast order. Jeff got up to leave and said, "I'll see you guys at the game." He went to get in his patrol car and check on the traffic which was building up with school bound drivers. Daniel began to read his Chicago paper and Tony got busy with more customers arriving.

Pamela and Leah were up, getting ready to go to work. They had worked out a schedule for taking showers and fixing breakfast. They took turns, one day one cooked breakfast while the other showered and the next day they switched. This day Pamela was cooking breakfast while Leah showered.

They had decided to wear semi-casual clothes that would be suitable for the football game since they would have to go right from work. They had checked with Rebecca the day before, about getting off a little early and she agreed. She told them that Daniel was picking her up out front of the building. Leah said they were being picked up at the apartment but they would have enough time to get there. Their apartment complex was closer than Rebecca's.

Rebecca had asked, "When is Pamela going to get her car back?"

Leah told her, "Sometime next week, they say it will be ready."

"I know she'll be glad to have it back. I'll probably see you at the game." Leah knew she was being dismissed and she went back to work.

Leah told Pamela about the conversation with Rebecca as they ate breakfast. Pamela said, "Yes, she's very nice but she is all business most of the time. I never am quite sure how friendly to be with her. I don't want her to think I'm sucking up."

"I don't think that would work with Rebecca. What do you think of her and Daniel? Isn't he a lot older than her?"

"Oh, I don't know how old he is but he's fine looking and Rebecca is probably in her late thirties. After that I don't think age makes that much difference. I wonder if she's ever been married. I don't know anything about her, do you?"

"No, but it would be interesting to know where she came from. She just sort of showed up one day, when Larry was the manager. Then she automatically became the manager when he left."

Pamela thought about it and the offered her opinion, "I think maybe Mr. Regal had planned to fire Larry anyway and he brought Rebecca in from another store to prepare her for taking over."

Leah thought about that for a minute and said, "That makes sense. You'd better get in there and get ready. We need to get going soon." She cleaned up the kitchen while Pamela showered and dressed for their day at work.

Ed was out taking Jazz for a ride on the golf cart and Karen was writing thank you notes. They had been up for several hours. The weather was looking threatening so they planned to enjoy one more day outdoors before the snow started falling. Melanie had called and told Karen her plans for coming home and made the arrangements to be picked up on Tuesday evening before Thanksgiving. Ed said he would get off early so he could go with her.

Karen heard someone in the driveway and it was the Barrys. When Joseph got out of the truck he said, "Thought we'd better come up and make sure our neighbors were okay after their trip."

Karen had gone outside to meet them, when Ed came up in the golf cart. Ruth was laughing when she saw Jazz riding with Ed and she said, "That dog is so spoiled, he thinks he's a person because you both treat him that way."

Karen said, "Yes, of course, he is like my baby and Callie is just as bad." They do sleep in the barn though, unless it gets real cold, then I let them in the house."

Ruth asked, "How was your trip?"

Karen told her about all the fun things they did and how much she had enjoyed it. She said, "I took Ed to his first play and he loved it."

Ruth gave her a jar of applesauce she had made and told her that they were going to have Thanksgiving dinner and would love to have Ed and Karen join them. Ruth said that the other single and widowed ladies at the church were serving the homeless dinners. She had helped with the cooking ahead of time.

Karen looked at Ed and asked, "Will that be all right with you?"

He wasted no time answering, "That sounds wonderful. I'll bet Ruth can cook up a great turkey dinner. Her breakfast was sure delicious."

Karen said, "Well, Melanie will be here, so there will be three of us if that's okay. I want you to tell me what I can fix. I'm a pretty good cook, too, you know and I won't think of coming unless I can help."

Ruth said, "Oh, of course I'll show you my menu and you can decide what you want to fix."

Karen said, "Now that's decided, so come in and have a cup of coffee with us." They all went into the house and sat around the kitchen table talking about the weather and the latest gossip in town.

Chapter 97

Tony and Maria closed the Café early and went home to get Mama and the kids. They were all well now, so they would all be going to the game. Snow was predicted to be on the way but they took plenty of heavy coats and extra blankets. The town of Dinsmore was completely football fanatic. No one would want to miss the homecoming game.

Pamela and Leah hurried home to wait for Jeff to pick them up for the game. Daniel parked out front of The Regal. He wanted to be there waiting for Rebecca when she came out. Ed and Karen left early so they could get seated and be there for Janet as Bill had asked.

It was a good thing they started early because the traffic was heavy and it took longer than usual to get into the parking lot.

When they got into the stadium, they looked for Janet but she wasn't seated where they were supposed to meet her. Bill was with the team in the locker room, giving them last minute encouragement, so they went ahead and sat down. It was a few minutes before Janet came up into the stands. Karen waved at her and Janet smiled as she approached them. Karen said, "It's so good to see you, Janet. Aren't you proud of Amy and Tom?"

She answered, "Yes, I really am so proud. That's where I've been. Helping Amy get ready for the ceremony. Tom is going to be her escort. He'll have to do it with his football uniform on since there won't be time to change and get back on the field." She leaned over to speak to Ed, "How are you, Ed?"

He had been dreading seeing Janet, since he had seen her in jail and hadn't been very kind to her because she had been so volatile and hard to deal with. He said, "I'm just fine and I'm glad you're looking so well. I know Bill and the kids are glad to have you at home."

She seemed a little sad as she said, "Well, it's only for the weekend." She quickly added, "But it's wonderful to be home."

Karen said, "You look so good. You've lost a lot of weight haven't you?"

Janet smiled broadly and said, "I'm so glad you noticed, I've been working on it and I feel much better, too."

By now the stands were full on both sides of the field. The Mavericks from

Mason came crashing through their paper sign and the crowd roared. The Dinsmore Dogs came from the other end and another roar went up. The Mavericks won the toss and chose offense. Their quarterback threw a short pass and only got three yards. They were not able to get a first down so Dinsmore took over and Tom threw a long pass to his favorite receiver, to gain thirty yards right away. It only took a few more minutes to get the first touchdown of the game. The kicker made the extra point and the other team had the ball. The opposing team didn't score at all in the first half so Dinsmore led by seven points.

Halftime came, the band began to play "Pretty Woman," marching onto the field. They got into a formation resembling a long aisle with band members lined up on each side. The announcer began to call out the names of the girls and their escorts in the homecoming court. The freshman maids were first and Amy came out on Tom's arm, looking so beautiful that it made tears come to Janet's eyes.

Karen hugged her and said, "You've got a beauty there."

Amy was in silver metallic gown with a halter style neckline. It was fitted and showed off her shapely body. She had her long blonde hair piled high on her head and she didn't look like a fifteen-year old, but then after all she was "going to be sixteen in December."

Tom had a big smile on his face, he was extremely proud of his little sister and it showed. The rest of the court followed and then they announced the queen, Megan Catron, the daughter of Sam and Carla Catron. She was a beauty, too. She was the senior class president and captain of the girl's basketball team, in addition to being a cheerleader. She already had scholarships to the university. Her escort was the captain of the boy's basketball team.

The crowd gave them a standing ovation and the band played "Send in the Clowns" as they all filed off the field. When the game resumed, the Dinsmore Dogs kept up their winning ways and won the game, twenty-eight to fourteen. The recruiter from Northwestern was in the audience again and everyone figured Tom would be hearing from him and others soon.

After the game Bill met Karen, Ed and Janet out in the parking lot. He said the kids were all going to McDonald's. He asked Karen and Ed to join him and Janet for a burger.

They agreed and got in the car to go, when they saw Daniel and Rebecca coming out of the stadium. Ed rolled down the window and asked, "Hey, want to meet us at McDonald's?"

Daniel looked at Rebecca questioningly and she nodded, "Okay, we'll see you there," he said.

There was an exceptionally big crowd at McDonald's that night but they were always prepared, knowing that the fans would be coming there and to Wendy's after the game was over. It was a given, on football night so they always stayed open late for the celebrators. The teens all sat in one section and the parents in another, of course. Everyone had a good time though.

The Wallaces and the Hawkins were seated at a table when Rebecca and Daniel came in. The men pulled another table up and they all sat down. Ed introduced them to Bill and Janet. The men rehashed the game while the women talked about the homecoming court.

When they all had their burgers, Bill got up and went over to the teens to talk to Tom and Amy. The kids were all shaking his hand and patting him on the back. When he came back, he said the kids had a ride with friends and that he and Janet had better get on home.

After they left, Karen said, "I thought Janet looked good and was very relaxed, didn't you?" Ed agreed.

Daniel explained to Rebecca what had happened to the Wallaces and Janet in particular. She was sympathetic and said, "I hope they'll be able to get over it. They seem like a nice family."

They all talked about the impending snowfall and the fact that it would be on the weekend so they wouldn't have to be out in it. When they went to their cars, it had started to come down in big wet flakes.

Ed said, "Do you think I should go back and tell those kids to go on home? They don't need to be driving in a snowstorm."

Everyone laughed at him and Daniel said, "They will run you off if you do that." They got in their cars and went on their way to their respective homes.

When Daniel walked Rebecca to her door, she invited him in. This time he accepted and they had a glass of wine while they sat on the couch and talked about the evening, the weather and other mundane things.

Finally, after much thought, Daniel put his arm around her and pulled her close. They kissed a long hard kiss. Then as if he was flustered or embarrassed, he stood up quickly. He said, "I really need to go now. I've enjoyed being with you and I'll call you."

She was a little surprised at his sudden move but she got up, gave him his jacket and walked with him to the door. He kissed her on the cheek and was out of the door.

She stood there a moment thinking, "How strange." When he got back to his apartment he gave himself a head slap, but he knew he had done the wise thing by leaving before things got out of hand. He could easily have stayed overnight and then been sorry tomorrow. He didn't want to become involved in a rebound romance. He fully intended to give it time.

When Ed and Karen got home, they were exhausted. The trip and the busy night had knocked them out. The burgers late at night didn't make for an energy lift but rather made them even sleepier. They didn't waste any time getting to bed and both were fast asleep in no time.

The phone rang in the middle of the night and it was the desk sergeant at the station. Jeff Collins and his date had been in an accident coming into town from Wendy's. Some kids had pulled out in front of him. The highway was slick from the snow and he slid into a light pole. They were okay, but Jeff had a broken ankle and his date got cuts on her face. The other girl was not injured.

The kids in the other car were okay. Some of them had been drinking though and Tom Wallace was arrested along with the driver, an older kid named Chris White, who was drunk. Tom had been acting drunk but was actually just mad and resisted arrest. The investigating cops had arrested both of the boys and took the girls home. One was Tom's sister and she was really upset.

Ed asked, "Do I need to go to the hospital?"

The sergeant answered, "Yeah, Jeff wanted me to call you and ask you to come and take the girls home. I think he thinks you're his dad." He joked in spite of himself and went on, "The kid was feelin' really bad and I told him, I'd send you down."

"Well, you did the right thing, to tell you the truth, he's the closest to a son that I've ever had."

When he hung up the phone, Karen was standing behind him looking frightened and asked, "What happened? Who got hurt? Was everything okay?"

He said, "Whoa, everything is going to be okay. Jeff got a broken ankle, Pamela got some cuts and Leah wasn't hurt. Tom and his friend, Chris White got arrested. Amy and Chris's date got taken home in a patrol car. I'm going to the hospital and take Jeff and his girls home.

You stay here. It's bad out there now. Just look at the snow. There will be more accidents tomorrow. It always takes a while for everybody to slow down and take it easy in the snow."

"Okay, I'll be waiting up for you so you be careful. I won't be able to sleep until you get back."

"I'll be back as soon as I get them where they belong. I won't bother with Tom and Chris. It will do them good to cool it in the jail for a night. Tom will need to keep his nose clean if he wants that scholarship, so he might as well learn now."

He got in his Cadillac and went to the rescue. Karen sat at the kitchen table waiting and worrying. After a while she got up and fixed some hot chocolate. Ed was back in about forty-five minutes and they sat there drinking hot chocolate while he filled her in on the accident details.

The Wallaces' were up waiting for their children to come home. Janet had been real quiet after they got home and Bill was too tired to talk anyway. They just sat in the den and watched television. When Bill heard a car, pull in the driveway he hurried to the door to let them in and was shocked to see Amy with a policeman.

It frightened him so much that he grabbed his chest. Amy said, "I'm okay, Daddy. We had an accident and the policeman brought me home." She ran in the house to her mother.

The cop said, "Mr. Wallace, Tom and Chris were arrested. Chris was drunk and he was driving. Tom got mad and he was arrested for resisting arrest. I'm sorry but it's all we could do. They'll be okay for the night. I'm advising you to leave it alone until morning, even if he calls you."

Bill said, "Yeah, I understand, I know you're right and that's what I'll do."

When the policeman left, Bill went in to talk to Amy and find out what Tom had done. He asked, "Did you know that Chris White had been drinking?"

Amy answered quickly, "No, I would never have ridden with him if I had known. Celia is a good friend of mine and she's been dating Chris for about a year."

Bill said, "Well, he is not a good influence on you kids. He messed up and didn't go to college. He just hangs around and works odd jobs. He's going nowhere and Tom doesn't need to be around him. He's trouble, that's all. Tom's risking everything doing stuff like this."

Amy said, "I don't think Tom was drinking, he just lost his temper. You know how he is. Flies off the handle and shoots off his mouth. The cop didn't like it and Tom just wouldn't shut up."

Bill noticed Janet was just sitting there looking like she was in shock. He went to her and said, "It's okay, Honey. They're just kids and need to be taken down a notch or two. I'll go get him out in the morning but he's going to pay a price. Just don't worry about it."

Amy hugged her mother and said, "I'm sorry we worried you, Mother. We are so glad to have you home. I don't want you to get upset."

Janet smiled and said, "I'll be all right. Don't worry about me, I'm on my medication and it keeps me calm. I won't be getting upset. I was so proud of you and Tom tonight. This is just one of those things that happens when boys are trying to be men."

Amy turned and hugged her father, "I love you, Daddy. I'm sorry that you have to worry with this mess."

He said, "It's going to be okay. Now you go on and get ready for bed. Then you can watch television with your mother and me."

Tom did call before long and Bill just said, "I'll see you in the morning, you'll just have to tough it out tonight."

He hung up the phone and smiled at Janet. She said, "Tough love, huh?"

Chapter 98

Saturday morning, Ed and Karen slept later than usual. They knew it was going to be a cold, snowy day and they wouldn't want to get out in it. Karen got up first and made the coffee. She looked outside and there were no animals on the porch but she saw their footprints in the snow. They had come up from the barn and gone back when no one came to the door. She had a cup of coffee and then put on a heavy coat with a hood and went to the barn with their food. She fed all three of her pets and talked to them for a while. They were fine with the cat and dog sleeping on the piles of hay. She brushed Candy for a few minutes and then she looked out the door and saw Ed standing in the door way in his robe.

She waved at him and went back to the house. He said, "I was surprised you were already up and going when I woke up."

She said, "Well, my children have to be fed and looked after."

"Now the baby in the family is hungry, too. But I've started breakfast already. Thought I'd treat you for a change. You haven't had any of my cooking yet."

She took off her coat and sat down and said, "Well, I'm ready, so bring it on."

He served sausage and eggs and toast. After they had finished, she went around the table and sat on his lap and kissed him. He said, "Hey, maybe I ought to cook more often."

They didn't dress until afternoon and then Ed said, "I'm going to call Bill and see how things went this morning."

When Bill answered the phone, Ed asked, "How's everything at your house today?"

Bill said, "Well, considering all that happened, it's okay. I guess they called you from the station."

Ed said, "Yeah, I had to go pick up Jeff and the girls. The real reason I called is that I forgot to ask you to find out from Janet, the name of the detective she hired and where he lives if you can. I don't want to cause trouble but I need to talk to him. I think he may know something I need to know."

Bill hesitated, "Well, I'll try but I really hate to bring that all up."

Ed knew that was troubling him so he said, "If you don't want to ask her, maybe she wrote him a check or there's a business card around somewhere. Just see if you can find out his name. It will help me a lot, if you can."

Bill said, "I'll see what I can do." Ed thanked him and they ended the call.

Later on in the day Ed said, "Hey, let's go see if the golf cart will run in the snow. We can go down and see the Barrys if they're home."

Karen called them and said, "We just wanted to make sure you were home. We'll be right down."

Joseph and Ed sat in the den and watched football while Karen and Ruth planned the Thanksgiving dinner. Ruth said, "Would you like to ask some other folks to come to the dinner?"

Karen said, "Well, maybe Daniel would like to join us. I don't know if Rebecca has family here or not. I'll check with him, if it's okay."

Ruth said, "The more, the merrier." So when they got back home Karen called Daniel but there was no answer.

Chapter 99

Sunday morning the sun was shining brightly and it had quit snowing. There was just a lot of slush on the road when they went to church. They had planned to go to lunch after church at the Holiday Inn so when they shook hands with Gary at the church entrance, Ed invited him and his family to go with them or to meet them there. Gary said, "That's really nice of you. Can you wait until I check with Christine?" Ed said, "Sure we'll be right inside the door. It's cold out here."

They went back inside and waited until he had greeted everyone. He went to find Christine When he came back, all three were with him. Christine said, "Hello, how nice of you to invite us. Are you sure you can take our little ones? Sometimes they're a handful out in public."

Karen said, "They will be fine. Surely the four of us can handle them."

They went in separate cars. When they got there, they chose to sit at a big round table. Actually the children were very good. They were hungry, so they were quiet while they ate. Then they colored the papers the waitress had given them.

They all ate from the buffet so they waited on themselves for the most part. The food and the conversation was good and they had and enjoyable time. Eric asked, "Miss Karen, how is your horse?"

Karen told him that Candy was just fine and promised him that when Melanie came home she would give him another ride. He said, "Oh, good. When will she be home?"

That's when Gary chimed in and told him that Melanie was away at college and wouldn't be home for a while because he figured the next question would be, "Can we go now?"

They all promised to do this again soon and went to their cars and homes.

Bill and his family had gone to church and when they were back home, Amy and Janet fixed lunch. Janet had put a roast in the crock pot earlier and when it was ready they all sat at the dining room table and enjoyed their first real family meal in weeks. Bill returned thanks and they all ate in silence for most of the meal.

Bill and Tom had been arguing for two days. Amy and Janet just didn't know what to say for fear it would start up again. When they were finished, the two girls cleaned up the kitchen and washed the dishes. Then they sat down at the kitchen table. Janet asked Amy about school and what she had been doing for fun. Amy said, "Well, not much because of cheerleader practice. Doing homework takes most of my time. I did go shopping one Saturday with Celia and her mother. Then the wedding took some of my time and that's about it. But of course getting ready for the homecoming was fun and that kept me busy, too."

Bill came in and said, "It's about time to head back to the hospital, Janet. Do you kids want to ride along?" Both of them said they had homework and didn't want to go with them. Bill said, "Just make sure that neither of you leaves this house. Tom, you may be out of jail but you are under house arrest. Don't forget it."

Tom just nodded his head and for once didn't spout off. He knew it would upset his mother and he didn't want her to go back to the hospital with that on her mind. He went to hug his mother and said, "I hope you will get to come home soon, Mom. We miss you a lot."

Tears were in Janet's eyes and she answered, "I hope so, too, Honey. I don't think they'll keep me much longer." Then she hugged Amy and told her, "I love you and your brother so much. Take care of each other and I'll be home soon."

Bill took her arm and picked up her overnight bag, saying on his way out the door, "I'll be back as soon as I can. Keep the doors locked and stay inside. I don't want either of you on the phone with your friends from Friday night. Remember we still have to go to court."

He opened the door to the truck for Janet and after she was in, he went around, climbed and cranked the engine. He didn't say anything for several minutes, and she thought maybe he was angry, so she didn't try to speak to him. Finally he asked, "Just what has your therapist told you about your condition? Will you always have to be on medication?"

Janet explained it as well as she could by telling him, "Yes, I will have to stay on medication and see a doctor on a regular basis, to check the level in my system."

"Well, I hope I can talk to the doctor and find out how much longer you'll be confined. We need to make plans for you coming home for good."

"What kind of plans are you talking about?"

"How you and I are going to handle it? You know, our relationship."

"I thought that we were going to family counseling."

"Yes, but in the meantime, how are we going to relate to each other?"

"I know you don't feel the same about me. I mean I don't think you love me anymore."

"Actually I don't how I feel. Things have certainly changed because of our fights and the constant turmoil in the past. You know I never cheated on you except when we were separated. I only saw Margie a few times, but I must admit that was her decision to break it off, not mine. By the way, Ed wants to know the name of the private detective you hired."

"I'm sorry I did that, but I was so frustrated. I was desperate and paranoid. That's why I contacted him. His name was Ken Barton. He was from Chicago. There's a card in the desk drawer if Ed wants to contact him. Why does he want to know?"

"I assume he wants to know if he has any more information about Margie. Ed and Karen don't believe that Margie committed suicide."

"Well, that is hard to believe, isn't it?"

"Yes, she was not the type and she seemed to be very happy to be back on her own and rid of Larry."

"Well, I don't know if you'll ever be able to love me again, but I hope you'll go to the counseling with me." They had pulled into the hospital parking lot by now.

Bill got out of the truck and opened the door for Janet, took her bag and walked with her to the entrance. When they were inside, he kissed her on the cheek and said, "We'll try to see you next week and I'll call your doctor and talk to him."

She smiled and told him, "Thanks for the nice weekend. I love you and the kids very much." She turned and went with the attendant to her room. Bill went back out to start his lonely trip home. He needed the time alone, to think.

Chapter 100

Karen finally got Daniel on the phone on Monday evening and invited him to Thanksgiving dinner. She asked, "Do you think Rebecca would like to come, or does she have family to be with?"

He said, "I don't really know anything about her family but I'll be glad to ask her if you think it's okay."

Karen told him, "Ruth says, the more, the merrier. I agree and I think you'll enjoy it. We're picking Melanie up tomorrow evening, so she'll be there and hard telling who else Ruth and Joseph will invite."

He said, "Well, I'll let you know about Rebecca, but you can count on me. What shall I bring?" She answered, "Just yourself or maybe a bottle of wine."

"That's a sure thing," He answered, joking, "Maybe two in case there's a crowd." That task done Karen went back to her studio to continue the painting she was working on.

Ed had gone back to work that morning after Karen fixed his breakfast. They sat talking over their coffee. When he got ready to leave, he came around to where she was sitting and kissed her long and hard. He said, "I am going to miss you today. This week off has spoiled me."

She answered, "You'll have to start thinking about retiring so we can be together all the time."

He said, "Oh, don't think that hasn't occurred to me. I'm not quite ready but it won't be long. Maybe sometime next year."

She smiled and told him, "When you're ready, not before. I'll be right here. I love you, you know that and whatever makes you happy is fine with me. Just take good care of yourself for me."

It was snowing outside again so he got a heavy coat on when he went out to get into his car. She watched him as he pulled out of the drive and after she had cleaned the kitchen, she went to her studio. She had already selected the photo she planned to use for this painting. It was one she had taken over the weekend of the snow in the pasture behind her barn. Candy was in it, standing by the fence with the snow coming down, but with her head held high and the wind blowing her mane. The sky was a gray blue with no clouds at all. The pasture was a golden field of sage grass with occasional snow drifts. It didn't cover the ground so there were patches of gold, in between the windblown snow drifts. She used broad strokes and impasto technique in the painting. The contrasting colors created a beautiful effect of a warm but wintery scene. Contrast and courage was the overall effect that would engage the viewer. It was the contrast of the cold landscape and the courage of the horse. At least that was her purpose and as it is, with all artists, she hoped her audience would get the message. She sat on her stool and used her third eye to critique the painting and decided it was worthy of her signature. She had done this painting in record time but she was pleased with it, so immediately got another canvas ready to paint.

She was going through some old photographs when the phone rang. It was Ed, and he said, "Hi, lover, I have missed you all day and wanted to check in. Everything okay?"

She answered, "I'm fine, I've missed you too but it's been a productive day in the studio. Anything going on there?"

"Not much with my partner gimping around on his broken ankle. He's using crutches so he's slow as molasses. Fortunately, we haven't had much happening. I wanted to tell you that I talked to Daniel and he said we could count on him and Rebecca for Thanksgiving."

"That's great. We should have a good Thanksgiving. By the way are you going to be able to go with me, to pick up Melanie?"

"Yes, I've already told the chief that I need to leave early and Craig Walker will fill in for me and help the cripple get around."

He was laughing and she heard Jeff in the background, "I'm going to get even with you old man, just you wait until I get back on both feet."

Karen said, "Sounds like he's feeling okay anyway."

Ed replied, "Yeah, he's just looking for sympathy. I've got to go now, but I'll see you later." He whispered into the phone, "I love you, my lady." He hung up before she could answer.

She heard Jazz barking and went to see what was going on. There was a bike rider in the driveway. As soon he saw Karen he turned and sped away. He had on a pullover sweatshirt with a hood, so she couldn't see what he looked like. She immediately called Ed and told him to get somebody out there to see if they could catch the biker.

Ed hung up, ran to his car and sped away with siren blasting and with the blue light he had placed on top flashing. As he turned on the road to the house, he met a bike rider coming toward town. He did a U-turn and went after him. The rider wouldn't stop, so Ed pulled over in front of him so that he crashed into the rear of Ed's car. Ed was out of the car and grabbed the rider as he got up. He had blood on his hands but didn't appear to be badly injured.

Ed pushed him up against the trunk of his car and searched him, put hand cuffs on him and looked at the ID he had pulled from his jeans. He pushed the hood off the guy's head and revealed a blonde head. To Ed's surprise, it was Tom Wallace.

Another squad car pulled up and the uniformed cop asked if Ed needed help. Ed shook his head, and said, "No, I've got it." He recited the Miranda rights to Tom and told he was under arrest for fleeing from the law.

Tom would not speak and just nodded his head when asked if he understood. He put him in the back seat of the other squad car and told the officer to take him in and book him. He said, "I'm going to check on Karen and I'll be back to the station soon, to do the rest of the paper work."

When he got to the house, Karen came out to meet him. He hugged her and said, "It's too cold out here. Let's go in and I'll tell you what happened. You're not going to believe it."

When she had sat down at the kitchen table, he told her he had just arrested Tom Wallace. She looked stunned and asked, "Why, did you do that?"

"Because he was your bike rider. I almost ran over him when I turned onto our road. I did a U and he wouldn't stop so I stopped him with my car."

"Oh, my God, is he okay?"

"He's not hurt badly, just skinned up. I'll have the doctor check him out when I get back down there."

"Oh, poor Bill and Janet. They are going to be sick. I wonder why he was running. He has known me forever. I surely didn't scare him just going outside."

"Yes, you did because he didn't think we were home. My car was gone and he assumed that you were with me. He didn't know I had gone back to work. I'll bet ten to one that after I get his prints they will match the one's on those dishes and the can in the Chicago FBI. I just wish I knew why. I'm hope it's not what I'm thinking."

"Oh, no, it can't have anything to do with Margie. Please don't tell me that."

"He had reason, if he knew about his dad and Margie. We'll find out soon enough."

"I hope you're wrong but go on back and get his story before he closes down."

"He already has. He wouldn't even speak. Acted like a deaf mute, just shook his head. What a mess! I hate my job at times like this. Those people just can't win and they're basically nice people. Just messed up in more ways than one."

"Are you going to call Bill?"

"I'll have to as a matter of law, because I shouldn't question him without his parent being there. I'll have to see what the chief says. He's going to raise hell when he finds out what I think of his "closed case" opinion."

"You can blame it on me. He can't do anything to me."

Then she kissed him on the cheek and said, "Get back down there now." He went out the door and back to the station, but he dreaded what he faced when he got there.

Karen couldn't get back to her painting after that. She sat in the kitchen going through the photographs, trying to make herself calm down.

The phone rang and it was Melanie confirming her plans for tomorrow. She would arrive at O'Hare at five fifteen. She would be staying until Sunday. Karen said, "That sounds so good. While you're here, we'll go to the bank and get in your Mother's safety deposit box. We've got to find a will or something to take to the lawyer after we find out who he was." She didn't mention the recent events to Melanie. She figured it would be better to wait until she was safely home and by then they would know more.

Melanie said, "Is the weather okay there?"

Karen answered, "Yes, it is now, it snowed over the weekend but the sun was shining all day today so there's nothing left of it. We'll see you at the airport. You take care of yourself. I can't wait to see you."

Melanie said, "Me, too, I miss home. I'm really planning on moving to Chicago so don't be surprised."

Karen said, "It's your life, you do what you think right and we'll support your decision."

Melanie was pleased to hear that and said, "I've got to go now, see you soon. I love you."

After she hung up the phone, Karen sat thinking about what could possibly be going on at the station.

Ed had called Bill at school and told him what happened and why Tom was under arrest. Bill went wild, called the assistant coach, Jerry Barker, to his office and told him to take over his duties. He just said, "I've got an emergency and I've got to leave right now. Don't tell Amy anything if you see her. She knows I'll come back for her."

Jerry said, "Okay, man, but take it easy. You look like you just saw a ghost. You'd better settle down before you have a heart attack." Bill just waved him off and went out to his truck and took off with tires squealing.

When he got to the station, he parked illegally in the police's parking place. He ran into the desk sergeant and asked for Ed. The sergeant pointed him to Ed's desk. Jeff was at his desk nearby. He spoke to Bill, "Come on Bill, I'll take you to the interrogation room. Ed's in there with Tom."

Jeff knocked on the door and entered, "Bill is here, Ed, can he come in?" Ed answered, "Sure come on in, Bill."

After Bill got in the room, he looked at Tom with astonishment. He said, "What have you done now, Son? Why are you here and not in school?"

Tom didn't answer. He just looked down at his hands. Bill looked at his hands, too. He said, "Your hands are bleeding, what happened?"

Tom was still silent. Ed spoke up, "You're not doing any better than I have been, Bill. He won't say a word. I don't know how we're supposed to find out what's going on, if he doesn't cooperate."

Bill looked at Ed and asked, "What are you talking about. Nothing's going on as far as I know. Why have you got my son here? I know he's supposed to be in school but is that a reason for arresting him?"

Ed explained that he had been at the house and when he saw Karen he took off. She didn't know who he was because his hooded shirt hid his face. He told him about the other house intrusion and the strange phone calls that Karen had been getting. He explained that it had something to do with Karen investigating Margie's death because the caller had mentioned it.

Bill just sat there looking stunned and disbelieving. He said, "Well, Tom has been acting strange ever since his mother went away but I don't think it had anything to do with Margie."

Tom looked at him and gave him an evil grin. It was a look of hate and he almost growled, "So you don't think so, huh? You drive my mother crazy and you wonder why I'm strange!"

Bill turned to Ed and said, "Should I call a lawyer?"

Ed said, "That's your privilege but I'm not releasing him until I find out what he's been up to."

Bill left the room and went to call Jack Carter, the lawyer that had taken care of Janet's case. He told him what he knew and asked him to come as soon as he could.

Ed came out of the room and told Bill, "I'm going to have Dr. Patterson come by and treat his scratches and make sure he's okay physically. There's a lot more to this than you or I know. I can't just drop it. I hate this as much as you do, but your son has a problem."

Bill said, "I know that, Ed. I'm not blaming you and I know you're right. Something is just not right so there's no use denying it. Our family is totally dysfunctional and I'm to blame."

Ed said, "Don't be too hard on yourself. Bad things happen to good people all the time. You need to keep your wits about you to work this out."

Ed went in to bring the chief up to date on what was going on and Chief Stone didn't look very pleased. He said, "So Karen has been snooping around, huh? What the hell does she think she's doing?"

Ed bristled at that and said, "Look, Margie was Karen's best friend. She doesn't think she committed suicide. That's a terrible thing to say about a person like Margie. It has had an awful effect on her daughter and it will probably affect her insurance proceeds. Even so it's a bad thing for people to think and Karen just couldn't let it go without checking it out. She was a good cop and she knows how to investigate. Why shouldn't she do it as a private citizen, if we can't?"

Chief Stone looked shocked at Ed's outburst and said, "Okay, okay, so now what? We going to keep the kid or what?"

Ed said, "Yes, we're going to keep him until I find out what he was doing coming to our house and running off like a scared rabbit." He went on to tell him about the vandalism but he didn't mention the FBI.

The chief said, "Okay, do what you have to do. Has he got a lawyer yet?"

"He's on his way here now. I'm not going to sit in on his interview. The kid won't even speak to me. I'll let the lawyer do his thing with Bill there and then have one of the other officers fingerprint the kid. He'll have to stay here tonight at least. I'll get back with him in the morning after he's had time to think."

"Well, that sounds like a good plan. You go on home and check on your wife. I'll see you in the morning."

Chapter 101

When Ed got home, Karen met him at the door. He hugged and kissed her and said, "Get this. The chief told me to go home and check on my wife. He's getting positively charming lately."

Karen shook her head and said, "No way. I'll bet he's mad at me, isn't he? I'm assuming that you had to tell him what I had done."

Ed grinned, "Yeah, I did. I surprised myself because I really went off on him and he took it."

Karen just said, "Oh, my!" Then she told him to sit down while she got dinner on the table.

He said, "This is the life, supper ready when I come home to my beautiful wife."

She smiled and told him not to count on it every night. Some days, "I'll be too busy painting to cook, but I'll try to take care of my man."

They had a ham and cheese casserole and salad. She had thawed of a couple of the apple dumplings and warmed them in the microwave. She served them with a dollop of whipped topping and then she said, "Let's go watch the news while we eat our dessert. You need to get comfortable, don't you?"

He was taking off his shirt and tie as she spoke and went to put the shirt in the hamper. He hung up the tie and came back to the living room to sit down beside her. He said, "Like I said, this is the life."

Back at the station, Jack Carter was interviewing his newest client and wasn't getting any further than Ed had. Bill tried to get him to talk, but had no luck. Finally, Jack said, "Well, I'm not going to be able to help you until you decide to talk to me so I'm going to let the officers do what they have to and you may be ready to talk tomorrow."

He got up and Bill followed him out of the interview room. Bill said, "What do I need to do?" Jack answered, "Go pick up your daughter and come back in the morning about nine. We'll try again then. There's no point in trying right now. He's too angry for some reason or maybe he's just scared but we're not doing any good."

Bill said, "Oh, my God, I forgot all about Amy. I'll see you in the morning.

Thanks for coming, Jack. I'm beside myself but you're right, maybe he'll have time to think it over. He's a smart boy but he's full of resentment right now." The lawyer told the officer to take over and they went out of the door together.

After they had finger printed him and took his mug shot. They got his personal items and bagged them. They took him back to a cell and locked him up. He sat there like a zombie for a long time.

The guard on duty brought him a sandwich and some coffee. He ate them like a starving refuge. He laid down on the bunk and tried to sleep. He thought, "If I go to sleep the time will go by faster." Then he began to cry quietly, because he didn't want anyone to know how upset he really was.

Chapter 102

Rebecca had called Daniel at the bank and invited him to supper. She had prepared the meal on Sunday so it would be easier to bake and serve after work. He was to be there at six thirty and he was on time. She had baked lasagna and salad. She had picked up a small cake at the bakery and served it with ice cream. He rubbed his stomach after the meal and told her, "That was superb. Best thing I've eaten in weeks."

She said, "Well, thank you, I'm glad you liked it. I really love to cook but don't get much of a chance."

"You can feed me anytime you feel like cooking. I'm afraid I can't return the favor. My cooking is a frozen dinner in the microwave."

"Well, the country club was very good."

"Yeah, I'm afraid you've got them beat though."

They went into the living room and she turned on the television but they weren't really paying attention to it because as soon as they sat down, Daniel leaned over and gave her a long tender kiss.

She moved away from him, on the couch and said, "Ooh, you caught me off guard, I wasn't expecting that. You know I've been thinking a lot about us. I mean our relationship, if you can call it that. I can tell you're hesitant, or at least you have been in the past. I understand that you're probably not over Margie yet. I don't really expect a lot of romance. I just enjoy your company and I don't want you to think I'm looking for more."

He was a little surprised by her candid pronouncement. He figured it was time for him to be candid, too. He told her, "Well, you've sure got me pegged, haven't you? You're right about Margie. She meant a lot to me. She didn't know I had been married. It wasn't that I kept it from her but it just never came up. We only had a few dates before she died. I don't know if I told you about my kids or not, but they're still in school and I did just get a divorce from their mother. It was a long time coming and Margie didn't even know about it. I was going to tell her the day I got back from finalizing the divorce. It was too late.

My daughter Allison is in medical school in Boston and her brother David is studying theater at Northwestern. They are great kids and have been very understanding about the divorce. They still visit and check on their mother but they can't live with her either. I just want you to know that I'm really interested in you, though. Past experience tells me that I must not rush into anything. I mean, I don't want to give you a false impression. I think we need time to get to know more about each other, don't you? How about you, have you ever been married?"

"No, I was engaged to a guy I dated for four years. We had set a date and then I found out he had another girl pregnant. It was a total shock and I couldn't handle it so I moved away to start over here and to get away from him."

Daniel asked, "Where did you live before?"

She went on, "I told you I'm from St.Louis, that's where I grew up and got my first job at Famous-Barr. My folks were not wealthy, we always had enough but with four kids, they couldn't afford college so I worked and went to night school to study marketing. I got an associate degree and did well at my job. My boyfriend was my high school sweetheart and I guess he didn't have enough time to sow his wild oats before we were engaged. Anyway, he managed to get himself in trouble with another girl and they're married now and have a darling baby girl. I'm over him but he seemed to think that I should still see him after he married. He was sort of stalking me and I don't want him to know where I am. I'm glad I moved because I love my job and Mr. Regal is so kind. I could never have had the position of manager in a big market."

Daniel had been quiet, listening to Rebecca's story. Now he asked, "So you're not going home for Thanksgiving?"

She smiled at him, "No, but I'll go for Christmas when I have more time off. You know the day after Thanksgiving is the busiest shopping day of the year. I need to be at work for that day."

He said, "That's true, I'm planning a trip with my kids for Christmas or after Christmas. They'll spend the day with their mother and then we'll go to Colorado to ski for a few days."

"That's wonderful! I'll bet they're excited about that." She declared and went on to say, "We always have a great Christmas. I have two nieces and a nephew under the age of five so it's a lot of fun to watch them opening gifts. Mother fixes a feast, I think she cooks for a month and freezes it for the big day. Daddy is a big old teddy bear kind of guy and he tries to pretend that he doesn't like any of the festivities but he has a great time with his grandchildren."

Daniel said, "You're very lucky to have a big family. My parents died within a year of each other, three years ago. I was an only child so all I have are my children. I'm not anxious to get old, but I do look forward to them getting married and giving me grandchildren."

Rebecca gasped at that news and told him, "Well, I hope you get your wish but don't be in too big a hurry to get them married off. You know the older we get, the faster the time goes."

He chuckled and said, "Yes, you're right and speaking of time, I'd better go and let us both get some rest. Can I help you with the dishes?"

She leaned over and kissed him on the cheek and said, "I wouldn't think of it. I'll have it cleaned up in no time. That's why they invented dishwashers. I have enjoyed the evening and I'm looking forward to Thursday. What time should I be ready?"

He looked puzzled, "You know, I didn't ask. I'll have to call you and let you know." He got up to leave and as he put on his coat, he said, "Thanks for the lovely evening, Rebecca, I really enjoyed it."

She smiled as she opened the door and he left, this time without a kiss. She sighed after she closed the door, and thought, "I guess he got the message. I'm not looking for a relationship."

Chapter 103

When Bill got back to the school, Amy was sitting on the steps outside, looking like she was frozen. She came to get in the truck and said, "Where have you been? I was about ready to walk home so I could warm up."

He looked grim and answered, "You won't believe where I've been. Your brother is in jail and I've been there with him and Ed and a lawyer. I don't know what's going on because he won't talk, won't say a word."

Amy started crying, "I can't believe it, he's acting so strange and now he's in jail. What is happening to us?"

"I don't know, I was hoping he had shared his feelings with you."

"He won't talk to me either. He's mad all the time and he sneaks out at night and runs or rides his bike. I don't know where he goes or what he does. It's crazy, our whole family is crazy."

Bill drove straight home and fixed some supper for them. They didn't talk much the rest of the evening. Amy went to her room and Bill sat alone in the living room watching the television. He got up and looked in the desk for the card that Janet had told him was there. When he found it, he called Ed and told him, "That private detective's name was Ken Barton, he's from Chicago."

He gave Ed the telephone number. Ed said, "Thanks for finding that for me, we're going to Chicago tomorrow and I'll probably call him. I'm sorry about Tom, I wish he would just talk to me but maybe Jack can loosen him up."

Bill said, "Yeah, well maybe. Listen, I'll talk to you later, okay?" He sat back down on the couch and began to beat himself up for his affair with Margie. He knew without a doubt that it had something to do with Tom's erratic behavior. What was he going to do?

When Ed got up on Tuesday morning, Karen was outside feeding the animals. He went to the door and said, "Hey, you're going to freeze out there."

She turned around and said, "No, it's really not that bad out. The wind isn't blowing today. Did you sleep well?"

He said, "Not really, can't get Tom off my mind, trying to figure out what to do about him. I'm going to fax his prints to Sam in the city and then when we get there I'll call him and see if they are a match. I also want to call that Ken Barton and see if he can be any help. He might have seen something that didn't seem important at the time."

Karen looked surprised, "Then we'd better leave early so you can do all that."

"Yeah, I'm going to try to get away at noon if you can be ready," he answered.

"I can be ready if you can get off. You don't think the chief will be suspicious?"

"I really don't care at this point. I'll talk to Jack Carter when I get to work and see if he can help any or if he will help. You know client privilege and all. I don't know how much he'll be able to tell me."

"Oh, that reminds me, I promised Melanie I would call him and find out if he was Margie's lawyer. Will you ask him for me?"

"Sure, I just hope I can remember it." He grinned and went on, "I'm just kidding. I'll remember it, that's important to know. Maybe you and Melanie can get some business taken care of while she is here."

Karen was in the house by now and fixing Ed's breakfast. He came over to the sink and kissed her on the neck and said, "Let's just have oatmeal today. Got to cut back on the fattening stuff and save up for Thanksgiving."

She turned and kissed him, "Okay, I don't want to make you fat and sassy." He patted her bottom and went to get dressed for work.

After they ate breakfast, Ed gathered up his briefcase and put on his coat and a hat. She looked at him, thinking how handsome he looked. She went over and kissed him and said, "You have a good day and I'll be ready to go at noon."

He said, "I'll see you then, love you." He went out to his patrol car and went off to work vowing to get Tom to talk today. Knowing he couldn't force him to, but trying to figure out a way to get some information from him. Ed couldn't imagine what was so troubling to Tom that he had just closed down.

When he got to the station Bill was sitting at his desk and he thought, "Oh, no, I don't need him here to bug me. Tom definitely is not going to talk with him in the room."

He said, "What are you doing, Bill? You know we're not going to release your boy today. He may be here for a while, unless he starts explaining his behavior."

Bill said, "I thought maybe I could see him."

Ed answered, "No, I'm afraid that's not a good idea. He obviously has some resentment toward you and I don't think he'll talk with you in the room. The best thing you can do, is go to work and let us handle it. I'm going to call Jack and talk to him soon."

Bill looked completely devastated. "Okay, you know best. I know Tom is mad at me but I love him so much, I hate seeing him in here. I wish I could trade places with him. It's all my fault, I know it is and he will never forgive me."

Ed told him, "Don't think that. Kids don't give up on their parents. He'll be back when this is over."

Bill got up to leave and then he turned around and said, "You call me, if you need me back here. Don't hesitate, okay?"

Ed was looking at paper work on his desk and answered him, "Will do." He was hoping Bill would get out of there so he could get on with it.

As soon as Bill was out of the door, Ed called Jack Carter. The first thing he asked after saying " Good Morning," was, "Were you by any chance Margie Sloan's lawyer?"

Jack answered, "Yes, I was, why do you ask?"

"Because, her daughter, Melanie, is staying with us when she's in town. We haven't heard anything about a will. We thought you might know something."

Jack said, "No, she didn't have me do a will for her. That's a shame, too. It would make it a lot easier on Melanie."

Ed said, "Well, thanks, we're going to check her safety deposit box on Friday, maybe we'll find one there. But now to the business at hand. How did you do with Tom Wallace?"

"Well, I didn't get anywhere at first, but last night he had them call me back down to talk. I hesitate to say much. He's a very distraught young man and what little he told me may incriminate him. I would hope he'll talk to you even though I told him not to. I guess that sounds crazy to you. What I mean is, I really think you can help him more than I can, in a way. I can't explain it but you're in a different position to help. I can tell you this, he is in trouble, he has done something that could be considered criminal. I don't think it is, but I'm not a judge. Does that confuse you enough? I've already gone further than I should, so don't ask for more of an explanation, please. I don't even know if I should tell his father, so you can see I'm in a tight spot."

Ed said, "Okay, thanks, I think."

Jack said, "Sorry, man. Call me if you need me."

They both hung up their phones and sat pondering that strange conversation.

Ed asked the jailer to bring Tom to the interview room and went to get two cups of coffee. He went in after Tom was there and gave him the coffee.

Tom didn't even look at him, just kept staring at the floor. Ed said, "I'm turning on the camera now, Tom. I want to have this interview on tape for evidence. I'd like for you to tell me why you refused to stop for me yesterday. I also want to know why you left my house in such a hurry when you discovered my wife was at home. Can you tell me?"

Tom didn't look up. He just sat looking at his hands. Ed went on, "Do you have something to hide? Did you have anything to do with Margie Sloan's death?" No response, whatsoever.

Ed said, "This interview has come to an end." He turned off the camcorder, went to the door and said to the jailer, "Put him back in his cell."

He went back to his desk. Jeff Collins had come into the station and was at his desk. Ed spoke to him and said, "Jeff, why don't you talk to Tom this afternoon and see if you can get him to say anything. Be sure to record it, I don't know what it's going to take but he's got to talk sooner or later. I'm going to leave for Chicago at noon but I'll call you as soon as I get back. Don't say anything to the chief but I faxed his prints to a friend of mine at the FBI and I'll find out if they match something I've already sent there. When I get back, I may have more to go on, whether he talks or not. I'd just feel better if he'd tell me on his own. I feel so bad for his family. He's such a great kid and this is going to affect his future, big time."

Jeff said, "I'll see what I can do. I don't know if I'll have any more luck. I'm not nearly as good at questioning as you are."

Ed answered, "Well, it's time you learned, I won't be here forever. You can even get Chip in on it if you want to. Double team him. Do whatever it takes. Play good cop, bad cop. What ever you do will be appreciated. Like I say, I'll call you when I get back. You going to be home or have you got a hot date?"

"I'll be home. Did I tell you that Pamela is cooking Thanksgiving dinner for us? Leah is going home because she lives close but Pamela can't make it to Missouri and back in time to go to work on Friday."

Ed said, "Well, that's great, I hope she's a good cook."

He went into the chief's office to tell him what he had done with Tom and that he would be leaving a little earlier than expected.

Chief Stone said, "That's fine as long as you've covered everything. I'll talk to you tomorrow. Now get out of here."

Ed said, "Thanks, I'll see you in the morning." Before he left, he called Karen and said, "I was just talking to Jeff about Thanksgiving and he tells me that he and Pamela are eating alone on Thanksgiving. What do you think about inviting them?"

Karen said, "I know Ruth would be glad for them to come. You tell Jeff that we'd like them to come eat with us. He should have Pamela call me or I'll call her. Find out from Jeff how to get a hold of her."

"Okay, I'll do that. The chief just told me to get out of here, so I'm coming home earlier, can you be ready?"

She said, "I am ready, come on, we'll get an early start."

After he hung up the phone he turned to Jeff and told him of their conversation and Jeff looked very pleased. He said, "I'll get with Pamela and let you know tonight."

Ed said, "Talk to you later, Kid." And he left the building, glad to be going away from the problem, hoping to come back with a solution.

Karen met him at the door when he got home. He said, "I'm going to change to jeans and be more comfortable."

She said, "That's what I did. There's nothing to dress up for, is there?"

He was soon changed and back in the kitchen. He said, "We'll have time to stop and eat on the way if we make good time. The Caddy is already filled up so let's go. Okay?"

She said, "I'm with you." She locked the door behind them, patted her pet's heads as she looked out at the pasture and saw Candy grazing. Ed had the door to the car open for her and was waiting impatiently.

Bill had a horrible day at work but he managed to teach his classes. He left the football practice to his assistant though. He sat in his office and called Jack Carter but didn't get any information from him. He was waiting for Amy to get done with cheerleading practice, so he called Janet's doctor and talked to him for a while. He got good news from him. He said that Janet would be ready to come home in two weeks, that she was doing very well. He warned that she must stay on her medication, so she would not have any more problems. He repeated his warning, because any lapse could create problems. Bill felt better after he hung up the phone.

Amy came in his office and he said, "Let's go to the Café and have supper, Honey. We need groceries and I don't feel like shopping. Okay?"

She said, "It sounds good to me. I'm starving."

When they got to the Café, he saw Jeff Collins sitting in the rear. He sat down at a table with Amy and then after Maria had their order, he walked back to Jeff. He asked, "Did you talk to Tom today?"

Jeff said, "Well, I tried, but I didn't have much luck. Ed tried this morning and then I saw him this afternoon. I even had Chip come in and see what he could do but the kid won't say a word. Not one word to anybody. It's the weirdest thing I've ever seen."

Bill said, "I don't what to say. It's just not like him to be this way but maybe if he sits in there long enough, he'll give in. Thanks for trying, Jeff. Don't let anything happen to him while he's there."

Jeff said, "He's in a cell by himself and we're watching him closely."

Bill got really upset then and said, "My God, you don't think he'll harm himself, do you?"

Jeff answered, "No, we don't, but we can't take any chances. He's hard to read and he's obviously unhappy so we're going to keep an eye on him. We've got good people there who will take care of him. Everybody knows he doesn't belong there but as long as he won't talk we have no choice."

Bill said, "There's my food. I don't want to upset my daughter so I'll talk to you later. Thanks again."

Chapter 104

Ed and Karen were half way to Chicago when they stopped at the truck stop and ate lunch. They had homemade beef stew with big homemade rolls. Ed said, "There goes my diet."

"Well, we'll skip supper. We won't need any after this."

They got back on the road and were at the airport at four o'clock. Ed got the car parked and joined Karen in the terminal. He went to find the phones and called Sam at the FBI office. When Sam got on the phone, he said, "Well, old buddy, we got a match on those prints. The ones you sent today matched the dishes from your house and the bottle from the other place. Does that help you out?"

Ed said, "It sure does, thanks a lot for all your help, I owe you one."

Sam said, "You can be sure I'll collect, too. Dinner next time you're in town."

Ed asked, "By the way have you ever heard of a guy named Ken Barton?"

"Yeah, he's a private eye here in town. I run into him occasionally. Never had a problem with him. He giving you trouble?"

"No, he was in Dinsmore, earlier this year spying for a jealous wife. I just thought he might have seen something to do with my case. I'll give him a call. Thanks again, Sam. Stop in if you're ever in Dinsmore."

Sam said, "Sure, good luck now, call me anytime I can help."

He looked for Karen but she had wandered off somewhere so he called the number Bill had given him. A grouchy sounding man answered, "Ken Barton, here."

Ed said, "Hello, I'm Ed Hawkins, police detective from Dinsmore. I wonder if you could give me some information."

Barton said, "Well, Detective Hawkins, I'll try. What is it you want to know?"

Ed replied. "Well, I understand you were in town working for Janet Wallace earlier this year. The lady you saw with her husband was found dead a few weeks later. Since you had followed them to get the goods for Janet, I thought you might have seen somebody else hanging around her besides Bill Wallace."

Barton hesitated and said, "Well, I really don't want to talk about something like this over the phone. I have no way of knowing if you're who you say, you are."

Ed knew he was right, but told him, "Okay, I'll tell you what. Could I talk you into coming back to Dinsmore and giving me any information you may have at the police department?"

Barton laughed at that and said, "Hey, I'll be glad to if you want to pay my going rate."

Ed was getting angry, he said, "Well, I'll tell you what else! I'll just come and arrest you and take you back with me. I'm at the airport right now. I can't come to your place or I would. I really need to know if you saw anything suspicious during your surveillance. Now do you think you can help me?"

Barton said, "Are you have a Thanksgiving dinner?"

Ed was puzzled, "Yeah, so what?"

"So you set an extra place, I don't have any place to go for Thanksgiving. I'll come to your place."

Ed began to laugh. Barton said, "I'm dead serious, I hate holidays with no family, so I like to intrude on others."

"Well, consider yourself invited. Do you need directions?" Ed asked.

"Just give me your number and I'll call you when I get in town."

Ed gave him the number and told him to get there before noon because the dinner was at the neighbors and there would be about twenty people there. "Anyway we'll be up at the neighbors at noon and I don't know their number." He explained, "Now I'm serious, are you sure you'll be there?"

Barton said, "You can count on it and I'll be hungry. See you Thursday, okay?"

Ed was delighted, "I'll look forward to meeting you and I'm counting on your help."

He went to look for Karen after he hung up the phone. It was a little after five by now and he walked down toward the inspectors station. As he passed the restaurant, he heard his name being called. Karen was sitting at a little table with a magazine and a latte'. He went in to join her.

He told her about his phone calls and the crazy private eye. She didn't believe him, she said, "You big joker. You know nobody would do that." He finally convinced her that it was the truth. He felt sure the guy could tell him something about Margie. She told him she was glad that he was able to get him to come back to Dinsmore.

He got a coffee and said, "Well, our girl should be here soon. This has been a good day. I'm feeling better all the time."

At six o'clock Karen was keeping an eye on the passengers going by and when she spotted Melanie, she called to her. Melanie looked around, turned and ran to them. There were hugs all around and she said, "You both look so good. I can tell you're happy to be together. I was hoping you would come with her, Ed."

Ed replied, "I wouldn't have missed it. We've had a good day. Shall we go collect your luggage or do you want something to drink?"

She said, "No, I'm fine. Let's go to baggage."

He walked with them and then said, "I'll go get the car and meet you out front. If they won't let me in, I'll just flash my badge."

Karen said, "We'll be right out."

They stopped at the same truck stop on the way back and had supper. Ed said, "I thought we were going to skip supper."

Karen answered, "But that was at lunch and now that it's supper, I'm hungry again. Besides Melanie is hungry."

Melanie quipped, "Yeah, the peanuts on the airplane weren't exactly filling, so I'm starving."

"Well, I'm not really hungry but I guess I'll eat with you girls. By the way" Ed said to Karen, "I forgot to tell you, I didn't know what time to tell Jeff to come to dinner. Have you and Ruth decided that yet?"

Karen said, "No, she hasn't told me. I'll have to check tomorrow."

Then he said, "Also you and Melanie need to know that Jack Carter was Margie's lawyer but he doesn't have a will for her. I sure hope you find one in the safety deposit box."

Melanie said, "So do I. I did some checking and they say probate is slow going anyway."

Karen said, "If you're up to it, we'll go to the bank tomorrow. Maybe we can get Ed to buy our lunch at the Café, if we plan it right."

The three of them talked and laughed, all the way home and it seemed no time 'til they were there. Jazz ran out to meet them as they drove in. The house felt warm and cozy after the trip. Karen showed Melanie that the guest room was now also Ed's office now but there was still plenty of room for her on the day bed. She helped her hang up her clothes and asked her if she needed anything else.

Melanie said, "No, I'm fine. I'm so glad to be here. You and Ed are very sweet to go to all this trouble." Karen assured her, "You are no trouble. We have looked forward to having you here with us."

Ed was on the couch with a big bowl of popcorn when Karen went to sit by him. He leaned over and kissed her, he said, "I'll share my popcorn with you if you'll get us a drink."

She went in and opened two beers and brought them back. Ed said, "Do you think Melanie will want a beer?"

Karen said, "I'll ask her if she comes out. I think she's tired and probably in bed already."

The words were barely out of her mouth when Melanie came out and said, "I'm not that tired and I can get my own beer."

Ed said, "I was about to say that no teenager is that tired."

Karen poked him in the ribs and said, "Oh, yeah, the worlds expert on teenagers. By the way she isn't a teenager any more."

Chapter 105

Jeff had tried to question Tom but didn't have any luck. Chip took a turn at it and he was not successful either. Bill came in and wanted to see his son but Tom refused to see him. So when Ed came to work on Wednesday, there was nothing new to report. He decided to try again but Tom was unresponsive.

He called Jack Carter, the lawyer, and told him, "There is evidence proving that Tom had been in Margie Sloan's apartment at some time." He told Jack about the affair between Bill and Margie. He went on, "I'm just telling you this so you'll know where I'm coming from. You might want to give your client this information so he can make up his mind whether to talk or not. If he doesn't tell his story, we may just file murder charges with the evidence we have."

Jack said, "I'll have to think about this, Ed. Thanks for keeping me informed. I'll get back to you later."

Karen called and said, "Tell Jeff to come to dinner at one o'clock on Thursday at Ruth and Joseph's house. I already called Daniel and told him the time. How is your day going?"

He said, "Well, I'm not having any luck with Tom but otherwise it's quiet. Want to meet for lunch at eleven thirty to beat the crowd?"

She answered, "That sounds good. Melanie and I are getting ready to go to the bank now. I'll see you at the Café. Bye now."

After he hung up, he thought about calling Bill, but decided not to, until he had talked to the private detective. He couldn't hold the kid much longer without filing charges. He decided to file vandalism and resisting arrest charges. Then Bill would have to bond him out and they could watch him. Bill would have to take responsibility for him to appear in court, so he would be keeping an eye on him, too.

He went into the chief's office and told him what he knew and what he planned to do. The chief surprised him by agreeing immediately. So with that decided, he did what he had to do. He called Bill to tell him that he would have to bond his son out. Bill was upset but so glad that he was going to get Tom out of jail that he didn't ask questions. Ed was relieved at that because he didn't want to answer any questions.

He then called Jack and told him what he had done. He told him just to hang loose until he let him know what was going after Thanksgiving. Chip Carter, the new young detective, was Jack's oldest son, he would know more if Jack wanted more information. Chip hadn't wanted to be a lawyer like his dad, but he liked law enforcement which sometimes put them on opposing sides. They had a good relationship though and it had never created problems.

Ed had done all that he could do and he left to meet the girls. They were not in the Café when he got there, so he went to his favorite table and sat down. Tony was busy cooking and didn't see him come in but Maria did and she came over with a cup of coffee. She asked, "Are you having lunch today, Ed."

He told her, "The girls are meeting me soon, so I'll wait to order. How have you been doing, Maria? Keeping Tony straight?"

She giggled and said, "You know that's impossible. It's so funny because you haven't been in for a couple of days. He's actually been worried about you. Thought he'd made you mad or something."

Ed said, "That is funny! Karen and I have both been busy. I just went back to work on Monday and then we went to pick up Melanie yesterday or rather last night. Nothing Tony does would make me mad after all these years. It's like water off a duck's back. He just full of it, you know what I mean, don't you?"

She was quick to answer, "I do, I do." She went on to another customer and as soon as Melanie and Karen came in, she was back to get their orders. Ed told her to bring them all a burger and fries. The girls told her what they wanted to drink and she went to tell Tony.

He turned around, waved and yelled, "Hi, Y'all, I've been missing you. Good to see you." They all just nodded their heads, not wanting to bring any more attention to themselves.

Ed asked, "So tell me, did you find the will? What all did you find?"

Karen said, "One question at a time. We did find a hand written will with Margie's signature which is great if it's legal. We found another bank account she had in her and Melanie's name for emergencies apparently. We also found the title to the car and it was all ready to change to Melanie's name, too. Margie was taking care of her little girl all the time. I expect she had planned to give her the car after one semester and then get herself a new one."

Ed said, "So I guess we'll go see if the car will crank after all this time of sitting unused. I've got jumper cables if we need them."

Tony brought their burgers over and said, "Hi there, Melanie, it's so good to see you again. Home for the holidays?"

Melanie said, "Yes, for that and to get a car so I can move to Chicago."

Ed and Karen looked at each other, surprised because they hadn't heard this news. Melanie saw the looks on their faces and said, "I was just waiting to see how things went and so far, so good. Don't you think?"

Karen just said, "Sure is."

They kept on eating, hoping busy body Tony would leave the table. Maria saved them by calling to him, "Where's my order, Tony?"

Ed whispered, "We're glad for you, Melanie. We just didn't give Tony any more to talk about. He's such a talker and the whole town doesn't need to know your business."

Melanie said, "Oh, my gosh, I thought for a minute you guys were mad at me."

Karen smiled at her, "No way, I'm all for you going to the Institute. Especially since you'll be closer to us and we can see you more often."

Ed said, "Do you need us to go with you, to help you move?"

"No, I don't think so, it's not that much. I'm going to need it when I move the stuff from Mother's place to mine, when I get one in Chicago. Then I'll need help for sure."

Karen said, "Well, before you drive all the way to Columbia, we'll have to make sure the weather is not going to get bad."

Melanie said, "Yeah, I knew you would say that and of course you are right."

They finished their lunch and went to the apartment complex to see about the car. It was sitting right where Margie had parked that last night and Melanie hesitated before she got in. She felt a shiver go over her, just thinking about it being her mother's car. She unlocked it and got in to try to start it. Amazingly it turned right over and she pulled it out of the parking place.

Ed waved her on and he drove Karen back to get her car. Before she got out of the car, she leaned over and kissed him, "Thanks for lunch and all that you do for Melanie and I."

He said, "Hey, just takin' care of business. I'll see you after work."

She got out and went to her car. She and Melanie had decided to wait til Friday to see the lawyer about the will. She went home to get some cooking done for Thanksgiving. Melanie was already sitting on the porch with Jazz and Callie. She said, "Is it alright if I go ride Candy?"

Karen said, "Oh, I know she'll be happy to have someone pay attention to her. I have neglected her since the wedding and all."

Melanie went in to change to her jeans and boots. Before long she was out the door and on the way to the barn. Karen was baking the pumpkin pies for the dinner so she got out the ingredients. Then she decided she needed to change to her jeans and an old shirt. She had also volunteered a broccoli casserole and some yeast rolls so she was into lots of flour and shortening for next few hours.

Ruth was doing turkey, dressing, gravy and mashed potatoes plus a dessert. Rebecca was bringing a carrot cake and salad. Pamela was bringing a corn casserole so there was going to be plenty of food.

When Ed came in from work, he stood there shaking his head, "Looks like there's been a snow storm in here." There was quite a bit of flour in the kitchen.

When Melanie had come in from riding she washed up and began to help. They still had a lot to do before they could relax. Ed said, "Tell you what I'm gonna' do, girls. I'm going to make us some grilled cheese sandwiches and a bowl of soup for our supper. You've got enough to do already."

Karen said, "Oh, I hate for you to have to do that, but it does sound good."

He said, "Hey, grilled cheese is my specialty." So you finish up what you have to do and then I'll do my thing."

He went to the bedroom to change to his jeans and when he came back, the phone rang. He said, "Hello, Ed Hawkins, here."

"Hello there. This is Ken Barton. I just got into town and I'm at the Holiday Inn. Just wanted to let you know."

Ed said, "Well that's great. You're right up the road from our place. Why don't you come by in the morning for breakfast and we'll get acquainted."

Ken answered, "That would be great if you're sure it's not too much trouble. Want to tell me where you are?"

Ed gave him the directions and told him not to come before nine. He went back to the kitchen to tell Karen that he had invited someone to breakfast.

"Well, you know what Ruth says, the more, the merrier." Then he told her who it was and she said, "Oh, that should be interesting to find out what he can tell us." He nodded and put his finger to his lips so she wouldn't say anything to Melanie. He started helping her clean up the mess. Then he got the supplies out to prepare his specialty.

She went to take a shower. Melanie was stretched out on her bed. When Karen got out of the shower, she looked in on her and said, "Are you feeling okay?"

She answered, "Oh, I'm just fine, I was just thinking that sometime tomorrow I ought to go to see Grandmother at the nursing home. It's been a while and she's probably wondering why I haven't been there."

Karen said, "That's a good idea, she'll probably be lonesome especially since it's a holiday." She went on to her room to finish getting into something comfortable.

When she came back into the kitchen, she had on her favorite warm robe. Ed had set the table and was warming a can of soup. He put the grilled cheese sandwiches on a platter and ladled the soup into bowls. He called to Melanie, "Come and get it, Melanie. A feast by the master is prepared."

She came out and she was in her pajamas. He said, "My goodness, looks the girls are tired out from cooking all afternoon."

Melanie said, "Oh, we're just warm and comfy. You can go put on your Pjs if you want to."

He said, "I'll pass on that. I don't wear those things and you don't want to see me in my boxers. Now eat up before it's cold."

They enjoyed their meal and all pitched in to clean up afterward. Ed asked, "Is everything ready for tomorrow's dinner?"

Karen answered, "All I have to do is pop my casserole in the oven in the morning. Everything else is done."

"Okay, then I'll cook breakfast in the morning, you girls can sleep in because you'll have a lot to do at the Barrys."

Karen and Melanie smiled at each other and Melanie said, "That's a great offer, Karen. Where did you find this guy?"

"Oh, he hung around just long enough for me to catch him."

"Who caught who. I think it was a tie and now I'm tied."

Karen pretended to slap him. He grabbed her, hugged and kissed her. Melanie acted shocked by covering her eyes. When the kitchen was clean, they all gathered in the living room to watch television until bedtime.

Chapter 106

After Bill got Tom out of jail with bond money, only $500 cash, he took him straight home. Neither of them said a word for a long time. Even after they were in the house they didn't speak. Bill really didn't know what to say. He was still in shock at his son's behavior and had no idea what to do about it. So instead of talking about the arrest, he began to tell Amy and Tom about what the doctor had said. Their mother would be coming home in two weeks and how nice it would be to have her home for good.

The kids looked at him like he had lost his mind. Tom walked out of the room muttering and Amy said, "What are we going to do about her? With all this mess, she'll really go mad. I may go mad, myself. I don't understand any of it. Do you?" She yelled, "Tom can you tell us how to understand the mess you've made of our lives?"

Tom came out of his room like a raging bull, went to Amy and started to shake her. Bill jumped and pushed him away. Tom started screaming, "I made a mess, what about him? He's the one that started all of this. Leaving home, screwing around and leaving us to suffer Mother's rants."

Amy just stood there with her mouth open, unable to speak. Bill said, "Tom, you go to your room and stay there. You've done enough damage for a lifetime. I don't want to hear any more of it."

Tom said, "No, you don't want to hear it, because it's true." He turned and went to his room and slammed the door.

Bill turned to Amy and said, "I'm sorry that he did that to you, I need to go think this through. Tomorrow is Thanksgiving, we must have something to be thankful for, but I've got to figure out what it is."

Amy said simply, "Good luck."

Daniel went to Rebecca's apartment after work. They were in the kitchen making a carrot cake. Daniel said, "I didn't know that a carrot cake was actually made with carrots."

Rebecca laughed at him and said, "I guess you didn't know turkey gravy was made with turkey either."

He said, "Oh, aren't you the wise ass?"

She laughed even harder, "While you're grating those carrots, grate enough for me to add them to the salad. I cheated on that and just bought three bags of salad greens with endive, spinach and all in it. We'll add the carrots and some cherry tomatoes. I'm going to make a special dressing that everyone will like. Kind of a sweet and sour that my grandmother used to make."

Daniel said, "Well, the career girl does have a little domesticity after all."

She whacked him with the spatula she was using to mix the cake batter. Now he had cake batter on his face. He swiped it off with his finger and tasted it. He said, "Um'm it's already good and it doesn't have any carrots."

She said, "If you don't hurry up, it won't have time to bake before Thanksgiving." She added some raisins and the spices and he handed her a bowl of grated carrots.

He said, "I believe that should be plenty for the cake and the salad."

She agreed and said, "Now you can spray those pans and flour them and we'll be ready to bake." He did as she said and she filled the pans to put them in the oven. She set the timer and said, "Now let's clean up and then we'll see what's on the tube. I cheated on the icing, too. I bought the canned kind so that will make it simpler."

Daniel said, "Do you cheat a lot?" Then he realized he shouldn't have said that, and added, "Just joking, don't hit me again. Not with that dish rag, you've got in your hand."

She looked serious and said, "Speaking of cheating, how about you. Do you cheat? You know I've been burned before, so I'm a little gun shy."

He was feeling bad about his stupidity and paused before he answered, "Well, I guess, I did cheat with Margie because I was still legally married but I had not had anyone for years. I had never cheated on my wife before. It was weird because the day after Margie and I were intimate, my divorce was finalized."

Rebecca was feeling a little sorry for him and said, "Well, I guess we can give you a pass on that one. You seem to be a pretty good guy, as guy's go."

"Well, thanks for that vote of confidence. I try." They spent the rest of the evening watching television until the cake was done.

When Rebecca got up to take it from the oven, Daniel said, "I'd better be going now. I want to be up early and walk in the morning and I need to call my kids and see how they're doing. They're both at their mother's for tomorrow and they'll be there for Christmas day. Then we'll have the rest of the time together. I can hardly wait for them to be here with me."

Rebecca said, "I guess, I can ice the cake without you, so go on and get your rest. What time will we leave tomorrow?"

He said, "I'll come get you at twelve fifteen or so." She was already starting to get the icing ready for the cake. He leaned down and kissed her on the cheek and went to the door.

She followed him and turned him around and kissed him hard and long. He just stood there, looking surprised and she said, "Thanks for helping me, I enjoyed having you here. Goodnight, now."

He said, "Goodnight, Rebecca." and went out of the door. On the way to his apartment, he was thinking how tempting she was and how he wanted to stay there but must not start anything that he couldn't finish. He was still thinking about that kiss when he got in his bed and he lay awake for a long time.

Jeff and Pamela were in her apartment after having pizza delivered. She had put her casserole together and it was in the fridge so they were on the couch munching pizza, drinking beer and watching the television.

Jeff said, "This is the life even if I do have to go to work tonight in order to have the day off tomorrow."

Pamela said, "What time do you go in?"

He told her, "At midnight. I traded with Chip. His family is not eating until six tomorrow and I'll have to go in then, too. Otherwise Ed would have to go in and that didn't seem fair. Craig wanted to go home to his folks in Lexington and I really don't mind. We worked it out so everybody could celebrate in their own way. There won't be much going on anyway."

Pamela asked, "Thanksgiving isn't a busy day? I figured a lot of people would be drinking and driving."

"Well, it's usually quiet but you're right, sometimes we do have to bring in a drunk driver."

Pamela said, "Chip is Jack Carter's son, isn't he?"

"Yes, he is. Jack wanted him to be a lawyer but he likes the other side of the law. Do you know Jack?"

"Yes, he got me my divorce and my last name back."

"Well, good for you. So what do I call you now?"

She giggled, "I'm still Pamela, just Pamela Dixon instead of Sloan. I'm sure Larry is glad, too. It was just a stupid mistake both of us made. I'm glad he took off, he didn't stand a chance here with all the dumb stuff he had done. I just got lucky with Rebecca recognizing that I wasn't an air head. She really stepped up for me and gave a chance to be somebody."

He leaned over and put his arms around her and said, "Hey, I think you are somebody. You're a great gal and you've taken some hard knocks and come back strong."

She said, "Thank you, I appreciate that and she kissed him on the lips for the first time."

He kissed back, a little too eagerly and she backed away.

She said, "I didn't mean anything by that, so don't think I'm being too forward. I just felt like kissing you, that's all. Understand?"

"I get it, no problem. I'll take any kiss I can get without questioning the reason."

He was grinning and said, "Really, I'm sorry, I just lost my head for a minute. I'm not trying to get you in the sack."

She poked him in the ribs and said, "I'm glad to hear that, now pay attention to the show."

They watched television for a while longer and then he got up and said, "I need to go on to the station now and check in with Chip. See what's going on and what I need to do."

She got up and walked with him to the door. He turned and kissed her on the cheek and said, "I'll pick you up at twelve thirty tomorrow. Be ready."

She waved him off and shut the door. She was thinking. He's a nice guy and a great kisser. I'd better watch myself or I'll be in another messy situation.

When Gary Oldham got home on Wednesday evening, Christine was in the kitchen preparing supper and working on the turkey for tomorrow at the same time. He went in and kissed her on the cheek and asked, "Do you have everything you need?"

She said, "Yes, but you can help me with this turkey. I want to get it ready to put in the oven and it's heavy and slippery. Could you wash it and get the giblets out?"

Gary said, "I sure can. Let me get out of these clothes and I'll be right back."

The little ones were involved in a Disney movie that Christine had loaded in the VCR for them so they were quiet for a change. Gary came back and after he washed the turkey he greased it good, put some salt in the cavity and plopped it in the roasting pan.

Christine said, "You did a great job of that. I guess that's something else, your Mom taught you, huh?"

He said, "Yes, she said we needed to learn how to be good husbands and the girls needed to learn to be good wives, so we all had to learn the same things."

"Well, you had a great Mom. I wish mine had been, I've learned more from you than I did from her."

"Don't be too hard on her. She didn't have an easy time of it. We always had Dad to make the living. Our mother didn't have to work and had plenty of time for us."

"Yes, I know that but it doesn't make me feel any better. She'll be here tomorrow and I guess I'm already getting worried. She's so critical and doesn't act like a grandmother."

"Hey, not to change the subject but I was wondering if we have plenty of food, I mean enough to have some more guests?"

"Sure, who do you want to ask?"

"I thought we could ask Bill Wallace and his kids. I don't know if you're aware of what's been going on there but he's got big problems."

"Why? Did Janet do something else?"

"No, not Janet. Tom has been in jail for two days. Bill just got him out today. I don't know all the details but something about vandalism and threatening phone calls. I tried to see him at the jail but he wouldn't let anyone visit with him."

"Well, you go call him right now. He might need to be with other people tomorrow. It's a sad day for a lot of folks. Especially when they have problems."

Gary called Bill and told him they'd like to have them come to Thanksgiving dinner. Bill said, "That sounds great to me if I can get the kids to agree. Let me call you back though, I really need to talk to you anyway. Maybe I can go in your office and talk some tomorrow."

Gary was agreeable. "That will be fine, I'll look forward to it and we're going to plan on you being here so talk to those kids and tell them I'll be hurt if they don't come."

"I'm afraid they don't mind hurting our feelings these days but I'll try that and see how it works. I'll call you back."

Gary hung up the phone and went back to Christine. "What's for supper, Wife?"

She just smiled at him and said, "I made some sloppy joes and baked some fries. We'll have ice cream for dessert. Let's get in on the table and then you can get the kids washed up to eat."

After supper was over and they were getting the little ones ready for bed, the phone rang. It was Bill and he said, "I just wanted to let you know we'll be there tomorrow. What time?"

Gary said, "Come at noon and we'll eat sometime after that. It depends on how the cooking goes but we can visit a while. I want to talk to you, too. I know you could use some help and I'd like to do whatever I can."

Bill said, "I appreciate that, we are going to need some good counseling in more ways than one." They ended their conversation and when Gary hung up the phone, he called to Christine and said, "Bill and his brood will be with us tomorrow."

She said, "Good."

Chapter 107

Ed was up early on Thanksgiving morning, frying bacon and sausage. He opened a can of biscuits and put them in the oven. The phone rang and Ken Barton wanted to know if it was too early to come by. Ed said, "No, man, I've almost got breakfast ready so you better get here before we eat it all."

He was just hanging up the phone when Karen came in rubbing her eyes, she said, "I thought you were kidding when you said you'd fix breakfast."

"Hey, you'd better get into something else, our guest is on his way here."

She groaned, "Oh, I forgot about him. I'll hurry so I can help you."

He said, "I don't need any help, just hungry people at the table."

Melanie came in and she was dressed, "So you're cooking again. Karen did well when she got you. I hope I can find a man that can cook because I'm only good at opening cans."

"Now I know that's not true. You fixed some mean chicken breasts for us one time. Remember?"

"That's right, but I need to keep that a secret. I still need a man that can cook so I don't have to."

He said, "Now the truth is out. Why don't you get the plates and silver on the table and as soon as Ken gets here, I'll scramble the eggs."

Karen came in and said, "Now let us have a cup of coffee before you start ordering us around, Mister."

He poured two cups of coffee and handed it to them as he said, "Now get with it, Lady."

She took her coffee outside while she fed Jazz and Callie and gave them the attention that they required. While she was outside, a car pulled in the drive and wiry little man in a felt hat and raincoat got out and came up to her.

She thought, "Oh, here we have a "Columbo" look alike. He stuck out his hand and said, "I hope I'm in the right place, I'm Ken Barton."

She took his hand and said, "Welcome to Dinsmore. I'm Karen Hawkins, come on in and we'll have breakfast. Ed's prepared us a feast."

They went inside and after introductions and returning thanks, they ate Ed's bountiful breakfast. When they were through with breakfast on their third cup of coffee, Melanie said, "Well, I'll let you grown up people go in the living room and I'll clean up Ed's mess."

"I resemble that remark. But I'll let you do just that anyway."

They went in the living room and Ed said, "I've been real anxious to talk to you even before all this new stuff happened."

Ken asked, "What new stuff?" Ed told him about arresting the Wallace boy and not being able to get him to talk.

Then Ken told him about his experience with Janet. He said, "I could tell that she had a problem. I mean, in more ways than one. When I got here, her husband was not living with them. She wanted to know what he was doing."

Ed interrupted, "Well, we know he was seeing Margie. When she found out that he had gone back home, she broke it off. He led her to believe he was getting a divorce, I think, but I don't know. We didn't have any idea this was going on. She was Karen's best friend. The girl in the kitchen is Margie's only daughter. We've made ourselves her foster parents, more or less."

Karen was just listening to the two of them and now she spoke up, "So, Mr. Barton. Exactly what did you find out?"

He said, "Please, call me Ken." He continued, "Well, they were meeting at the motel where Bill was staying. Then after he went back home, he would go to her apartment. He must have had a key because I saw him go in there when I knew she wasn't at home. Sometimes I would just stake out her place because he had already left the motel. I guess that's when she found out that he had gone back to the house."

Karen asked, "Did you take pictures?"

"I took some of her going into his motel room and him going into her apartment building but that's all. Nothing too personal."

Karen said, "I'm glad to hear that. I was shocked when I found out that Margie had been having an affair. It was not like her but I guess the divorce had put her in a different frame of mind. She and Bill had gone steady in high school and were a big deal until he went off to college and she started dating Larry. All of a sudden she was married to Larry and Bill was left out in the cold. I don't think he ever got over it."

Ken said, "Well, he wasn't the only person that went to her apartment. I saw Janet go there when Margie was at home and I saw a boy, I'm thinking it was the Wallace boy, go there when she was and wasn't. He went there several times."

Karen looked at Ed. She was distressed and on the verge of crying. He patted her on the back and said, "Don't take it too hard, Honey. We don't know anything yet."

Ed said, "You see, Ken, you were gone before they discovered Margie's body and she was in the bathtub, not under the water or anything. There was a bottle of pills on the floor by the tub and our chief of police decided it was suicide. He wouldn't let me investigate any further. But Karen is an ex cop and she did some investigating on her own. We just found out through the FBI that a wine bottle from the apartment and some dishes from a vandal that was here had matching finger prints. He didn't break in because Karen forgot to lock up when she was gone for a little while."

Ken asked, "So whose finger prints are they? Do you know?"

Ed answered, "Yes, unfortunately, we do. It's the Wallace's boy, Tom. I arrested him the other day. I booked him for resisting arrest so I could hold him. I allowed his dad to bond him out last night though. He never talked. Wouldn't say one word the whole time I had him in custody. I don't really think he did anything, or I can't bring myself to believe he did. But we want to prove that Margie did not commit suicide."

"Well, I can understand that. I don't know if I'll be any help but I'll try. I brought the pictures with me. Maybe I can help you with it when you question him again. I'll be there. I planned to stay in town for a few days, anyway."

Melanie had finished in the kitchen but had been listening to the conversation. When she came in she said, "Mr. Barton, if you can help prove that my mother didn't commit suicide, I'll be eternally grateful. It doesn't matter about insurance or anything like that. She'd had that insurance for years. It's her reputation I want to protect and I don't want a bunch of gossip about her affair with Bill Wallace either. So if we can solve this mystery without a lot of publicity, it will be good for all of us."

Karen added, "Lord knows the Wallaces don't need any worse news either. The less other people know the better."

Ed replied, "Well, we'll try to keep it as quiet as we can but if a crime was committed, it will have to come out. I'm sorry but that's a fact of life. Now let's quit worrying about this stuff for now. There's nothing we can do today but feel thankful."

Karen went to put her casserole in the oven and Melanie went to shower and change. Ed and Ken had another cup of coffee and checked to see what football games would be on later.

After she packed up everything but the casserole, Karen went to get her shower and change. She chose some black slacks and a red sweater, put on her sterling jewelry and got some black flats to be comfortable. She knew the women would be kept busy for most of the day. Melanie came out in a long denim skirt and vest with a white menswear shirt and brown high top shoes.

Karen thought, "She looks so much like Margie. It makes me sad to look at her sometimes."

To Melanie she said, "You look so pretty. Are you still going to see your Grandmother?"

"Yes, I'll go after lunch so I can get back early. I'm not used to driving and especially at night." By now it was almost noon, so they all got in their own cars and headed down the road to the Barrys.

Ruth and Joseph were both right at the door when they arrived, shaking hands and hugging everybody. They introduced Ken Barton as a friend from Chicago that just came into town. Not a lie, but shading the truth paid off right now. The men all made for the living room and the women went to work in the kitchen.

Ruth said, "Actually, girls, we could just sit down and have coffee or tea. I've got everything ready, just waiting for the guests. Unless you want to join the men at the television. You know they will be watching football all day."

Karen said, "I knew you'd have everything organized but I didn't want you to be worked to death so I thought we'd get here a little early. The others won't be here until one. I hope that's okay."

"Sure it is, I like to have a little time to relax before we start. Well, Miss Melanie, what have you been doing with yourself?"she asked as she poured the coffee and got out the cream and sugar which none of them used.

Melanie told her about her plans to move to Chicago and go to the Art Institute. Ruth told her that she had many old friends up there. She said, "I'll give you their names and numbers so if you ever need help, they'll be glad to help you. We loved Chicago but we wanted a quieter place to retire and a big yard and all to fiddle around in. So now we love Dinsmore just as much."

Karen said, "I'm going to be glad to have her closer, so we can visit more often. Of course I'm thrilled that she is going into art as a career."

Melanie touched Karen's hand and said, "I'm glad of that, too. I'll be there for your big opening at the gallery in January."

Karen told her, "You know if you're close in December, the Christmas parade is the twelfth and you can come for that. It's always a lot of fun, not to mention a lot of work. I always get stuck helping decorate. Tony wants me to help him and Maria with publicity."

Ruth said, "Yes, I'm in charge of the bake sale for the Women's Society."

Melanie said, "I'll sure try to be here, maybe early so I can help. I really don't know when we get out of school. I'll have to come home as soon as I find an apartment and get things ready to move there. I have a feeling December is going to be even busier that usual."

They heard car doors shutting outside and Ruth went to see who had arrived.

It was Rebecca and Daniel. Ruth welcomed them at the door and took the dishes they were carrying to put them on the counter top. After everyone had said their hellos, she took their coats and Daniel went to find the men.

Rebecca sat down with the ladies and thought, "Oh, so this is how it's going to be. I've got news for these folks. I'm watching the games with the men."

She smiled sweetly though and accepted a cup of coffee from Ruth's gracious hand. About that time another car door was heard and Pamela and Jeff were there, with Ruth at the door ushering them in and making them feel welcome.

When Jeff left to go find the men, Pamela smiled at Rebecca and they both knew what the other was thinking. She got her coffee and joined in the conversation with the ladies at the table.

In a few minutes Ruth got up and said, "Well, now that we're all here, I guess it's time to put the food out. I'm going to do this buffet style to make it more convenient. You girls can help me get it all out. Melanie would you put the ice in the glasses? I have sweet and unsweet tea to drink or just water. You other girls can arrange the food as you see fit. Joseph carved the turkey and ham already, and it's in the warming oven."

They all got busy and Karen checked to make sure everything was there. When they were all in the dining room, Joseph returned grace and everyone said, "Amen."

The next hour was filled with laughter, chatter, and groaning because they had eaten too much already but, "Yes, I guess I can hold dessert." was heard many times.

Everyone took their dishes to the kitchen when they had finished. Ed offered to help clean up but the ladies assured him that though they appreciated his offer, it would not be necessary. Ruth whispered to Karen, "You got a fine fellow there, my dear, a fine, fine fellow."

Karen smiled and said, "I know, I feel very lucky to have him. I'd been alone a long time and it still seems like a dream, to have such a wonderful companion."

After she had helped get the dishes ready for the dishwasher, Melanie said, "I'm going to drive over the nursing home and visit my grandmother. I hope you won't think that I 'm running out on you, Miss Ruth."

"No, my dear, I think that is wonderful. Your grandmother will be so glad to see you. I'm sure. Why don't you take some of this delicious carrot cake and pumpkin pie?"

Melanie answered, "Well, I guess it would be okay. I don't know what kind of diet they have her on but I'll check with the nurse."

Ruth got a plastic dish down and fixed it with some of each dessert. She said, "Well, if she can't have it, the nurse will I'm sure." They all laughed so hard at that remark, Ruth was embarrassed, "Sometimes I speak when I should keep quiet."

After Melanie had gone, Ruth said, "Now I know you young ladies like football, you go on in there and watch with those men. They're so rude, they haven't invited you but you'll just have to show them a thing or two." Then pausing and putting her hand to her mouth, she said, "Oh, my, there I go again."

They all had another good laugh at her expense but she joined them and tears were rolling down Karen's cheeks.

Ed came in and said, "I feel like we're missing all the fun. What is going on in here?" Then they laughed all the harder and he stood there looking stupefied. Karen let him wonder the rest of the day, but she told him later when they were in bed, talking about what a great day it had been.

Chapter 108

At the Oldhams, Christine, with Gary's help had created a feast fit for kings. Bill and his children were there at noon. After everybody was seated at the table, Gary returned thanks and then they started passing the bowls of delicious food.

Gary asked Tom if he was going to miss football now that the season was over and he said, "No, sir, I'll be playing basketball now so I'll still be busy."

Amy said, "We both play basketball, it's my favorite game. Did you know that Mother went to college on a basketball scholarship?"

Gary said, "No, that explains you and Tom being so athletic. Of course your dad is no slouch in the athletic department and some of the kids tell me he's a great teacher."

Bill was surprised at Amy being so talkative, but he was proud of her trying to be polite and make conversation. He knew Tom would not be making any great effort but at least he was polite and spoke, when spoken to.

Bill complimented Christine on her cooking and she said, "I'm so glad you like it, Bill. I was so happy when Gary invited you. It's always more fun to cook for a lot of people."

Gary said, "I don't know how she does it with these little house apes running around but she does a great job."

Bill told them about the plans for Janet's planned return. Christine said that was good news. They discussed the weather in between bites and when they were through eating the main course, Christine served the coffee and pumpkin pie with whipped cream.

Everybody helped clear the table and then the men made for the television and football. They took the little ones with them, so Amy and Christine could finish up getting the dishes in the washer. Christine said, "Amy, I'd like to take a walk, would you go with me?"

Amy said, "That's a very good idea, walk off some of the food I ate. I am so full that I'm afraid I will fall asleep if I sit down."

While they were walking, Christine told Amy that she knew that they had more than their share of trouble lately and if Amy ever needed to talk she was available. She told her that she and Gary did quite a lot of counseling and that they didn't gossip about other people's problems. She would never repeat anything told in confidence.

Amy said, "I'm doing fine in spite of Mother's problems, but Tom seems to be all bent out of shape. He doesn't act like himself, any more. He's moody and hard to get along with and poor Dad doesn't know what to do with him."

Christine said, "When your mother gets home, Gary plans to meet with all of you so maybe things will get better if everybody is working together. I know what it's like to have your mother not behaving normally. My mother and I were never able to become close. Even today, when she was supposed to join us for dinner. She called to tell us that she had another important thing to do and "Just couldn't make it." I know her well enough to know it's a man, who is the important thing, but never mind that. I would love for her to be a Grandmother but it's hopeless. She wants to stay "young." Young and grandchildren just don't work for her. But, back to Tom. He is just mixed up. He'll get over it. You know he's got so much to look forward to in college."

Amy told her, "He's going to lose his scholarship chances if he messes up much more. He's been in jail twice lately. That's so awful. I just can't imagine why he's behaving so badly."

Christine was shocked at that news, but she didn't let on and went on talking about other things, deciding to change the subject to happier thoughts. She asked if Amy was going to enter the Junior Miss Pageant and Amy said, "I don't know if I can. They have so many rules and without Mother, I'm lost. I can't ask Dad to help me with that kind of thing."

Christine said, "Hey, I can help you. Not only did I enter when I was in high school. I have worked with the program for years."

"Oh, that would be great! You'd know exactly what to do. Can I come by after school next week?"

"Sure, you bring all the information you have on it and we'll get it together. You don't have to worry about talent since you are such a great singer. I will love helping." Amy couldn't wait to get home and phone her friend, that had wanted her to enter. They had walked back to the parsonage by now and when they went into the house, they found three guys and two little kids asleep with the football game going full blast.

That night after they got home Karen and Ed were tired enough to skip the television and go straight to bed. Melanie had returned from visiting her grandmother and she was in her room, in the bed, reading.

Karen went in and asked about Mrs. Orson and Melanie said, "She was thrilled to see me and the dessert that Ruth sent was welcome. She isn't on any diet restrictions. She actually looked a lot better. She's a tough old bird, that's what she calls herself. Her mind is as sharp as ever. She wanted to know what you had found out about Mother's death. Can you believe she remembered that?"

"Yes, knowing her, I believe it. We'll have to go see her again as soon as we figure this out. I'm going to bed now. Don't forget we've got to go see the lawyer tomorrow and see what he can tell us."

"I haven't forgotten. Goodnight, Karen and thanks for everything."

"Goodnight, sweet Melanie."

Ed was already in the bed when she got there. She said, "Did you lock up everything?"

"Of course, would I forget a thing like that? Don't want any boogie man getting in here."

Then he asked, "What did you think of Ken Barton?"

"I thought he was a nice old guy, he was a lot older than I expected. You know. You think of a private eye being like Rockford."

"You've been watching too much TV. Did you know he was a cop for twenty years in Chicago? His wife passed away after he retired. He was at loose ends so he decided to become an investigator. That's why he was so glad to be here for Thanksgiving. He's one of those guys who dread holidays. They never had any children so he's lost at times like this."

"Well, I'm glad he could join us and I'm glad he's got some ideas about what went on at Margie's place. The visit from Janet was a surprise to me, wasn't it to you?"

Blunt as usual he said, "No, not really. I saw her in action at the station. She's a wack job for sure."

"That's a terrible thing to say, Ed. She's a sick woman and can't help being erratic."

"That's true but I don't envy anybody that has to live with her and her erratic behavior."

Karen looked surprised. "Are you saying that you don't blame Bill for cheating on her?"

"Maybe, but not really. It's his responsibility to get help for her, not to hang her out to dry."

She was having a problem with that remark, too. "Some people just won't accept help but I have a feeling that he just didn't care and she knew it."

Ed thought about it a while before he answered. "Well, I have a feeling that we're going to know something soon and it will mean more misery for that family."

"Let's change the subject, this doesn't make very good pillow talk, does it?"

"You're so right, Baby. Come here and let's get seriously sensuous, how do you like this?" He pulled her over closer to him and kissed her.

She said, "Don't stop, I love it."

Chapter 109

Melanie was already sitting on the back porch when Karen got up to make coffee. She opened the door and said, "I thought you would be freezing but it's really not that cold, is it?"

"No, it's nice. The sun was so bright, and I had to come out. Jazz and I have been playing ball and I went out to see Candy. We've been neglecting her, you know."

"You're right. We need to ride her today. It's going to be a pretty day."

Ed came to the door and said, "Would you ladies like to have this coffee out there?"

He came out holding three mugs of coffee and said, "It is great out here, isn't it? I can't believe this, the middle of winter and it's not very cold at all."

Karen said, "It's even warmer with this coffee, thank you. You are a really sweet guy, you know?"

"You're only saying that, because it's true. You have such good taste."

Melanie said, "Oh, please, what a bunch of mush. Do I have to listen to this?" They all began to laugh and Jazz started barking at them.

Ed said, "I guess I'd better go get ready for work. Think I can get a bowl of oatmeal from one of you women?"

Karen said, "It will be ready when you are." She sat down by Melanie and said, "We really are happy, you know. It's kind of like a miracle to find love at our age."

Melanie said, "My goodness, you talk like you're ancient. Love is great anytime you can find it. I'm just pleased that you found yours. He's been there all the time, hasn't he?"

"Yes, he was afraid I wasn't over Rich, though you're never over someone you love. You just go on living, hoping that you'll wake one morning, not thinking of them or their death."

Melanie said, "I know exactly what you mean, because that's what I do. My first waking thought is of my mother being gone. I still can't believe it."

She started to cry and Karen hugged her and said, "I'm sorry I didn't mean to make you sad. I should just shut up."

"No, it's just that what you said is so true. That's all. I'm okay, go fix Ed's oatmeal and I'll have a bowl with him. I haven't had oatmeal since, I don't know when."

Karen went in the house and got breakfast ready for all of them. She poured glasses of orange juice and made some buttered toast. She put some of Ruth's strawberry jam on the table and called them, "Come and get it while it's hot."

Daniel stopped at the Café on his walk Friday morning. It was very early and Tony had just opened up. He sat at the counter and Tony brought him a cup of coffee.

Tony asked, "How was your Thanksgiving?"

Daniel said, "We had a great day at the Barry's and I'm still feeling the pain from overeating. That's why I decided to walk today, trying to walk it off."

Tony was only interested in one thing, the facts. He said, "What do you mean, we?"

Daniel smiled and told him that he and Rebecca had gone to the dinner together. Tony beamed, "Oh, got us a new girlfriend, huh?"

Daniel answered, "Well, we have been seeing each other for a while."

Tony would have loved to find more but he had to go wait on another customer. He had been so interested in Daniel's love life that he forgot to get his order.

Daniel moved up close to where Tony was cooking and said, "Hey, I'd like a sausage biscuit, when you can get to it. If it's all right, I'll refill my own coffee."

Tony was embarrassed and apologized. He brought Daniel his order in a few minutes but he stayed too busy to pry out any more information. Maria came in before Daniel left and she said, "Good Morning, Daniel. Did you have a nice Thanksgiving?"

Daniel told her had a nice day and asked, "How was your day?" She answered, "With our big family, it was a mad house but we enjoyed it. Mama was worn out and glad when we went back to work."

Daniel said, "Speaking of work, I'd better pay this tab and get home. Got to shower and get to the bank. We should be busy today with all the people shopping and needing more money."

He had to hurry because he had taken longer than he planned and it was getting late. When he got back to the apartment complex, Rebecca was coming out of the drive. She stopped and rolled down the window. She said, "What are you doing out here in your running clothes? Aren't you going to work today?"

He explained, "I stayed out longer than I should have but I've still got time."

She said, "Well, I've got to get on, call me tonight if you're not busy."

He waved and headed up to his place. He was thinking, "Yes, I will call you, Rebecca, I sure will." He was beginning to think they might have something going. Maybe, just maybe, he would invite her to go to Colorado with him and the kids.

Bill Wallace and his children ate breakfast in silence. Tom still wasn't talking and Bill didn't know what to say. Amy just stayed busy cleaning up and keeping out of the way. She was hoping that she could get out of the house and go shopping with her friends. She was waiting until Tom went back to his room to ask her father.

When they were through eating, she cleaned off the table and got the kitchen cleaned up. By then Bill was in the den reading the paper. She went in and asked him, "I'd like to go shopping with my girlfriends today if it okay. Could you give me some money?"

He looked up and said, "Why sure, Honey. You've been working so hard taking care of this house. You deserve some fun and some money. I really appreciate all you do."

"Daddy, I'm so sorry that you have all these problems. You ought to go have some fun, too."

He groaned at that, "I've got to stay and play jailer. That's sure not what I had in mind for the holidays, but we do what we have to. I'll make it fine. Something will break soon. No point getting upset and worried. That would be wasted energy."

Then he sort of choked up and said, "I'm such a great philosopher. I'm worried sick because I don't know what to do with Tom. I don't know what to do with your mother either. This is going to be awful with her coming home."

Amy just nodded her head and said, "I know, it's awful but I don't know what to do either." She took the money he held out to her and kissed him on the cheek. She said, "Maybe Tom will talk to you later after he's had time to think about it."

She turned to go to her room and get ready to go out for the day. Bill went back to his paper. Tom stayed in his room all day.

After Ed went to work, Melanie said, "I'd like to go ride Candy for a while if it's okay."

Karen said, "Sure, go ahead. I think I'll go work on a painting. I haven't done anything for a long time and I've got a lot to do before January. We'll go see the lawyer this afternoon. I'll call him first though and make sure he can see us."

Melanie went to the barn and Karen to the studio. She had picked out a photo of a still life she had taken some time ago. She thought it would be a good contrast to her landscapes. She had stretched the canvas earlier in the month and she sketched the still life with a thin paint. She began to fill the negative space and was using a limited palette in burnt sienna and viridian green. She used naples yellow for the highlights. There were red apples, purple and green grapes with a big wine bottle and a glass half full of wine. It was all arranged on an antique cutwork table cloth which she had draped from the background to the mahogany table.

She had blocked in most of the colors and had been working a couple of hours when she decided to stop and get ready for lunch. She went to the back door to see if Melanie was back but could not see her anywhere.

Karen was in the shower when Melanie came in, she called to Karen, saying, "It's me, Candy and I had a great ride. I guess I'd better get ready, huh?"

Karen said, "Yes, I called Jack and he'll see us at one o'clock."

After they had both showered and dressed, they fixed sandwiches for lunch. Melanie asked, "What do you think Jack can tell us?"

"Well, he'll be able to tell us if Margie's handwritten will is legal and what we have to do with it, so you can take possession of her estate. We don't have to worry about the car title except to have it filed with the state. Maybe he can help with that, too."

Melanie said, "Yes, and then I need to go get insurance on it in my name, too. Have you heard the weather report for next week?"

"No, but we'll sure check before you start out for Missouri. I want you to tuck your hair up in a ball cap so you'll look like a boy while you travel. That way maybe no one will bother you. There's so much car jacking going on. You must always keep your car doors locked. Don't I sound like an old mother hen?"

Melanie smiled at her and said, "Yes, you do, or maybe more like a cop. I know you're right though, they're always warning us at school to be careful. Sometimes weirdos hang out at schools, just to see if they can catch someone off guard."

When they got to Jack Carter's office, his secretary told them to have a seat and he would be with them soon. Before long she said, "You can go in now. Mr. Carter will see you."

He stood up and came around his desk to shake hands with them. He said, "It's good to see you, Karen. How's married life?"

Karen said, "It's great."

Then he looked at Melanie and said, "I haven't seen you since you were a little girl. You sure do look a lot like your mother. I'm really sorry about her passing. It was a great shock."

Melanie said, "Thank you." And he went on, "Now tell me how I can help you?"

Karen told him what they needed help with, so he read Margie's will and said, "Well, all we need to do here is have this probated. That does take time but there should be no problem with it. You won't have anyone that will contest it. It just depends on how long the court takes and you will have to pay me, but I will try to charge the minimum amount. As to the car, just keep on using it and get insurance in your name. After the will is probated we'll take care of the title. Go ahead and get the furniture and anything else you need. It's just a matter of getting the court to agree that it's all yours now. Since your name is already on the checking accounts, there's no problem there. The insurance will come to you since you're the beneficiary so you'll have no money problems. I can't see any problems for you at all. Congratulations on having a mother that knew what she was doing."

Melanie said, "Thanks, Mr. Carter. I'll leave it up to you then and when it's done you can bill me. Karen will have my address when I get settled in Chicago."

Karen thanked him and they all shook hands and he walked them to the door. He said, "Good luck in Chicago, Melanie. Don't forget to come back to Dinsmore now and then."

She answered, "Oh, I won't. Karen will see to that."

She hugged Karen and said, "She's my mother now." Karen was overwhelmed and on the verge of tears, after hearing that remark. They went out to their cars after deciding to go to the Café for some of Mama's pie.

Chapter 110

Tony looked up from the grill when they walked in and said, "Well, Hello, girls! It's good to see you two. What can we get for you today?"

Karen said, "We'll have some of Mama's coconut pie and coffee." They went back to sit at Ed's favorite table.

Maria had come from the office in the back and she brought their pie and coffee to the table. She sat down and said, "How have you been, Karen? We haven't seen much of you since the wedding."

Karen said, "We haven't stopped running since then. Been to Chicago twice and then there was Thanksgiving and today we've been to the lawyer for Melanie's business. We're going to have a quiet weekend though, I hope."

Maria said, "Yes, I need a quiet weekend, too. Thanksgiving wore us all out." Then she asked Melanie, "How long will you be in town?"

Melanie answered, "I'll probably start back to Missouri tomorrow so I can be at school on Monday. I have tests to take before Christmas break and then I'm moving to Chicago to go to school."

Maria said, "That sounds great. You'll be closer to us then." While they were talking, Ed and Jeff came in the door.

Tony said, "Hey, he caught up with you, Karen. I think he may be a stalker. Want me to call the cops?"

Ed said, "Hey, you just leave this to me and get me a cup of coffee before I arrest you."

Jeff was still using his crutches and was slow to get to the table. Karen said, "I guess you won't be chasing any crooks on foot will you?"

Jeff just shook his head. He'd had enough o f the teasing by now. Maria got up to go get them their coffee and they sat down.

Karen said, "Did you come by accident or did you see our cars?"

Ed assumed a very serious look and said, "I'm a good detective, I had an APB out on you two." He smiled, but became serious when he said, "I talked to Bill Wallace earlier today and Tom still hasn't said a word. Not one word. I told Bill that we would let it go until Monday and then I would bring him back for another interview. I hate to make the kid miss school but we've got to get to the bottom of this thing."

Jeff said, "Then we'll start the water torture and get out the rubber hoses."

Melanie looked shocked and he said, "I'm only kidding, we don't do that. I hope you know that. That's what they do in the city."

She said, "Oh, great. I'm moving to the city. Of course I hope I won't be getting arrested anytime soon." Then she turned to Ed and asked, "Do you really think Tom had something to do with my mother's death?"

Ed put his fingers to his lips and motioned toward Tony. She knew what he meant so she began to whisper. "Seriously, do you?"

Ed said in a low voice, "No, but I think he knows something, and he's not telling. Then again he may be guilty. I don't know how we can find out if he doesn't talk. But let's not talk about it now. It will wait until Monday."

Karen changed the subject and said, "Melanie is planning on leaving us tomorrow."

Ed looked surprised and asked, "So soon?"

Melanie said, "I figured you'd be glad to get rid of me."

He looked hurt. "What are you talking about? I love having you with us. You're like a daughter to us."

That made Melanie tear up and she got up and went to hug him. "And you're like a father to me and Karen is like my mother. I feel very lucky to have both of you. I'll miss you but I've got to get on with life so I can earn a living one of these days."

"Well, I'm glad to hear that! I sure don't want to have to support you. I'm planning on you taking care of me in my old age."

Jeff said, "See what you get for being nice to this old man. You can't win. He's got an angle on everything. He made me work two shifts so he could be off on Thanksgiving. Then he cussed me out for being five minutes late this morning."

They were all laughing when Tony came over and said, "What's so funny over here?"

Ed said, "We were just giving Jeff a hard time."

Tony said, "I'm sure he deserved it."

Jeff just shook his head and said, "I know when I'm beat. Let's get back to the car, Ed. We need to get out there and protect the citizens."

Ed got up and kissed Karen on the cheek and said, "I'll see you girls after work."

Karen answered, "We'll be there. I'm going to go home and ride Candy for a while. What do you want for supper?"

He said, "Let's eat some turkey sandwiches and some of the leftovers. The lord knows that we've got plenty of those." He and Jeff went out. Soon Karen paid the bill and followed Melanie out to the street.

Melanie said, "I'm going to go by the florist and pick up something and then go to Mother's grave. I meant to do it before now, but we've been so busy."

Karen felt a shiver go over her for an unknown reason. She said, "I'll meet you there, I haven't been for a while."

When they got to the cemetery, they walked to Margie's grave site together. Melanie placed three pink roses on the grave and suddenly Karen knew why she had shivered. Every time she had gone there, seeing the pink rose was disturbing to her. It had always made her feel uneasy but there were no other roses there this time. She wondered where the person who had been visiting was now.

Now she was disturbed because there was no mysterious rose. She said a silent prayer for Margie and turned to go so Melanie could be alone for a few minutes. She waited at her car until Melanie walked up and said, "It doesn't get any easier. I still can't believe my mother is gone. She is in that grave and won't be back."

Karen said, "Honey, she isn't in that grave. Her spirit is with us and always will be. You'll feel her presence sometimes when you're quiet. At least that's how I feel when I'm quiet and think about her." Melanie just nodded and they went to get in their cars and go home.

Karen couldn't wait until she had on her jeans and boots so she could ride Candy. Candy seemed glad to see her, too. She was swishing her tail and tossing her mane as if to say, "Come on, let's go."

Karen and Candy galloped across the pasture. She rode for about thirty minutes and went back to the barn. She brushed Candy for a while and fed her before she went to the house. Jazz had come to the barn and walked or ran ahead of her to the house.

Melanie was in the kitchen making spaghetti sauce. She turned when Karen came in and said, "I know you and Ed talked about what to fix for supper but I didn't really want any more turkey. Did you?"

Karen agreed, "You will make a hit with Ed, I'm sure. Should I call and tell him to pick up some French bread?"

"No, I stopped and got some on the way home. I had planned to do this all day."

Karen patted her on the back and she went to check on her painting. She worked on it for a few minutes and decided to wait. She just wasn't in the mood. She was thinking of Melanie driving all the way to Missouri when she remembered they hadn't got the car insurance.

She went back to the kitchen and told Melanie that she would call her agent and get him to arrange it right away. After she had talked to him, she came back and said, "He's going to come by this evening and get your signature. Thank goodness there's enough time left for him to check everything out, so he can write it."

When Ed got home, he came in the door saying, "Ooh, my, it smells good in here. I could smell it clear outdoors."

Melanie smiled and said, "Well, I thought maybe this would be better than turkey sandwiches."

"You got that right! This is great. Where's that wife of mine?"

Melanie pointed toward the studio and said, "She's knee deep in paint back there. I haven't heard a peep out of her for an hour."

He started taking off his coat and tie on the way and went into the studio and grabbed Karen from behind and hugged her while he turned her around. He kissed her hard and long and she returned the same.

Melanie came in and they jumped when she said, "It's a dirty shame, you can't stand each other. What are you jumping for, I mean I am aware that you have a life and I love it. I hope someday I can find somebody I care that much about."

Karen said, "I hope you do, too, Honey. Just don't be in any hurry. As you can see, you never get too old to be in love."

They all went to the kitchen to eat the delicious supper Melanie had fixed. She had set the kitchen table with big salad at each place and a huge bowl of spaghetti covered with sauce. They had a glass of wine for starters and toasted Melanie's future in Chicago.

Karen told Ed, "Tad Lewis is coming by to finish up Melanie's car insurance. I completely forgot to do it today."

Then she told him about the cemetery visit and the fact that there was no rose. He looked puzzled and said, "H'm, I wonder what happened to the secret visitor."

She said, "My thoughts exactly." Then they had to explain it all to Melanie.

She said, "Maybe it was the person who had something to do with her death. Oh, God, you don't think she was murdered, do you?"

Ed said, "We don't have any idea how she died. We just don't believe she committed suicide."

Melanie said, "Well, I hope you can find out. I don't like people thinking she did." They both promised her they would find out if it was at all possible.

Someone was knocking on the front door. That rarely happened since everyone that knew them came in the back. Karen said, "That must be Tad."

Melanie said, "Well, I guess we'll have our coffee and dessert later. I'll start cleaning up while you take care of your guest."

Ed told her to go on. He'd do the clean up. She would have to sign papers and all. Karen went to the door and said, "Hi, Tad, come on in. It's really nice of you to go to all this trouble. Melanie wants to start back tomorrow and I forgot this today when we were taking care of our business."

He said, "Oh, that's okay. I didn't have anything else to do this evening. I'm just a lonely bachelor so nobody will be looking for me."

When Melanie came into the room, he said, "Hi, Melanie, I haven't seen you since high school. How are you doing? I was really sorry about your mother."

She had forgotten him but now remembered that he was a senior when she was a freshman and she thought he was really good looking. He still was, too. Blonde like a Norwegian god and tall with broad shoulders. She said, "I'm doing fine. It's nice to see you. Thanks for doing this for me."

He got out the papers she needed to sign and handed them to her. She read them and signed them. She asked, "How much do I owe you now?"

He said, "Well, it's seven hundred for six months. Since you're under twenty-five, it's really expensive but we have to have it, don't we?" She wrote a check and handed it to him.

He said, "Thanks, and by the way, the insurance from your mother should get to you before long. You know it took a while because they said it was suicide but she'd had the policy for four years so it didn't really matter."

"Yes, I know what they said. I don't believe it's true but I can't do anything about it right now."

Karen said, "Ed and I are working on solving that problem. We'll let you know if we find out anything."

Tad said, "Well, I'd better get going and let you folks go on with your evening…and…"

Melanie interrupted, "No, stay and have dessert and coffee with us. I fixed something special and we didn't have time before, but you're welcome to join us."

He said, "Okay, that sounds the best offer I've had all day." She went to the kitchen and set the table again for four this time. She had made a banana pudding for dessert and she served it up in glass bowls. Then she poured each one a cup of coffee. She put the sugar and creamer on the table and called them to come in and have a seat. The three of them oohed and aahed over her dessert. She said, "It's not much but it's the only dessert my mother taught me to make and we always loved it. I hope you like it."

She looked embarrassed and Karen patted her hand and said, "This is so nice. It's a good way to remember your mother."

Tad said, "Hey, my mom didn't teach me to make anything and I wish she had. I live on frozen dinners and fast food. Sometimes I drop in on the folks at supper time just so I can have a decent meal."

Ed said, "Now I call that a good plan."

After the dessert was wiped out, Tad stood and said, "Now I really am going. I've enjoyed being with you all. Thanks for everything."

Melanie walked with him to the door and he turned and said, "Hey, Melanie, could I call you sometime?"

She said, "Well, I'll be moving to Chicago but the next time I'm here I'll call you and maybe we can get together."

He smiled broadly. "That would be great. Good luck in Chicago." He took her hand like he was going to shake it, then he looked embarrassed and turned to go to his car. As he was going down the walk he turned to wave and she waved back.

When she had shut the door, she looked at Ed and Karen, they were grinning at her and she giggled. "He is some handsome hunk," she said.

Ed said, "I didn't notice, did you Karen?"

"No I thought he was an ugly duckling." She just waved them off and went to clean up the kitchen one more time.

Chapter 111

Gary Oldham called Bill Wallace to see how they were doing on Saturday morning. Bill said, "Not very well. Tom still won't talk to me at all. I've never seen anything like it. Ed is going to call him in again on Monday which means he'll miss school again and basketball will be out because he isn't keeping up his class work."

Gary asked, "Do you think I could come over and try my luck?"

Bill said, "Sure, there's nothing to lose except I hate for you to waste your time."

Gary was adamant. "It won't be a waste. I want to help. If I have to, I'll do all the talking. I'll be right over."

Bill decided he would get out of the house while Gary was there, he felt like he was in prison himself. He had called Janet at the hospital and told her they wouldn't be able to make this weekend. He told her Tom was sick. He thought, "I wasn't telling her a lie because there was something wrong with my only son and I feel totally helpless."

Gary was there in just a few minutes and Bill told him that he would be back in an hour. He explained, "I've been be in so long I'm getting cabin fever."

Gary smiled and said, "Go on, I'll stay til you get back."

Bill took off for his favorite hangout, the Town Hall, to shoot some pool and have a beer with friends. H e always enjoyed talking to Janet's friend, a waitress there. While he was there, Jeff Collins came in and Bill challenged him to a game. Jeff was still able to play, but just on one crutch. They played two games and Jeff said he had to get back to work.

Bill said, "Yeah, I need to get home and see if Gary had any luck talking to Tom. He's still as silent as a stone."

Jeff said, "I know you're worried about him. I can't say I blame you but I also can't imagine a good kid like him has done anything too bad. You keep a stiff upper lip, buddy. It will all work out eventually."

He went out to his patrol car and Bill went to his truck. He dreaded going back to the house but had no choice. When he got there, Gary was in the living room and just shook his head.

"Sorry, Bill, I didn't get anywhere with him. He thanked me for trying to help but said he wasn't in the mood to talk."

Bill said, "Well, he's going to regret it, because Ed is getting tired of his attitude and will probably arrest him tomorrow."

Tom was listening around the corner and he went back to his room and began to plan his escape. He put some clothes in his back pack and some snacks from the stash in his night stand drawer. He got money he had been saving out of his sock drawer and climbed out of the window. He got his bike and took off down the street as fast as he could go.

When Amy got home, Bill and Gary were still in the den talking. She went in and sat down with them for a few minutes and then she got up, excused herself and went to her room. She had been in her room talking to a friend on the phone. When she hung up, she went to Tom's room to tell him about her day of shopping.

Amy came running into the room where Gary and Bill were engrossed in a football game and said, "Daddy, Tom's not in his room. Did you let him go out?"

Bill jumped up and yelled, "Oh, my God, what has he done now?" He ran to see if the truck was there and it was. Then he checked the bike and it was gone. He turned to Gary and said, "He's on his bike. Maybe I can find him."

Gary said, "That could be impossible. Just call the police and they'll find him. Better them than you. He is going to need a shock to get him talking anyway. They won't kill him. It would be the best thing to happen at this point."

Bill said, "I have to agree with you. I have a feeling that he's already lost his scholarship possibilities." Bill called Ed at home and told him that Tom had taken off. He had checked his room and knew he took extra clothes so he didn't plan to come back. Ed said, "Just leave it up to me. I'll get with the crew that's on duty and explain it to them. I'll let you know when I hear anything."

Ed was in the living room with Karen when the phone rang. They had seen Melanie off early that morning with instructions to call when she got to St. Louis. He turned to tell Karen, "That was Bill Wallace. Tom has taken off and Bill is beside himself. I couldn't tell him that Ken Barton has been watching the house since yesterday morning. I'm sure he's following Tom right now. We'll just see where he goes. I expect Ken will call me soon."

Karen said, "Why you sneaky old man! They'll never know who he is, will they?"

Ed said, "That's the whole point."

They decided they had better stay home in case either Ken or Melanie called. Ed went to do some work in his office. He hadn't been in there since Melanie had arrived so he wanted to rearrange his things.

Karen went to her studio to work on another painting. She had one that wasn't finished but decided to think about it before going back to finish it. She decided to do a floral treatment this time and went through her photos to find one she wanted to use. She found one of a spring bouquet she had arranged with daffodils and quince and some dogwood branches. She had just begun her sketch when she heard the phone ring. She let Ed get it and he came in before long to tell her that Melanie was in St. Louis and planned to drive on to Columbia. Melanie had told him the weather was clear and it was so early she thought it would be better to go on to the campus. She would call from there.

Karen was relieved that she was that far but really had hoped she would wait til tomorrow morning to go on. Ed said, "Don't worry about her, she'll be fine. Go on and work on your painting. The time will go faster if you're busy."

She smiled and said, "You know me, don't you?" He nodded and went back to his office. He had written a list of possible reasons or ways that Margie could have died. He wrote down the list of possible suspects and sat there studying his notes. None of it made any sense to him. He had written, Tom, Bill, Janet, Larry, the apartment manager, Ben and that's as far as he got. He thought about Daniel and Pamela but dismissed that thought. The only reason he could think of, was the affair with Bill. That was so short, he couldn't believe that was a good reason for murder.

Then he thought, "What about an accident? That's a possibility." It made more sense than murder anyway. Karen came into his office and looked at what he was doing.

She said, "Making any sense of it?" He answered, "None. It just doesn't make any sense at all."

She told him, "I'm going to fix us something to eat. It's already two o'clock and we haven't eaten since breakfast."

He said, "I'm sick of doing this, I'll help you." He put his arm around her waist and they went to the kitchen. He asked her, "Do you want to do anything tonight?"

"Not really, it will be kind of nice just to sit and watch the tube and eat popcorn. What do you think?"

"That's sounds good to me, too." They made turkey sandwiches and warmed up some leftovers for their lunch. They sat at the kitchen table and talked about their plans for tomorrow. After that Karen went out to ride Candy.

Ed took the portable phone outside and played ball with Jazz. The sun was shining brightly and it was cool, but not too bad for November. Karen rode for about forty-five minutes and when she came back, Ed told her Ken had called. "He says he followed him about twenty miles. He says that kid can ride like a pro. Tom was asleep under a viaduct right then and Ken stayed away back so Tom wouldn't see him. He's headed north so I think he's headed for the hospital where Janet is. What do you think?"

Karen told him, "That makes sense but will they let him see her?"

"I don't know but they have been going there on weekends, so they probably know him. I think, I may need to go up there and talk to her therapist soon and see if he can tell me anything. I know it's privileged information but he can give me a hint. I have a feeling that she's got something to do with this whole mess."

Karen looked shocked and asked, "Do you mean with Margie's death?"

"Yes, Ken said he saw her go to Margie's apartment, remember?"

"Yes, but he saw Tom go there, too."

Ed said, "I don't know whether to call Bill or not."

"I think you should. He could go catch up with him. I don't think he ought to be going to see Janet. It might make her go off the deep end. I know Bill won't want her to know Tom's been in jail. Besides if they have something to do with this, we shouldn't let them get together to compare stories."

Ed called Bill and told him that it looked like Tom was headed to the hospital. He suggested Bill go catch him and bring him back. He told him that he would want him to come into the station first thing Monday morning for further questioning. Bill agreed and he got Amy to go with him and they started out to find Tom.

When Ken called back, Ed told him to come on back to town, after he was sure Bill had Tom in his truck. Ken told him that he would and then he asked, "What are you doing tomorrow?"

Ed said, "We'll be going to church, why don't you come by after noon and we'll buy your lunch. I'd like for you to stay until Monday and be with me when I question Tom again."

Ken told him, "That's a deal. I'll see you tomorrow."

When he hung up the phone, Ed told Karen, "I've invited Ken to come eat with us tomorrow. I hope that's okay."

She said, "Sure, we've got spaghetti sauce leftover, so I'll just make a salad and get some apple dumplings out of the freezer and we'll be in business."

"You are too good to me." He grabbed her and pulled her to him, she whispered in his ear, "It's because I'm mad about you. Come to my bedroom and I'll show you."

He said, "I can't pass up a deal like that." They spent the rest of the afternoon in the bedroom. They were both asleep when the phone rang. Melanie was back at school, safe and sound. She would be back in Dinsmore on December tenth. The Christmas parade was to be on the twelfth.

Chapter 112

Sunday came and went without any more disasters. Bill had called to say he had Tom back at home and Ken came to lunch. They spent the afternoon visiting with Ken. Then Ed suggested they drive up to the hunting camp. He said, "You may want to come back down during the holidays and go hunting with us. How about it, Karen, you up for a ride?"

She smiled at him, "Well, we have been staying in so maybe it would be nice to get out in the woods." Usually she didn't got to the hunting camp but she got her camera and decided to make the most of it from her point of view.

They all got in Ed's Caddy and drove the forty miles to the camp. When they got there, the guys went in the cabin and Karen started walking the paths to take her photos. Ken said, "This is great, you just bring your own gear when you come?"

Ed said, "That prevents any vandals taking off with anything of value. They might mess it up a little but it wouldn't be hard to repair any damage they could do. We've really never had any problems though."

They went out to find Karen. She had walked quite far into the woods and when she saw them coming, she put her finger to her lips and motioned for them to stop. She was crouched down behind a bush. A doe and her baby were standing by a little pond. She got some great shots of them and when she rose up they scampered away. She was thrilled and Ed said, "Well, that does it. You have to come hunting with me."

She looked upset, "There's no way I would ever shoot anything with a gun. I'll take the camera anytime."

Ken and Ed laughed at her and she quickly, continued, "What's more, don't plan on eating any deer at our house. I won't have it. Did Rich ever tell you that?"

Ed was still laughing and it was making her angrier, he answered, "No, he would never have admitted that. But come to think of it, the deer meat was always in my freezer and we ate it at my house."

Ken said, "You can't win, Ed. You may as well plan on donating any deer meat to the homeless."

Ed teased, "I wonder how Ruth feels about deer meat."

"You're welcome to find out. Just count me out if she fixes dinner with it."
She laughed with them.

They had walked back to the cabin by now and Ed said, "I think we'd
better get on back. It's going to be dark in a little while anyway." They all got
back in the Caddy. When they were in Dinsmore, Ed went through the drive
thru at Wendy's and got them each a burger and a bowl of chili.

In the kitchen at home they ate and talked about the agenda for Monday.
Ed and Ken had to question Tom. Neither of them looked forward to it. Ed
asked Karen, "Have you got any suggestions on how to approach him?"

Karen said, "Just tell him what it's going to cost him if he doesn't talk.
You'll have to charge him with trespassing if nothing else, won't you?"

"That won't keep him in jail. I've got to think of a way to put the hurt on
him. That's what it will take, to get him to open up."

Ken said, "What about his mother, do you think she might be involved.
She's not wired right. I thought she was very explosive."

Ed answered, "Yeah, she beat the hell out of Bill. That was after you left
town. She broke a rib for him with a baseball bat."

"Ooh, I'm not surprised. She was really wanting to get the goods on him."
Ken continued, "I sure hope my information didn't have anything to do with
your friend's death."

Ed said, "No, this has been coming on for a long time. Bill just couldn't
take Janet's moods any more and rather than get a divorce he resorted to an
old flame. If it's anybody's fault, it's his. He knew that his wife was mentally
unbalanced. I'm sure he tried, but gave up on her. Then she really went
bananas."

Karen said, "Yes, it's always easier to criticize, but I wouldn't have
wanted to be in that family. Those are great kids and Bill is such a nice guy.
He just used bad judgement and it may have cost Margie her life for all we
know."

The next day, Karen worked on her paintings all day. When Ed came
home she was surprised that the time had gone so fast. He found her in her
studio and said, "Looks like you've been busy. I like that painting."

"I'm glad. I have really enjoyed doing it. I had no idea it was so late. I need
to get my man some supper." She walked over to him and kissed him warmly.
She asked, "How did it go?"

"It's hopeless. The kid is just not going to give in. I've got to believe he is
afraid to open his mouth for fear, he'll say the wrong thing."

Karen said, "In other words, he covering for someone else." Then she asked, "Where's Ken?"

"He already went back home. He said he had other things to do and this was hopeless so he left right after lunch."

Karen cleaned her brushes and took his hand and said, "Let's go see what we can do for supper. I forgot to eat today."

"I don't think I've ever been that busy." She patted his tummy and said, "No, I guess you haven't missed many meals."

They decided on soup and sandwiches because it was quick and easy. He got the soup ready while she fixed tuna sandwiches. When they had sat down, he asked, "How would you feel about going to the mental institution to see Janet with me?"

"When would you want to go?"

"I'd like to go tomorrow if you could get away."

"That's no problem. I'll be glad to. I don't know what good it will do though. They probably won't let us see her."

Ed was quiet a moment and then he said, "Well, if I can talk to her doctor and explain the situation, maybe he can find out something without upsetting her."

"Yes, that's a good idea. When do you want to leave?"

"I'll call first thing in the morning and make an appointment. I'll use my official status to get it right away. We can leave after I buy you some lunch at the Café."

She smiled and said, "That's a deal. I'd like a little time with you away from the rest of the world anyway. The ride will be enjoyable."

They spent the rest of the evening watching some television and went to bed right after the news was over. Just as she was dropping off to sleep, Ed said, "Do you know just how much I love you?"

She turned over and put her head on his chest and answered, "I hope it's as much as I love you." They fell asleep with Karen's head resting in the crook of his arm.

Chapter 113

Ed already had the coffee ready when Karen got up in the morning. She said, "My you're up earlier than usual."

"Yeah, I want to get in early and call that doctor. Can you be at the Café by eleven thirty?"

"Sure, that will be no problem. You call me if it doesn't work out though. Okay?" By now he had a bowl of cereal and some orange juice on the table. He poured a glass of juice for Karen.

She was still drinking her first cup of coffee. She went to the door to see if Jazz had brought in the paper. When she went to pick up the paper, Jazz was wiggling around waiting for a treat. Karen let him in and got the treats. Callie was right behind him, ready to get her share as if she had earned it.

Ed browsed the front page of the paper for a few minutes and then got up to go. He put on his heavy coat and hat because the weather had turned cold overnight. He came around the table and kissed Karen on the top of her head as he said, "I'll see you at the Café unless I call you. Then we'll get on up the road to the hospital."

"Okay, I hope you have an easy morning. By the way, did you keep Tom in jail?"

"No, I don't see any reason for him to miss school. Bill will just have to keep him on a short leash for now." He went out the door and the animals followed him. They had begun to follow him to his car each day and watch as he left.

Karen poured another cup of coffee and read the paper until the phone rang. It was Daniel wanting to know when Karen could meet with his committee on decorating for the Christmas parade. Karen told him that she would call him later in the week and let him know for sure. After that they had discussed the weather and what they had done for the weekend. When the call was finished, Karen went to her studio. She just sat looking at her latest efforts and decided that she had better not start anything. She needed to shower and dress to meet Ed. She planned to go into town early and see what she could do to help Tony with the parade publicity. She sat down at her desk and wrote down some thoughts she had for the parade before she went to shower. She chose some gray wool slacks and a green sweater with her black loafers for the trip. Since it was a cold day, she got her camel colored car coat out of the cleaner's bag that it had been in since spring cleaning time.

After she went out the back door and gave the animals a pat or two, she decided to check on Candy in the barn. She got her some extra feed and did some horse whispering, promising to take her for a ride soon. Jazz and Callie decided to stay in the barn with Candy. On her way to town, she stopped and got the mail from the box at the end of the drive. There was a letter from John with a postmark from France. She put it aside to read later.

Tony was watching as Karen parked in front of the Café and when she entered he had a cup of coffee waiting. He said, "We haven't seen much of you lately. Been missing you."

Karen told him that she'd been painting and he said, "Oh, that's right. You've got a show to get ready for, huh?"

She said, "Yes, and I don't have a lot of time left. I was wondering if you were doing okay with the publicity for the parade."

"I think we've got it all taken care of. You might want to take a look at our plan. Come on back to the office and I'll show you what we've planned so far."

Karen was impressed with their plan for publicity. They had ordered big banners to place on the main street and several small signs to be put out at intersections. They had composed a nice press release for the news agencies. They were even contacting the Chicago outlets. She said, "Tony this is great. You didn't need my help at all."

He confessed, "Maria did most of it. She is real good with our advertising and knows a lot of people in the business."

They went back out to the front of the Café and Karen sat at the counter while Tony refilled her coffee cup. It was unusually quite with no customers coming and going. Karen said, "What is going on? It's so quite in town today."

"It's just the lull before the lunch crowd. I enjoy it while I can. Maria went to do some shopping while it was slow. Mama's got a birthday coming up and we want to do something special for her. She'll be seventy-five."

Karen said, "That's great. She's a great help to you, isn't she?"

"Yes, and she loves the kids. She keeps our home orderly so it's nice to go home at night and relax."

Ed came in the door with Daniel right behind him. He came over and kissed her on the cheek. Tony said, "Oh, my the honeymoon isn't over yet.

Can you believe it, Daniel."

Daniel just smiled and said, "It's good to see that it's never too late to fall in love."

Tony looked surprised and said, "Does that mean you might be thinking along those lines?"

"It was just an innocent remark, Tony. Don't go starting any rumors."

They all knew that was next to impossible for Tony. The three of them went back to their favorite table. Tony brought them all water. Maria came in and said, "I'll take care of these folks now. You'll need to fix their orders."

Ed and Karen decided to have a burger and fries. Daniel opted for the plate lunch. Karen said, "I think I can get with you and Grant on Friday if it's okay with you. How about the morning, about ten thirty?"

"That sounds great. I'll call Grant. Do you want to meet at the bank?"

"Sure that will be fine. Have you got any plans yet?"

Daniel said, "I really don't even know how they do this thing, but I understand they use the big stock barn on the outside of town to build the floats. Do we just supervise and help out where we're needed? Only four businesses have said they want to do a float."

Karen said, "Well, I'm sure there will be more that will wait until the last minute to sign up. You get an entry fee from each one. Then you make sure they follow the theme and help them when they need it."

They all concentrated on their food after Maria brought it and when they had finished, Ed said, "We should get started. I need to be there by two and it's an hours drive at least."

Daniel said, "Yes and I need to get back to work. Got a meeting with some of the Chicago crowd that are in town for a visit."

Ed went to pay the bill and Karen said, "Thanks for everything, Maria. We'll see you later."

Daniel followed them out after he paid his bill and said, "Take care and good luck. Hope you can find out something from the doctor. I'll be interested, you know. I still think about Margie every day." Karen nodded and said, "Me, too."

They got on the interstate and Karen tuned the radio to her favorite station and kept it low so that they could talk. She scooted close to Ed and he patted her knee and said, "This is nice. Just to get away for a little while."

When they got to the mental health facility the sun had come out. As they drove down the long lane leading to the entrance, Karen remarked about the beautiful landscaping. She said, "I'll bet it's beautiful in the spring."

They came to the guard shack. Ed showed his badge and told the guard that he had an appointment with Dr. Novak. The guard waved them on and they parked close to the entrance. Ed opened the car door for Karen and they went into the main foyer which was more like an atrium with lots of glass and plants everywhere. There was even a fountain on one wall. Ed went to the desk and told them he was there to see Dr. Novak. They said he should have a seat and they would let him know when to go back to the office.

He and Karen sat on a couch that faced the back of the building where a lovely patio with lots of umbrella tables and chairs were arranged. There was a bird bath and several bird feeders. In a few minutes a middle-aged man walked up and said, "Hello, I'm Dr. Novak and I'm guessing you are Ed Hawkins."

"Yes, sir, and this is my wife Karen. I'm glad to meet you and I sure appreciate you taking time for us."

"Well, let's go to my office and talk about this situation."

When they got to his office, he said, "Can I get you something to drink? I have fresh coffee and soft drinks." They agreed that coffee sounded good.

After they had all been seated and relaxed, the doctor said, "Now how can I help you?"

Ed told him the story of Margie's death and the mystery surrounding it. He told him about Janet's dangerous behavior and how Tom, her son had been behaving. "I know you can't reveal patient information but I would like for you to see if you can get her to tell you what she knows about it. Maybe you can tell her about her son's trouble. He is basically on house arrest. I didn't want to keep him in jail because I feel like he is covering up something."

He paused to let the doctor absorb the information and then continued, "I heard Janet is coming home soon and I thought it would be better for her to find out about her family's troubles while she is here and can get help with it."

Dr. Novak said, "Yes, you're right and I don't know how I'll be able to handle this information but I will definitely need to tell her."

Ed said, "If she reacts badly, or tells you something you think would be helpful, would you consider getting her to talk to me?"

Karen had remained silent while the two men were engaged in conversation but now she spoke up, "This may all just be a tragic mistake in a lot of ways. It may have been an accident that wasn't handled correctly. We just need to know. We're sure that our friend, Margie, did not commit suicide and we want to prove it. It's important to her daughter and to me. She was my best friend for many years."

Dr. Novak got up and walked around the room. He got the coffee pot and refilled their cups and then after he put it back, he walked over to the window and just stood there looking out.

Ed looked at Karen and shrugged his shoulders. She just smiled at him. Then she said, "Doctor, do you think you can help us?"

He turned and said, "I'm going to have to think about this and take great care in my approach but I definitely will let you know what I can do without breaking any rules of conduct."

Ed stood and said, "How about me giving you a few days and then I'll call you and see how it's going?"

The doctor said, "That will be fine. I certainly hope I can help and I'll wait for you to call."

Karen got up since it looked like Ed was finished and they all shook hands. Before long they were back in the car, headed for home.

Chapter 114

Meanwhile, in Dinsmore, Rebecca called Pamela to her office and told her to make an appointment with the high school to plan the Christmas Beauty Pageant. They would also need to get a committee to work on the float. Pamela said, "Well, I've never done any thing like this but I'll do my best."

Rebecca said, "You're young and the kids will like working with you on it. I'll give you plenty of time to do the job right. I'll be here to help if you need me. Just call the principal's office and explain what you need. He will know what to do. They've participated in this affair for years."

Pamela turned to go, then she went back and said, "Thanks for trusting me to do this, Rebecca. It sounds like fun and I really appreciate you letting me do it."

Rebecca smiled and said, "That's fine. You could use a little fun, couldn't you?"

Pamela just nodded and went back to her department to start making the calls. When she spoke to the principal, Carl Thomas, they decided to meet the next day. She found out that it wasn't a pageant, just the student body voting for their choice. The teachers chose two girls from each class and the students voted for their favorite from those choices. The one with the most votes was the Christmas princess and so on.

Then she asked him about workers for the float. He said that by the time she met with him, he would have a group selected and have them at the meeting. After that he would leave it all up to her. When she hung up the phone, she breathed a sigh of relief. Then she thought about how she could get a float so she called him back. He smiled when she asked, "Mr. Thomas, I was wondering, do you know how to get the trailer or whatever for a float?"

"Oh, you don't have to worry about that. We have a local farmer who provides a flat bed wagon and a tractor every year for the parade. Just tell him when you want to start decorating and he'll have it there."

She sighed again and said, "Thank you so much. This is starting to sound like fun now. I'll see you tomorrow at ten a.m." After she hung up she thought, "I'm going to get in touch with Karen Hawkins and see if she can help me get this started."

Bill had been so disturbed over Tom's problems that he hadn't been able to concentrate on his classes, but now it was time to prepare for tests before holiday vacation. He decided it would be interesting to assign some studies of the depression era and then to give the tests on that subject. He had heard his parents discussions of the worst time of their lives and he thought that he would enjoy doing some research on it himself. He also needed to give Amy a little more of his time. Since the squeaky wheel always got the most grease, he had neglected her because of Tom's troubles. Then too, there was the fact that Janet would be coming home soon. That was going to be a challenge for the whole family. He had hoped Ed would be able to get through to Tom but so far nothing had worked. Even the preacher had not succeeded in getting him to talk.

His phone rang and it was Mr. Thomas calling a teacher's meeting for tomorrow morning at seven thirty, to choose the candidates for the Christmas princess. He knew that meant getting the kids up early, to make the meeting on time. He got down a book that would help him with his planned test and began to read. Tomorrow he would make reading assignments for his classes.

Daniel called Grant in the afternoon and they decided to have the people who were entering floats in the parade meet with them and Karen on Friday. Grant was taking care of the entries and he said he had six entries all together. That was probably all the floats they would have but it didn't include the high school. The rest were bands from various area schools, horse riding clubs, motorcyclists, veteran groups and any other group that wanted to march the two miles down Main Street.

He gave Daniel the names of the businesses and each of them took three to call. Daniel was lucky enough to get each of his on the first try. They were all willing to be there on Friday for the meeting. He rang his secretary, Kathy, and asked her to arrange for donuts or the equivalent and coffee on Friday in the main conference room. He told her to let everybody know the room would be in use from ten thirty to noon. She asked, "Would I be nosy to ask what kind of meeting?"

"No, not at all. I will be wanting you to take notes for me, so that I will know what goes on. It's for the Christmas parade float planning. Six different businesses will be represented so plan for at least twelve. Then there's me and Grant and Karen. Count youtrself and order plenty. The staff will eat any leftovers. I'm sure."

She said, "I'll call the bakery as soon as I figure out what and how many to order." He told her that would be fine, turned off the intercom and sat back in his chair to think about how much he was looking forward to his vacation.

On the way home Karen had tuned the radio to her favorite again and they discussed the meeting with Dr. Novak for a little while. They decided it had been a worthwhile meeting. Karen mentioned that she needed to get a lot more painting done this week. That made her remember the letter from John that she had put in her purse.

She got it out and read it slowly. He was just telling her how much he loved France and hoped someday she could see it. Then he told her that he hoped she was working on her paintings for the show because they would need a lot to make a big splash.

He suggested that she not price anything until he was back and could advise her. The gallery would be getting 50 percent and he wanted to be sure she made money from the affair. He would be back in Chicago for Christmas. He would contact her and make arrangements to come down and help her with the pricing. They would be choosing which painting to put on the front of the mail out. He said he would take as many paintings back with him as possible to save her from being over loaded later on. He also wanted her to compile a list of acquaintances to receive invitations. Ask anyone and everyone she could think of no matter how insignificant.

She laughed when she read it out loud to Ed. She said, "Well, I could just go to city hall and get the tax payer's list for him."

"That would blow him away! It sounds like you're going to be a busy little lady for the next two months. Maybe Melanie will help when she's here."

"I'm counting on her to help me with Christmas, the parade, especially. I feel like we ought to have Joseph and Ruth for Christmas dinner. Don't you?
"

Ed said, "What about Daniel and Rebecca?"

"Oh, my, there's poor little Pamela, too. Do you think Jeff will invite her to his family get together?"

Ed shook his head, "I don't know if they are seeing each other steady or not. I hate to ask him about his love life. Daniel did say that Rebecca was going home for the holiday but might come back and go with him and his kids on a ski trip."

Karen looking surprised said, "That sounds serious. I wonder if he is serious. She's a beautiful girl and he did seem to like her a lot."

"Well, you never know. I think he was taking it slow, because he didn't want to have a rebound from Margie. You know he was really crazy about her."

"I know and it's such a shame. Margie deserved a good man in her life." By now they were pulling in the driveway of their home. When they got out of the car the animals were there to greet them. Even the usually indifferent Callie came out as if she was glad to see them.

Chapter 115

The rest of the week went by in a whirl. Karen painted from daylight to dark and now had thirty canvases finished. There were landscapes in all the seasons, a few still life arrangements and several floral pieces. She wanted to get at least ten more ready before Christmas. Thursday evening she prepared a steak dinner for Ed.

When he came in from work, he was pleased with the aroma of food cooking and his wife looking pretty in jeans and a flannel shirt with a funny ruffled apron on her front. He grabbed her and swung her around and kissed her hard.

She pulled back out of breath and said, "My goodness, what brought that on?"

He was grinning, "This is a wonderful end to a great day. Dr. Novak called me and said that he wanted to meet with me tomorrow, but that he would come down here. He wants to talk to Tom. I'll call Bill later on and make arrangements to have him bring Tom into the department."

"That is great news, no wonder you're so happy."

"Yeah, and then to come home to a beautiful wife cooking a great meal. What more can a guy want?"

She told him, "Go get out of your work clothes and wash up. I'll have it on the table in a few minutes."

She had a Greek salad for starters and then steak and baked potato. She had decided to cut down on the calories with a fruit and Jell-O dessert topped with Dream Whip.

When Ed had finished, he pushed his chair back and rubbed his belly, saying, "That was the best meal I've had since Thanksgiving. Actually, I think it was better than Thanksgiving."

Karen said, "Now you can help me clean up and we'll watch some TV for a change. I am painted out. I've got a meeting with Daniel and his committee in the morning so I probably won't paint again until Monday."

Ed told her she deserved a break. He said he would call her when Dr. Novak was finished, to see if they should take him out for dinner. They barely stayed awake for the news and were both too tired and full to stay up any longer. It didn't take either of them long to fall asleep.

Daniel had called Rebecca when he got home from the bank. She asked him to come over to her place and eat lasagna with her. He said, "That's the best offer I've had in a long time. I'll bring the wine and be right over."

She opened the door before he could knock and hugged him as soon as he was in. He kissed her and said, "I've missed you. Seems like a long time, doesn't it?"

She nodded and said, "Yeah, we get so busy that we forget to relax and enjoy life. There's so much going on with Christmas and all the other goings on. Of course this is the time for us retailers to make it out of the red ink. It's very stressful because you never know if it's going to work out."

They had a glass of wine and then ate a delicious meal with salad and garlic bread. Afterwards she served a delicious New York cheesecake for dessert with coffee.

He told her how pleased he was, that she had invited him. They cleaned up the dishes together and then went into the living room to watch TV. It wasn't too interesting so they caught up on the latest news in their lives.

He asked if she had decided whether she could go on the vacation with him. She said, "I really want to, if you're sure that your children won't mind."

"My kids will be delighted to know I have someone that I care about. They're great kids and want their old dad to be happy. They're very good to their mother, too. They know she is ill and they try very hard to make her happy and give her lots of attention. Can you tell that I'm a little proud of them?"

She smiled and said, "I look forward to meeting them. You can plan on me coming back from St. Louis in time to join you all for the trip."

"That's the best news I've heard lately so I'll be able to firm up the reservations tomorrow. Thanks, you make me very happy." He leaned over and took her in his arms and they kissed for a long time.

He was getting a little too passionate and Rebecca got up and moved away. He said, "I'm sorry. I didn't mean to upset you."

She told him, "No, I'm fine but as I told you, I want to take it slow so we don't get in over our heads until we're sure where we're headed."

He agreed and said, "I'm going to go now because I've got a big day tomorrow and need to be rested. I know you do too, so I'll get out of your hair."

She came to him and took his hand as he got up. She hugged him and said, "I like you in my hair but I'm just cautious and I don't want to rush into things.

I'm afraid I'm becoming too infatuated with you already."

He was surprised at her frankness and answered, "Don't hold back too much because the feeling is mutual and I love it."

He walked to the door and turned and said, "I'll call you tomorrow and see if you feel like dinner at the club."

She smiled and said, "Do that, it sounds good. I haven't been out since the last time we went."

He said, "Are you telling me I don't have any competition?"

She just shook her head and pushed him toward the door. He kissed her quickly and hurried out the door. When he got down the stairs, he stopped and stood there thinking about her and the evening, wondering if this was going to be a blessing or another heartache in his life.

Chapter 116

Bill got the kids up early and had a good breakfast ready for them. He said, "I'm sorry I have to get you out so early but the Mr. Thomas didn't ask me what time I wanted to come to a meeting.

Amy giggled and said, "Well, at least you got a great breakfast for us."

Tom said, "Yeah, Dad, this is really great."

They all put their plates in the sink when they were finished and when they had dressed, went out to the pickup and started to school. Bill had started it earlier so it would be warm. Amy and Tom went in the front entrance as usual when they got to school and Bill drove around to his office. He checked on his class plans and then made his way to the meeting.

It didn't take long for them to choose the girls for the competition. He was proud to know that the English teacher recommended his Amy. Mr. Thomas was pleased, that it went so smoothly and told them that he was meeting with Pamela Dixon at ten o'clock. He said if anyone was interested in helping with the float they should let him know because he was sure they could use the help. Then he told them, "I'm going to announce on the PA that I need students to volunteer for the work committee."

Bill said, "I'll be glad to help in any way I can and I can get my boys to help, too."

The shop teacher, Kerry Smith, said he would be available, too.

Mr. Thomas said, "Why don't you two come to the office at ten and meet with Miss Dixon and me?" They both agreed that they would if they could leave their classes. The meeting broke up and after they had another cup of coffee and polite conversation, they all made their way to their classrooms.

After Ed had left for work, Karen got into her jeans and flannel shirt and put on a heavy coat to go out and feed her animals. It was cold enough for them to be running around and wanting to play. She played ball with Jazz for a few minutes and then went to the barn to saddle Candy and keep her promise to ride. Since she and Ed had married, she hadn't spent as much time riding as in the past.

After they rode around the field for a while she decided to go check on Ruth and Joseph. When she got there, Joseph was coming up to the house with some wood for the fireplace. He said, "Hi there, girl. You've been a stranger lately. We miss seeing you."

She felt bad about that and apologized saying, " I know. We stay so busy and I've been painting like crazy to get ready for that show in Chicago."

He said, "You go on in the house. I'll bring this wood in and we'll get some coffee and sit by the fire. Ruth is going to be tickled to see you."

She held the door for him and Ruth squealed and said, "Oh, my lord, I'm so happy to see you. It's been a while."

She hugged Karen and said, "Sit down here and tell us all about your life. I know it's been busy or we would have seen you more often."

Karen told them all about their busy life and what she had to do today. She decided it best not to mention the trip to the hospital. Ruth sat filled coffee cups on the table and some fresh sticky buns.

They ate and talked for an hour or so and then Karen said, "I hate to leave such good company but I've got to get home and get ready for a meeting later today. Before I go though, I want to ask you to have Christmas dinner with us."

Joseph said, "Hey, that sounds great. Are you sure that won't be too much trouble?"

Ruth chimed in, "Yes, we would love to be with you but you'll have to let me help."

Karen answered, "We'll have plenty of time to plan what to cook and I'll sure want some of your good cooking."

They walked out on the porch when she got ready to leave and Ruth said, "I didn't know you rode the horse up here. Won't you freeze?"

"No, Candy is warm and she goes fast so it won't take long to get home. You get back in the house so you won't freeze."

She waved as she rode off. Candy seemed to be happy to be out so Karen took her out to the field again before she put her up in the barn. The other animals were sleeping on a stack of hay but got up and came to greet her.

By now it was close to ten so she went to her studio to look through her photos and plan her next painting. The phone rang and it was Ed. He said, "The doctor hasn't arrived yet but keep your evening open in case we can take him to dinner. Well, heck, even if he can't go, we'll go out to dinner. Okay?"

"Sure, I'm always ready to go out to dinner."

"Are you going to come by and see me after your meeting?"

Teasing him Karen said, "I guess I could do that. Would you like me to?"

"You know the answer to that. You tease. I'll let you go and see you later, my love."

"Ooh, you're such a flirt. I love it. Bye now."

Daniel was really pleased when he noticed that Kathy had ordered brownies and little petit fours instead of donuts. She had the coffee ready and everything looked good when his guests started to arrive. He greeted everybody as they came in and offered them refreshments.

By the time Karen got there, the rest of them had assembled and they all sat down to discuss the parade.

The theme was to be "A Country Christmas" and everyone seemed excited about getting started on their plans. The Regal was represented by Pamela and she said they planned to have a Snow Man Scene on their float with the Princesses.

Rachel Brent, the florist said she would have an old-fashioned pot belly stove and children trimming the tree with popcorn and singing carols.

Lewis Dalton said his float would feature the Night before Christmas with kids in bed and Grandpa reading the book.

Maria said the Café would have a big family around a table in an old-fashioned kitchen.

Marty Thompson from the Wal Mart said they planned to have a sleigh with Santa Claus and a fake reindeer, Rudolph, of course.

Sam Thomas said Fast Gas would have an old car with the Mayor and his wife and grandchildren riding in it. It would be pulling a trailer with kids and a tree on it.

Daniel said the bank planned to have a church scene with families in old fashioned clothing singing carols. He asked if anyone needed help with their project. Several held up their hands.

He said, "Just sign up, pay your fee and then we'll know how many volunteers we'll need. The high schoolers will be volunteering to help."

Pamela stood up and said, "Mr. Thomas at the high school is announcing that we need volunteers and also Bill Wallace, the coach and Kerry Smith, the shop teacher, said they would be available.

Daniel had positioned Grant at a separate table, to take the entry fees so the people began to line up to sign the roster and pay their fees. Daniel invited everyone to have seconds at the refreshments and said, "If there are no other questions, we'll just thank you for coming and encourage you to get right onto the production line at the barn."

Karen was feeling great relief because not one person asked her to help them when Maria came over and said, "I will be expecting you to help me, you know."

Karen smiled and said, "Oh, I thought I had escaped. I will be there helping with the high school anyway and sort of floating to help those who need it. We need to get started, too. It's only two weeks away. I'm hoping Melanie will be here to help out because I have simply got to keep painting for my show."

Maria said, "I understand, there won't be that much to do on ours but any suggestions will be appreciated. The city workers are going to install the signs this evening after the traffic dies down."

"Oh, that's good, because that is great advertising. I noticed the flyers are out in the stores, too. Are you mailing any of them?"

Maria said, "We just mailed them to the radio stations and newspapers with a letter of explanation. We sent one to the public television station, too. They have a calendar spot and that should go all over the state."

"It sounds like you've got it wrapped up. I'm going to see my husband at work right now so I'll see you later."

She went over to shake Daniel's hand and tell him he had done a great job. He told her Kathy had done all the arrangements. He asked, "What are you and Ed doing tonight? I've invited Rebecca to dinner at the club. Would you like to join us?"

Karen thought about the doctor and said, "I'll have to get back to you. It sounds great to me but Ed has some business going on and I'm not sure what he'll have planned."

"No problem, just give me a call later."

Karen went to the police department and the desk sergeant said, "Hi there, Karen, you've been neglecting us lately. Don't you love us any more?"

She said, "Your detective keeps me too busy these days. You know I love you guys but I like painting better than policing and that's what I've been trying to do."

Ed came out and said, "I'm glad to see you, Honey. The doctor is in there with Tom right now and he's been at it for quite a while. Maybe he's making progress. It would be so great to get this thing settled before Melanie comes home."

"That's good. Have you made any plans for this evening with the doctor?"

"I did ask him if he would be available, but he said that he has to get right back for a conference call with some other doctors."

Karen said, "Daniel wants to know if we can join him and Rebecca for dinner at the club."

"That sounds good to me. Tell him we're definitely available."

Karen said, "Should I wait to see the doctor when he's through? I'd like to go home and get ready for the evening if you don't need me."

Ed said, "No, you go on home. He may be a while and when he's through we'll let Bill come and get Tom. Then he and I will confer a little but I'll wait and see the tape of his interview. That should be a trip. I may bring it home and let you watch it, for your opinion on it's impact."

Karen was surprised, "I didn't dream he would let you tape his interview."

"It's the only way to let him talk to Tom without our presence which would have made Tom clam up."

Karen got up and said, "Well, I'm going then. You come home when you're finished. I'll tell Daniel that we'll meet them at the club in case you run late. Okay?"

Ed hugged her and said, "As usual that's good thinking. I'll see you at the house."

After Karen had left, Ed went to look in the one way window at the interrogation room and saw Tom was crying and Dr. Novak was holding his hand. Tom was talking at last. Ed did a high five to the air and went back to his desk. He had called Bill to come on down because he needed to be there with Tom. He wanted to talk to him before he let Tom go. Bill told Amy to hold back on supper until later and if things had gone well, they would go out to eat a burger or something.

Dr. Novak had told Ed earlier about his interview with Janet. He said he couldn't reveal her conversation because of doctor patient confidence, but that she would be willing to talk to the police when she came home. Dr. Novak said he was sure she would be able to handle the stress. In fact he thought she would be even better off, just to having it off her chest. Now all they needed was Tom to tell his story and they would finally know what really happened to Margie.

When Karen got back home, she called Daniel and told him they would meet him at the club but not to wait if they were late because Ed was finishing up some important business at work.

Then she got out her favorite little black dress and black high heels. She laid out Ed's best suit. It was a brown pin stripe she had talked him into buying the last time they went shopping. She got a white shirt out and chose a gold toned tie with little brown designs like fluor de lis on it.

The phone rang and it was Melanie telling her that she had managed to take her tests early because of her excellent grades. She would be home on the fourth of December. Karen was delighted and said, "I've missed you so much and I need you to help me with all this parade stuff when you get here."

Melanie answered, "I'll be glad to and then you'll have to help me move to Chicago. Of course first we'll have to find a place for me to move to."

"Yes, you will be needing a place."

Melanie asked if she had heard anything about the will or other news from the lawyer. Karen said, "I'm sorry but I haven't even thought of it. Do you need any money?"

"No, I'm fine. I was just wondering about it, kind of hoping it would be settled soon, so I would know how much I can afford for an apartment."

Karen asked, "Have you ever heard from your Dad?"

"Never. It's so strange. It's like he has completely forgotten me."

Karen told her that she would have Ed check on his whereabouts after Melanie got home.

Then after she told her how the animals were and what kind of weather they were having they said their goodbyes. Before she hung up, Karen told her to call from St.Louis, on her way home. She said, "I promise, Mommy."

They said good bye again. Karen went to the kitchen and warmed a mug of coffee in the microwave and was sitting at the kitchen table when Ed came in. He was beaming.

Daniel went to Rebecca's door at six thirty and she was ravishing in a red silk dress with sterling jewelry. She had her hair pulled up and it made her beautiful aqua eyes look even bigger.

He said, "Lord, you look beautiful."

She smiled and said, "Well, I'm going out with a very handsome man, so I want to look my best."

He helped her with her coat and took her arm as they went down the stairs to his car.

When they got to the club, the valet greeted him, as did the maitre de. He seated them near the windows that looked out on the patio. The water fountain was on and it changed colors from blue to orange to pink and back again.

When the waiter came, Daniel ordered their drinks and an appetizer. He told the waiter that another couple would be joining them so they would wait to order dinner. Rebecca looked puzzled and Daniel said, "I forgot to tell you that I invited Karen and Ed to join us. I hope that's okay."

"Of course it's okay. I really like both of them and they're always interesting to talk to."

"Yes, they're two of my favorite people. Of course, you know that."

Ed wouldn't tell Karen anything until they got to the club. He said, "I want to wait and tell you and Daniel at the same time. I think it will be comforting to both of you. I'll hurry and get ready so you won't have to wait long."

He was grinning so broadly that Karen wondered how anything about Margie's death could be that good but she didn't press him. She just said, "Okay, I'm ready so, hurry up."

He went to the bedroom and was pleased to see his clothes laid out for him. Ed wasn't into dressing up and hated making decisions about what to wear. He shaved quickly and decided not to shower so he wouldn't take long to get ready. He was back out in fifteen minutes and they were soon on their way to the club.

They left the Cadillac with the valet and went into the club. The maitr'e de welcomed them and took them to the table with Daniel and Rebecca.

Daniel stood up when he saw them and after greetings were exchanged the waiter came and took their drink orders. Ed said, "Well, I have interesting news for you and Karen, Daniel."

Daniel looked surprised and said, "What can that be?"

Ed proceeded to tell him about the visit they had with Dr. Novak. Then, about his visit today to try to interview Tom. He said, "Dr. Novak had much more success than any of us. He cleared up a lot of questions in my mind. You can tell me what you think after I tell you about it."

Ed began to tell the story as Dr. Novak had told him, "Dr. Novak had waited for Bill and introduced himself as Janet's counselor. Then they went into the interview room with Tom. I understand that the doctor told Tom that he had interviewed Janet and though he couldn't reveal what she had said, he knew that they had been together on the morning that Margie died. Tom told Dr. Novak that he heard his mother leave in the family pick-up at about four a.m.

He followed her on his bike. He had already followed his father and knew he was having an affair. Now he was thinking his mother was up to no good too. She parked across the street from Margie's apartment house and went inside. He followed a little later and saw her take out a key and enter the apartment.

Janet had stolen the key from Bill's key chain days before but Tom didn't know this. He went to the door and quietly opened it to see Janet standing there and Margie lying on the floor.

He panicked and ran to his mother and said, "What have you done?"

She started to cry and said, "I didn't do anything. She was just lying there."

Tom knelt down to check Margie's pulse and she was as cold as ice.

He said, "Oh, my God, she is dead."

Janet screamed and he shushed her. He said, "What are we going to do? If we call the cops, they'll think we killed her." There was a prescription bottle on the coffee table near Margie. She was lying on a rug on the floor like she had been sleeping there by the fireplace. Tom decided it would be best to put her in the bathtub and put the pill bottle beside her so they would think she had committed suicide. It didn't occur to him that she might have died of natural causes because she was so young. All he could think of was getting his mother out of there so she wouldn't be accused of killing her.

I went back to the evidence room and found the prescription bottle and found out it was made out to Melanie. It wasn't sleeping pills. It was an antibiotic. We, or I should say Dr. Novak, now thinks that she had anaphylaxis attack and died before she could get help."

Ed finally stopped talking and Karen just said, "Oh, my. I'm sure Margie didn't know she was allergic or she wouldn't have taken the medicine. You don't think Janet knew and made her take it?"

Ed said, "No, it seems that they were only there a few minutes. After they did their rearranging of the body, they dumped the wine, threw out the bottle and left the apartment. They were trying to get out before daylight and before Bill missed them."

Daniel said, "Margie and I did lay by the fireplace that night and that's where she was when I left. She also had said earlier that she had a cold and didn't feel all that good. We each had a glass of wine. Then too, we had drinks at the club. I hope that didn't have anything to do with her reaction."

Ed shook his head and said, "I'm not at all sure this is really what happened but it makes more sense than anything else we have come up with. I can understand how it was enough to send Janet into depression, causing her strange behavior."

Ed said to Rebecca, "I'm sorry to include you in this but I couldn't wait to tell them. We have been so puzzled for so long."

Rebecca assured him, "I am glad you have news that is better than what we thought before and it's fine that you shared it. I'm glad you trusted me enough to tell it here in front of me."

Daniel put his arm around her shoulders and hugged her, "Rebecca is a good sport. She has to be, to put up with me."

She smiled at him and said, "Oh, it's not such a hardship to be with you."

Ed hugged Karen, too and said, "Yes, I think we've got us a couple of good gals here."

Karen had been very quiet. Now she spoke up, "I am so relieved that this may turn out to be an accident. It's a horrible accident, but to know that Margie did not commit suicide is so comforting to me. What will happen to Tom and Janet now? By the way, why did they call the medicine sleeping pills?"

Ed said, "Pure stupidity. They didn't even check to see what they were. They, I should say we, jumped to conclusions because of the way her body was found. I'm as guilty as anyone. I let my emotions overtake my police training. I only found it out when I got the pill bottle out of the evidence room.

You see, the bottle was empty. Apparently Melanie had almost finished the prescription and Margie took whatever was left. It would have only taken one to kill her. It's like choking to death. One's throat just closes up and you suffocate. I haven't had time to talk to the district attorney yet but I imagine it will be taken before the grand jury which, thank God, will be private. It will be up to the grand jury to decide whether to prosecute or not. I really don't expect the D.A. to push for charges to be filed. I think both Tom and Janet have suffered enough. They may need to do some community service or something like that. Everything is on hold until after the holidays. The hearing or whatever will be sometime in January."

The waiter had come back and refilled their drinks and now was back for their orders. Daniel said, "Now I'm really hungry. Let's go for the big steaks. How about it, folks? Rib eyes for everyone?"

They all agreed on the rib eye but ordered their own versions of salad and potato. Karen said, "None of us will be able to sleep on such full stomachs."

Ed said, "I won't be able to sleep anyway. I'm really pumped from all that has happened today. You know I'm thinking that this might be a good time for me to retire and enjoy life for a change "

Everybody at the table looked shocked. Karen took a deep breath and said, "Where did that come from? I had no idea that you were seriously considering it."

He smiled and said, "I've thought about it a lot lately because now I have somebody to be with and won't be bored or lonely. I knew I couldn't until the mystery of Margie's death was solved. I promise I won't get under your feet. There are a lot of things that I would like to do. One of them is to be free to go with you to your art shows. That Chicago thing is just going to be the beginning. I want to be there for you. If nothing else I've got a good strong back and can help load and unload."

Karen said, "I'm certainly not worried about you being in my way. I'd love to have you around more and it's true that we may get to go to California if this show is a success."

Ed told her something he had been keeping a secret. "I am about to sell my house. They should sign the papers this week. I got a good price and I thought, if it's okay with you, that I would take some of the money and buy us a motor home to travel in."

Karen was too surprised to speak for a few moments. Then she said, "Why you old stinker. You've been planning this all along."

"Yeah, I was just waiting until I cleared up Margie's case so we could feel better having done all we could."

Karen said, "You are really something. Always coming up with a new idea and making my life a whole lot more interesting."

Daniel and Rebecca were just taking this all in and holding hands under the table. It was nice to see two people obviously crazy about each other and completely unaware that anybody else was in the room. They finally came to and rejoined the party when the waiter arrived with their salads. He apologized for taking so long and they assured them they hadn't noticed. Daniel said, "It's fine. We had a lot to catch up on so we aren't in any hurry."

When they had finished the salad, Karen turned to Ed and asked, "Did you find out who was leaving the rose?"

Ed nodded and said, "It was Tom. He felt so bad about the awful mess his mother had made. Since he wasn't sure what had happened. He would ride his bike over or go for a run and leave a rose for Margie. Of course we know he was the vandal at the house. He was hiding in the barn that day that you felt like someone was watching you. He also was trying to fake an English accent when he made the threatening phone calls. You know I'm thinking that he may have the same condition Janet has. He may need medication to control his moods. He has been under so much pressure that I can understand why he seemed out of control. The weird thing is poor old Bill didn't know any of this. His whole family seemed to be falling apart. I haven't talked to him yet because he was anxious to get Tom home. I was busy with Dr. Novak so I told him I would get with him later. I did tell him that we had cleared up some things and that he should just let Tom tell him, if he volunteered the information. I doubt very much if he will, because he was pretty upset and could hardly wait to leave."

The waiter arrived with the platters of rib eyes and baked potato covered with all the toppings and after they oohed and aahed they began to eat. There wasn't much conversation for the next few minutes. They were all feeling very good and really enjoyed the meal.

No one was able to order dessert but they did order wine and talked more after the meal. Daniel told them about his vacation plans.

Then they discussed the Christmas parade and what they each had planned for that event. Finally Ed said, "Listen, I've got a busy day ahead. We need to get home and get some rest. I probably need to apologize for dominating the conversation. I was just so excited to finally have some answers. This has been a great evening and I hate to end it."

Karen added, "Yes, it was so nice of you to invite us. I want to invite you two to Christmas dinner at our house. Do you think you can make it?"

Daniel said, "Well, I can, but Rebecca is going to her home for Christmas. I'm hoping she'll come back and join me and the kids for the ski trip."

Rebecca said, "Thanks for inviting me, Karen. I surely would come if I were going to be here but I haven't been home for a long time. My family is so big and crazy. I always sort of dread visiting but I feel I need to go once in a while. My mother will be happy that I'm there."

Then Daniel said, "Ed, let me assure you that you don't owe us an apology. The news you had is going to make our lives much better. It's still a sad situation in more ways than one but at least we know that is was basically an accident that got worse because two people overreacted and panicked. It would have been better if they had just left since there was nothing they could do for Margie. Obviously they felt some guilt or they wouldn't have reacted in such a bizarre way."

Ed said, "Well, Rebecca, you're not the only one with a crazy family as you can see from this event. You have a good time with your crazy family and we'll still be here when you get back. We'll keep an eye on Daniel while you're gone."

Daniel said, "The evening is on me so go on and get out of here. Go home and explain your retirement plans to your wife. I'm sure she'll be interested in them."

"Thanks for the evening, Daniel and for the fatherly advice. I guess we had better do that."

They went out, ordered their car and were headed home when Karen said, "You really did catch me off guard with that news, you know?"

"Yes, I know but it seemed like a good time to bring it up. I hope you'll be happy with me."

She scooted over close to him, put her arm around his shoulder and said, "It's a very good plan and I'm delighted."

Daniel and Rebecca left soon after and they were very quiet on the way home. When Daniel walked her to her door, Rebecca said, "Why don't you come in for a little while?"

He did and when they got inside, he grabbed her and kissed her. He said, "I've been wanting to do that all night."

She didn't try to move away from him but kissed him back. She said, "Would you like to spend the night?"

He just grinned like a little boy. She took his hand and led him to her bedroom. They would soon be spending a lot of nights together. He felt like Margie was finally at rest and he could go on with the rest of his life. He thought to himself, "Ed is not the only one with some plans for the future."

Ed talked to the district attorney the next day and he did decide to wait until January for the grand jury or a hearing of some sort. In the meantime Ed would write a complete report on all of his investigation. He had to be ready, to be the primary witness. Ed told him of his plan to retire the first of the year, but that he would still be available for the inquiry.

Then he went to Chief Stone's office and gave him notice of his planned retirement. The chief was totally surprised and said, "Are you sure you want to do this? You're not that old, Ed. What are you going to do with your time?"

Ed explained all the things that he and Karen had planned. Chief Stone said, "Well, it does sound as if you've got it all worked out and we'll sure miss you but I don't blame you a bit. Most of us wait too long to retire and then just die, so go for it, man. You and Karen deserve all the best."

When Bill got home with Tom, Amy was anxiously waiting for them. When they came in the door, she said, "Boy, am I glad to see you two. I was afraid they had kept you."

Bill smiled and said, "No, honey, we're fine. Let's all go to Wendy's for a burger or two. How about it, Tom?"

Even Tom was smiling and he said, "I could eat a horse about now."

They never discussed the police or anything about the interview because Tom didn't mention it so Bill figured he would find out what he needed to know tomorrow when he talked to Ed. It was the best evening they had been able to have in weeks and he didn't want to ruin it.

Chapter 117

Karen spent the day in her studio, painting her from her latest photograph. It was to be a landscape with Candy running across the field of sagebrush when it was a golden, reddish brown. The sun had been shining brightly that day and the sky was aqua blue with huge fluffy clouds. The neighbor's barn could be seen in the background. She was using a big brush and using big, bold strokes. This canvas was bigger that usual. It was four feet by six and she painted around the edges.

John had told her not to worry about framing because they would do that in Chicago. She didn't want this one to be framed. She stood back to admire her work and while she was deciding what to do next, the phone rang. It was Ed. He told her, "Well, I gave Chief Stone my resignation."

She said, "You are not wasting any time, are you?"

Ed was quite for a minute, "I hope it's okay. I thought it was all right with you."

She reassured him, "It's great. I'm just surprised how fast you moved."

"I won't be retired until the first of January. I'm going to sign the papers on the house in a few minutes and I just wanted to let you know that we'll be looking at motor homes this weekend."

She squealed and said, "That will be fun. I still can't believe you had thought of all of this and never even mentioned it."

"I wanted it to be a surprise. I hope it is a pleasant one."

She said, "It's very pleasant. You go do what you've got to do and let me get back to my painting. I'll talk to you more when you get home. I love you, you sneaky person."

"I love you more. I'll see you later." When she hung up the phone, she just stood there thinking about all the changes in her life, in the last few months. She never had expected to be this happy at this time in her life. Now she had so much to look forward to.

When Ed met with Bill at three o'clock, he told him all that he knew. He explained about the grand jury inquiry and told him not to be too worried. He said, "Unless there is more to Janet's story, everything will probably be dropped. We can't know what she told Dr. Novak, but she'll have to tell us when she gets home. I'll have to testify and I need to know exactly what happened."

Bill said, "I'm supposed to go pick her up this weekend. The doctor called me this morning and said that he's ready to release her. He said that she will need to stay on her medication and that I need to make sure she follows his instructions so that she won't have any more episodes."

Ed told him, "You bring her in next week so I can interview her. You can stay with her if you want to."

Bill said, "Okay, I'll call you the first of the week and set up a time to meet."

Ed shook his hand and told him, "Don't push Tom for information. He'll tell you his story when he's ready. He's been an innocent victim in all of this. Janet obviously was mentally deranged. Hopefully she'll have learned her lesson and stay on her meds. She may have to do some community service or may even have to serve some jail time but it won't be too bad. Don't say anything about it to anyone and it may never become public. The grand jury is secret and it should go no further, if they do as they are supposed to. You just take care of your little family as you have in the past and it will be okay." He paused for a minute and continued, "You screwed up when you started up with Margie but at least you were separated from your wife at the time. By the way if I were you I would have Tom checked by a reliable doctor or someone that Dr. Novak recommends. He may have some kind of chemical imbalance like his mother. I don't want to worry you unnecessarily but it's better to find out and take care of it before he gets in college."

Bill thanked him and said, "You know, you're right. I've been so messed up myself that it never even occurred to me. I'll check it out. I'll ask Dr. Novak when I pick Janet up. Tom won't even have to know what they're checking for because he'll need a complete physical to go to college."

Pamela had a meeting with her high school volunteers on Friday afternoon and they told her what they wanted to do for the float. They wanted it to look like a snow-covered field with a snowman. Someone in a snowman suit dancing to the music, throwing candy to the crowd. The Princess and her court would be sitting on seats that looked as if they were carved from a snowbank. They told her how they intended to achieve this result and she told them to be at the barn with all their supplies on Saturday the third of December to start on the float.

The school vote for princess was to be held on the following Monday. That evening Jeff called her and asked her to go to the movies in Lexington.

He apologized for not calling her in awhile. He said that after his ankle healed, he had been sick with the flu and couldn't even work for two weeks. She said, "Well, you should have called me. I would have brought you some chicken soup."

"I wouldn't expose anybody to that mess. I have never been so sick. I went home and let my poor mother take care of me." He said he would pick her up at six thirty so they could get there on time.

She was excited because she hadn't been out since their last date. She and Leah had been staying in to save money for Christmas. They had put up their little tree and had several gifts arranged around it.

When Leah came in from work, Pamela had supper on the table. "My, you are sure being efficient tonight."

Pamela explained that she had a date. Leah said, "Wow, what a treat. I wonder if Nathan will call me when he comes home for Christmas break."

Pamela answered, "I'm betting he will. I think he really liked you but he's got his mind on finishing his education. You can't blame him for that."

Leah said, "I don't blame him a bit. I just wish there were more eligible guys around here. It's slim pickings for anyone to date. Sometimes I feel like I'm already an old maid. Maybe we need to move to the big city and find some other possibilities."

Pamela giggled and said, "We could go back to school and meet some guys that way. You know what they say about girls going to college to find husbands. But I'm sure not interested in finding another husband. Been there, done that and it's not that hot."

After they had eaten, Pamela went to get ready for her date and Leah cleaned up the kitchen as per their work sharing plan. Then she went to the living room to watch television.

When Ed came home that evening, Karen had chili ready. He came in the door saying, "Boy, does it smell good in here." Jazz and Callie slipped in the door behind him.

He said, "You can tell it's getting cold out there. These animals are no dummies. They want in where it's warm. Let's keep them in here tonight. Okay?"

Karen hugged him and said, "It's fine with me. They have their beds right over there." The animals were already on their beds and pretending to be asleep.

Ed went to change into his comfortable sweats. Karen finished her cooking and had the table ready when he got back. They talked about their day and then planned their weekend. Ed said, "We need to go to church on Sunday. We've been missing too many Sundays. They'll be throwing us out if we don't show up soon. Let's call Gary and Christine and take them to dinner after church. I want to talk to him about Bill's situation anyway."

Karen agreed saying, "I'll call tomorrow and make the arrangements. How did the house closing go?"

"It was very simple. We signed all the appropriate papers, they gave me the check and we all went away happy. Now we can go motor home shopping."

After supper they cleaned up the kitchen together and then they watched television for the rest of the evening. Karen fell asleep with her head in Ed's lap. After the news he woke her up and carried her into bed. She kissed him on the neck and said, "You are such a romantic. Figured you could make sure I woke up, didn't you?"

He said, "There's motive to my madness, lady. It's time for romance."

They slept very late the next morning. The only thing that woke them was the phone ringing. It was Melanie checking in on her way home from Columbia. She was in St.Louis and was going to spend the night with friends. She said she would call when she left for Dinsmore. She might stay til Sunday. After they ended the conversation, Karen went into the kitchen.

Ed had made the coffee and was starting breakfast. He was whipping up scrambled eggs while the bacon fried. Karen poured a cup of coffee and drank it while she fed the animals. Then she let Jazz out to get the paper. Ed was about finished with the cooking and she made the toast. She said, "This is so good. I am starving, aren't you?"

"That's why I got started. You know me. I"m always hungry and today is fat Saturday."

She laughed at him and when Jazz scratched on the door she let him in with the paper. They read the paper and had a leisurely breakfast. When they had finished, Ed said, "Are you ready to go motor home shopping?"

"I had forgotten your plan. Yes, it sounds like fun. Where do you want to start?"

"Lets go to Lexington first. I don't see any in the paper. There's a sales lot over there. We can have lunch while we're there."

"Okay, I'm going to take a quick shower and get dressed." She got up and cleared the table.

He said, "I'll pass on the shower. After I dress, I'll go check on Candy and take the animals with me to the barn."

Daniel had spent the night with Rebecca again and when they got up, they dressed and went to the Café to eat breakfast. Tony was on duty by himself and greeted them as they came in.

He said, "You two don't have to work today?"

Rebecca said, "No, I took the day off and left Pamela in charge. I needed a break. Daniel and I are going to bum around today."

Daniel said, "How about fixing us one of your big country breakfasts with scrambled eggs, sausage and hash browns?" He brought them each coffee and went back to cook. Daniel had picked up a paper at the rack outside and he gave Rebecca part of it. Both of them sipped coffee and read.

He said, "You know what? I haven't been to a movie in ages. Would you like to take in a matinee in Lexington?"

"That sounds like fun. We can go to that big complex. There are several good ones playing. Can we go to the mall, too? I'd like to check out my competition." They finished breakfast and Maria came over to bring them more coffee. She sat down and visited with them until more customers came in. Afterwards they went out and got in Daniel's car and to headed out of town.

The Wallace family got up early and went to McDonald's for breakfast. Then they started their drive to the hospital to pick up Janet. She had gotten up very early too. She had all her belongings packed and ready to go. She was supposed to meet with Dr. Novak for her last session and get her instructions for living at home again. He was preparing all the instructions on paper so that she couldn't forget what he had advised her to do. She was to see the local therapist once a week and to stay on her medication. He had permission from Ed to tell her about his interview with Tom and to warn her that the police would be calling her in for an interview.

So, Janet and Dr. Novak had their meeting. Although she was upset to learn about Tom's interview, she was able to understand that it had been necessary. She knew she was in trouble but was just glad to be going home to face the music. When Bill and the kids got there she was waiting in the foyer. They all hugged and kissed, so glad to see each other.

Bill left them there while he went to talk to Dr. Novak. They met for only a few minutes but Bill was able to get his advice on Tom's mental health and the instructions for Janet's care. When it was over Dr. Novak went out with Bill, wished the family good luck and saw them to their truck. He waved as they went out of the driveway. He was thinking about what faced them in the next few weeks and hoping for the best. He felt that he had done all he could.

Ed went to feed Candy and the other animals while Karen showered and then they both dressed in jeans and flannel shirts. They put on boots and western hats to go on their hunt for their second home. When they went to the door, Karen said, "Don't we look cute today?"

Ed said, "That's the first time anybody ever called me cute."

They went out and got in the Cadillac for their shopping adventure. They looked at several motor homes after they got to Lexington and then they decided to go to lunch at Ruby Tuesdays. When they walked in, they were shocked to see Daniel and Rebecca sitting at a table and asked the hostess to seat them there. Daniel saw them approaching and stood up. He said, "What's going on? Are you following us officer? We haven't committed any crimes today."

Ed said, "Can't you see that I'm out of uniform? How about me and my lady joining you for lunch."

They all enjoyed their lunch and Daniel said, "Hey, we're going to a matinee. Don't you want to join us?"

Ed looked at Karen and she said, "That sounds like fun. "

The four of them spent the afternoon together and after the movie the girls did a little shopping while the guys sat on the bench and talked. At the end of the day, they all returned to Dinsmore. Ed had invited them to come to the house and play poker so they ended up spending the evening together too.

In the middle of the poker game, Karen said, "I forgot to call Gary. Hold up a while and let me go call them before it gets too late."

When she asked Gary if he and Christine could join them for lunch, he said, "That is the best offer I've had lately. I'll get a sitter for the kids so Christine can have a nice time, too."

Karen said, "We'll look forward to seeing you tomorrow then. Okay?"

That done, Karen returned to the game. While she was up, she got some more refreshments and drinks for everybody. Ed was taking all their money and after a few more hands, Daniel said, "It's getting kind of late. Don't you think we ought to get home, Rebecca?" She agreed and after exchanging thanks and telling each other how much fun they'd had. They left.

When Daniel walked Rebecca to her door, there was an uncomfortable moment and he said, "I think I'd better go to my own place tonight. My kids are supposed to call me tonight or tomorrow and you probably need some time to yourself."

She nodded and said, "That's a good idea. We need to slow down a little, I think. I love having you here but I don't want to mess up a good thing."

"You're right as usual. I have enjoyed the day and I hope you did." He pulled her to him and kissed her for a long time. Then he turned and left as she opened her door and went inside. He already missed her.

Chapter 118

On Sunday after the church service and lunch with Gary and Christine Oldham at the Holiday Inn. Ed said, "I think I'll go up the road in my golf cart and visit Joseph and Ruth. I'll bet you'd like to paint a little."

Karen said, "I'm sure they'd love that and I do need to paint. I'm getting worried about having enough pieces to suit John."

Ruth came to the door when Ed knocked and she squealed, "I'm so glad to see you. Joseph and I get kind of tired of looking at each other."

Joseph yelled from the living room, "Speak for yourself, woman. I know better than to ever say anything like that."

Ed said, "I put my wife to work painting and decided it had been much too long since I'd seen you folks. We went to church this morning and I didn't see you there."

Ruth said, "Joseph has been a little under the weather so we thought it best to stay in. It's been so cold. Didn't you freeze on that little cart?"

He grinned at her and said, "No, I've got on my thermal underwear, so I was warm enough. It didn't take long to get here." He visited with them for a couple of hours and told them all about his plan to retire and travel with Karen. They were happy for them and thought that was a great idea.

Karen was working on a big canvas of a snow scene when the phone rang. It was John Whitcomb. She said, "You must have gotten a mental message from me because I just told Ed that I needed to get some more done for you."

He said, "I don't want you to feel pressured. You won't do your best work if you are under too much pressure."

She assured him that she wasn't feeling that way and that she was looking forward to it. He told her that he planned to come down on the twenty seventh, to get whatever she had finished.

She asked, "What do you have planned for Christmas?"

He hesitated and then admitted, "I really hate to admit it but I don't have any plans. I have no family to be with so I just sort of hide out on Christmas."

"Well, you need to come on down here and have Christmas with us. We're planning a big dinner with lots of guests and I'd love for you to be here."

He was shocked and didn't speak for a minute, then he said, "That is so kind of you. I'd love to if you're sure I won't be in the way." They spoke a few more minutes and then Karen heard a knock at the door. She told John she would talk to him again soon and hung up the phone.

When she got to the kitchen, the door was opening and Melanie came staggering in loaded down with her luggage. She ran to her and took her bag and sat it down. They embraced and Karen said, "I am so glad to see you. It's seemed so long even though it hasn't been. I've just missed you. Come on, let's put your stuff in your room. Then I want to get your opinion on my latest work."

They were still in the studio when Ed came home. He hugged Melanie and welcomed her home. Then he went to watch TV while the girls caught up on the latest news. Karen told her that Ed had some news for her and then he told the whole story again. Stopping to answer her questions and to comfort her when she cried, because she had left the antibiotics there where her mother could take them. Karen and Ed both assured her that it was not her fault, that Margie knew better than to take someone's medication, without checking with a doctor.

All the committees met again on December sixth and everything was in order for the Christmas parade. The high school students had selected Megan Catron for Christmas princess and Amy Wallace was one of the girls in her court.

The shop teacher Kerry Smith had worked with the kids on the float and it looked great. Pamela was feeling really proud of herself because her project had gone so well. She and Kerry had become good friends and he had asked her out the night before the parade.

They went to the Café for dinner and then to her apartment to watch television. Leah had a date with Nathan who was home for the holidays and they all ate popcorn and drank beer until midnight. The guys finally went home and Pamela said, "We've got to get up early in the morning. I'm going right to bed."

Leah said, "Me, too. It was fun though wasn't it?" Pamela thought to herself, it was fun but Jeff is more fun.

Chapter 119

Ed, Karen and Melanie were up extra early on the Saturday of the parade. Melanie was going to ride Candy with the Equestrian Club. Karen had fancy rigging for Candy to wear on these occasions. They got her all ready and loaded her in the trailer. All three were in their western wear with thermal underwear because it was a very cold day. Ed drove with the trailer and the girls went in Karen's car.

It had snowed a little so it was beautiful. It wasn't deep enough to spoil the parade. The trucks had been out plowing what little snow was on Main Street. All the banners were still up and crowds were arriving in town for the big event. Some of the groups that had booths were able to set up inside the shops so they would be warm even though the weather hadn't cooperated. Others had butane heaters that kept them warm. There were bake sales from the churches and white elephant sales from garden clubs. The 4-H club had a booth with sandwiches, cakes, cookies and hot mulled cider. Everybody was in a festive mood.

Tony and Maria had done a good job of advertising because people were there from as far away as Chicago and tourists from other places that had just happened to come into town.

The Dinsmore High School Band led off the parade followed by Mayor Clint Baker, his wife Lynn and their grandchildren in an old Cadillac pink convertible with the trailer full of little kids. Then Melanie's big equestrian group rode by. Candy was enjoying herself immensely. The Lexington school band followed. There were motorcycle clubs and veteran's groups with young and old warriors. To Pamela's delight the float with the Christmas Princess won the best in show award. The one with Santa in his sleigh was last and he was throwing candy to all the screaming children. They loved it.

Ed and Karen went to the barn where they had left the trailer and waited for Melanie and Candy. After they had Candy loaded up, they went to the Café to have lunch. It was packed. They went to their favorite table in the back and soon Maria came and took their order for burgers and fries. She said, "I'd love to sit and talk to you but there won't be time today. I'm not complaining. This extra business will help get Christmas for all those kids I've got back there in the office. I didn't have time to take them home so Grandmother and they are hiding out until things quiet down."

Ed said, "Hey, we'll be glad to take them home after we eat if it will help."

Maria looked relieved and said, "That will be great. I know Grandmother will be glad to get out of here."

After Karen had delivered the Distefano family to their home, she went home, too. Melanie had ridden with Ed. She got Candy out of her fancy gear while Ed and Karen went to the house to fix a fire in the fireplace.

Karen said, "This had been a great day. I'm really getting the Christmas spirit now. Didn't Melanie look pretty?"

"Yes, she was gorgeous. You are just like a proud mother with her. All the girls were pretty. Did you notice Amy Wallace? I'm sure Bill was proud of her. She's such a pretty girl. I never thought that Bill or Janet were all that good looking but they sure had good-looking kids."

Karen snickered, "Well, I'm sure they would be glad to hear that. That reminds me. Did you interview Janet yet?"

Ed shook his head and said, "No, I'm putting that off until after Christmas. I think their family ought to be able to have a decent holiday. Dr. Novak told her that it would be coming up but didn't tell her when."

When Melanie came in, she announced, "I have a date tonight."

Karen was curious, "Well, when you manage to meet somebody to date?" Melanie giggled and said, "Remember Tad Lewis, the insurance guy?"

Ed chimed in, "Oh, yeah, the slick insurance salesman."

Melanie looked surprised and said, "I thought you liked him."

"Of course I liked him. I'm just teasing you. I hope you have a great time with Mr. Tad Lewis. Just don't run off and get married."

She shook her fist at him and went to her room. Karen said, "You sound like a doting daddy and you're always kidding me about being a mommy."

"Well, the shoe fits both of us and I love it. She's a great kid and I hate to think she's moving away."

Melanie came out of her room in a robe and said, "I heard that! I'm only moving to Chicago and you'll be able to visit in that fancy motor home you plan to buy. Besides, I'll be coming home to see my new mommy and daddy, because I love them. I will miss them, too."

She went into the bathroom to shower and they just sat there looking at each other. When she was dressed, she came out looking beautiful in a long, black A line dress with sterling silver jewelry and four inch black strap heels.

Ed whistled and said, "Good Lord, you look like your thirty. I mean you look great but you can't be old enough to dress like that."

She laughed at him and just then the door bell rang. She went to open the door and Tad came in looking handsome in a gray pin stripe suit with a pink tie. He spoke to Karen and Ed and then took Melanie's hand saying, "You look super. All the guys are going to be jealous of me tonight."

Karen said, "I don't want to be nosy but may I ask, where are you going?"

Tad answered, "We're going to my fraternity party at the Civic Center. It's a once a year thing we do with wives and girl friends for a holiday get together. I will take good care of her and needless to say I don't drink and drive so you needn't worry."

Ed said, "Well, that's good news. It wouldn't look good for me to have to get my kid and her date out of jail."

Karen hit Ed on the arm and said, "You nut. They won't be getting in jail. You two just have a good time and be prepared to tell us all about it when you get home."

Melanie said, "Don't wait up. We'll be very late, I'm sure. I'll tell you all about it in the morning." She kissed them both on the cheek and they hurried out the door avoiding any more conversation. Karen and Ed were left to try to find something to watch on the television.

Later in the evening the phone rang. When Ed answered, he sounded upset and said, "We'll be right there." He turned to Karen and said, "That was Jeff. He says Ruth called 911 and they had sent an ambulance to pick up Joseph. Heart attack, maybe. Let's get to the hospital. Ruth will need us."

Karen jumped up and got her coat off the rack by the door. Ed followed and after they locked up, they went down the road to see if the ambulance had left yet. It was still there so Ed pulled into the drive and parked out of the way. He ran to the house and found Ruth standing on the back porch wringing her hands. He took her by the arm and into the house.

He said, "You need to get a coat on. You don't need to get sick, too. Where's Joseph?"

She said, "They're working on him, giving him something to bring his blood pressure back up."

Ed went to the paramedic, whom he knew and asked, "How are we doing?"

The paramedic looked up and said, "Well, we've done some good. We're going to load him up and get to the hospital now. The doctors will be able to do more. I think he'll make it. It scared him, so we wanted to get him calmed down and breathing better."

Ed said, "I'll bring his wife to the hospital. You guys just get him there." They had him on a stretcher already. They lifted it and started out the door.

Karen was standing by the back door and said, "We're here Joseph. You're going to be all right and we'll take care of Ruth. We'll see you at the hospital." She went in to hug Ruth and tell her to get her coat. She asked, "Do you want me to do anything before we leave? Do we need to turn anything off?"

Ruth said, "No, we were already in bed when he began to gasp for air and said his arm hurt really bad. He was sweating and said he felt sick at his stomach. I got up and called 911 right away because I knew what it was. Can we go now?"

They all went out to the car after she locked her door. The ambulance was already on the road. Karen whispered to Ed that she would come back and leave a note for Melanie so she'd know where they were. By the time they got to the hospital, Joseph was in the emergency room and a doctor was checking him out.

After a few minutes, the doctor came out and said, "He's going to be all right. He has had a heart attack but he's doing very well now. We'll get him settled and run a few tests but we'll wait until tomorrow to run most of them. We'll have to see just what kind of shape his heart is in and then decide what to do about it. If you folks plan to stay, you need to go to the waiting room until we get him in a room. Then we may let you see him for a minute or two."

Ruth asked, "May I stay in the room with him?"

The doctor looked puzzled and said, "I can't say right now. Wait until I see how he does after the tests."

Karen said, "Let's get some coffee and go to the waiting room so the doctor can do what he needs to. Okay?"

Ruth just nodded her head. They went to the canteen for the coffee and when they had it, they went to the waiting room. They had all sat down in the comfortable overstuffed chairs and every one of them sighed. Karen said, "It's gotten so I sigh when I sit and groan when I get up." There was some nervous laughter and then Ruth started to cry and Karen put her arm around her and assured her, "Oh, honey, it's going to be okay. The doctor didn't seem too concerned."

Then Ruth shocked both Karen and Ed when she said, "I wonder if I should call our son." Karen said, "I thought you didn't have any children."

Ruth said, "We didn't want anybody to know. He was in prison for almost twenty years. He robbed a gas station when he was twenty-five and had a gun with him. He never showed the gun but because he had it they gave him armed robbery. Joseph is going to be upset because I told you. He has always been so ashamed of Stuart. We haven't seen him since he was released. Joseph doesn't want anything to do with him. He doesn't know that I have kept in touch all these years. He was my only child and I wasn't going to give up on him. He wouldn't have gotten in trouble if he hadn't gotten hooked on drugs. Joseph kicked him out. He lived on the streets until he got desperate enough to try to rob that gas station. He didn't even try to get out of it. He pled guilty and took his punishment. He went through rehab and he's working at a rehabilitation center now."

Karen and Ed just sat there, dumb founded while she told the story. Now, Ed said, "I'm shocked. I would never have guessed that you folks had a son who was in trouble. I mean, there's no reason I would, but it must be hard not to see him. You know people do learn and some can come back and straighten up their life. It is rare but he had good parents and I'm sure he knew better. His family background would give him a leg up."

Karen had been quiet until she said, "I don't know what to tell you, Ruth. I love Joseph and I can't imagine him not being able to forgive but that will have to be your decision."

The doctor came into the room and said, "Mrs. Barry, we have him settled down. The EKG didn't show anything too bad but he did have a slight heart attack and he'll need to keep quiet and let us run some tests before we let him go. You can see him for a minute or two but then you'll have to leave because he is in intensive care for the night and can only have visitors every hour for five minutes. He will sleep all night so why don't you go to see him before he goes to sleep and then these people can take you home."

He took Ruth by the hand and they went to the elevator. Ed said, "It's amazing that you can know people but never really know them intimately. I guess we all have skeletons in our closets. I would like to see them get together with their son though. You know I'm not going to be able to let this drop."

Karen said, "Yes, I know you. You're an old softy at heart and you and I both have seen enough sadness from drug addicts. We may have to contact him when we are in Chicago."

Ed said, "I may have to have a talk with Joseph, because he's missing out if his son is really rehabilitated. I know a lot of guys that really turn their lives around. You'd be surprised to know how many successful business men were addicts and still go to support groups. It can happen to anyone if they don't know what is involved."

Ruth came back then and they gathered up their coats and left the hospital. They went in with her when they got to her house. They offered to take her home with them but she said, "I'll be just fine. I'm not afraid to be alone. Joseph used to travel in his business and I got used to it. I really appreciate you kids taking care of me. I'll call you tomorrow and let you know how he's doing."

They went back to their car and when Ed started the engine, he chuckled and said, "That's the first time I've been called a kid in a long time."

It was well past midnight but Melanie wasn't home yet. Karen said, "I forgot to come back and leave her a note. I hope she hasn't been here."

Ed said, "Quit worrying, Mommy. She's out late, that's all." They went on to bed and heard Melanie come in about an hour later. She was being very quiet so they didn't let her know that they were both awake, anxiously waiting for her to get in.

The next few days were spent decorating the house for Christmas and visiting Joseph at the hospital. Karen and Melanie went to Lexington to visit Melanie's grand mother and told her that they would come and get her for Christmas day dinner. She was delighted.

Ruth and Karen planned the dinner menu and what each would fix. Melanie rode Candy every day and Candy loved it. Jazz would follow them out into the field. He was crazy about Melanie and she played ball with him every day. Karen told her she was spoiling him and that he was going to expect them to keep it up after she made her home in Chicago.

Ed had a busy week at the department. There were always a lot of arrests for drinking and the problems it brought during the holidays. The word had gotten around that he was retiring so he was taking a lot of ribbing about being old and worn out. He had lunch with Daniel one day and Daniel told him how much he liked Rebecca.

Ed said, "Uh, oh, I see another wedding in the future."

Daniel said, "I'm not rushing into anything but I would like to get married again. I liked married life. I just wish my wife had been able to handle it. I really loved her and she gave me two great kids. I just couldn't take her moods anymore. She was so unhappy. I really think she got better after I left and it took off the pressure."

Ed said, "Well, I just wish you the best. You make a great couple and there's no reason to rush. Look how long it took for me to tell Karen how I felt."

Daniel said, "Well, you're just slow. We know that, you old fogey."

Joseph came home after four days in the hospital. He didn't need anything special, except for some new medication and a little alteration of his diet. Number one, cut back on the biscuits and gravy.

He was so glad to be home, he just sat on the back porch even though it was very chilly. Ed visited with him several times and they talked about their work and Chicago and baseball season coming soon and were the Cubs ever going to win a series. Ed enjoyed being with the old guy and he wanted to know him better. He still had his mind on the son that Joseph didn't ever mention.

Karen was painting every chance she got. She did a palette knife painting of a spring scene with magenta, purple and yellow flowers. It was very impressionistic but the colors were vibrant and cheerful. She got Melanie to sit for her. She had her facing the window, looking out on the field at sunset. Then she got a photo of her lying on her bed reading a book and she secretly painted it. She used a limited palette on that one with shades of blue and sienna. Then she decided to stretch some smaller canvases to add variety to the show. Most of those were florals and still lifes. She used some of her favorite pottery and other objects around the house. She had never felt so inspired and was in another world when she painted. She liked it there. Life was good. The studio was full of pots, vases, wine bottle and other knick knacks. Melanie helped her with some of the arrangements and she was a good critic.

Christmas week came and it was time to cook, which was another favorite pastime, especially at holiday time. Most people thought of it as work but she loved it, when it involved a lot of people, who would enjoy eating it. She was fixing a turkey and a ham, a sweet potato dish and broccoli casserole. Ruth would do the dressing. Karen took her some turkey parts to boil for the broth. They would add the turkey drippings when it was ready to be baked. Then there were the desserts to think about.

She planned to make apple and pumpkin pies and Ruth would do the mince. Ruth said she would bring the baby lima beans that she had put in the freezer last summer. Everybody loved those. Each of them were to make a salad of some kind. They decided the canned cranberry sauce would do.

The guest list was growing by leaps and bounds. Ed had called Ken in Chicago and invited him since he had no family. Karen called Pamela to check on her plans and she said she was invited to Jeff's family for dinner but she might come by to see everybody. Then she called Gary and invited him and Christine and the children. There would be at least thirteen counting the little ones.

They had everything planned and in order for the holiday, so two days before Christmas Karen and Melanie decided to go Chicago and look at the apartment that Melanie's friend had found for her. If she liked it, she would sign a lease agreement and move the first of the year. They wanted to do some shopping, too.

Karen hadn't bought a gift for Ed yet and couldn't decide what to get him. Melanie wanted to find something for him, too. Ed didn't feel he could take off work so it was a girl's only outing. Karen decided to invite Ruth to go with them. She made arrangements with Ed to check on Joseph during the day. When she went to see them, Joseph was in the living room watching soap operas and Ruth came to the door, smiling as usual with her arms out for a hug. Karen said, "I just came to see if Joseph was behaving himself."

Joseph bellowed, "How could I do anything else. She won't quit hovering over me. I'm just fine. The doctor said I could do anything I wanted to, just to watch what I eat and take the meds. I'm not gonna die just yet."

Karen said, "Well, that's good news because I came to invite Ruth to go to Chicago with Melanie and I tomorrow."

He jumped up and said, "Please, take her. I need to have some time without a nursemaid in my hair. What little is left of it."

Ruth looked confused and said, "Oh, I'm afraid I really shouldn't be gone right now. I know he's tired of my fussing but I'm afraid to leave him alone."

Karen assured her, "I have made arrangements for Ed to come by and check on him. He might even take him down to the station to watch the goings on. He'll be all right and you need to have some fun with us girls. We won't stay overnight because I've got to finish getting ready for our Christmas get together."

Joseph said, "Go, Ruth, I mean it. You go and you have a good time. I'm just fine." After a few more minutes of encouragement, she agreed. Karen told her to be ready at six in the morning so they would have plenty of time in the city. She gave them both a big hug and went back home.

After school, Bill took the kids home and then he went to see Ed at the station. When he got there, Ed was on the phone and motioned for him to sit down at his desk. Ed hung up the phone and said, "I was ordering flowers for my girls. Going to send them on Christmas Eve."

Bill smiled and said, "Things must be slow around here if you don't have anything more pressing than that."

Ed smiled and said, "Yes, thank goodness, it has been slow. Not much crime in Dinsmore right now."

"I just wanted to find out where we stand on Janet and Tom. When do you plan to see her?"

Ed answered, "I'm waiting until after Christmas. You go on and have a good time with your family and I'll call you to set up something. The grand jury meets in January so there's no big hurry. I just need to get her version of the accident in writing and we'll go from there."

Bill said, "Then you do believe it was an accident?"

"Well, it was a stupid thing to do. Some may see it as involuntary manslaughter because we can't prove she was dead when they got there. But I really do believe it was accidental. I'm not promising she won't have to stand trial but the DA may want to make a deal to avoid the expense of a useless trial. I hope he will, so your good name won't be trashed by the publicity. Your affair with Margie was really stupid, too."

Bill hung his head down and said, "Yes, I know. I feel that I'm more responsible than either of them. If I hadn't started with Margie, we wouldn't be having this conversation. I think Margie would still be dead though. It was obviously an allergic reaction to the medication."

Ed said, "You're right and we'll just have to pray the grand jury sees it that way. You're much loved in this town and I think that will help Janet's case. Just try to put it on a back burner and enjoy the holidays. By the way, your Amy looked very pretty in the parade. I'll bet you were proud of her."

Bill was beaming, "Yes, I am. She's not only pretty but she's a very good girl and helps me a lot. Did you notice Tom was riding on that float, too? He helped build it and rode with the football starters. Principal Thomas has been so good about helping him catch up on his school work and not questioning his frequent absences."

Ed stood up and held out his hand to shake Bill's. He repeated his advice, "Just enjoy the holiday. Merry Christmas. I'll see you at the Christmas Eve Midnight service."

Chapter 120

When the girls got to Chicago the next day, they went to the gallery first. After visiting with John and his partner for about an hour, they went to see Melanie's future apartment. They met her friend, Alicia, at the apartment building.

It was close to the art institute and in a fairly good neighborhood. It was a small building by Chicago standards but it did have private parking underground, which was well lighted. It was a studio size apartment, with a Murphy bed in the living room and a tiny kitchen and bath. It smelled of fresh paint and new carpet. The best thing was that it fit Melanie's budget. There was a possibility that she would get a room mate but she wanted to wait and see how she did on her own for the first time in her life.

After they looked it over, they went to the super's office to sign the papers. Her office was a desk in her apartment. Her name was Terri Wynn, and she was a young single mother of a toddler who was busy playing in the middle of the floor. She told them that she was the manager days and then had a sitter at night so that she could finish getting her teaching degree.

When they finished their business, they made plans to move in on the second day of the new year. Then they decided to find lunch. They went to a Pizza Hut that was close by so they wouldn't have to be in traffic at lunch hour. While they were waiting for their pizza and Melanie was in the rest room, Karen said, "Ruth, I was wondering if you'd like to contact your son while we're here."

Ruth looked surprised and said, "Oh, my, you've been reading my mind. I've been thinking of him ever since we got here."

Karen went on, "Let's call him and find out how to get to him. I'd love to meet him."

Ruth said, "Joseph would be very upset if he found out."

"Well, we'll just keep it our secret, then. Do you want to?"

Ruth answered quickly, "I'd love to."

Karen asked, "Do you have his number at work?"

"Yes, he lives there, too."

"Then go call him right now."

Ruth got up and went to the pay phone. Melanie was surprised to see Ruth at the phone in the hall next to the rest room but could see she was talking to someone, so she went on to the table. By now their food was delivered. When Ruth came back to the table, she was smiling broadly. The rest of the meal was spent explaining things to Melanie.

They weren't far from the rehabilitation center and Ruth got driving directions but she said, "He told me that he would rather come here and meet us. I told him it would be okay. Can we just take a little longer eating?"

Karen smiled and said, "I think that can be arranged, since we're talking more than eating. Then we'll have to think about dessert. Do they have dessert here? We could order another pizza and let Stuart help us eat it."

Ruth said, "He said he would be here in a few minutes. It's within walking distance. Can you believe that we chose to eat here so close to my boy that I haven't got to hug for almost twenty years? I wonder if I'll recognize him out of that prison garb. Oh, I'm getting butterflies just thinking of it."

A few minutes later, a handsome white haired man in a bright, tie dye T-shirt came in the door of the restaurant. He was medium height and very muscular. Karen thought to herself that had to be him because he looked just like a younger Joseph. He came over to the table and put his hands on Ruth's shoulders. She jumped and turned to see him. She was up in a flash, hugging him and quietly crying.

He kissed her on the cheek and said, "Now don't cry, Mom. This is the best day of my life. I never thought it would happen. What do I owe this to?"

She took his hand and motioned for him to sit down. She said, "We owe it to this kind young lady and my good friend, Karen Hawkins. She said that she was bringing me for a day of fun but I think she had this on her mind all the time. I just told her about you a few days ago."

He held out his hand to Karen and said, "Well, I sure am glad you tricked her into coming."

"Oh, I didn't really trick her. I did think she needed to have a little fun and Joseph agreed."

Ruth said, "I'm sorry." She repeated, "I just told her about you a few days ago. Your dad had a heart attack and I was wondering whether I should let you know. Don't worry. He's fine now. Just as ornery as ever."

Stuart said, "That's good news. I do hope you'll let me know if it's ever safe to come visit. I miss you both so much. I'll be there, even if it takes years to get him to forgive me."

"I intend to tell him about this when I get home. He needs to know and he needs to forgive and forget. You just keep up the good work and we'll get together, yet."

Melanie was just sitting there, still stunned by the news and then later she asked, "How do you like it here? I'm moving here soon. It's the first time I've really lived away from Dinsmore except for school. I'm kind of frightened by the whole thing. You know, a big city, new school, new life."

He nodded and said, "You're going to love it. There's so much to see and do. There's never a dull moment and it's quite safe if you watch where you go." Then he said, "I'll give you my card and you can call me if you're not afraid of an ex-con, I'll show you around the sights. Do you like art?"

She smiled at that and said, "I'm enrolled at the Art Institute. That's why I'm here. My other mother here, is an artist and has been teaching me since I was a little girl."

He looked at Karen now and asked, "Is that so? How do you and Mom know each other?"

Karen said, "We're neighbors and they've always helped me out whenever I needed them. I'm here to arrange a show at The Rose Gallery in January."

He was impressed and said, "That's great. I go to all their openings. It's a great gallery."

Karen asked, "Ruth, we want to do some shopping. What do would you like to do?"

Ruth looked confused and before she could answer, Stuart said, "I don't want to be pushy and interfere in your plans but could I go with you? I took the afternoon off after Mom called and I would love to have more time with her. I can help you find the stores, too."

Karen said, "Sure, let's go find those stores."

They all climbed in Karen's car. Ruth sat in the back with Stuart, holding his hand the entire time. He showed Karen the best way to get to the big department stores and when they got there and found a parking place, he and Ruth decided to stay in the car and visit while the girls shopped.

Karen and Melanie checked out several of the stores before Karen decided to buy Ed a heavy, plaid robe and a pair of slippers. Melanie bought him a pair of socks and some suspenders with Santa Clauses on them. Karen said, "He's going to love those."

After they had their gifts wrapped, they looked at some of the other clothing and when Melanie raved about a sweater with a Christmas motif, Karen bought it for her, even though she protested. They each got some perfume. Since it was getting late and Karen wanted to get back home before dark, they decided they would have to do this again when Karen was visiting.

When they got back to the car, Ruth and her son were still talking away. Before she started the car, Karen turned to Ruth and asked, "Why don't we invite Stuart for Christmas dinner?"

He quickly said, "Oh, no, I have plans with my patients and I don't want to come to Dinsmore until Dad asks me."

Ruth said, "I intend to tell Joseph that I have been to see Stuart and how well he is doing. It may upset him but he needs to face his problem."

Karen said, "I understand, I'm sure you both know best. I do want you to know I have been delighted to meet you. I love your folks and wouldn't have done this if I didn't think it was right. You hang in there. Joseph is a good man and he'll come around. I imagine he thinks about you more than we know."

They took Stuart back to his place and he told them the best way to get out of town. He hugged and kissed his mother for a long time. Then he stood on the curb and waved as they left.

Ruth was crying softly as she said, "I'm not crying because I'm sad. I'm so happy I got to see him. It's hard to imagine that he is so much older, but twenty years is a long time. I sure hope he can have a good life." Melanie and Karen both said, "Me, too."

They only stopped once on the way home for a rest room break and a soft drink. They made it back at six thirty, a little after dark but still early. Ed was at the Barrys when Karen pulled into the drive. They all got out and went in.

The two men were playing poker at the kitchen table. Joseph said, "Karen, your husband is robbing me. He's won two hundred pennies from me."

Then he asked, "Well, sweetie, did you have a good time in the big city?"

Ruth said, "It was wonderful. I might go back when Melanie moves to her new apartment. Besides we'll have to go to Karen's art opening, won't we?"

He looked surprised and said, "I guess we will at that."

Ed gave him back all his pennies and said, "One of these nights, I'll get Daniel and Jeff and we'll have a real poker game. How about that?"

"I'll be ready when you are."

Karen said, "Well, I'm tired. I want to get out of these clothes and into something comfortable. Tomorrow will be busy, getting ready for our dinner. I'll talk to you then, Ruth."

They went to their cars and back home feeling tired but happy. Karen could hardly wait to tell Ed about the day.

Chapter 121

Down at the Barry's house, Ruth fixed a nice supper for Joseph following his new diet. They were eating a dish of fruit and yogurt when Joseph said, "Tell me about your trip. Did you have a good time?"

"Yes, it was just wonderful. Best day I've had in ages."

"Where did you eat lunch?," he asked, "I'll bet you had something I can't eat now."

"We weren't worried about fancy. We just went to Pizza Hut because it was close to Melanie's apartment. Karen didn't want to do a lot of driving in city traffic."

He nodded and said, "Yes, I can understand that."

She went on, "But something wonderful happened while we were eating. Stuart came and joined us for lunch."

Joseph jumped up from the table and yelled. "What do you mean? Stuart! How did he know you were there? You've been keeping things from me, haven't you?"

His face was blood red and it was scaring Ruth but she went on to answer him calmly. "I called him from the restaurant. He works close to it and Karen suggested I call him."

He was still yelling when he asked, "How did Karen know about Stuart? When did you tell her?"

"I told her when you were in intensive care and I was wondering whether to contact Stuart. I've been writing him for years. You may have disowned him, but I never gave up on him. He's paid his debt to society and I have never quit loving him for even one minute."

Joseph just threw up his arms and sat back down. He said, "I can't believe you would deceive me for twenty damn years. You knew it went against me to contact him."

Ruth was not being backed down now that she had started. She said, "He was my only son. My only child. You had no right to keep me away from him no matter what he did. Everybody makes mistakes and a lot of good people ruined their lives with drugs. Now Stuart is helping those very same kind of people get their lives straightened out. I didn't get to visit him often. You know those few times, when I went to my sister's? Well, I really went to Joliet and saw Stuart."

Joseph just sat shaking his head. He finally got up and stomped off to the living room and Ruth cleaned up the kitchen. For the first time in forty-five years of marriage, Ruth got her nightclothes and went to the guest room, locked the door and went to bed.

Joseph did not object.

Chapter 122

It was early, Christmas Eve morning. They had a lot to do, to prepare for their big Christmas dinner. Ed had the day off, so he was going to help Karen as much as he could and then he planned to visit Joseph.

Karen had told him all about the Chicago visit and they were curious to know if Ruth really had told him, as she planned. They ate a leisurely big breakfast after the animals were taken care of and Jazz had brought them the paper. Karen had made a list of "To Do" chores for the day and laid it in plain view for Ed and Melanie to see.

She had already prepared her desserts and frozen them so the last minute cooking would be easier. The turkey was thawing and would go in the oven very early Christmas morning. She would prepare as much as possible and refrigerate it all, until tomorrow. There was silver to polish and the table to be decorated today. They would go ahead and set the table, then turn everything upside down. The plan was to make Christmas day as relaxed as possible. At about seven Melanie joined them at the breakfast table.

Karen asked, "Would you like me to fix you some eggs?"

"No, I'll just have some cereal after I drink my coffee," she said, as she poured a cup of it. She took a section of the paper and began to read it. Suddenly she shrieked, "Listen to this. It's an article about the rehab center where Stuart works and he's mentioned in it. It says he has twelve patients that he counsels and that he has a degree in counseling. He must have finished college in prison. Isn't that something? If we hadn't met him yesterday, this would mean nothing to me."

Karen said, "I wonder if Ruth will see that article."

"It would be hard to miss. There's a big picture of the building in the local news section . The article is very flattering to the center, to Stuart and the other counselors."

Ed said, "Maybe Joseph will read it and get a different outlook on his son."

Karen mused, "Well, Joseph is a pretty stubborn old curmudgeon, you know. He may be hard to impress."

"You're right about that. I know it's hard for him to trust again, but twenty years ought to be enough for anybody to get over it," Ed muttered under his breath.

Daniel had gone to Rebecca's apartment early in order to take her to the local airport so she could go home to St. Louis for Christmas with her family. She had arranged to be off work for three weeks in order to come back and go to Colorado with Daniel and his children.

He dreaded spending Christmas alone, except for having dinner at Ed and Karen's. After he had seen her off, he went back into town to the Café. When he went in, Tony greeted him warmly. "I'm glad to see you. It's been so quiet this morning that I thought maybe the town had shut down and forgot to tell me."

Daniel smiled and said, "It is quiet out there but a lot of folks have Christmas Eve off so they're sleeping in and not getting out until later. We're closing the bank at noon so they'd better get out if they want to do any banking." Daniel sat at the counter and Tony brought him a cup of coffee.

He asked, "Going to have breakfast today?"

Daniel said, "Just a biscuit and sausage. I've got to get to work so I can tie up loose ends. I'm going to be off for a couple of weeks and I don't want to leave things undone. I don't want to get emergency phone calls while I'm on my vacation."

Tony said, "Wow, that sounds good. I haven't had a vacation in so long, I've forgotten how it feels. What are you going to do with two weeks off?"

"We're going to Steamboat Springs for some skiing."

"Who's we?" Tony tried to look as innocent as possible.

Daniel smiled and said, "Oh, now I'm going to have to swear you to secrecy or I'll have to kill you."

"So kill me. I'm kidding. I can keep a secret in spite of my reputation for being a blabber mouth."

Daniel decided to take a chance and tell him, "Rebecca is going with me and my kids for a few days of fun in the snow."

"That's great. You and her are a real item, huh?"

"You might say that. I do think a lot of her. She's a real lady and a good person. She's been real good for me." Daniel paid for his biscuit and got up to leave. "Now remember if this get's out, I'll be back to get you."

Tony smiled and said, "Have a great time and bring back pictures."

Gary Oldham was in his home office preparing his words for Midnight worship services. Christine was baking a coconut cake to take to the Hawkins for tomorrow's dinner. The children were watching favorite sing along tapes on the television, so the house was peaceful. It was a rare treat for Gary and

Christine.

Bill had an appointment with Gary for some counseling later in the afternoon. Gary wasn't sure what Bill had on his mind and from time to time his thoughts wandered from the message. He kept wondering what he could do to help Bill and his family. Bill was at home since school was now out and they were all getting ready for Christmas, in their own way. Amy was in her room wrapping gifts and Tom was in his room reading. Janet was baking some pies and preparing yeast dough for rolls. They had a turkey thawing. Bill always made the dressing early in the morning while the turkey baked. They had Christmas tapes playing and they seemed like a happy little family. Not one of them had mentioned the trouble they would face soon after the holidays.

Pamela was working harder than usual, because she was acting manager in Rebecca's absence. Leah had taken off to go home for the holiday weekend. Jeff was working double shifts today so he could be off tomorrow when Pamela would join him at his family home for dinner. Pamela had planned to prepare something to take, but Jeff insisted she just bring herself so she decided she would take a box of fancy candy or cookies . She was a little worried about meeting new people and especially the parents of a guy she was dating. She was painfully aware that everybody knew she had been married to the town drunk.

Back at the Hawkins, the phone rang and it was Larry Sloan. When she answered the phone, he asked Karen "Do you know where Melanie is? I called her school but they said she had quit."

Karen said, "She's right here with us. Where are you?"

There was a pause and then he said, "Well, actually, I'm right here in town staying at the Holiday Inn."

"That's great. Would you like to speak to Melanie?"

"Yes, if you think she'll talk to me."

"Sure, Melanie, it's your father, comes talk to him."

Melanie came to the door and just stood their looking confused, "It's Dad?"

"Yes, come take the phone. I've got to check on my pies in the oven."

Melanie took the phone and said, "Hi, Dad. I thought you had forgotten me."

Larry said, "No, Honey, I'm just a jerk for not contacting you sooner but I have been trying to get my act together and I'm afraid I haven't thought about other people. I know that sounds selfish but that's what they tell you in rehab. You have to put your recovery first. I'm not very good at personal relationships anyway. I have this overwhelming sense of guilt."

Melanie said, "I guess I can buy that but I've never judged you. I always gave you the benefit of the doubt. Where are you, anyway?"

"I'm at the Holiday Inn right down the road. I'll be going back to LA day after tomorrow but I sure do want to see you before that. Can you get away to come have dinner with me tonight?"

She said, "Well, we're going to Midnight Worship but I've got the evening free. What time?" He told her to meet him in the restaurant at seven and she told him she would be there. When she hung up the phone, she turned to Karen who was standing there listening to the conversation. "What do you know about that? You never know when he'll turn up."

Karen said, "I'm just glad he called. I'm sure it took some nerve, knowing how he has neglected you in the past."

"Yes, that's what he said, more or less. I'll go meet him and treat him with the proper respect but I really don't think of him as a father. He has just never been there for me, so it's hard to have a relationship with him."

Karen asked her, "Do you want to invite him to dinner tomorrow?"

"No, if he had called and made arrangements to see me before, I would. It would just spoil the day for me. I doubt if he's changed that much. You know how overbearing he can be. He must have some kind of plan or else why would he be here?"

More to herself than Melanie, Karen said, "I wonder if he has contacted Pamela. I hope not. She's doing so well."

Melanie said, "Well, we'll know what he's up to after our meeting." She turned and went to her room to get ready.

Ed took his golf cart down to see Joseph and Ruth. Ruth opened the door when he knocked. She was busy cooking and didn't hear him drive up. When he was inside, she said, "Joseph is in there watching the television as usual."

Ed said, "What? I don't get a hug today?"

She giggled and said, "I'm sorry. Of course you get a hug." She hugged him and asked, "How's Karen doing on her preparations?"

Ed said, "She's got it all under control. Melanie and I have done what we can to help. It's winding down now because there are some things that have to wait until tomorrow morning very early. We're going to Midnight Worship. Are you and Joseph going?"

Ruth said, "I am. I don't know what Joseph is doing. He's sulking and I'm not paying any attention to him."

Ed was surprised to hear that and he said, "Ooh, have I come at a bad time?"

"No, it's fine. Maybe you can make some sense to him. Anyway I'm sure he'll be glad to see you." She handed him a cup of coffee and said, "You go on in there and talk with him. I've got to get back to my chores."

He did as told. Joseph smiled and stood up to shake Ed's hand. He said, "I'm glad to see you. It's been as quiet as a tomb here today." He put the mute on the television and asked, "What have you been up to today?"

Ed told him, "I've been helping the wife get ready for tomorrow. How about you?"

Joseph looked grim and said, "I've just been staying out of the wife's way. She's mad at me and I'm not paying any attention to her."

Ed said, "Gosh, I didn't think people that have been married as long as you two got into these kind of impasses."

Joseph said, "Well, I'm sure you've been told about my convict son and the fact that my wife has been contacting him all these years in spite of my feelings."

"Don't you believe in forgiveness, Joseph."

He glared at Ed now and growled, "Damn it, I forgave that boy so many times I lost count. But when he humiliated us by being sent to prison, it was the last straw."

Ed said, "Well, I'm not going to ruin my friendship with you by getting in the middle of yours family's private business but I would give you this bit of advice. Sometimes we have to swallow our pride and take back harsh words and try just one more time. You only have one child and it's been twenty long years. He's done very well to come out and be able to have a decent life without ever asking you for help. So think it over and don't be too stubborn to admit that sometimes people do change. By the way, you definitely need to read today's paper."

Joseph asked, "What's that got to do with it. I read the front page. There's never any news in the damn thing." Ed felt Joseph's anger rising and didn't want to risk upsetting him further.

He waited a minute and then said, "There's an interesting article in one of the inside columns. You might be in for a surprise."

He got up and said, "I've got to get back and see if I can help Karen. I'll see you tomorrow. Bring your appetite."

Joseph looked up at him and said, "You think I'm wrong, don't you?"

Ed thought about it a minute and then he said, "I'm not here to judge you.

I've never been in your shoes. I just want you to keep an open mind and not hang onto an old grudge. It won't help your health any and it sure doesn't help your marriage. You don't want to make Ruth unhappy, I know."

Joseph held out his hand and Ed took it and shook it. Joseph said, "You're a good man, Ed. I'm glad you and Karen are together. Now go on home so I can read that paper."

Ed stopped in the kitchen and gave Ruth another hug and said, "Hope you can go to Midnight Worship. Let me know if you need to ride with us." She nodded her head and he thought it looked like she had been crying. He didn't say any more. He just went out, got in the golf cart and headed back to his house.

Back home, the girls had cleaned up the kitchen and were sitting in the living room. When he came in the door, Karen got up and went to hug him. She asked, "How were things at the Barrys?"

He shook his head and said, "It's hard to say. Ruth was busy and seemed to make a point of staying in the kitchen. I did take advantage of the situation and spoke to Joseph about his feelings. I sure hope I didn't offend him. He seemed to take it all right but he's not the kind of guy to express his feelings. He did get a little angry with me."

"Well, Melanie had a phone call from Larry while you were gone. He's at the Holiday Inn. Do you think we ought to ask him to dinner?"

"That's up to Melanie. I sure wouldn't object. How do you feel about it, Melanie?"

She didn't answer for a minute and then said, "Well, I feel like I should ask him. I really don't have any feelings about it or about him. You know he hasn't bothered contacting me in ages, but I know he had to work on getting his act together. If you and Karen don't mind, I guess we should ask him."

Karen said, "John called, too. He and Ken are in town. They came together. Ken went to the gallery and introduced himself to John and they got to talking about Christmas and found out they were both coming here."

Ed said, "That's great. So our guests are all lined up except for Melanie's grandmother. When are you going to get her?"

Melanie spoke up, "I'm going to get her in the morning after breakfast."

"Okay, so we're all set. What's for supper anyway? I'm starving."

"Well, we've been cooking all day but I didn't fix anything to eat for supper. I have sandwich makings. We can grab a sandwich and chips and eat in the living room. I'll cut one of the apple pies and we'll have apple pie ala mode for dessert. How's that?"

"Let's do it and then I'm going to take a nap until we go to Midnight service."

They went to the kitchen. Melanie went to make her phone call to Larry. She canceled their meeting for tonight and invited him to tomorrow's dinner. He reluctantly accepted the invitation even though he was disappointed that he wouldn't see her until tomorrow.

Midnight services were beautiful. Gary spoke briefly about the real meaning of Christmas and Christine sang the "Lord's Prayer." Then the congregation sang several Christmas carols. Bill Wallace read the story of Christ's birth and the children's choir closed the service with their rendition of Silent Night.

Refreshments were served in Fellowship Hall by the Women's Society. Ruth was helping serve the refreshments and Karen asked, "How are you doing. I'll bet you're worn out from all the cooking."

Ruth smiled and reminded her, "You know I'm happiest when I'm cooking. I was so glad Ed came to visit. Joseph's whole attitude seemed to change after that."

Karen said, "I'm assuming that is good news, huh?"

Ruth nodded, "You assume correctly. I'll tell you about it tomorrow."

Karen moved on and spoke to several other friends and then went to find Ed. He was busy telling some men about his upcoming retirement and the plans he had. She waited for him to finish and then said, "Can we go now. I've got to get up at dawn to get that turkey baking."

He took her arm and said, "You are so right. Let's get Miss Melanie and go." He signaled to Melanie who was talking to Amy and Janet Wallace. She nodded and came to join them. They said their goodbyes and went out to the car.

Chapter 123

Karen had set the alarm for four thirty and she was up making the coffee when Ed joined her in the kitchen. She had the turkey ready for the oven and out of the fridge. The oven was warming up for the job at hand.

Ed came up behind her and put his arms around her waist, kissed her on the ear and said, "Merry Christmas, darlin'."

She turned around and kissed him on the lips and said, "and the same to you, honey. I can't believe I feel this good at this hour of the day."

"Well, you're probably all excited about opening that gift I got you."

She smiled and confessed, "Hey, I looked and there's nothing under the tree for me from you."

He shook his head and said, "I'd never gave you a chance to peek. I know you and your snoopy detective habits." Then he went to the coat rack and got her coat and his and said, "Put this on and come with me."

She was puzzled but complied and they went out the back door. He led her to the barn. At the barn he opened the doors which usually were left open. She saw a big motor home parked therein the barn. She squealed and said, "You crazy man. I can't believe you did this. It's beautiful."

She climbed in and looked around and said, "You got the really nice one, didn't you? This is going to be so much fun. I'll bet you spent every cent you made on your house."

Ed was delighted at her reaction and said, "I may be nuts but not that nuts. I'll need to have money to gas this thing up."

She sat in the driver's seat and he said, "Why don't you crank her up and pull her out in the drive way so everybody can see it."

"You've got to be kidding. I can't drive this big thing. You do it." After he had pulled it out into the drive, they just stood there admiring it for a little while.

Melanie was at the back door yelling at them, "Hey, you two, get back in here. I want to open my presents." He had shown Melanie his surprise while Karen was in the shower.

The three of them just had toast and coffee so that they would be extra hungry for dinner. Actually they were all in a hurry to get to the presents.

Melanie, like a child, was especially anxious to get to hers so they let her open hers first. She was thrilled with the pretty satin robe and slippers that Karen gave her. Ed gave her a gift certificate from the Regal. Then there were some diamond earrings from both of them that made her cry.

Ed gave the same earrings to Karen and the same gift certificate, too. He apologized for not being good at picking out things for ladies. They both assured him that they were very happy to be able to go shopping.

He really liked the robe and lambs wool slippers that Karen gave him and tried them on immediately. Melanie gave him a tweed wool cap that made him look like the Irish man he was. He modeled it for them and they told him how handsome he was. This pleased him immensely.

When all the gifts were opened, they had another cup of coffee. Melanie went to shower and dress because she had to go pick up her grandmother at the nursing home. Ed and Karen both decided it was a flannel shirt and jeans day. He put on his Santa suspenders and after they had dressed, it was back to the kitchen to finish up the cooking.

Karen checked the turkey and dipped out some of the juices to send up to Ruth for her dressing. She called Ruth and asked her if there was anything else she needed. Then she asked Ed to take the extra turkey broth and drippings to Ruth.

He said, "Well, I'll take it but I hope I don't get into a long conversation with Joseph."

"You just tell him you have to get back here to help me. He'll understand." He got his coat and went out to the car. He decided that it was a little too cold for the golf cart. Ruth met him at the door and insisted he come in. She tempted him with sticky buns and coffee so he told her that she would have to sit down at the table with him.

She said, "That's fine." She got them each a coffee and sat down saying, "I need to take a break anyway. I've been up for hours. Did you open gifts yet?"

"Oh, yes, with Melanie there, we had to, before she had a fit. It was really nice. Having a young person around makes it more fun. Did you know her dad is in town? He's coming to eat dinner, I think. He hadn't contacted her since the funeral so I'm glad that he finally got around to it."

Ruth said, "Yes, it's about time. I guess he's had a lot of problems, so maybe he's better."

Joseph came into the kitchen and said, "Who's better? Are you talking about me?"

Ed said, "Merry Christmas, Joseph. We were talking about Melanie's dad, not you."

"Merry Christmas to you, Ed. It's good to see you."

Ruth got up to get Joseph a cup of coffee and he said, "Thank you, dear."

She patted him on the back and Ed thought to himself, "I guess everything is okay again." Then he said, "I hate to leave good company but I have orders to get back and help with all the dinner arrangements. I've got a new toy to show you when you come down, Joseph."

"Well, I'll look forward to that. You're not going to tell what it is?"

"No, I want to surprise you. I'll see you all later. Thanks for the refreshments, Ruth. Let us know if you need anything else."

Ruth said, "Listen why don't you take the pies I've baked with you. That will save me loading them up later." She began to put the pies in a box for Ed to take home with him.

He was surprised to see a strange car in the drive when he got home. He put the pies on the kitchen table when he got in the house and looked for Karen. He heard voices in the studio and then he realized that John must have arrived.

He went back to the studio. Both John and Ken were there with Karen. After all the handshakes and greetings, he said, "Well, what do you think of this lady's efforts?"

John smiled and said, "I couldn't be happier. They are great. I had no doubt that she would do a great job, though."

Ken said, "Hey, I don't know a thing about art but I like this stuff."

John was smiling when he said, "Listen we need to appeal to the people that know nothing about art. The people that like our "stuff." All the critics in the world do nothing for an artist's pocketbook." He turned to Ed and said, "You are a lucky man, because not only can she paint, she can cook. When we came in the house the aroma was overwhelming and I can't wait til dinner."

He was thinking that if Ed hadn't got her first, he might have been tempted to approach her. He shook off the thought, knowing that it would probably never have worked. A world traveler and small town girl. All three of them liked their place in the world, just the way it was so it all had happened for the best. They could be friends, good friends. Good friends are hard to find.

Ed said, "Did you see our new travel home in the drive?"

"Yes, and she tells me that you are retiring so you can travel together. That is so great. I'll be planning her San Diego show as soon as we finish in Chicago."

Ed put his arm around Karen and said, "I guess I'd better keep her painting then, huh?"

They were all still talking when they heard Melanie holler, "Hey, where is everybody. I've got a special guest in here."

Mrs. Orson was seated in the living room and they all went to greet her. She looked much better than she had the last time Karen saw her. She said, "I'm so happy that you remembered me. This makes Christmas so special. Everybody at the home was jealous."

Karen said, "Well, you're looking so well and we are so glad to have you. Would you like to have some tea or coffee?"

"I would love to have a cup of coffee, the real stuff with caffeine. We don't get it at the home because they don't want to keep us awake."

"Well, we want you to be awake because we're going to have a great day."

Melanie gave her the gift she had bought for her and she opened it immediately. It was a pretty chenille robe and a bottle of perfume. She almost cried when she said, "Thank you so much, Melanie. You are as sweet as your mother was." That made Melanie almost cry and she hugged her grandmother and said, "We inherited that trait from you, Grandmother."

That scene sent everybody scurrying from the room, so they wouldn't cry. Ed and the other guys went out to inspect the motor home. Karen went to the kitchen and checked on her turkey. She got out the casseroles that needed to go in the oven and reviewed her list to see what else she needed to prepare.

They planned to eat at one o'clock and it was eleven now so the guests would begin to arrive soon. The phone rang and it was Ruth. She asked Karen if Ed could come over and help her load the food in the car. Karen called to Ed and told him what she needed.

The men all crowded into Ed's cart and they headed down the road. Karen went to get her camera so she could take a picture of the three of them when they got back. She went back into the living room to visit with Mrs. Orson and Melanie. Mrs. Orson said, "I'm so glad that you have been taking good care of my granddaughter. It's very nice of you and your husband."

Karen shook her head, "It's our pleasure. She's like a breath of fresh air and we are going to miss her when she moves."

Melanie was waving her hands at Karen but it was too late, the cat was out of the bag so she had to explain, "I'm moving to Chicago to go to school there, Grandmother."

"Whatever for?" she asked. Melanie told her about the art school and her plans for the future. Then she said, "Come with me, I want to show you what

Karen has been doing." They all went to the studio.

Melanie went to her room and came back with two canvases in her hands. Karen was surprised to see that Melanie had been painting, too.

She said, "Oh, Melanie, these are great. They are nothing like mine but they are great examples of abstract impressionism."

Melanie thanked Karen. Grandmother Orson just said, "Yes, they are very pretty colors." Melanie giggled and told her that she understood that a lot of people didn't understand her style but that it didn't matter as long as they liked the colors.

Karen told Melanie, "Leave them out because I want to show them to John."

"Oh, no, I'd be scared for him to see them." Melanie objected.

"He won't say a thing to hurt you. He's very honest, but he might give you some helpful criticism, if any. You need a professional opinion. I'm too prejudiced to judge but I have a feeling that he will be impressed. I'll show them to him when we're alone so no one else will hear his opinion." Melanie grudgingly agreed and they went back to the living room.

The kitchen door opened and the men all came in accompanied this time by Daniel. Karen went to greet him with a hug and Ed said, "I'm going to have to keep an eye on you with all these bachelors around." The men had brought in Ruth's dishes and Karen went back to her cooking and shooed the men to the living room and den.

Ed put some Christmas music on the stereo and they all sat around talking about everything from hunting season to the future of the country while Karen and Melanie made the final preparations for dinner. Karen interrupted them long enough to get a group photo in front of the tree.

Soon Ruth and Joseph arrived and right after them, Gary, Christine and their children. The children livened up things and the men ended up in the floor playing with the toys they had brought with them.

Christine and Ruth stayed in the kitchen but Karen told them that she had everything under control and it would be more helpful if they went and sat down until she needed them. She was the only one in the kitchen when Larry Sloan knocked on the back door. She opened it and greeted him warmly, "Well, I'm so glad you're able to be here with your daughter. Come on in and meet everybody."

She called to Melanie and when Larry saw her, he looked shocked. He said, "God, you are so pretty and grown up. I've missed a lot, haven't I?"

Melanie just shook her head, "I don't know. You never seemed too interested."

He looked crushed and she quickly said, "I'm sorry that was unnecessary. Merry Christmas, I'm glad to see you. You're looking good, too. I've heard that you have been working on a new life and I'm glad you're doing well. Come into the living room. Grandmother is here and I'm sure she'll be glad to see you, too. I think you know most everyone."

When they got to the living room, she said, "Grandmother, look who's here. My long lost father."

Mrs. Orson held out her hand and said, "It's good to see you, Larry."

Ed said, "It has been a long time, Larry. Let me introduce you to John Whitcomb and Ken Barton. John is representing Karen and her art and Ken has helped me on some cases at the department."

The men all shook hands and after they had some small talk, Larry turned back to Melanie. He reached in his jacket pocket and brought out a little gift box which he gave her. She opened it and it was a beautiful diamond encrusted heart pendent. She gasped, "Oh, it's beautiful. Thank you so much."

She put her arms around his neck and kissed him on the cheek. He kissed her back and said, "I'm glad you like it. Merry Christmas, Baby. I love you."

Chapter 124

At one o'clock they all gathered around the table that had been extended as far as it would go. Ed had poured a flute of wine for each guest and he made a toast.

He said, "Karen and I are very happy to have all of our friends here for our first Christmas as man and wife. Merry Christmas to all." They all clinked their glasses and then Karen took a couple of pictures. Then she asked Gary to return thanks.

With the Amens said, Ed ordered, "Okay, let's eat. I'm carving so pass your plates and give me any special requests." They all enjoyed a leisurely dinner. When the dishes were cleared, Ed and Daniel both went into the kitchen to help Ruth and Karen with the coffee and desserts.

After they were finished everyone took their dishes to the sink and rinsed them as if someone had told them to. Karen was surprised that all she had to do was load the dishwasher. She put some of the scraps out on the porch for Jazz and Callie.

She said to Ruth, "I don't usually feed them table scraps but today is special."

Ruth hugged her when she came back inside, "It's been a wonderful day. I'm so glad you planned it. It would have been a lonely day if you hadn't done this."

"Well, it's always more fun to share it with friends and family. Next year we'll make sure Stuart is here, too."

Ruth murmured, "Oh, I hope so. That would be so wonderful."

They spent the rest of the afternoon visiting and playing games. Some of the men played poker in the kitchen and Melanie challenged Ruth to a game of Scrabble. Christine was busy with the children, trying to keep them out of trouble but she managed to help Ruth with some good words in the Scrabble game.

Karen visited with Mrs. Orson and Larry. He told her about his experiences in California. The phone rang and when Karen answered, it was Rebecca. She called Daniel from the kitchen and gave him the phone. He took the phone to the hall for some privacy and when he had finished, he said,

"Rebecca said to tell everybody Merry Christmas."

Karen said, "That was nice of her to call. Is she enjoying her visit with her family. Yes, but she said she couldn't wait to get back, so we could go on our trip." Then he had to tell Ruth all about the vacation he had planned with Rebecca and his children.

Ruth said, "I want to see your paintings, Karen. Can you give us a preview of your show?"

Karen said, "I guess it will be okay. Come on back to my studio." Several of them went with her and everybody had nice things to say like, "I don't much about art, but I know what I like." or "This is very interesting."

Karen got a kick out of the comments. She had heard them so many times but she knew that her friends wanted to make her feel good and she was happy with their commentary. When everyone started back to the living room, John hung back and asked, "Karen, what are these?" He was holding one of Melanie's canvases.

Karen reminded him that Melanie was studying art and that she had done a few while she was visiting. He said, "These are exceptional examples of abstract, do you realize how good these are?"

She nodded and said, "Yes, I told her that they were great. You know she's enrolled at the Art Institute and moving up there next week."

John replied, "I remember that you told me about it. I've just been concentrating on your show and hadn't thought any more about it. We need to get her lined up for a talk with my partner."

Karen was really surprised now and asked, "You don't think that it's too early in her career?"

He smiled, "Hey, if she can produce this kind of work on a consistent basis, it's not too early. We will be keeping an eye on her and her progress. I just don't want to lose her to another gallery."

Karen said, "That's great but I still want her to continue her education. That degree will give her more self esteem. I've always felt like I was missing something by not having the degree."

John answered, "Not everyone needs the degree. You have a natural talent and that's remarkable, so thank your lucky stars." John patted her on the back and said, "Let's get back to your guests. We'll talk about it later."

When Karen got back to the living room she asked the group, "Does anyone want more dessert or another cup of coffee. The little kids jumped and yelled in unison, "I do."

"Okay, come right this way and I'll fix you up." She sat them at the kitchen table and gave them each some banana pudding and a glass of milk. The grown ups began to drift in and sample the desserts, too.

Ed had made another pot of coffee and several filled their cups with the steaming brew. Karen fixed a plate and took it to Mrs. Orson. She said, "That's so sweet of you. I have really enjoyed this day but I've got to get back to the home soon."

Karen said, "Yes, Melanie will take you in a little while. It is getting late but she'll get you back before dark."

When they had finished eating again, Christine said, "Gary; we need to get these children home so we can settle them down before bedtime."

He agreed and began to gather up their coats. He turned to Karen and said, "This has been a great day. Thank you so much for including us."

The rest of them chimed in and agreed that the day couldn't have been better. Karen assured them that it had been a pleasure for her and Ed. Melanie went to get her grandmother's wrap and told Karen, "Dad is going to ride with me to take Grandmother back and I might visit with him at the motel for a while."

Karen nodded, "That will be good for both of you."

Soon everyone had left except for John, Ken and Daniel. Daniel went into the kitchen and began to rinse the dessert plates, preparing for the next dishwasher load. Karen had gone outside to see everyone off and help Ruth and Joseph load their car.

She was surprised to see Daniel at the sink when she came back in. When she objected, he said, "Hey, I've had such a good time and why should you have to do all of this?"

Ed had gone to take Ken back to the motel. John was not ready to leave yet. When Ed came back in, he said, "Karen, you go sit down. Daniel and I will take care of this."

John was still in the living room and she went in to join him. They began to make plans for getting her canvases to Chicago. He would take several back tomorrow and she would bring more when she helped Melanie move.

He said, "Would you mention to Melanie that I'd like to talk to her tomorrow before I leave?"

"Sure, it won't be so hectic then. Just don't come too early. I want to sleep late. I feel like I've been up for days."

He said, "Yes, I'm sure this has been a long day and I need to get back to the motel so I'll be fresh for the trip home." He stood up and went to get his coat.

Karen said, "I didn't mean to run you off."

"You're not running me off. I've been up a long time, too. I've got a full day waiting after I get back to the city." He went to the kitchen where Ed and Daniel were finishing up and they all shook hands.

Karen walked with him to his car and he said, "I really appreciate you inviting me today. It was nice to spend time with a happy family and their friends. I hope I can repay the kindness someday."

She was quick to respond, "Oh, I think you have already done a lot for me and mine. I'm starting to get the jitters about my show and meeting all those strangers. I hope I won't look like a complete hayseed."

"Shame on you, Karen. You're a very sophisticated lady and I'll be proud to introduce you to the art connoisseurs of Chicago. I just know they are going to love you and your work."

They shook hands and then she hugged him.

He said, "I'll be back in the morning. Late morning. I really do want to talk to Melanie."

"Okay, I'll see you then. Hope you rest well tonight."

"After all that I ate, I'm sure I will have no problem sleeping." She watched and waved as he left the driveway and when she got back in the house she found Ed and Daniel sitting at the kitchen table with more coffee and dessert.

Ed said, "Come sit down, darlin' and have some more dessert with us." He got up and pulled out a chair for her.

She got a cup of coffee before she sat and said, "I couldn't possibly eat another bite. I can't believe you guys can eat again."

Daniel said, "Well, we just didn't want it to go to waste and there is still room in the dishwasher. I've got to get going. I need to get packed and ready for the kids tomorrow. I'm getting excited. I haven't had a real vacation in so long, I'm not even sure I'll be able to relax and enjoy it."

Ed said, "Oh, I imagine you'll relax as soon as you see Rebecca. Why don't you ask her to marry you while you're out there?"

Karen poked Ed in the ribs and said, "What are you talking about. When did you get to be cupid?"

Daniel grinned and said, "Well, Karen, it has already occurred to me, I'm not dead, you know."

She squealed with delight and said, "Oh, that would be so great. I really like her and you need somebody so you can be as happy and Ed and I."

He said, "I'd like that."

Ed pretended to be angry and said, "Now, who's playing Cupid?"

She put her arms around his middle and said, "I'm sorry. I didn't realize you guys had probably already had this conversation. I'm so happy to hear that there's a possibility we can have another wedding."

"Whoa," Daniel said, "Wait until I ask her, if I do, before you start planning the wedding."

"Oh, okay, but if you do, you call me and tell me so I can get started."

They were still laughing when Melanie came in the door. She asked, "What's so funny?"

Then she asked, "Are you still eating? Your stomachs must be bottomless pits."

Ed got up and pulled out a chair for her. "Can I get you something, Little Miss?"

"Well, I could probably force another piece of that apple pie. Have we got any ice cream?" Ed proceeded to get her pie and ice cream. He asked, "How about a cup of coffee?"

"That will be good. I love being waited on. I know somehow this is going to cost me."

Ed feigned shock, "I can't believe you said that. What could I possibly do to you? However, maybe you could finish cleaning up the kitchen since Daniel and I got a good start on it."

She just shook her head and began to eat. "Just leave it to me when you're through. I haven't done that much today."

Karen said, "I've got some news, really, good news for you. John was very impressed with your art and wants to talk to you in the morning before he heads back to the city."

Melanie shrieked, "Oh, my lord, you've got to be kidding. I don't believe it. Do you believe it?"

Karen smiled and said, "Yes, I believe it but I told him that I still want you to concentrate on your education and he promised that he would not interfere in that."

"Oh, Karen, too many good things are happening. I can't believe how lucky I am. I get to stay with you and Ed when I'm home. I get accepted to the Art Institute. I find a place to live. I've got a boyfriend and my dad wants to keep in touch and help me with expenses."

Ed piped up, "Whoa, now, what's this about a boyfriend? I didn't think you had time for a boyfriend. When did this happen?"

"Well, you're the one who introduced us. Remember the insurance

437

salesman? I went out with him once and we've stayed in touch ever since. He's been out of town visiting his family in Lexington so I haven't seen him yet but I intend to when he gets back."

Ed patted her on the back and said, "I do approve. As far as I know he is a nice kid and I'm glad the two of you hit it off."

Daniel had gone to get his coat and now was ready to go out the door. He said, "Don't let him intimidate you, Melanie. The cop in him just makes him think he's in charge. You can pick your own boyfriends, as far as I know."

He was smiling and Melanie knew he was kidding Ed but she said, "Well, I do trust his judgement but in the end it will be my decision. Just in case I meet an axe murderer, I want to make sure Ed knows who I'm dating."

Daniel kissed Karen and Melanie each on the cheek and shook hands with Ed. He said, "I will remember this day for the rest of my life. It has been the best Christmas I've had in many years. Since my kids have been grown, the divorce and everything, Christmas usually seemed like a very sad, confusing day."

As he turned to go out the door, Karen reminded him, "Well, maybe next year you will have another great one with a new wife."

Daniel shook his head and said, "Oh, lord, if she turns me down, I'll be humiliated since I had to open my mouth and reveal my plans."

Karen told him, "She won't turn you down. I can tell that she's crazy about you and her biological clock is ticking. She'll accept and before you know it, you'll have another family."

He almost ran out the door at that and as he left the drive he honked his horn all the way.

After Karen closed the door, she turned to Melanie and asked, "How did it go with your dad?"

Melanie told about their trip to Lexington. She said that he had apologized to both Grandmother Orson and her for his bad behavior in the past. He promised that he was going to renew his relationship with them and keep in touch even though he did plan to stay in California where his reputation was good. He felt there were too many ghosts in Dinsmore. He figured he wouldn't be able to live down his drunken antics. She had dropped him off at his motel and promised to meet him in the morning for breakfast.

Karen agreed, "That's great. I'm so glad that you can start over and have a decent relationship and I'm sure Margie would be pleased."

Ed said, "Yeah, that's good but remember I'm still your other dad and I love you, too. Don't go breaking my heart."

She got up and went to him and hugged him. "There's no way I could forget that. You've been so great and you know, I love you."

Chapter 125

The two of them were eating breakfast the next morning when John came to the door. Karen offered to fix him something to eat but he said, "I've already eaten but I will have coffee with you. Sit still, I know where it is."

After he had filled his cup and sat down, he said, "I saw Melanie and her father at the restaurant. Is she coming back?"

"Yes, she'll be back shortly. Larry is leaving this morning to go back to California. We can go back to the studio in a minute and look at her work. Then you can talk to her when she comes in. I'll leave you alone so you can discuss your ideas."

They sat there and talked about how much fun Christmas had been, Karen's upcoming show and where they would go in the new motor home. After a few minutes Melanie came in. John said, "I'd like to look at your work again and then talk to you about showing your work at our gallery."

Melanie became very excited, "Well, come on and I'll show you what I have here. I have a lot more packed up for my move." They went back to Karen's studio.

Ed and Karen went to get dressed for the day. After they had dressed in their jeans and flannel shirts, they went to the barn to check on Candy. Jazz and Callie were right behind them. Sometimes Jazz would run ahead and then come back to walk with them. Karen decided to saddle Candy and go for a ride. Ed got into the motor home and sat in the driver's seat, imagining he was on the road to somewhere exciting.

John had finished his talk with Melanie and came out of the house with her. They walked down to the barn. Ed got out of the motor home and said, "Did you two come to some agreement?"

John said, "Yes, I'm going to see what I can do about having her show very soon. I've got to get on the road right now. I hate to leave before Karen gets back but I have a lot to do when I get back to the city, so you tell her I'll call and finalize our plans next week. Okay?"

"Sure, I'll tell her. You drive carefully going back. The traffic will probably be heavy."

They shook hands and John got in his car which was full Karen's paintings. He honked his horn and left to go pick up Ken for the trip back to Chicago. Melanie had gone out to the field to look for Karen. When Karen came back to the barn, she was on foot. She said, "Melanie stole my horse. Let's go in and get another cup of coffee."

Everything was back to normal at the Café and Tony had been in a good mood when Larry Sloan came in the door. "Hi there, Larry. It's been a while since we've seen you. How's the world treating you these days?"

Larry was glad there was no one else there since it was very early. "I'm doing fine. I just had breakfast with my daughter at the motel but I wanted to come by on my way out of town, just for old times. I know, I owe you an apology for some of the things I said and did in the past."

Tony shook his head, "Hey, man, it wasn't that bad. You were drunk and it was bound to happen sometimes."

"Well, I'm in a twelve-step program now and one of the things I need to do is make amends. So, please, accept my apology so I can work my program."

Tony stuck out his hand after he put a cup of coffee on the counter. He said, "Apology accepted. Good luck and have a safe trip. Don't be a stranger. Nobody holds a grudge around here. Everybody makes mistakes, you know."

Larry drank his coffee and when he tried to pay, Tony said, "It's on the house. Glad you came by."

Larry went to his rental car and headed for the airport. It was the last time he was ever in Dinsmore. For years after that, he would visit Melanie in Chicago or she went to California at least once a year.

For the next three days most of Dinsmore was getting back to normal after all of the holiday hustle and bustle. Bill and his family were using the time to get ready for the grand jury that would be held the first Thursday in the new year. Janet finally admitted what she had done and how Tom had tried to help her. All of them were under a lot of pressure and worried but they managed to have a good Christmas. Just being together had now become very special. They were learning to appreciate each other again. They even began to play board games instead of watching TV in the evenings. When Sunday came they were all in church together.

Gary gave a wonderful sermon on the joys of family and the celebration of Christmas. He emphasized the real meaning of the holiday. He spoke of how he and his family had been with friends for the day and about how meaningful it had been. He talked about how important the extended family was and how it didn't necessarily mean relatives. He said sometimes friends become one's family, especially since families are scattered all over the country and few people get to put down roots in this day and age. He kept his sermon short and the congregation sang extra hymns to fill out the hour. When the lay preacher had said the final prayer, he hurried to the door to shake hands and greet everyone. Christine and the children joined him to wish everyone a Happy New Year.

On Friday at the police department, while he was still off work, the troops were planning Ed's retirement party. They decided to have it at the National Guard Armory because they wanted to invite the whole town. For the entertainment, they planned to have a roast with all of his co-workers and friends involved. They would hire a band and hire food catered to make it a really big affair. They planned to sell tickets to cover the expenses and set the date for the Saturday before the grand jury session. They put Jeff Collins in charge of ticket sales, Craig Walker would get the printing done and the Chief said he would get the Armory and the band. Chip Carter would be in charge of the catering and seating arrangements. They decided to keep it non alcoholic so that entire families could come if they wanted to. They put Jeff in charge of calling Karen to let her know the plans. They would try to keep it low key so that Ed wouldn't know any details. They knew he would be busy helping Melanie move and Karen prepare for her opening so they thought they could work around him. The chief said if he had to he would send him out of town for a meeting or something.

Chapter 126

After Daniel's kids had come into town on Monday, they all went to the airport to pick up Rebecca. She was surprised to see all of them waiting when she de planed. Daniel hugged her and kissed her on the cheek. He was delighted to introduce her to his kids and they were really friendly and seemed happy to meet her. They were very glad that their dad had someone he could be close to.

On the way back to town they talked about their plans for the ski trip. They would leave on Thursday and get back on Sunday morning. Rebecca said, "That sounds great. I'm off until next Monday so that will work for me. I'm glad I'll have a day or two to rest up from my trip home. It was exhausting. My parents are getting old and senile and they argue non stop now. We did manage to have a good time in spite of them but it is difficult to be around such unhappy people."

Daniel said, "Well, you're back with happy people now and I'm so glad. I really missed you."

Allison poked David in the ribs when he said that and David just smiled. When they got to the apartment house, Daniel helped Rebecca get her luggage and started up the steps. The kids said they would see her later and went to Daniel's apartment. When they got to the apartment, Allison said, "I think he's in love, don't you?"

"Hey, I don't blame him. She's a looker and seems nice."

When Daniel came in the door, Allison said, "Hey, Dad, tell us. Are you in love or what?"

Daniel's face turned bright red.

He said, "Am I that obvious?" Both of them answered, "Yes."

He sat down and said, "Well, I had planned to talk to you guys about her but I might as well do it now. I'm thinking about asking her to marry me while we're in Colorado. How do you feel about that?"

David spoke first, "Go for it. You don't need to be alone and she seems like a really nice person. Besides if you don't, I will. She's a real beauty."

Daniel had to laugh at that and he turned to Allison. She said, "Dad, nothing would make me happier than to know you had someone to love and she seems like a good choice. I can tell you're crazy in love."

Daniel just shook his head and said, "What a great couple of kids you turned out to be in spite of your mother and I. Just don't let on, so I can make arrangements for a special dinner while we're there. If I can get up the nerve to ask her, I'll do it then." There were high fives all around.

Ed went back to work for the first time since Christmas and nothing important had happened in the police department while he was off. He went to talk to the district attorney about his upcoming testimony to the grand jury. Everyone was discussing the latest murder on the national news. It had saddened the whole country. The consensus of opinion was that they were glad to be in a quiet little town.

But Ed still had to tell the DA what he thought had happened to Margie so he reminded them that crime can happen anywhere. When he got to the DA's office he began to tell him the story just as he had told the group that night at the country club…Tom had told Dr. Novak that he heard his mother leave in the family pick up at about 4:00 a.m. and so on and on. He told the whole awful story.

"After talking to Dr. Novak, I went back to the evidence room, found the prescription bottle and found out it was made out to Melanie. It was an antibiotic. Apparently Margie was allergic to the medication. We're thinking now that she had anaphylaxis attack and died before she could get help and before Janet or Tom had even entered the apartment. All this time Tom was thinking that his mother might have killed Margie. He was just trying to protect her. That explained his strange behavior and refusal to talk. That's it in a nutshell. Accidental death.

It was simply an unfortunate accident with two people who were trespassing in more ways than one."

He told him that Daniel had spent part of the night with Margie and would testify that she wasn't feeling well earlier in the evening. The DA said, "The grand jury will meet on Thursday the ninth of January and I doubt if anyone will be charged but I do feel that they should receive some kind of punishment for withholding evidence."

Ed explained, "I'd like to avoid making a public spectacle of the Wallaces. The whole family has suffered. Could we make it a private hearing and maybe the judge will sentence them to some community service or something to that effect?"

The DA quickly answered that question. "Ed, you know we can't have private hearing but we can encourage the judge to close the court room and the grand jury will be sworn to silence for six months. Then it's going to be public knowledge, but it won't be of as much interest. The public will have gone on to another subject of discussion. They tend to have a short attention span. The Wallaces will just have to deal with it the best they can. I think the community has enough admiration for Bill to give them a break. They'll survive and it will be forgotten very soon. They may well be the better for the experience. You know the old adage, "circle the wagons." when the Indians are coming."

"Yes, I know you're right. They are really good people but it just proves even the good people can make great mistakes and look very bad." The two men shook hands and the DA said, "See you in court."

Karen and Melanie had planned to meet Ed for lunch so they took care of the animals early. After they had gone through their morning ritual, they got in the car and went to town. They stopped by the cemetery and Melanie put some flowers from Christmas on Margie's grave.

Then they went to the Regal to do some shopping. Pamela was in her department when they got there and she was glad to see them both.

Karen asked, "Did you have a nice Christmas?"

"Yes, I did. I was really worried because I had never met Jeff's family. They were all so nice and we had a lot of fun. It's a big family so it was a busy household and the food was delicious. I didn't want to take my one dish wonder so I took a tin of fancy cookies instead and they seemed to like that."

Melanie said, "What is your one dish wonder?"

"It's the only thing I know how to fix. At least the only thing that I can take to a dinner. A corn casserole that I did take to the Barry's Thanksgiving dinner and Ms Ruth was very complimentary. She may have just been being nice, though."

Melanie said, "I can understand that. I've tried cooking for Ed and Karen. So far, they haven't objected. I've sure got a lot to learn before I can have a dinner party."

Karen changed the subject and asked, "Have you talked to Rebecca?"

"Yeah, I did, right after she got back in town. She's met Daniel's kids and says they are great. She seemed so happy to be going on a real vacation."

"I'm sure she is. Seems her family visits are not too pleasant for her."

Pamela asked, "What are you girls shopping for today?"

Melanie said, "We're shopping with our Christmas gift certificates. We really don't know what we're shopping for yet. Just shopping."

"Okay, if I can help, just let me know." She excused herself to go help another lady. They went to the lingerie department because Melanie had said that she needed some warm Pjs. Karen decided to get a new nightgown and after they had finished shopping, it was almost noon. Karen said she would wait until Ed was with her to redeem the one Daniel had given them.

When they got to the Café, Tony greeted them as usual, warmly and loudly. "I haven't seen you girls in a long time. Where you been keeping yourselves?"

He brought them their water because Maria was busy with some other customers. Karen joked, "Well, in case you didn't notice it was Christmas and we cooked at home for that occasion."

"You're kidding. I didn't notice? Have you ever had Christmas with five kids? It was a mad house. I was glad when it was over and I could come back to work."

They all had a good laugh at that. Karen told him that Ed would be there soon and they would wait to order. She added, "But I could stand a cup of coffee." Melanie nodded in agreement.

After he brought their coffee, he rushed back to the grill to fill Maria's orders. Maria came by and said, "Hello, ladies. I've missed seeing you. Hope you had a nice holiday."

Karen said, "We sure did and we already heard Tony's version of yours. Did you enjoy it?"

"Of course. I love watching the kids and all their excitement. He does, too but he likes to pretend he doesn't."

Ed and Jeff came in and Maria said, "Well, here are your lunch partners. I'll be back to get your orders in a minute."

Ed hugged Maria and said, "It's good to see you. Looking beautiful as usual." She blushed and said, "You never said anything like that before you were married."

He said, "Well, I'm getting braver in my old age."

Jeff chimed in, "Yeah, you have to forgive him. He's so old and feeble that he has to retire. So just overlook him. It's senility setting in."

Ed pretended to give him one in the chops and after they sat down, Karen said, "You two are sure in a good mood. What's going on?"

Ed explained, "I went to the district attorney and I think we are going to get done with Margie's case in a good way. I hope it will be okay with you, Melanie."

He explained what they had decided and Melanie said, "I think that will be fine. I know it was really accidental and Mother would not want them punished. She didn't know those pills had penicillin in them or she wouldn't have taken them. I had bronchitis last time I was home and the doctor had prescribed them. I was supposed to take the whole prescription. I forgot to take them with me when I left. The whole thing was a terrible mistake. I feel responsible, too."

Ed took her hand and said, "Honey, you can't feel that way. As I told you, your mother was old enough to know better than to take someone else's meds. She was probably sleepy and feeling bad and just didn't think." Then he said to the group, "We need to keep this between us. We're going to try to protect the Wallaces as much as possible so don't say anything to anybody and maybe we can take care of it without a lot of publicity. We will let the news hounds know that Margie did not commit suicide but accidentally took the wrong medication which caused the anaphylaxis attack which killed her." They all busied themselves with the menus when Maria came back to the table though they knew exactly what they would order.

School was still out for the holidays so Ed and his coworkers would be busy ticketing teenage drivers that thought the streets were their personal drag strip. There was very little other crime. There would be some drunkenness which led to abuse at home and in the bars. They were not looking forward to the celebrations that would take place for New Year's Eve. The jail got over crowded on that night.

There would be a fireworks display at the park outside of town and hundreds attended that every year and there was usually a fender bender or two. They would have to hire extra help to direct traffic. Karen would even be out there to help with that situation.

Chapter 127

Daniel, Rebecca and the kids spent Wednesday packing and when they were done, they decided to go out to eat. They went to the Café because Daniel wanted Tony and Maria to meet his family. It was early when they got there around five thirty because they wanted to eat early and get to bed. They had an eight o'clock in the morning flight to Colorado.

When they came in, Tony looked up from a book he was reading. Daniel said, "My has business dropped off so much that you have time to read?"

Tony jumped up and as he stuck out his hand to shake, he said, "No, not really, it's just the slow time of day before the hectic one starts."

Daniel introduced David and Allison to Tony and Maria, who had come out of the office when she heard them talking. Maria said, "We all love your dad. Not just because he's the banker but he's really a great guy. I guess you know that, though."

Allison said, "Yeah, we sort of like him, too." They all sat down and after Maria brought their water, she took their orders. When she brought their drinks, she asked, "Why are you eating so early?"

Daniel told her about their vacation plans and she looked at Rebecca and said, "Aren't you the lucky one to get to go on a ski trip?" Rebecca said, "Yes, I think so, too."

After they had eaten, they went back to the apartment complex. Daniel went to Rebecca's apartment but he told her, "I'm going to go now and finish getting ready. You go to bed early. I'll call you in the morning to make sure you're up. Okay?"

Rebecca looked a little confused and she said, "Well, yes, that will be fine. I thought you would stay a little while. What's your hurry?"

"I just think I need to make sure the kids and I have everything ready. I'm getting kind of jumpy or excited or whatever you want to call it."

Rebecca smiled at him and said, "Well, then go on. I've got plenty to do, too." She went with him to the door and hugged and kissed him hard on the lips. He returned the kiss and then hurried out the door.

He practically ran to his car because he was late for an appointment, he had made with Karen. They met at Jacob's Jewelers. He wanted Karen to help him select a ring for Rebecca. When he came in the shop, Karen was standing by the counter with the owner, Jacob Jakowski. She was smiling, "I am really worried about this because I don't know Rebecca that well. I know she's a very stylish girl and always looks like a fashion model."

Daniel said, "When she was in the shower, I got this out of her jewelry box." He held up a birth stone ring. "She doesn't wear it often but I know it fits."

Jacob showed them box after box of diamonds and they finally narrowed it down to three. Daniel was so confused that he finally just closed his eyes and told Karen to mix them up. He picked one up and bought it immediately. Jacob said, "I'll get it ready for you right now."

Karen said, "You need to calm down. I can almost guarantee the answer will be "Yes."

"Yeah, almost guarantee. Even though you just said, " I don't know Rebecca that well." She doesn't get that close to most folks. She does think a lot of you but have you ever discussed her love life?"

"No, I guess not, but we've always been with you and Ed. No chance for girl talk."

He said, "That was a mistake. I should have given you a chance to get to know each other. Let's face it. I'm like a puppy dog around her. She makes me weak in the knees. I'm a basket case."

By now Karen was laughing hysterically. She hugged him and said, "I've got the picture, Daniel. I love it. Quit worrying. The girl would not be going on this trip with you if she wasn't serious."

The jeweler came out of his work room and handed him the red velvet box that contained the key to his future life. He tucked it in his coat pocket and wrote the check to pay for it. Mr. Jakowski said, "If for some reason she doesn't like your choice, I will exchange it."

Karen said, "There is no way the girl will part with that rock. It's beautiful and she'll love it."

Daniel walked Karen to her car and said, "I'll call you and let you know how it goes."

Karen said, "Please, do, I'll be so anxious to hear but I know it will go fine. You deserve to be happy, Daniel. If Rebecca can make you happy, I'm all for it. By the way, you know you're going to have to testify before the grand jury right after you get back."

He looked sad, "Yes, how could I forget? I'm dreading bringing it all up again. It makes me very sad to think that I left Margie feeling so bad, but I had no idea that she was that ill."

Karen took his hand and said, "Listen, she wasn't that ill. She just took the wrong thing for a cold or congestion or whatever was bothering her. She should never have taken something not prescribed for her. It had nothing to do with you. I'm sure she was very happy to have you in her life and it's a shame that it couldn't be, but you are completely innocent."

"Well, I feel kind of bad about getting involved with Rebecca so soon after Margie's death."

Karen stopped walking and took him by the arm, "Hey, we're not getting any younger. If we want to have a relationship, there's no point in counting the days. As far as I'm concerned Ed and I should have been together long ago but we waited. We missed a lot of time when we could have had the happiness that we have now. You go for it. Life is just too short. Listen to me preach. I'm sorry."

They had reached her car and he hugged her and said, "Thanks for the pep talk, coach. I needed that. Take care of yourself and I'll see you when we get back."

When Karen got home, Melanie was sitting on the back porch with the animals. She went to meet Karen on the driveway and she asked, "Karen, would it be all right if I asked Tad to dinner one night this week?"

"Well, sure. What night do you want to do it?"

Melanie paused and then she said, "Well, he volunteered to help pack up my stuff at Mother's apartment so I thought that inviting him over would be a good idea." Hesitantly she said, "So tomorrow if that's okay with you."

"Sure, I'll just leave the apartment early to prepare the dinner. What shall we serve?"

Melanie wasted no time answering that question, "No doubt about it. Nobody makes better lasagna than you. Salad and lasagna and a dessert will do great."

"Well, I won't have to grocery shop for that. I have all the ingredients on hand and a pie in the freezer so actually I can put the lasagna together in the morning and that will give me more time to help with the packing. Do you think we can finish packing in one day?"

Melanie said, "I hope so because I would like to move on Friday if you can get away."

Karen said, "Well, I'm fine with that but we'll have to check with Ed and see if he can, because he'll have to drive with the U-Haul trailer. I've driven with the horse trailer but not all the way to Chicago. I don't want to do that.

If he can't get off, we'll have to wait until Saturday. Okay?"

Melanie hesitated a minute before she answered, "Well, Tad could drive. He wants to go to see my place."

Karen stopped walking and looked at Melanie. "Maybe you don't even need us to go. That would be fine if you don't need us. Do you plan to come back for Ed's retirement party?"

Melanie looked surprised at Karen's response and said, "Oh, I didn't mean that I didn't want you to go. I was counting on your help and I really planned to come right back so I could be here for the grand jury hearing and for the retirement party."

Karen said, "Well, that sounds great and we'll just wait til Ed gets home and see what he wants us to do. Anyway if he decides to drive, Tad can ride with us. We won't have to take your car since you'll be coming back. Don't mention the retirement party, just tell him you're coming back for the grand jury. The guys at the department really want to try to surprise him, even though I think that might be impossible."

They were still in the yard when Ed came home. He got out of his car and when he walked up, he put an arm around each of them and said, "What's for supper, ladies? I'm starving."

They looked at each other and Karen said, "Well, would you settle for a snack while I fix something? I've been out shopping for an engagement ring and lecturing our friend Daniel."

He smiled and said, "Sure, I'll have a peanut butter sandwich while you cook. What possessed you to lecture Daniel? He's a big boy and doesn't need a mommy."

After they finished dinner, Melanie cleaned up the kitchen while Karen went to her studio to sort out the paintings that she planned to deliver when they moved Melanie. She made a list and then put tags on each one with her name, the title and medium. Then she wrapped them in the brown paper she had bought from the U-Haul people when they made arrangements for the trailer.

Ed came in the room and said, "What's going on back here? Can I help?"

She told him about Melanie's plans and asked if he could get off on Friday. He said, "I'm sure I can. They are all taking over my jobs these days. I really don't have much to do. I think they'll be glad to be rid of me."

She was smiling at the thought of him losing control. "Oh, I doubt if that is true. They probably are just trying to make it easy for you. I hope you aren't sorry you resigned."

He put his arms around her and kissed her a long hard kiss. "I am not sorry in the least. I can't wait to take you in that motor home and go see the world."

"That's good. I just told Daniel that I wish we hadn't waited so long to get together. I'm looking forward to having more time with you, too. Daniel was worrying about how it would look if he married Rebecca so soon after dating Margie. I told him that life is too short to worry about that."

Ed said, "You're a wise woman, woman. We are going to enjoy life and I'm retiring so that we'll have time while we're still healthy. I don't feel old, do you?"

"Honey, when I'm around you I feel like a kid, just starting a new life."

Later when they had gone to bed, she said, "I just hope Daniel and Rebecca will be half as happy as we are." As he reached to turn the lamp off, Ed said, "Me, too."

The Wallace family met with their lawyer Jack Carter on Thursday. They told him the details of their experience in Margie's apartment just as they had told Dr. Novak. He told them that he had no idea what would happen but that he would meet with the district attorney and find out what he had in mind. He told them not to worry because it wouldn't help any of them. Just to be as honest as they possibly could.

He told them how the grand jury operated and what to expect. He said, "I feel like they will understand that it was an accident and that you were both in the wrong place at the wrong time. Needless to say you re-acted in a weird way and didn't do what you should have, by not calling 911. Then to compound things, you withheld information for a very long time. I know there will be some punishment but I'm not sure what it will be. We'll just have to take what they hand out. The grand juries are not allowed to discuss what they hear for at least six months so the gossips won't be able to spread rumors right away. If they do they can go to jail or be fined. We'll try to keep it out of the news. Bill is such a great coach, I don't think his job will be jeopardized since he wasn't involved in the situation at the apartment. Besides when he was having the affair, you were separated. My best advice is to just keep on living your lives as usual and wait to see what happens. I will represent you as well as I possibly can."

They left the office feeling a little better, but still not comfortable. On the way home, Bill pulled into the church parking lot and went into Greg's office. He said, "Greg, I wonder if you would pray with me and my family. We're in trouble and need the Lord's help."

Greg told him to come on in and he went to get the rest of his family. When they had all assembled in Greg's office, they formed a circle and held hands and Greg led them in prayer. He didn't know for sure what kind of trouble they were in and he didn't ask or really care. He just prayed for the Lord to forgive them their sins and to give them peace. When they left the church, they all felt much better.

Chapter 128

Karen was having her morning coffee on the back porch. The weather had warmed in the last few days. It was still cold enough for her coat but the sunshine was just too appealing. She had been there about thirty minutes when Ed joined her. She laughed at him in his pajamas and heavy coat.

He said, "What are you doing, dressed so early?"

"It's packing day at Margie's apartment. Tad, Melanie and I are going to be busy. Wanna' come?"

He grinned and shook his head, "I think I'll pass but I will be there to load and then to unload in Chicago."

Karen told him about the guest they would be having for dinner and then she said, "That's why I'm up extra early. I want to put the lasagna together before we leave so I won't have much to do when I come home. I know I'll be tired. Would you be a dear and stop and pick up a loaf or two of French bread at the bakery?"

He sat down beside her. "I think that's the least I can do for a lasagna dinner. I'll even perk it up with some garlic butter as my donation to the cause."

She leaned over and kissed him, "Sounds good. I'd better get in there and fix breakfast first." He followed her into the kitchen and then went to shower and dress for work.

When Melanie came into the kitchen, she was dressed for the chores of the day. She got a cup of coffee and sat at the table. She said, "I really appreciate all you've done for me, Karen. I don't know what I would have done without you. I hope I can repay your kindness someday."

Karen went over to where she sat and bent over to hug her. She said, "Melanie, as far as I'm concerned, you're the daughter I never had. Don't worry about repaying me. Besides, you know I'll expect you to take care of me and Ed in our old age."

They both were laughing when Ed came into the room and said, "Are you talking about me?"

Karen said, "Oh, yes, it's all about you. You're so vain!"

Melanie told him what Karen had said and he said, "I know you probably think we're already old but we don't think so. You won't have to worry about us for a long time. We'll wait until you're a famous artist and filthy rich. Then we'll just move in with you."

Melanie said, "Have I told you that I plan to live in Paris?"

Ed roared with laughter but replied, "I can learn to speak French. You don't get off that easy." They were still at it when Tad came to the door.

Karen said, "My word, don't you think it's a little early for supper?"

He looked startled and she said, "Never mind, we've just been acting silly and I was joking with you."

After they finished breakfast, Ed left for work. Karen started on her lasagna, while Tad and Melanie cleaned up the rest of the kitchen. That done and the lasagna in the fridge, they left for Margie's apartment. It made Karen despondent to see all of Margie's things being packed and moved out of place. It made her death seem so final.

She tried not to let it show to Melanie. The girls packed all the dishes first while Tad packed books and odds and ends. The clothing, they put in garbage bags to take to the Crisis Center. They packed up condiments and other food items so that Melanie would have a start in her new apartment without grocery shopping.

The major appliances all belonged to the landlord so they only had a couple of chairs and a couch that were extra heavy. They took the beds apart and stacked everything in the living room.

Ed would bring some extra help on Friday to load it all. At noon Karen said, "Let's take a break and go get something to eat."

When they got to the Café, Ed and Jeff were there, as well as Pamela and Leah, all sitting at the cop's favorite table. Karen said, "Uh huh, caught you out with strange women. You just can't trust a cop these days."

The guys stood up and pushed another table up to theirs.

Tony was busy cooking but he didn't miss that move. He said as loud as he could, "You caught him now didn't you, Karen?"

Ed said, "You just stick to your cookin', buddy or I'll run you in. We've got some hungry hard workin' folks here."

Maria came over with water for the three new customers and said, "What are you up to? It looks like you've been working hard."

Karen said, "Do we look that bad? I haven't even looked in the mirror since morning. We've been packing up for Melanie's move and it is hard work."

Maria said, "I can't believe you are leaving us, Melanie," as she wrote down their orders.

Melanie answered quickly, "Oh, I'm just trying to get an education. I'll be back on weekends a lot. This is home and I'll miss Karen and Ed." Tad gave her a puzzled look and she said, "I'll miss you, too. Don't worry." He just smiled and said nothing, but he patted her on the knee under the table.

Karen left the two young people vacuuming the apartment and finishing up the packing so that she could shower before dinner. She was in the kitchen making the salad when Ed got home. He came up behind her and kissed her on the neck. He said, "Ooh, you smell so good and you look good, too. I know you had a hard day in more ways than one."

"Yeah, it was sort of depressing, but I didn't want Melanie to feel bad so I toughed it out."

He went to change into his jeans and was back in a flash to fix his French bread. He said, "I told them I needed to be off on Friday and I'll swear they seemed glad to get rid of me. I guess I retired just in time because I don't feel needed any more."

Karen patted him on the back and said, "Well, I'll be glad to have you with me so don't worry about it."

He had no idea that the department was busy making last minute arrangements for his retirement party on Saturday night and they were thrilled that he would be out of town. They had asked Karen to keep him away as long as possible.

When Melanie and Tad came in the table was set and ready for them.

Karen said, "I know you'd probably like to shower but I don't want my supper to get cold, so just wash up and let's eat."

Tad said, "It smells so good that I don't care about a shower. Show me where to wash up, Melanie."

She took him by the hand and said, "Right this way."

Karen went to her bedroom to get her slippers and saw them in the master bath wrapped in each other's arm and completely oblivious to her presence. She waited to come out of the bedroom until she heard them talking and figured it was safe. After they all had enjoyed Karen's delicious dinner, Ed and Karen went to the den to watch TV. Tad and Melanie cleared the table and put the dishes in the washer.

Ed said, "I think that I'll pick up the trailer after work tomorrow so that we'll have it early Friday morning. Jeff and Craig are going to come by and help us load. I told them to be there by seven. I figured if we could get out of town by nine we'd be in the city before the traffic got too bad. We'll load your paintings tomorrow evening if that's okay."

Karen was lying with her head in his lap and she said, "Sounds like a plan to me. Then we can take them by the gallery on our way out of town. I don't know if the kids are riding with us or going in a separate car."

Tad came into the room and said, "I think we'll take my car, so we can stay and put some of her things up. Then it won't be such a mess when she actually moves in. I thought if you two can stay long enough to help set up the beds, we'd be able to take care of the other things."

Karen said, "That sounds like another good plan. You men have got it together and I'm glad because I'm so pooped I don't want to think."

Melanie said, "John wanted me to bring some of my paintings, too. He wants his partner to see them so I hope you can drop them off with yours. Okay?"

Ed told her that would be fine and then he asked Karen, "Are you ready to call it a night?"

"I could go to sleep right here but I guess I'll go to bed if you insist."

He laughed and said, "I think that you will be a lot more comfortable. I'm going to stay up and watch the news and then I'll be in."

"I won't wait up." She said, as she stumbled off, "G'nite, kids. See you later."

"Goodnight, thanks for everything." Tad said, "The dinner was fantastic, Mrs.Hawkins. Thank you." She just waved her hand over her head and was gone.

After Tad had gone, Melanie sat down with Ed and watched the news. She said, "I hope you know how much I appreciate you and Karen."

He patted her hand and said, "We're happy to help, Honey. You mean a lot to both of us. I want you to be really careful while you're out in the city. I hear about so many awful things that happen, but if you stay aware of what's going on around you and don't go to dangerous neighborhoods, you should be okay."

She promised she would keep that in mind and when the news was over, she kissed him on the cheek and said, "Goodnight, Ed. I love you."

"I love you, too. Don't you ever forget that Karen and I both love you and we want the best for you."

Chapter 129

Karen was busy all day Thursday getting her paintings ready to deliver. Melanie worked on hers, too. Then they spent some time in the barn with Candy and played fetch the ball with Jazz. The weather was so nice they didn't want to stay in the house. Later on Melanie rode Candy while Karen fixed supper. Ed had planned to come home early. She wanted to have dinner ready so that they could all go to bed early.

Tomorrow was going to be a long hard day. Tad called for Melanie. Karen told him she would get Melanie to call him back. Then she talked to Jeff about the retirement party and it seemed to be working out great. Jeff was so excited. He could hardly quit talking about it.

She asked him how he and Pamela were doing and he said, "She's a really nice person and I like her a lot but neither of us are ready to be serious. We just enjoy doing things together and aren't in a sexual relationship because neither of us believes in sex outside of marriage."

Karen was surprised at that bit of news but she told him, "That's very admirable of you both in this day and age."

He replied, "I don't worry about what others do but I see too much unhappiness from people who don't take responsibility."

Karen said, "You're so right of course. I guess I'll see you early in the morning. It's good of you to help us out."

He said, "It's no problem. I sure hope you can keep Ed occupied on Saturday. I don't want him to find out after we've been able to keep it quite this long. You won't believe how many people are coming. We are going to have a blast."

After they had finished talking, Melanie came in and Karen gave her the message from Tad and they talked on the phone for a long time. Karen heard Ed's car in the driveway and went outside to meet him. He had the U-Haul trailer hooked up so they began to load the paintings before it got dark. The temperature was beginning to drop, so they didn't take long getting the job done.

At the dinner table, Ed said, "Wouldn't you know that snow is predicted for tomorrow. I hope they're wrong because that will make it rough driving."

They were eating their dessert of bread pudding when the phone rang. Ed got up to answer it. He said, "Hi, Daniel. How's the skiing?" There was a pause and he said, "Well, sure. I'll get her."

He motioned for Karen to come to the phone and he whispered, "He didn't want to talk to me. He wanted you. What's with that?"

Karen just smiled mischievously and didn't answer him. She took the phone and said, "Hello, Daniel, how's it going?" and then she squealed, "Oh, that's so great. I knew she would. I know you're a happy camper. Was she surprised?"

"We'll tell you all about it when we get back. Keep Sunday night free. I want to take you all out to dinner at the club with my family. Okay?"

Karen said, "I can't wait. Travel safely. We'll see you then." When she hung up the phone, she said, "Daniel and Rebecca are officially engaged. She accepted his ring." She told them about the Sunday night plan and Ed said, "Well, that will be interesting, won't it? Will you be here, Melanie?"

Melanie said, "Sure, I'm coming back Saturday so we can…" She paused and hastened to say, "So we can go to church on Sunday with you."

Karen's face had lost all color and when she got her breath back, she said, "That's right. You'll need to come back early, too. We need to check out the apartment one more time and turn in the keys to the super. Besides there's the hearing."

She was hoping that Ed hadn't noticed the gap in Melanie's sentence. Melanie got busy right away clearing the table and Karen said, "Let's go watch TV a little while, Ed."

He said, "Is that all Daniel had to say?"

"Isn't that enough? Aren't you surprised?"

"Not really. I knew he was crazy about her and I figured they would get together eventually. I wanted to know about the skiing."

She took him by the hand and led him to the couch. "He'll tell us all about it when he gets home." Ed didn't know that Daniel had changed his plans to come back by Saturday night so they could be at the big party.

Friday morning they were all up extra early. They had oatmeal and orange juice after their coffee. Karen fixed a thermos of coffee for the road. The weather was not looking good. The wind was blowing and the sky was cobalt blue. It looked like it would snow any minute. They all got their warmest coats and hats before they went outside.

Melanie had fed the animals in the barn, so that they would be warm. At six thirty they loaded up in the Cadillac with the U-Haul on the back and started out to the apartment. When they got to the apartment building, Tad was waiting there in his car. Soon after Jeff and Craig arrived.

They loaded the heavy stuff first so that Jeff and Craig could get to work at the station on time. Tad and Ed left to take the large couch, one chair, the bedroom suites and some odds and ends of tables to a temporary storage facility until Melanie could decide whether to sell them or not. Jeff and Craig followed them to help unload and then they went to work. Ed said, "Thanks a lot, guys. I'll repay the favor sometime."

He shook hands with each of them and Jeff said, "I'll remember that when I move out of the house."

Ed said, "I've been meaning to speak to you about that. Don't you think it's time to leave the nest?"

Jeff looked sheepish and said, "Hey, I don't cook as good as my mom."

When they were back to the apartment they got the rest of the bigger items and loaded them. That done they started carrying boxes down. Ed got in the trailer and arranged everything, so they could get it all in. They put the bags of Margie's clothing in the trunk so Karen could take them to the Crisis Center on Monday. The work went smoothly and they were ready to leave by nine o'clock, just as it started to snow. Tad was driving his Jeep which had four wheel drive so he would be safe on the road and the Cadillac would be fine even though the trailer made driving a little trickier.

They stopped halfway there as usual, had a rest and coffee. Ed and Tad decided the drivers needed a donut for energy. Before they left there, Ed checked on the load and found everything was staying in place. It was packed so tight, it could hardly move anyway. The snow was coming down in bigger flakes now and the highway was starting to be covered but it wasn't deep.

Ed said, "We just need to be careful and drive at a safe speed." He checked again with Melanie on the exit he should take and directions to her apartment. They all loaded up and took off again, after about thirty minutes of rest.

They got to the apartment house at just before noon, barely beating the lunch traffic. There was underground parking. When they found an empty space, Tad parked his Jeep. Ed pulled up close to the elevator to unload.

Ed and Tad would have to move the heavy stuff by themselves this time. Karen would keep watch on the remaining goods and Melanie would help the men when she could.

After they had unloaded everything but the paintings. Ed pulled the car and trailer back out to the street. It took him some time to find a place to park the rig. He finally went to a filling station and offered to pay them to let him park there for a couple of hours. They agreed and he began walking back to the apartment. He noticed the fact that it wasn't a real nice neighborhood and made a mental note to give Melanie some more advice about her safety.

There were young men hanging out on every corner, that didn't seem to have anything better to do. A little kid that should have been in school, came up to him and asked him if wanted to buy some weed. He told him to "go home to your momma" and the kid cussed him out. He just laughed it off knowing the kid didn't know any better.

When he got back to the apartment building, Karen said, "I was starting to get worried about you. Where have you been?"

He told her what he had done and they began the chore of hauling Melanie's belongings to the fifth floor. They took the love seat with a couple of small items first and after the heavy items were all in the apartment, they loaded the boxes on the elevator with Melanie. The three of them took the next elevator.

Tad was fascinated by the Murphy bed. . He kept letting it down and putting it back up.

Ed said, "You're going to wear it out if you don't quit playing around."

Karen was helping Melanie arrange the furniture, when Ed said, "I think that they can do the rest and we should get on to the gallery, don't you?"

She stopped to survey the situation. "Okay, you're right. I want to get that done and get back on the road before the snow gets worse. Are you kids coming back this afternoon?"

Melanie said, "Yes, I wanted to stay and get every thing set up but with the weather like it is, I think maybe we'd better get back as soon as possible, too. I'll have time to get it all done before school starts."

Ed said, "Okay, we'll go on then and see you back at the ranch this evening."

He shook hands with Tad and said, "You drive carefully coming back." Then he hugged Melanie and told her, "I really like your little place. It's perfect for starting out." Then he told her about his experience walking back from the station and said, "Just don't go walking around here. When you go to the store, make sure it's a good neighborhood. Remember what I told you about staying aware of your surroundings. You always carry that whistle and pepper spray that I gave you."

Melanie hugged him back and said, "Yes, Daddy."

He blushed and said, "I like that."

She said, "Okay, Daddy."

Karen hugged them both. Tad went down to drive them to the station. When Ed went to pay for the parking, the station owner said, "You don't owe me anything, man. I'm glad I was able to help. Some kids were getting curious about your trailer. When I saw them checking it out, I ran them off."

Ed said, "Well, I really appreciate it. We've been moving our daughter into an apartment not far away. I'm going to tell her to buy her gas here. Her name is Melanie Sloan and I want you to take good care of her for me."

The station owner said, "I'm Stan Labowski and you tell her to ask for me and I'll see that she gets taken care of."

"Will do."

They shook hands and Ed went to the car where Karen was already waiting. He told about his conversation with Stan and she asked, "Did you really call her your daughter?"

He said, "Sure, that's how I feel about her, don't you?"

"Yes, I'm so glad you do, too."

Chapter 130

The local police in Dinsmore, were not doing much policing on Friday. They were all going to the Armory checking on their party plans. The tables and chairs had been delivered.

Tony and Maria were catering the affair and they had rented dozens of checker table clothes, dishes and warming trays. They planned to serve Ed's favorite, spaghetti and meatballs. With salad, garlic bread, and cheesecake for dessert. Of course they would have a big decorated cake with thirty candles on it for his year of service. They had little boxes with Ed's name and dates of service on them. The guests would each take home a souvenir piece of the cake in the box.

Tony was there working when Jeff stopped by one time. Jeff said, "I really would like to stay here and work on everything but I need to get on patrol."

Tony told him, "Don't worry. Everything is going to be okay. We'll get it all done by tomorrow." Later that afternoon the country band they had hired came in and sat up to practice. Several of the cops were there to watch them.

They had sold four hundred tickets already. Chief Stone was there, too. He was going to be one of the participants in the roast. It would be Chief Stone, Jeff, Daniel, Greg and Tony sitting at the head table with Ed and Karen. They would get together on Saturday to make sure they each had a different embarrassing story to tell about Ed.

Gary Oldham would act as the master of ceremonies. Chip Carter worked the evening shift at the department and he went by to see how things were going.

Back at the station he said, "Chief, are we done selling tickets?"

Stone said, "Yes, I'd say, we're sold out. That place won't hold more than five hundred and if we've sold four hundred already, it's safe to say, it will be full if you count the invited unpaid guests. Our expenses are easily paid and we'll be able to give Ed at least a thousand dollars, maybe more."

Chip said, "Hey, that's great! He'll be able to fill that motor home's gas tank."

Stone said, "I hate to admit it but I am going to miss him and I'm really jealous. He has a plan to enjoy his retirement. I can't imagine retiring because

I don't what I'd do with myself. Drive my wife crazy, probably."

"You need a hobby, Chief."

"Right." He went back to the paper work on his desk and Chip figured it was time to leave.

Jeff was going to see each person who was speaking and ask them to give him a copy of the remarks they would make. Most of them had no idea what they would say but he insisted and they finally got something on paper. All of them had an embarrassing moment or incident of Ed's to share.

Gary as the master of ceremonies said, "I will not be telling any stories on Ed. I will introduce the others but I want to keep him as a friend."

Tony said, "I can't wait. It will be fun to see him squirm." Tony and Maria had hired extra help to do the catering so that they could enjoy the party.

The mayor was going to present him with a plaque in recognition of his years of service. Since it was going to be a non-alcohol occasion there would be whole families there. Jeff was more excited than anyone else, since Ed had been his partner and mentor for five years.

Ed maneuvered the trailer through the busy Chicago streets to the Rose Gallery. Karen ran in the gallery while he circled the block. She saw John immediately and asked him, "Where can we park the trailer to unload it?"

John told her to stay right there and he would go get in with Ed and show him how to get to the alley behind the gallery. John went to the sidewalk and on Ed's next pass he went to the street and hailed him. He jumped in the car and directed him to the alley. He got out and rang the bell. Ed began to unload the paintings.

John said, "You don't have to do that. I'll get some help out here to unload. Come on in and we'll have a drink or a cup of coffee while they unload."

Ed didn't need to be begged. By now he was getting pretty tired of loading and unloading. Two young men came to the door and John gave them their directions. He and Ed went in to find Karen. She was already in the break room drinking coffee with Harry Rose, the official owner of the gallery and John's partner.

John introduced Ed and they shook hands even though they had met briefly before. Ed said, "What do we need to do here? I mean what does Karen need to do? I'd like to get started back before the weather gets any worse."

Karen explained that she had made lists of everything and the minimum that she would like to have for her work. She said, "But the final prices will be your call to make, John. I have so little experience in selling and I don't know your clientele so I'll be happy with whatever you decide."

He looked her list over and said, "This looks very good and I see you have a list for Melanie also."

"Yes, we brought her paintings, too. She said that you wanted to let Harry have a look. She's busy setting up her little apartment right now or she would have come with us. I'll have her call you for an appointment next week."

Ed was getting impatient and said, "It sounds like everything is in order so can we go now?"

Karen said, "Yes, I know you're worried about the weather and we need to miss the evening traffic, too. What about it, John? Everything, okay?"

"Sure, if I have any questions, I'll call you. We'll plan to have the opening on Friday night the twenty fourth. Is that still okay?"

Karen said, "That will give me three weeks to work up my nerve. I'm scared to death."

"You don't have a thing to worry about, Karen. It will be fine. I will need the names and addresses of the friends you want to invite and we will be sending invitations to several hundred of our patrons so you'll have a great opening. It will be a formal affair so dress appropriately and just prepare for a very nice evening."

Karen smiled, "Easy for you to say. I'll do my best but you know I'm just a small town girl, so I'll need help making conversation with strangers."

"Harry and I will be there every minute."

Karen hugged him and said, "Okay, we're going now. Call me if you need anything else from me. Come on Ed, let's get on the road. It's been a very long day."

Ed thanked John and Harry and took her arm as they went back to the car to make their way out of the big city.

They got back to the interstate with no problems. When they got to the half way stop, they went in and ordered pie and coffee. Karen went into the rest room and was shocked when she looked in the mirror. She hadn't even put on lipstick all day and she looked very tired. She wondered what John and Harry had thought when they saw her in such a state. She plashed some cold water on her face and brushed her hair and put on some lipstick. She decided that helped a lot. When she got back to the table Ed said, "You look much better. I was concerned that you might have overdone it."

"No, I didn't realize how bad I looked. I am tired though and I will be glad to get home."

They took their time eating and a few minutes after they started to eat, Melanie and Tad came in the door. They sat down in the booth with them.

Karen said, "I didn't think you would be starting back this soon. Did you get a lot done?"

Melanie said, "We did a lot but I'll finish up when I come back. Tad was worried about the weather and I knew he was right. We thought it would be wiser to start back early."

Ed said, "Tad, you are a smart young man. I would have been worrying all night until you got back." They ordered hot chocolate and a big cookie. After everybody had finished eating, they went to their cars and started the trek to home. The snow was still falling in big flakes but the roads were not covered. The trucks were out with sand and gravel for the slick spots."

They got home at eight thirty. After the men left to take the trailer back to the dealers, Karen and Melanie started to prepare some dinner. They decided that soup and sandwiches would be good for a snowy night. Karen kept homemade soup frozen and it didn't take long to thaw it, first in the microwave and then the pot. Melanie boiled some eggs to make tuna salad. When the meal was well on it's way, Karen went to shower and get into her Pjs.

Melanie sat the table for four and when the guys came in, it was almost finished.

Ed asked, "Where's my lovely wife?" Karen appeared in her robe and slippers.

"You weren't kidding about being tired, were you?"

She said, "I don't know which is worse being hungry or sleepy."

When they were seated and began to eat, Tad said, "This could get to be habit forming."

Karen said, "What do you mean."

"Eating home cooking. You don't know how much I miss it. I do the frozen dinner thing just to stay alive. This is heavenly."

Karen smiled and said, "Well, you'll just have to come more often. We always have enough for another mouth."

They made ice cream sundaes for dessert and Karen had coffee with hers. She said, "I love to drink coffee with ice cream."

Ed said, "I thought you wanted to go to bed early. Won't the coffee keep you awake?"

"Nothing will keep me awake."

As soon as she had finished, she said goodnight to everybody and went to the bedroom. Tad decided he had better get back to his place. After he was gone, Melanie and Ed watched the news before they went to bed.

When Ed crawled into bed, Karen turned over kissed him and went right back to sleep. Ed lay there awhile considering how lucky he was to have such a great life. He dreamed about traveling all over the country with Karen in the motor home that night.

Chapter 131

The three of them had a long leisurely breakfast the next morning with pancakes, bacon and eggs. Ed commented on the high fat content but hastened to add, how much he had enjoyed it. After they had read the paper and drank multiple cups of coffee, Ed went to get dressed.

Karen told Melanie in a whisper that they had to keep Ed from going to town today no matter what. Melanie suggested that they pack a picnic lunch and go check on the hunting camp. They could take some pictures and see what they needed to bring when gun season opened.

Karen said, "That would be great. Let's ask Ed."

Ed came back to the kitchen and said, "Ask Ed what?"

"How about going up to the hunting camp today? I'll fix a picnic lunch and we can spend the day. I'd like to get some new photographs to paint from while there is still some snow on the ground."

He immediately agreed that it was a great idea and said, "How about going in the motor home, just to test it out?"

Taken by surprise, Melanie and Karen looked at each other, and then Karen said, "Well, I guess that would be fun. We really haven't checked it out. It is full of gas?"

"Oh, yeah, I've just been waiting for an excuse to drive it."

Karen said, "We won't have to fix a lunch. I'll just put the groceries in there and we'll fix it after we get there."

She got some soup, crackers, cold cuts and bread and put them in a bag. Melanie got the drinks and mayo out of the fridge. Ed grabbed a bag of chips and said, "We've got a feast here, let's go, girls."

"You go pull it out of the barn, Ed, and I'll be right there."

Melanie went with him and Karen went to the phone and called Jeff. She told him their plan and he was delighted to know Ed would be out of town. He told her to tell Ed that they needed him at the armory about seven and she could insist on going with him.

Melanie had a date with Tad and would already be at the armory. Karen was to tell him there was a disturbance at a dance there and they needed all the help they could get. Ed was honking the horn and she told Jeff, "I've got it and

468

we'll see you then. Good Luck."

She called Jazz and picked up Callie to take them on the trip. When they got into the motor home, Ed said, "What is this?"

She said, "You may as well face it now, where we go these guys go, too. I can't leave them at home alone for weeks."

"So this is a test run, huh?"

"Right." End of conversation.

The roads were all clear now and the sun was shining brightly as they headed up the highway to the camp. Melanie watched the TV in the back while Ed and Karen just enjoyed looking at the scenery. He made his usual stop at the little store by the camp road. The owner of the store was very impressed by the motor home. Ed bought a cigar and some candy bars from him.

When he got back in the vehicle, Karen looked in the bag and said, "What is this cigar for?" "I always have a cigar when I come up here."

She said, "Ed, that's a weird habit, you know that don't you?"

"I know but it's become a tradition."

Karen pled, "But you will smoke it out of doors, won't you?"

"Of course, I'm not stupid." Melanie giggled and Ed said, "What's so funny, missy?"

"Oh, I think I just witnessed your first argument and it's such a ridiculous reason for an argument."

Ed's answer was, "Most arguments are ridiculous."

Karen said, "Right." End of conversation.

When they got to the cabin, it was obvious that some vandals had been there before them. Someone had spray painted dirty words on the front of the building. They all just sat there for a few minutes without speaking.

Then Ed said, "Well, I'll have to come back up and give this place a new coat of paint. I don't know what I did to deserve this but I bet I'll find out."

When they opened the door Jazzy jumped out and ran barking to the back of the building. He barked even louder when he got around the corner and someone screamed, "Get him off of me."

Ed went around to see what was going on and a very thin young boy was up against the wall, looking terrified. Jazzy was just growling now, but not backing down.

Ed said, "Well, what do we have here? A spray paint artist, perhaps? One with a dirty mouth or mind, should I say?"

"I'm sorry, I just wanted to get even with you for putting my old man in

469

jail. He's all I've got, I'm hungry and there's no money to buy anything. I was going to break in and look for some food but I couldn't get the door open. Then I found the spray paint out there by the tree stump."

"How old are you, boy?" He was at least six feet tall and skinny with long, sandy hair that could use a shampoo. "I'm 11." Ed was thinking, 'This is the tallest eleven year old I've ever seen."

He asked, "Do you play basketball?"

"Nah, I don't go to school. We don't have the right clothes and I have to help Dad cut wood so we can eat."

Karen and Melanie were just watching while Ed questioned the kid.

Karen said, "Ed, why don't we get him something to eat while you check him out?"

Ed was surprised by the question. He had forgotten that they were there, in his haste to catch the culprit. By now Jazzy had backed off and was standing beside Karen.

"Sure, come on, Son. We'll get you something to eat before we talk any more." He took him by the arm and lead him to the motor home. Karen and Melanie began to prepare lunch.

Ed went to check inside the cabin and Karen told the boy to sit down at the table.

She asked him, "What's your name?"

He said, "Beau Hayes."

"How long since you had something to eat?"

"I don't know. It's been a while. The food ran out at my shack a few days ago. Mr. Smith at the store gave me some candy the other day. I didn't tell him it was all I had to eat."

Karen said, "Why not? You know he would have fed you."

"I was ashamed. It's so embarrassing to have your dad in jail and to be so poor that you can't even buy your own food. He's always been real nice to me and I didn't want him to know about the mess I'm in."

Ed was back and he put his arm around his shoulders and said, "Son, it's not your fault and it's no sin to be poor. I'm going to see to it that you get taken care of."

He screamed, "No, sir, don't do that! They'll take me away from my dad if they find out."

Ed was surprised at the boy's panic and asked, "Who will take you away?"

"Those people at the welfare department or child department or sumthin' like that."

Ed patted him on the back and said, softly, "Well, we just won't let them find out anything. We can handle this. I just have to find out why your dad is in jail and then go from there. Now let's eat."

They all sat around the little table and had their first meal in the motor home. The kid ate as though he were starving and he probably was. He had good table manners but he was eating fast and Ed put out his hand and said, "Listen, you can eat all you want but I want you to slow down so you won't get sick. Sometimes when you haven't eaten for a long time, your stomach gets upset. So take it easy. We've got plenty of food and time. You just relax. When we get through here, we'll go to town and get you some clothes."

He looked at Karen and she was nodding her head. She was thinking, "How am I going to keep him from seeing what's going on in town." Then she said, "We can go to Wal Mart." Knowing it was outside of town and he wouldn't see all the in town activities.

They all cleaned up Beau's handiwork with paint thinner and cleansers as much as they could. Then they checked on the inside of the cabin again. Karen walked into the woods for a few minutes to get her pictures. The snow was almost gone now but some remained in the shady secluded spots. She saw some rabbits scurrying away and squirrels but that was all the wild life that came out. They loaded up and went back to town. It was now about four thirty. Melanie was in the back talking to Beau. Karen tried to eavesdrop but couldn't hear above the sound of the engine.

At the Wal Mart they bought everything from underwear to a coat for Beau and when they were through shopping, they went to the house. They encouraged him to take a shower and put on some of his new clothes. While he was in the shower they decided that Ed would check on his dad tomorrow, but for now he would stay with them.

Karen said, "Let's go to town to eat pretty soon and then we'll see what else we can do to entertain the kid."

Melanie smiled and said, "I've got a date with Tad but I can get him to pick me up at the Café."

Karen was checking her watch and knew it was getting late and they needed to get to the armory by seven. She planned to have Ed drive by the armory and then she would say, "I wonder what's going on in there tonight. Let's go see. It must be a concert and Beau might enjoy that." Jeff's plan wouldn't work now.

Beau came out of the bedroom in his new jeans and a flannel shirt. He looked so befuddled that they all laughed. He looked embarrassed, he thought they were making fun of him until they told him how great he looked. That was all he needed to make him smile broadly. "Goll, thanks so much. I ain't ever had my own clothes before. They've always been hand me downs that didn't really fit."

Ed told him, "Well, you are quite welcome. Now you need to get that new coat on because we're going to town to eat supper."

Beau asked, "What about my dad?"

"I'll have to take care of him tomorrow. He's safe and the food's not bad at the jail. We'll see what the problem is and what we have to do to solve it, later."

That seemed to satisfy him and he went to get his coat. Karen cut the tags off and Melanie said, "Okay, I got Tad and he's going to pick me up at the Café at six thirty so let's get going." She wanted to be in the armory before Ed and Karen got there.

They got to the Café about five forty five and it wasn't too busy since almost everybody was at the armory. They got their orders quickly. Karen was glad Tony wasn't there because he might have accidently let the secret out. Maria was doing the cooking and a local teenager was serving the customers.

Beau ate slower this time but it was obvious he was enjoying his burger and fries. Tad came in the front door and walked back to the table. They introduced Beau to Tad. Melanie finished her meal quickly. She said, "I'll see you all later if you're up when I get in."

Ed said, "Last one in gets the couch." When Melanie looked surprised, he laughed and said, "I'm only kidding. Beau will be on the couch so don't be scared when you see him or maybe I should say, don't you scare him."

When they finished and Ed went to pay the bill, Maria said, "I'm going to close early since the town seems to be quiet tonight."

She winked at Karen and Karen nodded saying, "Yeah, it's unusually quiet for a Saturday night."

The three of them went to get in Ed's Caddy. Karen said, "Let me drive. You guys can talk while I take a ride around town."

Ed looked puzzled but said, "Oh, okay, but just remember this is my pride and joy, you'll be driving."

She gave him her best hurt look and said, "I thought I was your pride and joy."

"Oh, you know what I mean. Beau, this is an example of how women can twist your words."

She was still laughing when they came to the armory. She did her best to be sincere, when she said her pre planned lines. "Let's go see what's going on in there. Must be some kind of concert."

Ed said, "Are you sure you want to go in there. What if it's one of those hard rock, metal bands playing or something?"

"Well, we'll just come right back out, if it is." She had a hard time finding a parking place but once parked they walked to the building. The band was playing country music that could be heard in the parking lot as they got closer.

Ed said, "Well, that sounds pretty good. I'm surprised we haven't heard about this before. I guess we were too busy moving and getting ready for your show."

Jeff had Craig on the look out in the parking lot and he radioed to tell them, "The joker is here!"

So when they entered the building the band began to play "He's a jolly good fellow." Ed looked totally confused. He turned to Karen and she just took his hand and led him to the front of the room.

Jeff was standing there with a microphone in his hand. He shook Ed's hand and said, "Welcome, Ed, this is your big night and we're all here to help you celebrate."

At that Ed turned to look at the crowd and couldn't believe his eyes. There were hundreds of people, most of whom he recognized, standing at tables and applauding for him. He just shook his head and said, "I hope you don't expect me to say anything. I'm speechless. What the Hell is going on?"

That brought on gales of laughter and Jeff told him, "This is your retirement party and nobody forgot to come. They love you and Karen. They just want to give you a proper send off. So have a seat and prepare to enjoy the evening. We have a lot of people who want to speak, so you won't have to worry about speaking unless you want to defend yourself later on."

He led them to the table of honor where Melanie and Tad were already seated with the speakers. Ed shook his finger at Melanie and said, "So you were in on this, I take it."

Melanie said, "Oh, Ed, the whole town has been in on this for weeks. The only person that didn't know was you."

She stood and hugged him. Karen had not let go of his hand and Beau's. She squeezed Ed's now and kissed him on the cheek. She whispered in his ear, "Gotcha!"

That made him smile. When he was seated, the band began to play again as Jeff made his way to his seat at the speakers table. Karen finally took time to explain to Beau what was going on. He just said, "Oh, Goll, this is great."

Jeff made a short speech about his work with Ed over the years and how much he had learned from him. He said, "Later on I tell you a few secrets about Ed Hawkins methods. Right now, we will have a short intermission so we can eat."

The teenage waiters and waitresses from the high school started bringing out salads and taking drink orders. Ed leaned over to Karen and said, "How can I eat after the supper we just had?"

She said, "Just do the best you can do so Tony won't have his feelings hurt. He's worked so hard getting this done for you."

Melanie said, "Now you know why Karen and I only had salads."

Ed retorted, "Yes, and you never even gave me a clue. What do you think of that, Beau?"

Beau just grinned and said, "I'll eat enough to make up for you, Mr. Ed. I could eat for a week, I think."

Ed slapped him on the back and said, "Well, maybe they'll give us doggie bags and we can take it home. I'm so shocked, I don't think I could eat even if I hadn't already pigged out."

When the crowd was almost finished eating, Jeff took to the speaker's lectern again and introduced Gary. Then Gary made a few remarks about his relationship with Ed and Karen after which he introduced speaker after speaker to praise or vilify Ed for the next hour.

Ed laughed as hard as anyone else at his own escapades. Especially the ones about his methods of law enforcement. They had made room for dancing and when the speakers were through they had an hour for dancing.

Ed took Karen's hand when Jeff had asked them to lead off the dancing. Many other people joined them on the dance floor. Ed whispered, "This is the first time we've ever danced, isn't it?"

When Tad cut in, Ed and Melanie danced. She said, "Well, we got you good didn't we?"

He nodded and said, "I have never been so surprised in my life. It makes me feel good but it makes me sad, too. I really want to think of this as a new beginning not the end."

Melanie squeezed him and said, "We're not thinking of it as the end either. Your buddies just wanted to let you know how much they thought of you. They have had such a great time planning all this. They really love you, Ed and so do I."

He kissed her on the cheek and said, "And I'll tell you again, love you like a daughter. I hope you remember that. To Karen and I, you are our child and we want to be there for you. Don't ever forget that." She assured him she would not and when the music stopped they made their way back to the table just as Gary started to speak again.

He said, "Now we would appreciate it if the honoree would make his way up here so we can give him an award."

Ed got Karen by the hand and said, "You have to go with me."

She got up and said, "Okay, but don't expect me to hold you up." She giggled as he gave her a pained look and she said, "Come on now, it's not going to hurt." She ended up leading him to the lectern, as the crowd stood and applauded. The band played "Jolly Good Fellow" again.

When they got to the lectern, Chief Stone was there to greet them. He praised Ed for all his good police work and humanitarian acts over the years before he presented him a plaque that was engraved with his name and years of service. Then he presented him with a check for one thousand dollars. Ed got weak in the knees and Karen thought for a minute that she really would have to hold him up.

She knew he was having a problem, so she went to the lectern and said, "I'll have to add my two cents worth of praise for my husband. As you know we worked together for years. He and my late husband were best friends. It took a long time for the two of us to figure out that we would make a good couple. He's a wonderful companion and the biggest booster in my new art enterprise. We are looking forward to many years of traveling and just enjoying our life with each other and our friends. I am so grateful that you all have chosen to honor him and to give him such a generous gift. Now maybe he will be able to say a few words of appreciation. How about it, Ed?"

He smiled and put his arm around her waist. He began to speak but choked up and had to pause a moment to regain his composure. "You folks have made me feel very humble tonight. It hasn't been a surprise, it has been shocking. I am so grateful to have friends like you and I'll never be able to repay your generosity. I thank God every day for giving me Karen and Melanie to love and I surely thank Him for friends like you all. Thanks is certainly not enough but I can't think of another word that would cover my gratitude."

Jeff stood up and said, "Okay, that's enough. You can sit down now. We were just kidding. This is not really for you. We just wanted to have someplace to go dance and this was as good an excuse as any."

He paused, "Oh, look there. I do believe that another good friend of yours just came in the door."

Ed looked out toward the entrance. Daniel was coming in and walking toward him with a big smile on his face. Ed turned to Karen looking puzzled. He whispered, "I thought he was in Colorado."

Karen said quietly, "Sh…He changed his plans for your big night."

When Daniel finally made it to the lectern, he shook Ed's hand and began to speak. He said, "I want to congratulate you on your thirty years of service to this community and tell you that the Bank of Dinsmore and it's board of directors wanted to do something to honor you. We decided to give a thousand dollars to a charity that you have always supported, the Crisis Center. This is made in your name, Ed Hawkins, in honor of your years of support for their cause and coming to the rescue of many needy families in this community."

At this point Ed couldn't take any more. Tears were rolling down his cheeks and he just grabbed Daniel and hugged him. When he pulled himself together, he held his hands up and said, "Thank you, everybody."

He sat down pulling Karen on to his lap. The crowd applauded again, the band played, "You are My Sunshine" and everybody began to laugh. Gary came to the lectern again and said, "That is the end of our part of this ceremony. You are welcome to stay and dance until the band quits." People began to rush up the where Ed was and shake his hand, offering their congratulations. It was midnight before they could leave.

The following weeks would prove very busy and time would fly by. The Wallaces were back together as a family. Janet was doing community service at the Crisis Center. Tom was being interviewed by various colleges. Bill was considering an offer from a college. Amy was selected most beautiful freshman.

Daniel and Rebecca were planning a Spring wedding. Rebecca took a leave of absence to plan the nuptials. They would honeymoon in Paris.

Melanie was doing well in school. She still was seeing Tad and came home every other weekend. She visited her grandmother at least once a month. Margie's grave now had a new headstone that read, "Too soon gone, but not forgotten."

Beau and his dad were back together living in much better conditions. Beau's dad was working as the caretaker at the hunting camp. The members had built a small, but new, modern cabin for them to live in. The members were able to fix up their own cabin and leave equipment there, now.

Tony was still greeting the citizens of Dinsmore at the Café every morning. He had hired a full time waitress, so that Maria could just cashier and keep the books.

Stuart came to visit his folks, on his dad's eightieth birthday after receiving an invitation. Enclosed was a letter of apology from the one and same, his father, Joseph. They held the party at the Methodist Church fellowship hall.

Gary preached a sermon on the magic of forgiveness on that Sunday. Joseph, Ruth and Stuart sat together in the front row with Christine.

Karen's art gallery opening was a huge success with half of Dinsmore in attendance and when spring came she, Ed, Callie and Jazz were on their way to San Diego in the motor home with a sign on the wheel cover that read "The Artist and the Cop."

Oh, yes, Jeff went out to the Hawkin's place every day on his patrol to feed Candy and at least once a week he went riding. Sometimes Pamela, who was the new manager of the Regal went with him.

Printed in the United States
59415LVS00003B/31-51